# DEAD IN THE WATER

"Jake, my God, look at the core temperature," Alex said. The temperature gauge needle had crept out of the Normal range.

Botkin burst into the reactor control compartment with a wild, terrified look on his face. "The warning signals—a radiation leak—"

"A coolant leak," Scott corrected Botkin. He saw Abakov ease into the compartment behind Botkin. "Calm down."

Botkin, pointing at the temperature gauge, threw himself at the control console. The gauge's black needle wiggled at the edge of the red zone. "The fuel will melt," he cried. "We have to surface right now—" Botkin grabbed an SC1 microphone. "We have to emergency blow—"

Scott tore the mike from Botkin's fist. "Belay that!"

"We're all going to die—"

Scott grabbed two handfuls of Botkin's coveralls and threw him against the console. "No one's going to die!"

## Nonfiction by Peter Sasgen

*Red Scorpion: The War Patrols of the USS* Rasher

PETER SASGEN

POCKET STAR BOOKS
New York London Toronto Sydney

An *Original* Publication of POCKET BOOKS

A Pocket Star Book published by
POCKET BOOKS, a division of Simon & Schuster, Inc.
1230 Avenue of the Americas, New York, NY 10020



ISBN: 0-7434-8359-6

First Pocket Books paperback edition December 2004

10 9 8 7 6 5 4 3 2 1



Cover design by James Wang

Manufactured in the United States of America

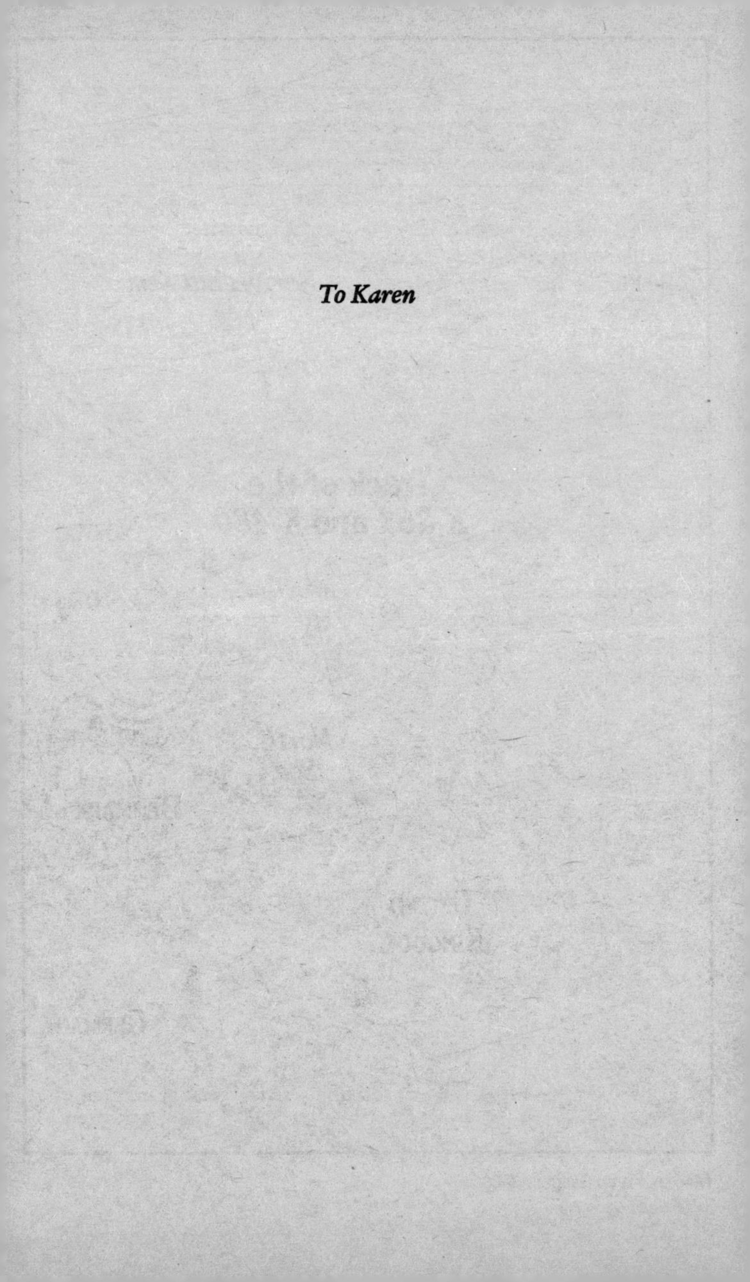

*To Karen*

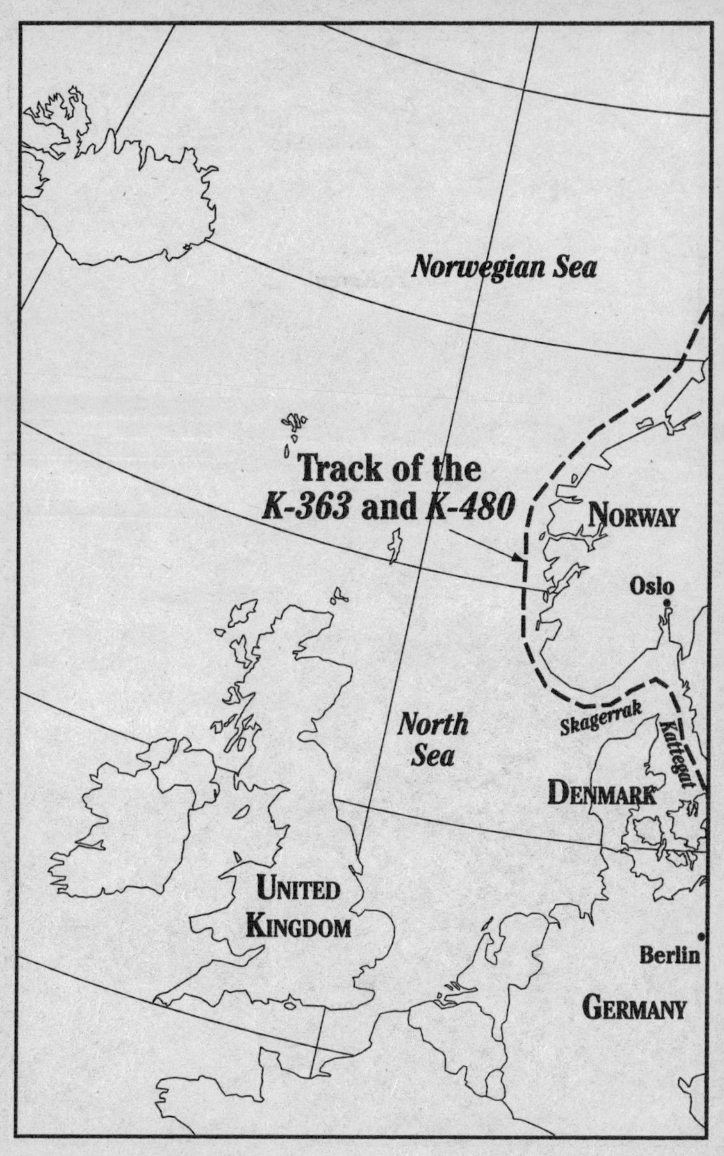


Map by Karen Sasgen, 2003

Barents Sea
Murmansk
Archangel
SWEDEN
FINLAND
Gulf of Bothnia
Helsinki
Gulf of Finland
St. Petersburg
Stockholm
ESTONIA
RUSSIA
LATVIA
Baltic Sea
LITHUANIA
BELARUS
Warsaw
POLAND

# Part One

## THE PLAN

# CHECHEN SUICIDE BOMBERS KILL MORE THAN 1,000 HOSTAGES IN MOSCOW CONCERT HALL

## Separatists Press Fight Against Russian Forces

MOSCOW (RIA-Novosti: 15 SEPTEMBER 2006) FOR IMMEDIATE RELEASE—Chechen separatists killed more than a thousand hostages when they blew up the Tchaikovsky Concert Hall, home of the State Symphony Orchestra. The hall was packed with 1,600 men, women, and children attending a Rachmaninoff concert.

The attack in the Russian capital was carried out by 50 heavily armed men and women, members of a Chechen suicide squad, seeking the withdrawal of Russian troops from their country. The terrorists, armed with automatic weapons, grenades, and explosives, held Russian security forces at bay by threatening to kill the hostages if their demands were not met.

A masked rebel told a correspondent for RIA-Novosti, the government information agency, that the theater was wired with explosives and that the hostage-takers were ready to "sacrifice themselves for Chechnya's independence." They warned that any attempt to storm the theater would set off the explosives. The Russian president's refusal to negotiate with the terrorists brought denunciations from the unidentified rebel leader, who had demanded an end to Russian occupation of Chechnya.

The standoff ended when security forces attempting to enter the hall via an underground service tunnel opened fire on the rebels, who then detonated their explosives.

# 1

## Murmansk, the Kola Peninsula, Russia

Radchenko hunched his shoulders against the bitter Arctic wind and swung down off the Number 8 electrobus onto Ulitsa Kipnovich. His boots crunched on the early October snow that had swept in from the Barents Sea across the taiga and low surrounding hills with their glistening stands of birch. The city's mask of white hid its dark, crumbling heart. Like a whore made up to fool an unsuspecting customer. A whore paid to turn tricks, thought Radchenko.

The dimly lighted street was a canyon of deserted apartment blocks bisected by the shimmering electrobus catenary. Radchenko felt utterly alone and for a moment wondered if he had stepped into a trap. He crossed the street and stood in a block of shadow, waiting for something or someone to move. He lit a cigarette, waited a beat, then set out, keeping to the shadows.

The Novy Polyarnyy Hotel was an ugly pile of yellow brick that Radchenko entered through an unlocked rear service door. He walked past the drunken night porter dozing before an ancient black-and-white TV broadcasting an eerie blue light into the worn lobby. Radchenko shunned the lift, thinking of the noise it would make, and instead took the stairs, their risers and treads creaking under his weight. He reached the second landing, stopped, but heard only muffled voices behind closed doors. Somewhere a toilet flushed.

Radchenko reached the third floor, turned left, and found the room. He took a deep breath, knocked twice. The door shivered open and Radchenko slipped into the room. He quickly inventoried the double bed, the battered greasy dresser and chair, the rusty washstand, the drawn blinds.

"Relax. We're alone."

Radchenko faced the tall American. He had a weathered face and short iron-gray hair. He wore well-cut khakis and a bulky black turtleneck sweater. His Russian was elegant, faultless.

Perhaps he had a beautiful blond wife; didn't all American men have blond wives? What would she think if she knew her husband was with a Russian sailor in a hotel in Murmansk?

"Vodka?" The American opened a fresh bottle of Sinopskaya, a premium brand Radchenko had never heard of. "Smoke?" He pointed to a carton of Marlboros that lay open on the bed.

Radchenko downed the vodka, smoother and sweeter than any vodka he had ever tasted. The American refilled Radchenko's drink, then refilled it again.

"I said relax; no one knows you're here."

"You have money to pay?" Radchenko said. He went to the window, peered through a gap where the blind met the wall. All he could see was a forest of TV antennas and satellite dishes on the roof of the apartment building next door.

"Yes."

"Dollars?"

"Yes."

The American watched Radchenko pace the room drinking vodka. He stopped to tear open a pack of cigarettes and light one.

"Take the whole carton; I don't smoke."

Radchenko heard that American men and their blond wives didn't smoke. Unhealthy. But they liked alcohol and sex. Usually taken together. He considered the American through the curling smoke from his cigarette.

The American sat down on the bed. He hadn't touched his drink. At length he said, "You had no trouble getting away?"

"The idiots who guard the base don't pay attention. We come and go as we want."

"No one else saw you leave? A shipmate, perhaps?"

"No one."

"Are you on the fleet duty roster?"

"I have the midwatch: midnight to 0400."

The American rucked a sweater sleeve to uncover a chunky stainless-steel wristwatch. "Then we have plenty of time. Take off your jacket and be comfortable."

Radchenko stopped pacing. He refilled his glass but didn't remove his jacket. He said, around the cigarette stuck in his mouth, "How much will you pay?"

The American swung his legs up on the bed and leaned back against the headboard, glass of vodka balanced on his chest. His feet were shod in a pair of scarred Wellington boots. "What I promised: five hundred. Another five hundred if you do what I want."

A fortune, thought Radchenko. More money than he could ever make as a sailor serving in the Russian Navy, which had seemingly run out of cash to pay its rankers—

its officers too. Desertion and suicide were common, as was talk of mutiny. To make matters worse, Radchenko's commanding officer, an iron-fisted disciplinarian, had also become disillusioned. Radchenko remembered being scared to death by what he had overheard him discussing with other officers in the wardroom of the submarine *K-363*. And when Norwegian nuclear scientists surveying radioactive waste at the Olenya Bay submarine base brought the tall American and his assistant aboard the submarine to interview the crew, Radchenko, sensing an opportunity to earn some money, made an approach.

Radchenko stripped off his jacket, threw it on the bed. The American responded with a look of expectancy. Radchenko felt the vodka but poured more. The alcohol would make it easier to provide the service the American was eager to pay for. Wind rattled the window glazing. Somewhere a door slammed. Radchenko heard the elevator start up. He chewed a nail. He hadn't ever done this before and wasn't sure how to get started.

The American had five folded hundred-dollar bills in his hand. "For you."

Radchenko felt the tension mounting in his body. He reached for the money even as he realized something was wrong. The American heaved himself off the bed an instant before the door splintered inward off its hinges and two men burst into the room.

A barrage of raindrops exploded against black steel. A filthy morning topside at U.S. Navy Atlantic Fleet Headquarters, Norfolk, Virginia, had the watchstanders' chins tucked into their sodden peacoats. Belowdecks, where it was warm and dry, the canned, conditioned air smelled from ozone. Commander Jake Scott waved his executive officer, Commander Manny Rodriguez, into the small stateroom that doubled as his personal quarters and private office aboard the USS *Tampa*, a Los Angeles–class nuclear attack submarine.

"What's up, Skipper?" said Rodriguez.

"ComSubLant, that's what's up," Scott said. "The squadron commodore just called. Ellsworth wants to see me."

"You in trouble?"

"No more than usual."

"The commodore give you a hint what the boss wants to see you about?" Rodriguez asked.

"Possible change of orders."

"Hell, Skipper, we already have our orders."

"Change of orders for me."

"What?"

The *Tampa* had just completed a refit and was scheduled to depart Norfolk for sea trials and, later, deployment. Scott had been the *Tampa*'s commanding officer for over two years and she was his home. Whatever it was that Ellsworth had in mind for him, the admiral was in for a fight. Especially if it meant giving up command of the *Tampa*. She was his ship and he didn't want anyone to take her from him. He thought about Tracy. Someone had taken her from him; now this. No, that wasn't true: Tracy had left him. Big difference.

There had been all those intelligence-gathering patrols into hostile waters, all those weeks and months away from her. She had complained that he was more intimate with his sub crew than he was with her. The phone calls had hurt too. Like the one on his first night ashore after a hellish sixty-day patrol off North Korea. He had picked up the phone and heard loud music in the background. A man's voice said, "Trace, it's Rick. Wanna party, wear that red-hot outfit of yours?" "Not tonight,"

Scott had said icily. Click! At least he hadn't walked in the door and found Rick's face buried between Tracy's legs. Why blame her? She just wanted a normal life, not the one he'd given her. He wondered if she had found her new life satisfying, if the things she liked to do in bed excited the guy she was running with now. . . . He caught himself in time and reeled back from the edge of misery.

Scott stood. "I'm to report to Ellsworth at fifteen hundred."

"What about the party at the O club?" Rodriguez brayed. "You gonna make it?"

"Better stow it for now."

Scott looked at all the untouched paperwork piled on the desk, reports and correspondence awaiting his review and signature. What he really wanted to do was shit-can all of it and get back to sea. He took a dirty work jacket down from a hook on the bulkhead. "Take care of my ship, Manny."

Vice Admiral Carter Ellsworth, commander, Submarines Atlantic, peered through a pair of thick wire-rimmed glasses that magnified his pale blue eyes. The benign look on his face masked a cunning personality. His desk, except for coffee in a fine china cup, had been cleared of papers. Flags, framed photos of the president, the civilian service chiefs, and plaques bearing the names of U.S. submarines were the only items on display in Ellsworth's spartan office.

"Consider yourself detached from the *Tampa,*" Ellsworth said without preamble.

Scott felt he'd been gut-punched.

"You're detached for TDY. Chief of staff has your orders. You can pick them up when you leave, *Captain.*"

"Captain?" Scott said.

"You've been frocked for your new assignment." Ellsworth tossed Scott a plastic bag containing a pair of silver eagle collar devices. "Meanwhile, see if these fit."

Scott's frocking was a mixed blessing. He'd bragged, had even worn as a badge of honor, that he was probably the oldest commander in the Navy, passed over for promotion to captain once and doomed if he was passed over again. But reassignment meant giving up command of the *Tampa* and he'd worked too hard rehabilitating himself to do that.

"Karl Radford wants to see you," Ellsworth said. The cup rose to his lips; gold braid on his sleeve sparkled like a bolt of raw electricity.

Scott digested this. Karl Radford, a retired United States Air Force major general, headed the Strategic Reconnaissance Office, a supersecret intelligence agency with intelligence-gathering assets in place world-wide. Scott had a lways suspected that most—if not all—of the missions he'd conducted at sea had been ordered by the SRO. Perhaps even the one that had almost ended in disaster. And had been hung around his neck.

Ellsworth looked at Scott. He saw a man in his early forties, tall, with dark hair flecked with gray. He had rough-edged good looks and a bearing that indicated he knew how to handle himself in tough situations. "Any idea why he'd want to talk to you?"

Scott shrugged. "No, sir. Do you?"

Ellsworth ignored this and said, "Wrap up whatever you have pending. Radford wants you in Washington day after tomorrow. Any problem with that?"

"Perhaps he'd consider someone else in my place."

Ellsworth set his jaw. "What are you saying, Scott?"

"That I'd prefer to retain command of the *Tampa*.

Whatever General Radford has in mind for me can't be more important than what I'm doing now."

Ellsworth pushed the coffee aside. His pale blue eyes had turned dark. "Let me tell you something, Scott. You're still hanging by a thread. You've had your second chance and admittedly you've made the most of it. A lot of men who have been in your position are out of the Navy. Some are selling appliances for Sears; others are reading the want ads."

Scott felt pressure building at the base of his skull.

Ellsworth plunged ahead. "Those men didn't deserve a second chance, but you did. I don't intend to give you another."

"Admiral, I fought hard for it and I don't plan to end my career on the beach all used up."

"Apparantly General Radford agrees. He wouldn't ask for one of SubLant's best skippers unless it was damned important. More important than driving subs. He knows your background and all the rest. He wants someone with a brain who knows how to use it. I told him you wouldn't disappoint him."

"Thank you."

"Now let me give you some advice, Scott. A lot of people around here think you're a hero and that you got the shitty end of the stick–that we brass hats needed a scapegoat and you were it. No need to go over old ground, what's done is done. But keep this in mind: I know Radford, and he isn't impressed by heroes. He'll dice you up if he thinks even for a second that you might customize the orders he gives you. This time try sticking to the rules–his rules, not Jake Scott's. I don't think you'd be very successful selling appliances."

Ellsworth stood. "That about does it. Oh, one more

thing. Rodriguez. In your judgment, he's fully qualified for command?"

Scott stood too. "He is."

"I'll be riding the *Tampa* during her shakedown. See how he handles it. The pressure, I mean."

Scott put a hand to the base of his skull.

Ellsworth saw Scott to the door and shook his hand in a mechanical fashion. "By the way, it was Radford who wrangled your frocking out of BuPers, not me," Ellsworth laid a finger beside his nose. "I gather it wasn't easy."

Scott finished a beer and wrapped up the remains of Chinese takeout in a brown paper sack. He gazed numbly at a muted CNN female talking head with plastic hair and Chiclet teeth yapping about the president's upcoming summit meeting with his Russian counterpart in St. Petersburg, city of the czars. And on Capitol Hill, the Senate majority leader . . . He punched the power button and she vanished.

Broken noodles, greasy paper bags, and cardboard containers went into a garbage pail. Was garbage picked up on Thursday? Or was that recycling day? He was out of sync with the daily rhythms of life ashore. But his apartment was cheap and close to the base, which was all he cared about. And that his neighbors minded their own business. A Marine Corps colonel two doors away had never spoken a word to him.

Scott started packing a bag for Washington. Radford's summons, like everything about him and the SRO, was a mystery. Black ops and a secret budget to carry them out gave Radford enormous power to influence events around the world. Like the Yellow Sea operation. Scott shuddered inwardly. It had been a nightmare. And even though the board of inquiry had exonerated him, it had not erased the uncertainty about his fitness to command a nuke that lingered in the minds of many of his superior officers. Maybe the summons from Radford would change some minds.

Scott finished packing, then looked around to make sure he hadn't forgotten anything. His gaze settled on the door to the spare bedroom, which held boxes filled with the remnants of his former life as a husband. He kept the door closed so he wouldn't be reminded of it. Yet, it was hard not to be, especially when he heard the couple next door arguing, their fights punctuated by exploding crockery. Not like the Scotts, he thought. They had always fought their battles in thundering silence.

The memory of the last time he saw Tracy was burned in his brain. Her lovely wide mouth a tight, angry slash, she had held him in a withering gaze, violet eyes dark with anger. To avoid a scene when Rick arrived in his new Corvette to pick her up, she had aimed her cell phone at him like a gun and screamed, "Get out! Get out or I'll call the police." When Scott returned the next morning, Tracy was gone.

That night Scott dreamed he was looking through a periscope at a North Korean frigate. Her twin stacks vomited smoke as she swung around and charged. *Christ, they've spotted us!* In a heartbeat the frigate's bow began to fill the periscope's field of view. Fear rippled through his guts. Too late now to run for it: He was committed; the SEALs had to be recovered. He had to fire torpedoes, had to save the men, but his orders went unheeded, shouted down by Tracy yelling, "Get out! . . . Get out! . . . Get out!"

# 2

## St. Petersburg, Russia

Thick clouds pressed down on the golden spires and gilded domes of the imperial city. A snarl of traffic wormed around Moskovsky Station at the Square of Insurrection, with its tangle of southbound rail lines, trolley buses, and trams. On Nevsky Prospekt the traffic inched past a narrow street, at the dead end of which was a scrubby car repair shop surrounded by rusty Volgas, Moskvichs, and Zhigulis. Parked out of sight in a lot next to the shop strewn with crumpled fenders and car doors was a burgundy BMW sedan and a gray Volvo station wagon.

Alikhan Zakayev warmed himself at a kerosene heater in an unoccupied bay of the shop. Greasy tools, engines, and dismantled transmissions littered the floor and workbenches. Zakayev, a smallish man, wore a cashmere navy topcoat like a cape over a double-breasted suit. His hooded eyes took in several thickly built, unshaven, menacing-looking men sitting on a bench. One of them stroked a thin black-and-white cat happily kneading his pant leg. Another man toyed with a SIG 220 .45 pistol equipped with a laser sight, its red dot coursing over walls, ceiling, and Zakayev's body.

"Put that away," Zakayev said.

The SIG disappeared instantly.

Zakayev didn't like the flamboyant display of arms for which his followers had a penchant much like their penchant for expensive German cars. Zakayev's taste in cars ran more to Volvo station wagons.

Zakayev touched his pencil-thin mustache and said, "What are you doing?"

A beautiful young girl perched on a stool, her leather miniskirted bottom protected from grease by a clean shop rag, looked up from a thin paperback book. "Reading."

"You can read later." Zakayev jerked his head in the direction of a storeroom off the main part of the shop from which a desperate keening sound emerged. "Find out what's taking so long."

The girl was very tall and had huge, heavily made-up eyes. She had on dark purple stockings and spike-heeled boots. She strode across the shop on a pair of long, wonderfully shaped legs and, with a handkerchief to her nose and mouth, entered the storeroom only to emerge a moment later.

"He says it is no use," the girl said from behind the handkerchief.

"No use?"

"See for yourself."

Zakayev stepped gingerly across the shop floor, avoiding patches of grime and oil. He entered the storeroom. The strong smell of shit and piss shocked his nostrils, but he ignored it. He couldn't ignore another smell: burned flesh and hair. A naked man built like a bull hung by his wrists, which were bound with wire, from the hook of a chain fall rigged from a ceiling beam. Mechanics employed the chain fall to lift engines out of cars; now it held what looked like a charred side of beef.

The bull had been badly beaten and his hair and scalp had been burned away, leaving only a blackened skull. Zakayev's eyes went to the man's groin, where his genitals had been. What he saw was the charred stump of a penis and carbonized testicles. That he was still alive was a tribute to his physical condition or perhaps all the vodka he drank.

Another man, a huge hairy ape wearing dark glasses and with a black cloth band wound around his head, stepped back from his work. He had on a leather apron over black clothes and in one hand held an acetylene torch, its roaring tapered blue-white flame capable of biting through case-hardened steel.

Sweat glistened like diamonds on the ape's forehead. He shrugged and thumbed the gas valves closed. The flame sputtered, popped, died. "You won't get anything else out of him, General."

"So it's the Winter Palace."

"He swore it. And I believe him." The ape looped the torch and hoses over a pair of gas tanks lashed to a hand truck. He wiped sweat from his eyes.

Zakayev gazed at the bull—what was left of it—hanging from the hook. The stench was overpowering. It reminded him of another time, in Chechnya. He and his men had waited all night in a soaking drizzle, hidden in rubble off the main street in Grozny where it intersects the city's main square and the Sunja Neva.

To their rear was Minutka Square, where refugees came to seek family members and buy food and medicine, and which Russian forces repeatedly attacked with artillery and air strikes. After more than eight years of fighting, thousands of Chechen civilians had been killed there.

The Russian assault unleashed at dusk had left more than two dozen women and children mangled in their own viscera near the market, which had been reduced to a pile of broken sticks and mortar. Zakayev assumed that Russian Spetsnaz—special forces—would launch a follow-up probe to assess the damage. He looked around at his men, most of whom were young enough to be his sons. Gripping their weapons, eager for revenge, they huddled against the cold. It was a spectral scene: a jagged landscape lit by yellow gas flares from broken pipes, smoke blacker than night roiling skyward. Nothing moved but a few stray cats and dogs and a homeless old man on crutches seeking shelter.

He heard it first. "Listen."

A snorting diesel engine. A Russian BTR-80 armored personnel carrier poked its camouflaged boatlike prow around a sharp bend in the road and rocked to a halt. The BTR's turret, sprouting machine guns, smoothly traversed the killing field. Zakayev silently urged the Russians on. He knew they were wary, especially at night.

Another snort and the BTR inched forward, its big tires throwing off clods of mud. Perhaps these Russians were new arrivals and still fearless or just plain stupid. Whatever, Zakayev got ready. He stripped a plastic bag from an RPG-7 grenade launcher, pulled the safety pin from the conical warhead, and, shouldering the weapon, poked its nose through an opening in the rubble. He took aim on the lumbering vehicle and, as it drew abreast of his hide, squeezed the trigger.

Zakayev ducked behind the wall yet felt the heat from the blast rake his face and hands. Ammunition in the BTR cooked off and sent the Russian three-man crew and seven Spetsnaz sprawling out of the vehicle's flung-open hatches into fierce Chechen small-arms fire.

Zakayev stood over a badly burned Russian soldier, a teenage conscript begging for his mother. The stench of burning diesel, of scorched flesh, of shit and piss, hung in the night air. The other Russians were dead. How long had this boy been in Chechnya? Zakayev wondered. Not more than a few days, judging by his new cammies and polished boots. But his eyes were already old and filled with fear and pain. Sorrow too. Not for what his comrades had done to the Chechen women and children in Minutka Square, but for his bad luck to have been sent to this living hell of a country. He probably had no idea why the Chechens wanted freedom from Russia. Perhaps he had been thinking of his girlfriend back in Moscow and dreaming about becoming a rock star. But all he could do now was cry, *"Mat', Mat', Mat'."*

Zakayev shot him in the head.

"Who was he?" she asked.

"Who?"

"The bull." The girl had on a luxurious black sable coat. The silky pelts caressed her purple-stockinged thighs, which held Zakayev's attention for a moment. Together in the Volvo, driving away from the repair shop, they looked like successful Russian entrepreneurs on their way to a meeting with foreign venture capitalists. Or a man with his young mistress.

"Nobody." Zakayev put his eyes back on the road. Traffic was still heavy. Linked metal barricades had been spotted along the prospekts in anticipation of the crowds sure to be drawn to the presidential motorcades sweeping through the city. He changed lanes, made sure the turn signal went *ka-pick, ka-pick, ka-pick.* An infraction might draw the attention of the militia. Their identity cards would hold up to scrutiny, but he was not eager to test them.

"Ali, tell me." She twisted around in her seat, peeled off a purple kid glove, and reached over the console to fondle his crotch.

"An FSB officer."

The girl stopped manipulating him. She slowly took her hand away and faced forward again. "Ali, an FSB officer?" The Russian Federal Security Service—Federal'naya Sluzhba Bezopasnosti, or FSB—had responsibility for providing security at the summit.

"We weighed the risks," Zakayev said. "They were acceptable."

Instinct had told him that the Winter Palace—Russia's Versailles, recently restored to its former imperial splendor—would be the focus of the upcoming summit meeting between the American and Russian presidents.

"A Chechen woman who works for a St. Petersburg catering service that has a contract to supply meals for the FSB—she told us that one of their men assigned to the press motor pool had access to the summit schedule. She said that sometimes this man didn't show up for work at the parking lot because he was drunk and that his FSB supervisors didn't seem to mind because his friends filled in for him."

"And you took him?"

"Late last night, after he completed his shift. I concluded that if he suddenly disappeared he wouldn't be missed for days."

Snow flurries had changed to rain; the wipers *zick-zick*ed over the greasy windshield glass.

For more than a month St. Petersburg had been teeming with American and Russian security personnel preparing for the summit. Parts of Dvortsovaya Ploshchad had been sealed off and access to the Hermitage and Winter Palace, former residence of Czar Nicholas II and the Russian imperial family, had been severely restricted. Already a whole section of the city from the Neva south to the Obvodnyy Canal had been sealed off to traffic and pedestrians.

"He told us what we wanted to know about the summit. The schedule. Times and dates. Everything."

Zakayev had learned that after all the pomp and circumstance attending the American president's arrival, he and the first lady would be given a tour of the Winter Palace by the Russian president and his wife. They would see personal items from the imperial family on display in the Malachite Room and stroll the White Dining Room, where the Bolsheviks seized power in 1917 from Kerensky's provisional government. After all the festivities and a state banquet, the real business of the summit would take place in one of Catherine the Great's private apartments in the Hermitage.

"But, Ali," said the girl, "eventually they'll go looking for him."

"By the time they get themselves organized, it will be too late."

Zakayev turned onto Nevsky Prospekt and pulled up at the Nevsky Palace Hotel. It was popular with successful European businessmen who liked to show off their mistresses while prowling the lobby or cutting deals in the restaurant over caviar and sturgeon mousse. It was the perfect place for a wanted man like Zakayev to hide in plain sight.

Scott's eyes went to the two-inch-thick file folder emblazoned with diagonal black stripes and labeled, DIRECTOR—PURPLE.

Karl Radford, standing behind his desk, ignoring regulations that prohibited smoking in government buildings, shifted a cigarette to his left hand so he could pick up the folder with his right. In a husky voice that matched his thick build, he said, "I was told you know Frank Drummond."

"Rear Admiral Frank Drummond? Yes, sir, I do."

Radford viewed Scott through a scrim of cigarette smoke. "How well do you know him?"

"He's an old friend. My patrone. I served two tours under him—as exec on the *Nevada,* then a shore billet at Net Warfare. He also straightened out a few problems I had a while back. . . . But then, I assume you already know this."

Radford nodded.

Scott was on a hair trigger, his instinct for sensing trouble alive. "Why the questions about Frank?"

Radford said, "How well do you know his wife?"

"Very well. She and Frank are two of a kind. Always looking out for the hired help. Vivian's a wonderful, gracious lady. They never had children, but they'd have made great parents." What he didn't add was that long deployments at sea were tough on a marriage—tougher on children who grew up without dads. "They're certainly devoted."

Radford, collecting his thoughts, gazed out the window of his office in Crystal City, Alexandria, Virginia, at an unbroken stream of headlights and taillights crawling past the Pentagon on I-395. He watched late arrivals high-stepping through puddles in the parking lot downstairs. Across the Potomac, the tip of the Washington Monument scraped the bottoms of dark clouds filled with more rain. Scott thought the scene mirrored his own mood perfectly.

Radford rounded on Scott and said, "Do you know if Drummond was a homosexual?"

Something caught in Scott's throat. Had he heard right? Radford saying that Drummond was a homosexual? *Was* a homosexual?

"Well?" Radford insisted.

"Frank Drummond is not a homosexual," Scott said firmly.

"How do you know?"

"Because I know the man intimately. I worked with him for years—"

"Doesn't mean a damn thing. Plenty of men hide it. Men in the Navy."

"What's this all about, General? My orders to report to you didn't say anything about Admiral Drummond."

Radford lurched back to his desk. He mashed out his cigarette in a thick cut-glass ashtray and, looking down at the twisted, flattened butt, said, "Frank Drummond is dead."

For a long moment Scott held Radford's gaze. "Dead? How?"

"Suicide. In Murmansk."

An ugly picture was forming and Scott refused to believe what he saw.

He and Drummond had been friends for over ten years. They had met when Scott had been ordered to the USS *Hampton*, an Improved Los Angeles–class SSN, as Drummond's exec. Drummond had immediately recognized Scott's exceptional skills as a submariner and had helped push his career along the track to a command of his own. The chemistry between them had been right, and later, when Scott followed Drummond ashore, their professional interests intersected and their friendship and mutual respect deepened. Drummond was there with sound advice and wise counsel when Scott had to endure the pain of a shattered marriage and the near destruction of his career over the Yellow Sea operation.

Scott, numb, disbelieving, got to his feet. His words boomed across Radford's desk. "Impossible. Frank would never commit suicide. Never."

Radford opened the purple file. Parts of pages spiked to the folder were highlighted in yellow marker. "Three days ago we received a Flash report from our embassy in Moscow. Frank Drummond was found dead in a hotel in Murmansk. Also found dead in his room was a young Russian sailor stationed at the submarine base in Olenya Bay, Kola Peninsula. The FSB report states that the men were"–Radford put on a pair of black half-frame reading glasses and consulted a highlighted page–"found in bed together, naked, each shot in the head. The weapon used, a small-caliber pistol of Russian make, was found in Drummond's hand."

"That's bullshit."

Radford gave Scott a flinty look over the tops of his glasses. A college professor exasperated by a stubborn but brilliant student. "Read it for yourself."

It was all there. The Novy Polyarnyy Hotel. Liquor, cigarettes, money. An American officer identified as Rear Admiral Frank Drummond, U.S. Navy. The dead sailor Andre Radchenko, age nineteen, able seaman assigned to the Russian Northern Fleet submarine *K-363*. The suicide weapon a Russian 5.45mm PSM automatic. Drummond's body waited at Moscow's Central Morgue, pending instructions for disposition from the United States Embassy.

The report, compiled by the investigating FSB officer, one Yuri Abakov, had been countersigned by the embassy's second secretary. Scott was familiar with the

FSB, the successor to the old KGB, and its reputation for being inept if not corrupt. But the report was clear-cut and Scott couldn't see how ineptitude, much less corruption, could have mistaken this apparent suicide for murder. What business Frank Drummond had in Murmansk wasn't disclosed in the report.

"Does Mrs. Drummond know that Frank is dead?" a shaken Scott asked.

"She was informed yesterday, minus certain, ah, details. She was told that he was killed during an attempted robbery."

"You spoke with her?"

"Not personally. My deputy. Mrs. Drummond had just returned from London. She'd spent a week with her husband in St. Petersburg, then flew to London to visit friends before returning to the States. She wanted to turn right around and fly back to Moscow, but we persuaded her that that was not the best thing for her to do. I told her that instead I was going to send you to Moscow to escort Drummond's body back to the States for burial. Since you speak fluent Russian and know your way around over there, she agreed with my decision. She wanted to talk to you but didn't know where to reach you."

"Then I intend to see her today."

"Before you do," Radford said, "there are a few things you need to know. Please sit down."

Scott heard Radford's icy tone soften. He offered Scott a cigarette, which he declined, then lit one for himself and blew out twin plumes. "I should have immediately offered my condolences. Please accept them now. I know that learning of Drummond's death in this fashion is not pleasant."

Scott said nothing.

Radford removed his glasses and massaged the bridge of his nose between thumb and forefinger.

"Drummond was on special assignment for the SRO. I personally approved his selection for it. He has an impeccable record, four-oh all the way. An exceptional officer in every respect. Brilliant, really. As you know, he was also an expert on nuclear physics and fissile materials. But a man's record—the cold facts, if you will—doesn't tell you everything. You have to weigh the intangibles, try to read his character, rely on intuition, etc. Given your past difficulties, I know you understand this.

"I accept that you believe Drummond was not a practicing homosexual. I, on the other hand, have to weigh the evidence the FSB presented. And in this case their report has undercut you. Until I receive evidence to the contrary, I have no choice but to believe what I've read about Drummond. And in that respect, when you speak to Mrs. Drummond, you will not reveal any information that's in the report. Is that understood?"

"Understood."

Radford paused to click a computer mouse, which activated a flat-screen monitor. Data appeared, then a picture of Drummond. Radford typed in a word, clicked the mouse, and waited. The screen data changed and he swung his attention back to Scott.

"We've a delicate situation on our hands. As you know, the President is scheduled to attend a summit meeting with Russia's president in St. Petersburg ten days hence. Many issues will be discussed, chief among them economic assistance and international terrorism. The President will likely support Russia's continuing battle to eradicate Chechen terrorism, which is responsible for that recent concert hall massacre in Moscow.

We need Russia's support in the UN Security Council for our ongoing reforms in the Middle East, especially in Iran. Another issue on the President's agenda is securing Russian fissile materials from dismantled submarines. It's piling up at their naval bases on the Kola Peninsula.

"Fissile material from decommissioned submarine reactors," Scott said.

"Yes. Drummond was in Russia working with a Norwegian group called Earth Safe. They're trying to inventory and prepare the fissile materials for transfer to secure storage facilities that are being built with U.S. funds. He was working with Earth Safe when he disappeared and was later found dead."

Scott knew that Drummond and Earth Safe faced a daunting task. Russia's helter-skelter approach to the dismantling of their old nuclear submarines, and the defueling of their reactors had not only contaminated huge tracts of land in and around northern Russian cities, the fissile materials also presented a tempting target for terrorists bent on constructing a nuclear device. The Russians had as much to fear from terrorists as the U.S. did. A nuclear device in the hands of Chechen terrorists was too frightening to contemplate. But with the Russian economy only now beginning to recover from years of Communist control, funds for the disposal of nuclear materials had dried up.

Scott said, "And you're thinking that while Drummond was up in Murmansk, he stumbled into a personal situation and took advantage of it?"

"Yes, that's how I see it."

"Well, I don't. Drummond wouldn't pay for sex. Not from a high-class call girl, much less a young man. Besides, his wife had just visited him in St. Petersburg."

"Whatever," Radford said, unmoved by Scott's argument, "Drummond's death can't in any way interfere with the summit or cause embarrassment."

"I presume the President has been informed."

"I briefed Paul Friedman. I thought it better that the national security advisor know about it first so he can maneuver the President around any land mines waiting in Russia."

"Do the Russians know?"

"If you mean the Kremlin, I can't say. I assume the FSB keeps them informed about everything, but about this, who can be sure? In any event, it could prove embarrassing to both sides."

Scott didn't see anything embarrassing about Drummond's death. If anything, he wanted to prove the FSB wrong and clear the man's name. And the best place to start would be in Moscow.

Radford clicked the mouse. "Drummond had possession of sensitive materials, documents, CD-ROMs. He billeted at the embassy so you'll have to find the materials, seal and return them via diplomatic pouch as soon as possible. Also, take care to sanitize his personal belongings. We wouldn't want Mrs. Drummond to have a nasty surprise."

Scott ignored this last admonition. "Who's my liaison at the embassy?"

Radford looked at the monitor. "Chap named Alex Thorne. Second science attaché. Don't know anything about him, only that he was apparently working with Drummond and has connections with Earth Safe. He may know something about Drummond's movements around Murmansk. But be discreet. Your orders state that you're a CACO–Casualty Assistance Control Officer–and the embassy staff may be able to help you cut through any bureaucracy attending the release of Drummond's body."

"Where do I billet?"

"At a hotel in Moscow. We want you out of sight as much as possible. The Russkies still watch the embassy and it's best they don't see you going in and out every day. You're authorized to wear civilian clothes, which may help you keep a low profile. All of this is spelled out in your orders. You'll also find manifests for the return of the body via U.S. commercial air carrier. And payment vouchers for mortuary services. You will report your progress to me and for that purpose you'll be issued an armored cell phone by the embassy's chief of security. It'll have preselected channels, but use it sparingly. The Russians have gotten better at breaking our signals."

"When do I leave?"

Another glance at the monitor. Another scroll. "Tomorrow night. From Dulles to London, then Sheremetyevo II. Someone from the embassy will meet you. Oh, and one more thing: You'll be working with this Abakov fellow, the FSB officer who wrote the report. Be careful with him. A lot of their people are former KGB and they're not to be trusted. Tell him nothing."

"Aye, aye, sir."

Radford's face took on a steely look. "Admiral Ellsworth told me you're one of his best skippers. That's despite what I've seen in your file."

Scott felt pressure at the base of his skull. "Well, General, as you said, the files don't always tell the whole story."

"Indeed. Just don't prove me wrong."

Scott spotted the strip mall on Route 7 outside Falls Church, Virginia. A quarter mile beyond it, Scott turned onto a narrow street and drove past 1960's-era split levels and ranchers until he came to a house surrounded by a fence in need of repair. He pulled into the driveway and parked behind a silver Buick.

The Drummond property looked unkempt and weedy, but the house had been recently painted. He spotted a barbecue kettle and lawn chairs stacked against the garage, forgotten since summer. Who would take care of these things now? he wondered. Now that Frank was dead.

A radiator knocked but inside, the house felt chilly and damp, perhaps something to do with Frank's absence that was palpable. The house felt familiar. The vanilla-colored woodwork and neutral carpeting. A glass-fronted cabinet filled with knickknacks from the Far East: porcelain, carved ivory Buddhas, lacquered rice bowls inlaid with mother-of-pearl. Drummond's collection of Navy memorabilia on shelves in his study: a cracked coffee mug, a nickel-plated ashtray, cigarette lighters emblazoned with the logos of the subs he'd served in. Evidence of a life lived.

"I made us something to eat," said Vivian Drummond. Her face looked drawn, eyes liquid.

They sat in the kitchen, which gave onto a deep yard bounded at one end by a copse of leafless maples. Vivian pushed up the sleeves of her mauve sweater and poured coffee. She set out freshly made chicken salad on beds of lettuce, and chilled white wine. Always the perfect hostess. Everything just right even in tragedy. Then she broke down.

Scott held her, rocking her like a child.

"I don't understand it," she said. "I just saw him in St. Petersburg. We had a wonderful visit. Romance, dinner, the theater. He was looking forward to wrapping up his work and coming home. It's beyond belief. I can't comprehend how such a thing could happen. All those years in the boats, the dangerous missions that scared the hell out of him and me—not a scratch, and now this. A robbery in Murmansk."

Scott knew that the story concocted by the SRO, of a robbery gone bad, would not ease Vivian's pain. And there was nothing he could say that wouldn't make him feel less guilty for betraying her.

"Vivian, did Frank tell you what he was doing in Murmansk?"

Vivian dabbed her eyes, tried to limit the damage to her makeup. "I look a mess. No. He never talked about his work. Never. And a good Navy wife doesn't ask."

They tried to eat their meal that suddenly had lost its appeal. Instead Vivian drank a glass of wine. She got up, sat down, got up again. "I don't think I can stay here, Jake. Not now. Too many memories. I'll sell and head south. Or maybe California."

"Things may look different later. We can talk about it when I return."

Vivian went to him. "Jake, I don't know how to express my gratitude. It's got to be terribly difficult for you, too, bringing him back."

"I owe him. I owe him everything. He knew what they planned to do with me. He made them admit the truth. They knew we were lucky to get out alive, lucky to save the ship. Everyone involved in the mission knew the risks we ran—Ellsworth, the rest of them . . ." He caught himself. "Sorry, Viv. I didn't mean to bring it up. Not now. It's just that—"

"I understand. Frank would understand. Didn't he always?"

"Sure."

Jake sensed Vivian's resource of stoicism had been drained dry. Her shoulders sagged and her fine features were about to crumble. He kissed her on the cheek and stood back. "It shouldn't take me more than a week. I'll take care of everything."

"Will they catch the person who murdered Frank?"

"I understand the Russian security service is working closely with the embassy. I'll look into it." It was one lie he could live with.

When it seemed Vivian didn't want to talk about it anymore, Scott knew it was time to go. But she caught his arm and said, "There is one thing."

Scott had started to shrug into his coat and stopped.

"When I saw Frank in St. Petersburg, he seemed distracted," Vivian said. "Oh, we were having fun, but beneath the surface I could tell that something was working on him. I knew how he was, how he had that damnable ability to be two people at the same time. He knew how to hide behind a mask of absurd good cheer even while his guts were churning."

"Did he say anything—anything at all—about what might have been bothering him?"

"No, the only thing he said was something I knew he meant as a joke about how my being in St. Petersburg had saved him from himself."

"What did he say?"

"That he had a blind date lined up in Murmansk."

# 3

## The Inner City, St. Petersburg

The girl's long booted legs strode over cobblestones. One false step on stiletto heels would end badly for her. Demonstrating phenomenal poise, she negotiated the narrow street without a mishap. The street paralleled the Fontanka River, which was south of the Neva. It ended in a pleasant little park complete with benches and a fountain that served as a hub from which, like spokes in a wheel, three equally narrow streets branched off to other parts of the city. A few pedestrians lugging groceries in net bags or walking their dogs crisscrossed the square lost in their own reveries.

Alikhan Zakayev sat on a bench near the fountain, which had been turned off at the onset of cold weather. Bundled up in his cashmere topcoat, he looked like a successful businessman who had sought a haven from the bustle of the city. On the bench next to him was a soft black leather zipper portfolio like those favored by Westerners. Instead of paperwork and a cell phone, the bag held a Heckler & Koch 9mm P7 pistol and a Czechoslovakian fragmentation grenade.

Zakayev admired the girl's performance as he watched

her clip-clop over the stones, sable coat and all, long black hair parted down the middle spilling over her shoulders like wings.

He had found her when she was fourteen, living on the streets in Grozny and suffering from starvation and dysentery. She had been raped and sodomized by Russian soldiers and left for dead. Her family had simply disappeared. One night the Spetsnaz showed up at her house and took them away. She had hid in the barn, and after her family had been forced at gunpoint aboard a truck, she watched Russian boys shoot the livestock and loot what little food was left before tossing phosphorus grenades into the house and barn. She escaped with only the clothes she had on and her parents' wedding album wrapped in oilcloth.

The girl had bound her life to Zakayev's, even considered herself his "wife," which he didn't discourage. But Zakayev's devotion to his cause didn't allow attachments. Enemies could use them to destroy you. A woman made you vulnerable. Love made you weak, and a man devoted to the cause had to be strong. He had early on learned to purge himself of sentiment. To Zakayev the girl was simply a beautiful object that gave him pleasure. But there were moments when he saw what might have been if the world he knew had not been destroyed.

The girl came up to Zakayev. He watched her casually finger-comb her hair, fascinated how she had transformed that ritual into a viscerally erotic act. "You saw him?" he asked.

"Yes," she said. "He's on his way. And he's alone."

"He never travels alone." His hand brushed the leather portfolio, then patted the bench. "Sit. It will distract him while we talk."

The girl sat, crossed her legs, and began swinging a pointy-toed boot in the direction of a heavyset man walking slowly toward them from the direction of the river. He had a slight limp from an encounter with a Russian antipersonnel mine in Grozny. The shattered leg had not been set properly but he never complained. There were more important things to worry about. The meeting with Zakayev, for one.

Ivan Serov. The unassuming manner, workaday clothes, and halting walk belied the fact that Serov led one of the most ruthless Russian *mafiya* gangs in all of Russia. His network had not only penetrated the Russian economy, it trafficked in everything from drugs and weapons to human organs. Zakayev knew that Serov also fronted for many high-level Russian bureaucrats involved in bank and credit card fraud, loan-sharking, and smuggling. For Serov, maintaining control of his billion-dollar empire was worth fighting and dying for.

"I almost didn't recognize you without your beard, Alikhan Andreyevich," said Serov. "And that dapper mustache." His eyes roamed Zakayev's face, his clothes, the bulging portfolio. "You are suddenly prosperous, no?" He gave the girl a slight head bob; his gaze lingered on her for a moment.

"How is the leg, Ivan Ivanovich?" Zakayev looked into a pair of dark eyes under bushy eyebrows. The battered face was pale and doughy, raw from the cold. Serov wore a bulky down-filled coat, and Zakayev wondered if under it he had on body armor.

The leg? Serov shrugged. It was nothing. He gazed around the square, perhaps judging distances, assessing escape routes. He sat down beside the girl. She made a move but Serov put a hand on her thigh and said, "Please, stay."

At length Serov said, "It's a long trip from Moscow to St. Petersburg. I haven't been in the city of the czars for a while. I almost don't recognize it, it's changed so much. All the construction. The Winter Palace is beautiful. I hope the American president will appreciate it. They say he's not interested in culture, just money."

"They say his wife is devoted to the arts," Zakayev snorted.

"She's a former actress. Married to a black politician who once marched with that—what was his name? King. And became president. Only in America. That's why he's coming to Russia. He wants to talk about business. No harm in that. If business between the U.S. and Russia is good, we all benefit. Even you, Ali."

"He also wants to assure the Kremlin that in return for privileged oil deals and continuing support for America's war on the Middle East, the U.S. will not object to the massacre of Chechen civilians and the destruction of our country."

Serov frowned. "We all have our business interests, Ali. Some of us have even been willing to compromise to get the deals we want. Perhaps you should consider it. The Americans are not indifferent to your concerns but are caught in the middle. They think they can bring the Kremlin around to accepting that independence for Chechnya is inevitable. But it will take time."

"We don't have time. Our people are being murdered. The Russians torture children and old women, destroy cities and homes . . . But you know all that."

"You're too impatient."

"Am I? The war has gone on for over ten years. It won't end until the Russians are defeated, until their people and cities are destroyed too."

"You tried that and it didn't work. The bombing of

the Tchaikovsky Concert Hall was a disaster. Killing a thousand Russian civilians—women and children too—only hardened their resolve."

Zakayev turned flaring eyes on Serov. "And now they know our resolve is unbreakable. Now they will fear the worst."

"What, killing a million Russians instead of a thousand?"

"Those are only numbers."

"This time, if you kill even a hundred Russians, the Kremlin will declare martial law."

"Which will be bad for business. Ivan Serov's business."

"Yes."

An elderly woman walking a schnauzer on a lead said, *"Dobry den'!"*

Zakayev nodded good day.

Serov leaned against the girl sitting between them and thrust his big head toward Zakayev. He smelled of tobacco and garlic. "I asked for this meeting, Ali, to discuss mutual concerns, not to listen to one of your speeches."

"And I told you there was nothing to discuss. Anyway, I'm done giving speeches. It's too late for that."

"In business, my friend, it is never too late to discuss a mutually beneficial deal." Serov got to his feet. "Come, the three of us, we'll take a stroll. My leg hurts when I sit too long."

Serov linked his arm through Zakayev's and turned him toward one of the narrow spoke streets that led back to the river. With a sudden deft move that surprised Zakayev, he took the heavy, bulky leather portfolio from Zakayev and gave it to the girl. "She can carry it for you, eh? Your cell phone may go off. I don't want any distractions while we talk."

Serov steered Zakayev toward the Anichkov Most, one of the city's most beautiful bridges. "I have a message for you from the Brotherhood." He was referring to the Muslim Brotherhood, an Islamic organization based in the Middle East that supplied Zakayev and his men with money for weapons through one of Serov's many front organizations, for which Serov extracted an exorbitant fee. "They promise that they will supply you with whatever you need to continue the fight against Russian control inside Chechnya's borders. But they won't support any plan you have to launch another attack on Russia itself. In other words, they won't support another operation on the scale of the concert hall massacre."

"Do they think—do *you* think—that the Kremlin will pull its troops out if we suddenly give up and ask for a negotiated peace? No. As long as the Russian Army occupies our country and commits atrocities, we will continue to fight. As for the draft of a new constitution, we will never accept one drawn up by the Kremlin because the moment they think we have lost our resolve, they will attack in force. That's the only thing they understand: force. And we will meet them with equal force. If the Brotherhood won't support us, so be it. We'll get help from other organizations who are sympathetic to our cause."

"The moment may be approaching, Alikhan Andreyevich, for you to consider alternatives. For the Islamic extremist movement, funds are becoming harder to raise. If you alienate the Brotherhood, how can you hope to find the money needed to fund your operations? They control the flow of money to organizations like yours from the Saudis, Syria, Libya, Iran, even the North Koreans, and will simply cut you off."

"You forgot to mention your own organization."

"I'm only a simple middleman. I control nothing. You seem to think I have more power than I actually do."

Zakayev snorted. "You have unlimited power, Ivan Ivanovich, and unlimited resources. Why pretend you don't? You don't care about our cause. What you care about is losing your fat brokerage fees if the Brotherhood cuts off our funds. Well, let me tell you, we have other ways of dealing with that. Our people are dedicated. They will do whatever must be done."

"That's what troubles the Brotherhood. And what troubles me. They're not stupid. We both know how you think. We both know what's possible."

The trio reached the hub where the narrow cobblestone streets met the roundabout with the fountain at its center. The streets themselves were lined with three-story czarist-era buildings recently restored to their former glory and resplendent in their creamy yellow and white paint.

"And what is it that you think you know, Ivan Ivanovich?" said Zakayev.

"I know, for instance, about the death of an American in Murmansk. Rumor has it that your people were involved. Why?"

Zakayev stopped and unlinked his arm from Serov's. He faced the *mafiyosoi* and said, "The rumors are wrong. You shouldn't believe them."

Serov took hold of Zakayev's coat lapels. "You're not listening to me Ali. We will lose everything we have gained if you go ahead with another large-scale operation. If you are planning something big—bigger than the concert hall operation—and you succeed, the Russians will turn Chechnya into a wasteland."

"But they have already turned it into a wasteland."

For a moment his eyes went to the girl taking it all in, then back to Serov. "Ask her, if you don't already know this, and she'll tell you."

One of the most dangerous men in Russia gave Zakayev a menacing look. He took time to light a cigarette. When he spoke, his voice was cold and flat. "Not only are you pigheaded, Alikhan Andreyevich, you insult me."

Zakayev said nothing.

"As a practical matter," Serov said icily, "whatever it is you are planning, I suggest you change your mind and put it off."

Zakayev gave Serov a crafty smile. "Is that a threat?

Serov, looking down, rolled the flattened brown cigarette between a thumb and forefinger. "I don't believe in threats," he said.

"Then go back to Moscow," said Zakayev. "We have nothing more to discuss."

Serov took the cigarette out of his mouth and made a face.

Zakayev, alert, saw an almost imperceptible gathering of feral energy in Serov's body. The *mafiyosoi* raised his arm over his head and, with a sweeping gesture that gave the appearance of being staged, threw the cigarette he was smoking into the dry fountain, where it landed with a shower of sparks among withered leaves and dried bird droppings.

A split second later Zakayev heard the thunder of tires on cobblestones echoing off the fronts of buildings. He spun around and saw terrified pedestrians flatten themselves against the walls of buildings as a black BMW hurtled down one of the narrow streets.

Behind Zakayev a burgundy BMW, its tires thundering over the cobblestones and scattering pedestrians, hurtled down another street from the direction of the river toward the hub. The two big sedans, tires howling, engines roaring, raced each other round the fountain as if playing tag. A man wearing a balaclava leaned out an open front window of the black car and opened fire on the burgundy car behind him.

Serov the gimp, backpedaling toward the fountain, had drawn a heavy automatic from his coat pocket. Zakayev heard a powerful explosion, then another. He saw Serov slam against the rim of the fountain. The girl, aiming the pistol she'd pulled from the portfolio, was ready to shoot Serov again. But before she could, Zakayev dragged her to the cobblestones out of the line of fire, breaking her fall with his body.

Bullets whined off the fountain and cobblestones. Someone in the burgundy car returned fire. Bullets thunked into BMW sheet metal, slapped through windshields. The black car swung too wide and sideswiped an iron bench, then fishtailed, jumped the curb, and slammed head on into a stone wall fronting one of the czarist-era houses. Steel shrieked and buckled; diamonds of shattered safety glass exploded against the wall. The car rebounded, leaving both the driver's and gunman's heads tangled in the bloody folds of the deflated air bags that had punched through the bulging windshield.

The burgundy BMW slewed to a stop; its doors flew open and pairs of strong hands dragged Zakayev and the girl into the car. Zakayev felt brutal acceleration, heard tires spinning, fighting for traction on the cobblestones. The girl lay sprawled on her stomach in the backseat across the lap of one of the brutes from the auto repair shop. Her long hair flew every which way and her stockings had been torn at both knees. Zakayev, lying on his back on the floor of the car, saw that she still had a tight grip on the pistol and an exultant look on her face.

"I shot him," she said. "I shot Serov."

*"Dobro pojalovat'v Rossiyu*—welcome to Russia, Captain Scott."

He saw a pretty woman with short blond hair and a serious look on her face. She had on sneakers, jeans, and a down-filled jacket over a turtleneck. Not the typical U.S. Embassy greeter sent to fetch a jet-lagged VIP, thought Scott, but just as well. Low profile, Radford had said.

*"Spasiba*—thank you. I'm supposed to meet—"

"That's right, I'm Alex Thorne," she said.

"But I thought—"

"I know what you thought. My name is Alexandra, but everyone calls me Alex."

They shook hands while passengers departing customs and immigration flowed around them like a river.

"Sorry for my getup," she said, "but they didn't tell me I was to pick you up until an hour ago. Shall we go?"

Outside the terminal she muscled a black Embassy SUV from the parking lot through airport traffic and sped for the Moscow Ring Road via the International Highway.

"Where are you quartered, Captain?" she asked, all business now.

"Jake."

She smiled. "Right. Jake."

He looked at her profile, the straight line of nose, taut chin, and full lips. She pushed blond hair behind an ear and gave Scott a glance.

"The Marriot Grand," he said. "They broke the budget for me."

"I take it you've stayed there before."

"During my last tour."

"Ah. Then you know your way around Moscow."

He glanced out the SUV's tinted windows at a forest of construction cranes rising over the Russian capital's skyline. "But I hear it's changed a lot."

"It sure has. Parts of Moscow are like a Potemkin village, while other parts of it are more like the States than the States. Shopping malls are popping up all over. Want mall rats? We have 'em. Rap stars too." She wrinkled her nose. "And terrorism."

"That attack on the concert hall must have everyone on edge."

"Sure does. People here are frightened of what might happen next. Things won't return to normal until Russia pulls out of Chechnya. Even if they do, it may not end the bloodshed. The Chechens have been brutalized and are bent on destroying Russia by any means possible."

"What's your role in this?"

"It's my job to see that Chechen terrorists don't get hold of fissile materials from decommissioned nuclear subs to make a radiation bomb or a nuke. It's a frightening situation. There's so much nuclear rubbish laying around up north that it's almost like another Chernobyl."

"I know it's the most radioactive place in the world," Scott said. "The Russian Northern Fleet has decommissioned—what?—sixty nuclear submarines, nearly their entire fleet. That's more than a hundred reactors to safeguard. Can it be done?"

"Not the way things are. The Russian Navy's main concern is when they're going to be paid. A crew in charge of a laid-up nuclear submarine is hardly thinking about security. Plus, many of the crews are unfit for service. A month ago a sailor at the sub base in Olenya Bay went berserk and killed five people before he killed himself. A week later a guard at a nuclear reprocessing plant in Siberia killed his boss and two coworkers. A terrorist could easily walk onto a base and steal enough nuclear fuel to make a dirty bomb. Just mix a couple of kilos of strontium 90 with Semtex and set it off in Moscow."

"What are the Russians doing about secure storage?"

"It's a joke. Most of the boats are rusting away at their piers and in danger of sinking. In Murmansk, for instance, an old Hotel-class sub laid up in a fjord is in such bad shape that the navy's afraid to move it for fear it'll sink. As for storage, the concrete bunkers are overflowing with solid and liquid waste. Worse yet, they've dumped scores of naval reactor assemblies into the Barents Sea. Talk about shitting in your own backyard."

Alex whipped the SUV around a line of slow-moving lorries hauling precast concrete pilings to a Moscow construction site. Another motorist seemed to take offense and sped past the SUV with a middle finger raised defiantly.

"The Russian economy is just starting to climb out of the tank and they have no money for cleaning up the mess," she said. "Norway and the U.S. have signed agreements with Russia to help build a processing plant. But it will take years. Meanwhile there's the war in Chechnya— Uh-oh."

Scott saw her eyes flick to the rearview mirror. A pale gray car with flashing red and blue lights on its roof came up fast and tucked in behind the SUV. He heard the familiar hee-hawing and knew what it was.

"Shit," said Alex.

*"Gaishnik*—traffic cop?"

"GAI—traffic inspector. He sees the diplomatic plates and knows he can't get a bribe out of us, just wants to give us a hard time." She braked and pulled onto the shoulder to stop.

"Like I said," Scott said, "nothing has changed."

The officer, in creaking leather and mirrored sunglasses, got out of his patrol car and approached. He motioned that Alex should lower her window.

*"Vaditel'skie prava."* The cop looked past Alex, at Scott.

Alex fixed the cop with a disapproving gaze. *"Nyet. Ya Amerikanski diplomat."* She pointed to herself and Scott.

"Your driver's license," the cop demanded again, this time in English.

She handed it over and he kept it as he made a slow circuit of the SUV, thumped a fender, and returned to the open window. Alex held out a hand for the document.

"This vehicle has a burned-out brake light."

"Thank you for pointing it out, Officer. I'll be sure to tell the motor pool mechanic at the American Embassy," she said, emphasizing *American* and *Embassy*. "Now, if you don't mind, we're on our way to a meeting with an official of your government."

"It's dangerous to drive with a burned-out brake light. It can cause an accident and you can be arrested." The cop eyed Alex from behind his mirrors, perhaps weighing whether or not he could wrangle a bribe after all.

"I'm sure you're right, Officer," Alex said. She reached out and plucked her license from the cop's hand. Before he could react, she upped the power window and drove off. "Prick."

Scott smiled but said nothing. The only thing he and

Alex had in common so far was an interest in Drummond's death. But he was beginning to like her a lot. He also liked the way she took charge and admired her determination not to be intimidated, which was a tall order when dealing with dangerous materials scattered across the Kola Peninsula or bribe-hungry Russian cops.

Alex got on the car phone with the embassy duty officer and detailed their encounter with the *gaishnik.* She also gave an ETA at the Marriott Grand. "Just in case," she said to the duty officer.

She was an attractive woman and Scott wondered if she'd gotten involved with Drummond–and if she had, how his death, in a hotel room with a naked Russian sailor had affected her. It wasn't idle erotic speculation on his part: He'd need her help and had to gain her trust if he was going to discover how Drummond had died. There was little to go on and little time to find answers.

"Sorry," Alex said, hanging up the phone. "I thought it best they know."

They caught up to and repassed the lorry convoy. She took the next exit to the inner ring road and crossed the Krymsky Bridge over the Moskva. Traffic had thinned, and, wrist draped over the wheel, Alex relaxed and permitted herself a look in Scott's direction.

"I know you must have a lot of questions about Frank," Alex said.

"I do. I have orders to escort him home, but that's not the only reason I'm here. I know you worked with him on the nuclear security side. That he was liaison to the Norwegians and Earth Safe. What else?"

"He was a great guy. We were more than colleagues: We were friends. He always had a good sea story to tell. He never got impatient, never got angry. He was a good listener too. We worked well together. When he died, I was devastated."

"Do you believe the death report the FSB filed with the embassy."

Her mouth tightened. "I don't know. It didn't seem possible . . . I mean, that Frank was . . . gay. I know he was married, that his wife paid him a visit in St. Petersburg, but still, I don't know what to believe."

"What was he doing in Murmansk that night?"

"I'm not sure."

"You were there with him, weren't you?"

"Actually, I wasn't. We'd been in Murmansk for two weeks, digging through records, photographing sites, interviewing Russian naval personnel. We had been aboard several submarines waiting to be dismantled in Olenya Bay, tagging equipment and such. But we'd also been aboard a nuclear sub that was being readied for a patrol."

"A sub still in commission?"

"Yes, a fairly new one, as they go."

"Do you remember which one?"

"An Akula, the *K-363.*"

"What were you doing aboard her?"

"Interviewing the crew. We try to develop a baseline on crew proficiency and training. As you know, active submariners in the Russian Navy are trained at their nuclear power school. From them we sometimes select individuals for special training in the handling of nuclear materials ashore."

"Go on."

"I'd returned to Moscow to file a report a day before Frank was due to wrap up in Murmansk on Tuesday. But my train was delayed by bad weather and I didn't get to Moscow and to the embassy until Thursday morning. I found a message from Frank on my embassy voice mail system, but it was so garbled I couldn't understand it. He had used a cell phone and it sounded like he was heading back to Moscow on Friday, but that something had come up. Anyway, when he didn't show on Saturday, I called the Norwegians and the base commander at Olenya Bay. They both said he'd left for Moscow Thursday night. That's when I notified the authorities in Murmansk that he was missing. They found him on Sunday. With the dead Russian sailor. And the gun."

Alex touched the corner of an eye. "I don't know what to believe," she added again after a long, thoughtful silence.

Scott told her about his friendship and naval service with Drummond, and about Vivian.

"Then you don't believe the FSB report," Alex said.

"No."

"Then, what do you think happened to Frank?" The way she asked the question seemed to imply that she knew what his answer would be.

"I think he was murdered."

"But the report said–"

"I know what it said: suicide. But it's bullshit."

"Who would murder him?" Alex said.

"I don't know. But I need you to help me find out."

They crossed Tverskaya Prospekt, an exclusive shopping street lined with expensive boutiques and hotels. Even so, Scott spotted a new McDonald's restaurant going up next to a Prada store.

She gave Scott a look. "How can I possibly help you?"

"You were with him a good part of the time he was in Murmansk. Maybe there's something you can remember that'll help. Like his cell phone call."

"Forget that. I told you, it's useless. Totally garbled."

"Did you know the sailor who died?"

"No. All I knew was that he was assigned to the *K-363.*"

"Then, how did Drummond know him? What personal business would a Russian enlisted sailor have had with an American naval officer?"

"Beats me, Jake."

"Those are things we have to know."

"But how can you hope to find the killer if you're here only to take Frank's body back to the States. You don't have time to investigate anything."

"I'll make time."

"Jake, the ambassador wants Frank's affairs wrapped up before the summit. And you know the Russians: how their bureaucracy moves at a glacial pace. The FSB's not going to help you because they've already investigated and submitted their report."

"I've got a meeting tomorrow morning with the investigator who handled the case," Scott said. "Yuri Abakov. Do you know him?"

"I saw his name on the report and I gave a statement to one of his people, but I've never met him."

"Tomorrow we'll try to find out what else Abakov knows."

" 'We'?"

"You're coming with me. I want him to know we're working together."

"Uh-uh. I'm not getting involved, Jake. I'm the second science attaché, and my jurisdiction is limited to finding loose nuclear material, not investigating a murder."

"Then, you do think they were murdered. Right?"

Alex said nothing.

"You said Frank was a friend not just a colleague," Scott said.

Alex pursed her lips.

"Well, he was my friend, too, and we owe him."

She started to say something, but he pointed. The Marriott Grand had appeared on the right. She pulled in under the arched portico. Scott got out with his things but, before closing the door, leaned back into the SUV and said, "Tomorrow, Lubyanskaya Ploshchad. Know it?"

"Of course," Alex said.

"Good. Pick me up here zero eight hundred sharp."

"Jake, I told you—"

"Do it for Frank."

# 4

## FSB Headquarters, Moscow

Outside, a pair of guards in a glassed-in booth checked IDs. Inside, helmeted officers in battle dress armed with Heckler & Koch MP5 submachine guns strolled the remodeled former KGB headquarters lobby. The city and its entire security apparatus were on alert after the Chechen massacre at the concert hall. Everyone was suspect.

Scott and Alex waited at the elevator banks. Alex wore a tailored black suit and white silk roll-neck top. A medley of gold bracelets glittered on her wrists. Light from the recessed ceiling fixtures illuminated her even features and flawless makeup. Her eyes sparkled, and she obviously enjoyed the attention her transformation had elicited from Scott.

A ping, and a pair of elevator doors hissed open. Their escort, a young FSB officer, motioned them inside. The doors closed, the car rose, and Scott was struck by the irony that in another era he and Alex would have been riding this elevator to an interrogation cell in the basement from which few people had ever emerged alive. All he heard was the hushed sound of the car's ascent, not the screams of prisoners undergoing torture. As if guessing what was on his mind, Alex gave him an almost imperceptible nod.

They got off on the tenth floor, in one of the oldest parts of the three high-rises that made up the FSB headquarters. The hallways were floored in worn linoleum and illuminated by buzzing fluorescent lamps. Office doors had old-fashioned pebbled glass inserts, behind one of which was the blurred silhouette of a man gesturing expansively while haranguing someone unseen.

"Please." The escort led them through an open door labeled Investigations Directorate, into a tiny, overheated office.

Yuri Abakov had on a *ushanka* hat, its ear flaps tied securely together on top. His pasty-looking face was expressionless behind a drooping black mustache. He looked up at his visitors from behind a worn wooden desk and, as if shooing a pesky fly, flicked a hand at the escort who departed without a word.

"Inspector Abakov?" Scott said in Russian.

He gave Scott a once-over, noting his leather bomber jacket. "*Colonel* Abakov," he replied. Before Scott had a chance to correct himself, Abakov shifted his gaze. "Who is this?" he asked, as if Alex were incapable of speaking for herself.

"Doctor Alexandra Thorne, Ph.D.," she said. "I'm the second science attaché, United States Embassy, Moscow."

"I wasn't told she'd be present for this meeting," Abakov said to Scott. "Who authorized it?"

"I did," Scott said. "You have a problem with that?" Without waiting to be asked, he pushed a chair toward Alex and took one for himself.

Abakov removed the *ushanka* from a head that was bald except for a fringe of short, dark hair, the tight skin reflecting light like a mirror. His expression had changed from boredom to one of outright annoyance.

"You're not in the States, Commander."

*"Captain,"* said Scott.

"You have no authority here, so don't think that just because you're an American who speaks Russian, you can come into my office and start throwing your weight around like Bloody Harry."

"It's Dirty Harry." Scott put his orders on the desk, in front of Abakov. "There's my authority. As you know, Colonel, I'm here to escort Admiral Drummond's remains back to the United States. I was told that I would have full cooperation from the FSB. And from you. Dr. Thorne was Admiral Drummond's liaison with the U.S. Embassy and the Norwegians. She's agreed to assist me. And since I don't have time to waste cutting through bullshit, I'd like to get started as soon as possible."

Alex's knuckles went white on the chair arms.

Color rose in Abakov's face and spread across his bald pate. He rose from his chair behind the desk. Though he was several inches shorter than Scott, he had thick shoulders and huge, meaty hands that appeared capable of causing severe damage to whatever they grabbed hold of. A heavy vein started pulsing in his neck.

"You Americans," Abakov said, switching to very good English. "You think you own the world. You use your power to crush opposition to your capitalist policies and to force your values on the rest of the world. In Russia, if we resist, you threaten us and say that we are irrelevant. Everything you do is for the purpose of enriching American business. Everything you do around the world has strings attached. You are hypocrites!" Abakov's voice rose until it boomed like rolling thunder. "You would like nothing better than to conquer Mother Russia so your business conglomerates can suck us dry! Your military too!"

The door flew open and a man stuck his head in and looked around. "Yuri, I can hear you all the way down the other end of the hall. Is everything all right?"

Abakov caught his breath. "Yes, go away."

The man looked around, shrugged, and left. Abakov, slightly winded, sat down.

"Are you finished lecturing us?" Scott said.

Abakov ignored this and read Scott's orders while touching the pulsing vein in his neck.

"What can you add to your report on Drummond's death?" Scott said, as if Abakov's outburst had not occurred.

Abakov bristled. "Nothing. Everything is in the report. Admiral Drummond and another man were both found dead in bed together. Ballistics confirmed that the bullets in their brains had been fired from the gun we found in Admiral Drummond's possession."

Scott waved that away. "I'm not questioning the basic facts of the case, Colonel. But allow me to explain something to you." Scott told Abakov what he knew about Drummond and detailed their professional and personal relationship. He finished, saying, "I assure you, he was not a homosexual."

Abakov, a blank expression on his face, appeared unconvinced.

"Now let me tell you something," Abakov said evenly in English. "I've been an investigator for almost thirty years. I understand human nature. I learned to think not only with my brain"—he tapped his head with a thick finger—"but also with my eyes. Sometimes the truth is right in front of you and all you have to do is look at it. Sometimes it even jumps up and bites you in the ass. There in Murmansk, in that hotel room, was Admiral Drummond, dead, shot in the head. Lying next to him was the young sailor, Andre Radchenko, also dead. Admiral Drummond had in his hand the pistol used to kill the young man and himself. What the report doesn't say is that the two were found lying very close together, embracing, you might even say. Each had a hand on the other's genitals, more or less, rigor mortis being what it is."

Alex put a hand to her mouth.

"Experience told me that these two had had a *gomoseksualist*—homosexual—encounter. But something went wrong. Perhaps they had had a lovers' quarrel. It happens all the time. Or perhaps Admiral Drummond realized that one day he would return to his wife and couldn't bear the thought of losing his young male lover."

"Nonsense," Alex said. "None of that fits the Frank Drummond I knew. What you've described is totally out of character."

Abakov's gaze fixed on Alex. At length he said, "Dear lady, you were intimate with Admiral Drummond?"

"What do you mean by 'intimate'?"

"Did you have sexual intercourse with him?"

Alex started. "Of course not. Our relationship was strictly business."

"Then how do you know he wasn't gay or bisexual?"

"A woman can tell."

Abakov shrugged dismissively. "Of course."

"I want to view Drummond's body before it's prepared for shipment to the States," Scott said. "Alex?"

She nodded faintly.

"Can you make the arrangements, Colonel?"

Abakov looked exasperated.

"What's the problem?" Scott said.

"The problem, Captain, is that my department lacks manpower. The few men I have are overworked. Visiting a corpse uses up time better spent solving crimes. I myself have not been home for supper in a week and my children have forgotten what I look like. My wife is not, as you Americans would say, a happy camper."

"Sorry," said Scott.

"Sorry, yes." Abakov pointed to a stack of case folders on his desk and on the floor. "The FSB has a backlog of these and not enough men to handle them." He picked up a file and slapped it with the back of a hand. "Here, for instance. We've had to send a team to St. Petersburg to find an FSB officer who has been missing for several days. We have no idea what happened to him. On top of that, there was also a *mafiya* shoot-out in St. Petersburg in which a man ended up dead, another perhaps badly wounded, but we don't know for sure. It appears the dead man was a member of Ivan Serov's organization, which has links to Alikhan Zakayev, who we believe was behind the bombing of the Tchaikovsky Concert Hall. The pressure from the Kremlin, to say nothing of your Secret Service, to find Zakayev before the summit opens is unrelenting."

"He's your number one suspect?" Scott said.

"Yes. He's a monster who enjoys killing Russians. Can you imagine killing a thousand innocent civilians? The sooner we find and capture him, the sooner we can end this nightmare of terrorism."

"Any leads on his whereabouts?" Scott said.

"All we know is that where one finds Serov, one often finds Zakayev."

"Interesting. What do you make of the fact that Zakayev may have been in St. Petersburg?" Scott said.

"At the moment, nothing. In any event, I am eager to

wrap up this Drummond business," Abakov said, shifting subjects. "After all, we don't want something like this unfortunate incident in Murmansk to affect U.S.-Russian relations."

"My thoughts exactly," Scott said.

Abakov jammed the *ushanka* on his head and reached for the phone. "I'll let the morgue know we are coming."

A 9mm slug had furrowed Zakayev's left forearm just below the elbow. The girl had fussed over him until the painkillers made him drowsy and he fell asleep. He awoke hungry and in pain. While he ate, the girl demonstrated by poking a finger through a bullet hole in the sleeves of his cashmere topcoat and suit jacket, both stiff with dried blood, the track the bullet had taken.

"Get rid of them," Zakayev said. "Your fur coat too."

The girl tied everything in a bundle and took them into the work area of the car repair shop for disposal.

He had no recollection of having been shot. Only later had he discovered that his clothes were wet with blood. After he'd been stitched up by one of his men, the pain had set in. He was familiar with bullet wounds: He'd been shot twice by Russian *Spetsnaz* in Grozny and had the ugly red scar tissue to prove it. There was no way to know for sure, but he wanted to believe that it had been Serov who shot him.

It had been a setup from the start. No one could be trusted now, not even the Brotherhood. The girl was sure she'd shot Serov, but even if she had, he might still be alive and plotting another trap. Still, Serov would have a mess to deal with in the aftermath of the shootout that could only be cleaned up by bribing members of the St. Petersburg militia and editors and journalists at newspapers and TV stations. He would also have to deal with an FSB already on high alert for terrorist and criminal activity, scouring the city for the missing bull. The thought of Serov feeling heat from the authorities made Zakayev feel better.

The girl returned and watched while Zakayev changed into a nondescript outfit that made him look like a *uchitel*—a teacher—perhaps from some small, provincial technical school. He shaved off his pencil mustache, donned a *ushanka*, and wound a wool scarf around his neck to complete the transformation. The girl, in boots, leather pants, and bulky sweater, would pose as one of his students.

Zakayev heard the hiss and crackle of a transceiver. The man with the black headband who had savaged the bull entered the shop's small office that had served as Zakayev's temporary headquarters.

"Anything?" Zakayev asked.

"Not yet, General," said the man. "There's been no sign of Serov or his men. We checked everywhere, even the hospitals. Maybe he's dead."

"You've done well," Zakayev said. "But Serov is like a cat with nine lives. I have a feeling we'll hear from him again." He looked around the squalid quarters. "Tell the others we'll be done soon."

The man and his crackling radio departed. The girl helped Zakayev pack a small black suitcase with wheels and a retractable handle. Inside were outfits he'd wear later. She had packed her own things in a red nylon backpack similar to those favored by college students the world over. When they were finished, Zakayev summoned his men.

His eyes roamed their faces. They had taken a blood oath to avenge the brutal slaughter of their families in Chechnya and to prove their unquestioned loyalty to him. They had fought at his side, shared the hardships and tragedies the war in Chechnya had unleashed, and together had killed scores of Russian soldiers.

Zakayev recalled an incident during which he and his men had seemingly been driven mad by their unquenchable lust for revenge. He had sucked the coppery taste of blood from the stump of a tooth shattered by the butt of an assault rifle slammed against his face. He spat blood in the Russian's face before driving the butt of his own assault rifle into the soldier's guts, then watched the man choke to death on his own vomit. Zakayev, bleeding from his mouth, head swimming from the blow to this face, leaped over a crumbled wall that once had been part of a house in a small village outside Grozny and, with the girl at his side, took cover.

Locusts shrilled in the midsummer Chechen heat. The landscape rose and fell in unruly heaps of green around decaying homes and farms. Dilapidated houses lined the town's deserted main street. He saw punched-out windows with torn curtains and, farther on, burned-out buildings and piles of rubble. A fire-blackened Russian truck lay upside down, its undercarriage looking like the exposed belly of a giant scorched bug. Six corpses lay scattered around it.

The Russian Zakayev had just killed brought the total to seven. There were at least five more Russians trapped in the barn. The evidence of their crime was in plain view: On the side of the barn in which the Russians hid were the naked crucified bodies of a young Chechen woman and her infant. The Russian soldiers had raped the mother, then nailed her and the child to the side of the barn, driving long iron spikes through their hands and feet. The pale corpses hung, spread-eagle, from the weathered planks. Zakayev and his men caught the soldiers standing around the barn laughing, smoking, drinking vodka.

Hit by an RPG, their truck had roared into the air and crashed back to earth in a ball of flame. The dead lay where they had fallen, twisted, formless, some headless. The others had put up a brief firefight from inside the barn but knew it was hopeless.

After they surrendered Zakayev, made them take the woman and child down and dig their graves. Then, while the Russians, herded back-to-back in a circle, begged for their lives, Zakayev tied them up like a bundle of cordwood. After they were thoroughly doused with gasoline, he set them on fire.

"Ali?"

The mention of his name jolted him from the memory of that day.

"Fighters! You have proven your dedication to the battle for Chechen independence," Zakayev said. "We are fighting a war that we will gladly sacrifice our lives to win. There are still more battles to come, and because our work here is finished, I am releasing you from my command so you can return to Chechnya. There you will organize yourselves, form new cadres, and prepare for the collapse of Russia. When the collapse comes, it will come quickly, perhaps within days. Regional pro-Russian administrators will try to maintain stability in Chechnya, but they and their puppet prime minister will fail because Russia as we know it will cease to exist. Align yourselves as quickly as you can with the new forces of independence that will emerge from the old regime. They will be Chechnya's future."

Each man made a short, awkward speech and renewed his vow of loyalty to Zakayev. The girl produced a bottle of vodka. She filled glasses, jars, and tin cups, which the group, Muslims drinking Russian vodka, raised to toast Zakayev. *"Za vashe zdarov'e!"* Afterward each man had a private moment with Zakayev before departing. The man with the black band around his head waited until the others had departed before speaking to Zakayev.

"I volunteer to stay behind, General, to make sure that Serov is dead. If he's not, I will kill him."

Zakayev poured the man another vodka and one for himself. "Forget Serov. He can't stop us now. No one can. Go back to Chechnya with the others."

"It has been a privilege to serve with you, General. Perhaps someday you will visit Grozny and I will have a new wife and children to present for your blessing."

"Yes, someday," Zakayev said. He thought about what he himself had lost and what this man might gain. "Name one of your children for me."

The men loaded their gear in two cars and departed. One by one, the girl began shutting off the lights in the shop. The man who owned the shop, a Chechen, was due to return from a visit to his wife's family in Pskov and scheduled to reopen for business in the morning without having laid eyes on Zakayev or his men. Or knowing that a freshly dug grave behind the shop had been hidden under parts from wrecked automobiles.

Outside, Zakayev looked at the girl. The backpack hung from her thin shoulders. She had tied her hair back in a long ponytail sticking out from under a knit cap pulled down over her ears. To Zakayev she was just a beautiful child. "Are you afraid?" he asked.

"Afraid of dying?"

"That too."

She kissed his cheek. After a last look around the shop, she closed and bolted the door.

# 5

## Moscow Central Morgue

**The flesh looked cold** and hard like alabaster. Scott didn't touch it, just observed while the technician held up one end of the sheet like a tent flap.

He almost didn't recognize Drummond, which made his task bearable. With several days growth of beard—patchy gray stubble like iron wire—sprouting from a face with a pair of badly sunken cheeks, Drummond looked like he'd been hauled out of a Moscow gutter. Scott imagined Vivian waiting patiently in Falls Church to deliver Drummond's dress blue uniform, freshly pressed and in a plastic bag, to the funeral home.

Scott examined a small hole in Drummond's left temple plugged with cotton stained pink. On the opposite temple he saw a large bulge sutured shut with coarse black thread where, the attending pathologist explained, under a mass of brain tissue and skull fragments he had excavated for and found the bullet that had burrowed laterally through Drummond's head.

Alex, hand to her mouth, hung back. "It's him, isn't it?" she said, unable to tear her eyes away.

"Yes, it's him," Scott said.

The morgue stank of death and antiseptic. It was a miserable concoction of cracked white and green tile and peeling paint. The only light came from fixtures hanging over the double row of stainless-steel autopsy tables, some of which held sheeted corpses waiting their turn. In a nod to the Americans, two aproned and gloved technicians had agreed to delay their work until the viewing was complete.

"He's been autopsied," Scott said, observing the long, sutured scar on the torso. "Why?"

The pathologist started to say something, but Abakov spoke up. "Standard procedure. We check to see if there could be contributing circumstances."

"A heart attack or a seizure," the pathologist added.

"It's pretty obvious what killed him, isn't it?" Scott said, motioning that the sheet should be lowered.

"It would seem so," Abakov said, "but there are strict rules we must follow."

"Where's the kid that they found with him. Radchenko."

"Gone," said the pathologist.

"What do you mean, 'gone'?"

"Released to his family for burial," Abakov said. "I can tell you he had a nearly identical wound to the head. Right-side entry but in his case the bullet exited on the left and did quite a bit more damage than you see here in Admiral Drummond."

"Do you have the bullets?" Scott asked.

"I can get them," the pathologist said, his eyes shifting to Abakov.

Abakov gave a nod.

They waited in silence for the pathologist to return. Abakov smoked, drawing it deep into his lungs. The smoke masked the faint odor of putrefaction lurking under one of the sheeted corpses on a nearby table. Alex looked pale.

The pathologist returned with a blue plastic Ziploc bag containing two small-caliber bullets. Scott dumped them into the palm of his hand. The bullet taken from Drummond, the pathologist explained, was almost pristine. The other bullet had been badly distorted.

"The bullet completely shattered the boy's skull," Abakov explained.

"Where's the pistol these came from?" Scott said.

"Ballistics has it."

"I have a question," Alex, still looking pale, said. "During your autopsy, did you check for semen on or in either body. In other words, could you tell if they had had sex? Did you find any . . . *prezervativy?*" she asked, using the word for condoms.

The pathologist shrugged. "We found no such evidence. It would have been obvious if they had. Usually the rectum shows evidence of trauma—"

"We assume," Abakov broke in, "that they hadn't gotten around to it. There was no evidence of any sexual activity, nor did we find any condoms."

After an awkward interval Abakov said, "Is there anything else you'd like to see?"

Scott put the bullets back in the plastic bag and zipped it shut between a thumb and finger. "The hotel room in Murmansk where they died."

"What did the ambassador say?" Alex said. She handed Scott an iced vodka.

"This is a nice apartment," Scott said. Hers was in a block of modern but uninspired redbrick apartments within the U.S. Embassy compound. Alex had brightened it up with travel posters of California sunsets and

Florida beaches. The furniture was barely serviceable, but by introducing a collection of vases and figurines made of blue-and-white traditional Russian Gzhel porcelain, lacquer boxes, and *matryoshka* nesting dolls purchased on the Arbat, she had created a warm, personalized environment.

"What did he say?" she repeated.

"I didn't talk to him. I met with the deputy chief of mission."

"Stretzlof? He's a pompous ass. And a boor."

"So I discovered," Scott said. He picked up and examined a beautiful reproduction of a sixteenth-century Russian icon, a painting of the saints Comas, Jacob, and Damian dressed in colorful robes and with gold discs radiating saintliness floating behind their heads. "You have a good eye for this sort of thing."

"You have to be selective. The shops in Moscow sell a lot of junk to tourists, but if you shop around you can find exquisite things. Like a Chekhov first edition out of my price range."

"Mine too," Scott said. "Stretzlof wants Drummond's body shipped home as soon as possible. I got the impression it's terribly inconvenient to have a senior military officer murdered in Russia."

"Stretzlof is the ambassador's hatchet man. He fronts for the political section too. Did you meet the political affairs officer?"

"No. Should I have?"

"He's Stretzlof's handpicked man. He and Stretzlof have gone out of their way at times to anger the Russians. I don't get it, because we need them as much as they need us. We want a free hand in the Middle East; they want the same in Chechnya. But hey, I try to mind my own business."

She sat, chin cupped in a fist and looked at Scott. "This is a close-knit community and it's hard not to step on toes," Alex said. "Be careful which ones you step on."

"I had a chat with Brigadier General Carroll," he said. "The defense attaché."

"He offered to help expedite matters, but I told him we could handle things. I didn't tell him that we were going to Murmansk."

"Maybe you should have. If Stretzlof finds out, he'll have a fit. He'll say you've overstepped your orders."

"Wouldn't be the first time," Scott said.

She looked at him guardedly. He sensed a cool, analytical intelligence at work and knew that nothing would likely escape her notice.

"It's a long trip," she added.

"Only twelve hundred klicks. We'll be back before dinner. Besides, it's Abakov's helicopter and gas, so it won't cost Uncle Sam a penny."

"What do you hope to accomplish by going to Murmansk?" Alex said.

Scott prowled the living room. He seemingly was bursting with energy, the room barely able to contain it. "I don't know. But I want to find out what the hell happened. Somebody killed Frank and that sailor and I want to know why. Maybe there's something Abakov's men overlooked."

She threw him a questioning look. "Are you saying that the FSB is covering something up?"

"You tell me. What were you two doing in Murmansk that would be so sensitive someone would kill Frank? Remember what Abakov said? He believes the U.S. is trying to conquer Mother Russia. If someone believes that and killed Frank, they could have killed you too."

Alex gnawed at a fingernail. "We don't do classified

inspections of nuclear weapons—don't go anywhere near them. Abakov believes that nonsense because he can't adjust to the new Russia. He wants things the way they were under Brezhnev, when the KGB ran the country. Then he got regular paychecks and could go around scaring the shit out of Russian citizens. Now he has to be nice to people, especially Americans. He's a dinosaur who can't adjust to a kinder, gentler Russia."

"Can you think of any reason someone would kill Frank and that boy?"

"I told you, Jake, all we did was inspect and inventory reactors and their fuel, and monitor radiation levels at the sub bases. Sometimes it was pretty boring work. What kept it from being boring all the time was that Frank was fun to work with; plus, he kept scrupulous notes, which made the job of writing reports easier."

Scott slugged down his drink. "Then maybe that's where we should start looking: at Frank's notes."

Alex punched a code into a wall-mounted keypad and shut off the embassy's nodal security system inside Drummond's apartment. She and Scott stood in the foyer listening to a hum from the refrigerator and a ticking clock on a table in the tiny living room. Like Alex's apartment, Drummond's was spare, and he'd made no effort to personalize it. A few well-thumbed Russian-language magazines and a *National Geographic* lay on a Scandinavian-style coffee table in the living room. Other than a coffeemaker and box of sealed premeasured packets of coffee, the kitchenette was bare.

Alex said, "Frank took all of his meals at the embassy mess."

"He always used government mess whenever he could," Scott said.

"He kept his papers here," Alex said. "Each apartment is equipped with a safe. Sensitive materials are held at the chancery, but then, he and I didn't handle top-grade material."

She led Scott past a small bedroom that held Drummond's personal effects to an even smaller room off the hallway that had doubled as his office.

A laptop computer, neatly stacked file folders, a laser printer, and reams of packaged copy paper took up all the space on a trestle table. Pens and pencils, points carefully aligned, stood at attention in a ceramic cup with a smiley face on its side next to a pair of radiation monitors equipped with belt clips. To the left of the table a paper shredder on a stand hung over an empty wastebasket. More files and papers had been left neatly stacked on the floor. Drummond had squared everything away before going to Murmansk. Even his caster chair had been parked just so under the table.

Scott sat down and turned on the desk lamp. He selected a thick file from the stack on the floor and opened it. A rough draft of a report had blue-penciled corrections scribbled over the pages and margins. Scott skimmed the first page of a report on the threat posed by loose fissile materials in Russia.

"Tell me what you're looking for," Alex said. "Maybe I can help. This stuff is pretty technical."

"I don't know what I'm looking for, and that's the problem. Maybe there's something here that might give us a hint."

"Jake, the only thing I know for sure is that Radchenko was assigned to the *K-363*. We went aboard the sub and did a walk-through and met the crew, but I don't specifically remember meeting him. I mean, they are all young and look alike with their short haircuts.

Frank interviewed some but not all of the *K-363*'s sailors in private ashore to see if any would be suitable to work with Earth Safe securing materials. We had some problems with that, but nothing we couldn't handle."

Scott's senses came alert. "What kind of trouble?"

"The captain of the *K-363* made it clear that he didn't want us on his boat and that he definitely didn't want us talking to his men ashore—or anywhere else for that matter."

"What was his name—can you remember?"

"How can I forget? Kapitan Third Rank Georgi Litvanov. A prick."

"Kapitan third rank—a full commander. What did he do?"

Alex frowned. "He flat-out told us to get the hell off his ship. He even ordered one of his—what do you call them?—*michman*—"

"Warrant officers."

"Right—to escort us off the boat."

"So what happened?"

"Well, you know Frank. He used that charm of his to defuse the situation, and the next thing he and the *michman* were swapping sea stories."

"What did Litvanov do about that?"

"What could he do? We had permission from the commander of the Russian Northern Fleet as well as the Interior Ministry to do our work. Litvanov sure as hell didn't like it but he had to go along with it. I know that the captain of a naval vessel is God, but he had to relinquish his kingdom to a higher authority."

"This Radchenko was a *krasnoflotets*—an able seaman. What did he tell Drummond?"

"I don't know, because I didn't sit in on the interview."

"But Frank rejected him."

"Yes. Radchenko had hardly any experience in nuclear power. He was just a striker getting on-the-job training. I think he doubled as a mess cook."

Scott raked fingers through his hair. His eyes roamed Frank's desk, darting from object to object. "It doesn't make sense. Frank was always looking out for the welfare of his crew, especially the enlisted men. He understood their problems and knew that a ship and CO is only as good as its crew. But Frank wouldn't necessarily sit down and knock back a few cold ones with his boys. And not this boy. Yet, there he was in Frank's hotel room."

"Maybe he had information Frank wanted."

"What information?"

Her mouth tightened. "I don't know."

"Okay, say he did, but why meet him in a shit hole of a hotel? And why the need for secrecy?" Scott considered for a long moment, gazing down at the gray carpeting as if he might find the answer written there. He looked up. "Did Frank say anything at all about a meeting?"

"Not a word. Just that he was going to wrap things up and head back to Moscow."

"By the way, any idea what happened to his cell phone? I didn't see it listed on the FSB's inventory of his personal effects."

She shook her head. "It's missing. Someone must have stolen it."

"It's useless without his activation code," Scott said.

At length Alex's shoulders sagged. "Maybe . . ."

"Maybe what?" Scott said.

"Maybe Abakov was right. Maybe Frank and the sailor . . ."

"Come on, Alex. I know you don't believe that."

"I don't want to, but I can't think of any reason that Frank would have met with a half-illiterate navy conscript in a hotel near the base. Everything would have been covered in the private interviews."

"Then there's got to be another explanation." Scott turned back to the desk. "What about his computer? Maybe there's something useful on it."

"I doubt it," Alex said. "Most of the stuff he copied to the hard drive was encrypted technical material, and I don't have the access codes."

"I thought you said he kept the high-security stuff in the chancery."

"He did. Even so, this stuff is sensitive, and that's why he used a twenty-eight-bit encryption code."

"Isn't that overkill?"

"Probably, but he was careful."

"Right, and a man who's that careful wouldn't meet a sailor from Olenya Bay in a hotel room in Murmansk unless it was damned important."

Alex said nothing. She knelt beside Scott and booted the laptop sitting on the table. He inhaled her scent, a light fragrance in her hair from the shampoo she had used. The desktop came up on the screen. Alex stroked keys and waited. A dialog box asked for an ID. She tried various combinations of words and letters but kept getting *Access denied.* Scott suggested a few more, but she got the same result.

"See what I mean?" Alex said. She shut down the laptop.

Scott stood. He blew through his teeth in frustration. "What are you doing for dinner tonight?"

They had a table in one of Moscow's elegant new restaurants on Ulitsa Petrovka, complete with tinkling crystal, waiters wearing tuxedos, and a chef imported from Paris. Over drinks Alex said, "Why are you so interested in my background?"

"For one thing, we're going to be working together. For another, I don't meet a woman every day who knows how to build a twenty-megaton nuclear weapon."

Alex laughed behind a hand. "That's not true at all." She lowered her voice. "I don't know how to build a bomb. I know how they work and what goes into one, that's all."

"That's plenty. So tell me about you."

"There's not much to tell. I grew up in California. My father was a journalist and I wanted to grow up and be one too. I thought a life interviewing presidents and foreign leaders was the most exciting thing in the world a person could do. Instead I discovered I had a knack for science and studied physics at USC. After I completed graduate work, I got a job at Brookhaven National Laboratory on Long Island. I arrived when they discovered that radioactive tritium had been seeping into ground water. I was on the team that worked to solve that problem, and later I was offered a position with the U.S. Department of Energy as an embassy liaison with the Norwegians in Russia. That's how I ended up in Moscow."

"I'm impressed," he said.

"You make it sound as if I'm bragging. I'm not. You asked for my résumé and now you have it."

"I don't think you're bragging. Some people take a lifetime to get where you are."

"I'll save you the trouble with the math," Alex said and laughed. "I'm thirty-eight."

"And single?"

A hesitation. "I was married—for a while. Single now."

"What's it like for a single woman living in Moscow?"

"Culturally it's exhilarating, socially it's deadening. But I do interesting work and meet interesting people like Frank Drummond. We had a fun time together."

"What kind of things did you do?"

"Frank was interested in Russian history and I took him places that simply amazed him. We went to museums—not just the usual places like the Pushkin, but smaller ones I'd discovered, little gems tucked away in apartments and homes on the backstreets of Moscow where hardly anyone ever goes. He was amazed at what he saw."

"Frank was that rare individual one seldom meets in the military," Scott said. "He was well read, culturally aware, and introspective. And he wasn't afraid to fight for what he believed."

"What's his wife like?" Alex said. "I can't stop thinking how difficult this must be for her."

Scott told her about Vivian. He told her about the hardships and heartbreak. "It goes with the job of being a Navy wife," Scott said.

Alex, perhaps sensing a hint of acidity in that observation, said, "If you don't mind my asking, is there a Mrs. Scott?" She raised a glass of white wine to her lips.

"There was." Scott's face hardened. He looked at his watch. "Considering the time difference, I'd say she's probably in bed with the U.S. military attaché she flew to Tokyo with last month."

"Oh. Sorry."

Scott slugged down vodka.

"Kids?"

"There wasn't ever time."

Alex sipped wine and met his eyes when he looked up. "Too much sea duty, is that what you're saying?"

"You spend a lot of time at sea in subs if you want

command. I was exec on two boats, then CO of the *Chicago* and *Tampa.*"

"Now I'm impressed," Alex said.

"Tracy sure as hell wasn't."

"So, what's she like?"

How to describe a woman he had lived with for fourteen years? He wanted to say that she was a beautiful satin bitch. He remembered that Tracy's voracious need for emotional support had drained him dry. So had her fits of manic jealousy and bouts of deep depression. Their breakup had been shattering. Coming as it had on the heels of his mission in the Yellow Sea, it had left him feeling alienated and cold.

Alex reached across the table and put a hand on his. The contact seared his flesh. "Sounds as if she didn't like sharing you with that sub." She took her hand away and returned his penetrating gaze with one of her own.

"So, what were you doing running around under the ocean in your sub?" Alex said after their dinner, which arrived on a silver cart accompanied by four waiters and a sommelier, had been served.

"Gathering intelligence," Scott said.

"Spying on the Russians?"

"Not always."

"It sounds dangerous," she said, looking up at Scott from her salmon and pastry *kulebiaka.* "Tell me about it." Her intensity made it hard for him to refuse.

"We went to extraordinary lengths to get what we were after. We took some terrible risks, had some close calls, and . . . well, sometimes things didn't work out." *And sometimes men get killed,* he could have added, but didn't. And when the Navy had to have a scapegoat, he was it. From the start he'd been against a mission into the northern Yellow Sea between China and North Korea. The Yellow Sea was too damn shallow for sub ops, and, like the NKs, the Chinese considered it their private lake. So why send a submarine into the Yellow Sea on a virtual suicide mission where the Chinese and NKs had been waiting to set loose their antisub forces like a pack of wild dogs against a trapped hare?

"What kind of intelligence did you snatch from under the noses of the people you spied on?"

"Arcane technical stuff that would bore you."

"What you mean is that you can't talk about it."

"I've already told you too much."

"Maybe you haven't told me enough," she said cryptically.

He put down his fork and touched his mouth with a stiff linen napkin. "What exactly do you mean?"

"Jake, think about it. You and Frank are cut from the same cloth. You both were involved in intelligence work; it's what you do. Is it possible that Frank, posing as a liaison officer with Earth Safe, was actually working for the CIA or someone else and was in Murmansk to gather intelligence and instead ended up dead?"

"Frank would never serve two masters—never let himself be used in that way." As soon as Scott said that, he realized how wrong he was. Like Scott, Drummond had worked for the SRO before and had been working for them when he was murdered. It would have been easy enough for Drummond to slip into a role that would give him access to what was at one time some of the most inaccessible submarine bases in the world. But for what reason? There was little the SRO and CIA didn't already know about the once-mighty Russian sub force and its now crumbling bases on the Kola Peninsula and in the Far East. So why send Drummond to Russia when Alex

Thorne and the Norwegians were capable of handling the cleanup work on their own? Scott didn't have an answer.

"I keep asking myself why someone would kill Frank," Scott said. "He was an American naval officer, not a professional spy."

She made an explosive sound. "You met Yuri Abakov. To some people in Russia, there's no difference."

After dinner, bundled up against Moscow's cold, they strolled a mostly deserted Ulitsa Petrovka. Scott said, "Tell me about Frank's files stored in the chancery."

"What's to tell? Individuals, even those who are assigned to the embassy on a temporary basis, are provided with B-level secure storage for sensitive materials. They're kept in the same underground vault as the embassy's A-level top-secret materials are, but in a different area. Frank was assigned a lockup and had access twenty-four hours a day. Jack Slaughter is chief of security. He also handles the comm center and the embassy's voice mail net. Did you meet him?"

"Stretzlof introduced us," Scott said. "I told Slaughter that I had orders to round up Frank's papers and ship them out via diplomatic pouch. He seemed eager to help out."

"That's Slaughter."

Scott suddenly stopped walking. "And you say that we can access the B-level lockup twenty-four hours a day?"

"Yes," she said, turning around, walking back to him.

"Then, let's go," Scott said, and hailed a taxi.

Alex led Scott through the embassy's elaborate security apparatus, consisting of retinal screening devices and voice recognition monitors at B level, far below the streets of Moscow. The duty officer accompanied them to the lockup area, where Scott took custody of a metal box filled with Drummond's papers. Once they were settled in a conference room, the duty officer closed the door and departed after making sure that he had displayed the Occupied sign outside.

Scott noticed the room's oddly shaped sound-suppressing wall and ceiling tiles, which greatly attenuated their voices and imparted a palpable sense of claustrophobia. Filtered air hissed from a ceiling fixture. It was like being aboard the *Tampa*.

"Are you cold?" Scott asked.

Alex lifted and dropped her shoulders, hugged herself with both arms. "No, just wired."

Her mood of expectancy had affected Scott too. "Then let's get to work."

Drummond's papers, reports, and CD-ROMs had been carefully organized. Most of the material bore a Confidential or Secret heading.

"Should I be looking at this stuff?" Alex said. "I don't have a clearance for Secret, only Confidential."

"Never mind that; does any of it look familiar?"

Alex read a document. "Yes, some of it. This one, for instance, pretty much covers the time line we had established to search the Kola Peninsula for loose fissile materials. I don't think you're going to find anything in here that will be useful."

"First rule of intelligence work: Don't jump to conclusions," Scott said.

"It's also the first rule of science."

"Then, follow the rules." Most of the material made no sense to Scott, but he knew it would be easy to overlook something important. "It's like looking through the periscope of a submarine: Things you think aren't there sometimes are. Believe me, I know."

The evening quickly ran its course. And though the conference table was a storm of papers, notes, and CD-ROMs containing only dry technical information on the storage and handling of fissile materials, Scott refused to admit defeat.

"Will you be using the conference room all night, Dr. Thorne?" said the duty officer when he called from his station at midnight.

Alex sucked a paper cut on her finger. "No, Hank, we're about to wrap up. Give us another fifteen minutes."

She gave Scott a look and said, "Face it. We're on a wild-goose chase."

There was a rap on the door and it opened. A man with dark blond hair and dressed casually in jeans, penny loafers, and a flannel shirt entered the conference room without bothering to ask permission.

"Hello, David," Alex said pleasantly, trying hard not to show that she was annoyed by his intrusion. "Have you met Captain Scott? Jake, this is David Hoffman, my boss. David's head of the embassy's department of energy–the DOE office."

Hoffman, his face a mask, ignored Scott. "Where've you been, Alex? I haven't seen you for a couple of days."

Alex brushed loose strands of hair from her face and said coolly, "I thought I told you, David, I've been helping Captain Scott wrap up Admiral Drummond's affairs. Jake's here to escort the Admiral's body back to the States and–"

"So I hear," Hoffman said. "I also hear that you've signed out for Murmansk tomorrow. May I ask why?"

"We're going to take a look at the hotel where Frank and that sailor died," Scott interjected. "Alex agreed to be my escort."

"I don't think that's a good idea, Alex," said Hoffman

sourly. "There are some important things that need attention here. For one, there's the summit briefing document."

"David, I've already promised Jake that I'd go," she said, chagrined.

"If you'll permit me, Mr. Hoffman," Scott said, "I've been ordered to report all the details of the incident in Murmansk to my commanding officer in Washington. The FSB report is quite thorough, but there's nothing like seeing that place firsthand. While we're there, I might want to visit the sub base in Olenya Bay, and Alex knows it like the back of her hand. I'd say that's pretty important."

Hoffman turned his gaze on Scott. "Alex works for me, Scott, and the DOE, not the U.S. Navy. I don't lend my people out for use as tour guides."

"This is no tour we're taking," Scott said acidly. "An American flag-rank officer has been murdered in Russia. I need Alex's help to find his killer."

"I heard," Hoffman said, gazing past Scott to the blizzard on the conference table, "that Drummond took his own life."

"You heard wrong," Scott said. The look he gave Hoffman said further discussion about Drummond had ended.

"David, we're packing up Admiral Drummond's papers right now." Alex swept an arm in the direction of the table. "Another day and we'll be finished."

Hoffman moistened his lips. "All right, one more day. But that's all. I expect everyone in the office to turn to."

"Thanks, David," Alex said to Hoffman's departing back.

She wouldn't look at Scott. Arms folded, she paced the room with her head down and said, "I'm sorry, but

I should have warned you. David's very defensive."

"And he's jealous too," Scott observed.

"Jake, that's ridiculous. He's simply worried about the budget cutbacks at State. They're looking hard at DOE and usually start by cutting frills."

Scott moved papers around on the conference table. "Securing loose fissile materials is considered a frill?"

"State prefers to leave the hunt for nuclear material to private organizations with money like Earth Safe. David worries that he'll be sent stateside to oversee the dismantling of an old nuclear power plant. Would you want a job like that?"

"Have it your way." Scott picked up a batch of documents and squared their sides.

"Look, I'll smooth things out with him later. I have to live with him after you're gone."

"Is he your lover?"

She stopped pacing and gave Scott a hard look. "Of course not. I told you, he's my boss. We've worked together a long time, I like David, and–" She caught herself and looked away. "God, why am I telling you this?" She waited a bit before she turned back and saw Scott looking intently at a document that he had found tucked inside a report that he held spread open on the table with his other hand.

"Bingo," Scott said.

Alex moved to his side. "What?"

"It's him," Scott said.

"Who?"

There was no mistaking the significance of what he'd discovered. He planted a thumbnail under a name in capital letters in the text of a decrypted message. "That Chechen terrorist. Alikhan Zakayev."

Scott and Alex read the message together.

////PURPLE//INTERCEPTS INDICATE (GEN)
ALIKHAN ZAKAYEV OPERATING ST
PETERSBURG VICINITY AND NORTH//
CONCERN REGARDING TIMING RE POSSIBLE
OPERATION(S) COINCIDE SUMMIT//URGENT
YOU IDENTIFY-CONFIRM//CONTACT
AUTHORIZED//USE EXTREME CAUTION//RISK
RED DIPLOMATIC INCIDENT//PURPLE END////

"What does *contact authorized* mean?" Alex asked.

"That Frank had permission to meet with and talk to Zakayev."

"Why? Zakayev's a terrorist. He kills people."

"We must have information that Zakayev is planning an operation to coincide with the summit. Washington wanted Frank to get information and if necessary meet with Zakayev, try to head it off."

"Head it off? How?"

"Offer him something. Or kill him."

Alex's voice came out strained. "What you just said. Do you know what that means? It means the United States government has a connection to Alikhan Zakayev, who just killed a thousand civilians in Moscow."

"And Frank Drummond too," said Scott.

The Mi-28 helicopter, rotors clattering, lifted off the pad from Tushino Aerodrome, north of Moscow. As it gained altitude it swung north toward the Kola Peninsula. Moscow's gray suburbs quickly disappeared, replaced by the barren, snow-streaked Russian steppe stretching to the horizon.

Scott and Alex, belted into their bucket seats in the divided cabin, faced an impassive Yuri Abakov across the aisle like paratroopers headed for the drop zone. He had on his *ushanka* hat and wore a short, heavy coat over civilian clothes. Their breath plumed in the biting cold, which a pair of overhead electric heaters had so far failed to overcome.

Twenty minutes after departing Moscow, Alex twisted around, pointed out the Perspex window, and said above the noise of the chopper's rotors and turboshaft engine, "Amazing. We're almost over Rybinsk."

Scott looked out and saw a clump of factories and smokestacks and to the north, a huge body of water shimmering like beaten metal. "How do you know?"

"Because that's the Sea of Rybinsk down there. And if you look to the south, you can see the city of Rybinsk on the Volga."

"She's right," Abakov said, passing them two cups he'd filled with coffee from a thermos. "Rybinsk is a big manufacturing center. In '41 they dammed the upper Volga to make a reservoir, one of the biggest in the world."

Rybinsk quickly slipped aft and disappeared.

Scott sat back in his seat and sipped hot, black coffee. Abakov briefly met his gaze, then looked away. Scott took it as his opening.

"Tell me about Alikhan Zakayev."

This time Abakov met and held Scott's gaze. "Tell you what?"

"What he's like. Why he hates Russia."

"He hates Russia," Abakov said, "because he wants independence for Chechnya and we won't give it to him. So he started a war and he's losing it and wants to make us pay for his mistakes. It's that simple."

"The truth is," Alex said, "the Russian Army killed Zakayev's entire family: wife, children, parents, and grandparents. That's why he hates Russia. Why won't you admit it, Colonel?"

Abakov glared at Alex, then looked out the window.

"Is that true, Colonel?" Scott said.

"Zakayev was a former KGB major," Abakov said, his gaze on Scott. "I knew him in Moscow in the late 1980's. Even then he was a hard man, driven. He moved up the ladder and made full colonel. Then, in 1991, during the failed coup in Moscow, he disappeared. We thought he had defected to the West, but instead he had returned to Chechnya, where he joined the rebel forces who had declared their independence. Yeltsin sent in troops to put down the rebellion, and Zakayev, who by then had risen in the ranks of Chechen guerrillas to general and commanded a huge rebel force, put up a hell of a fight. We offered to negotiate but Zakayev refused and"—Abakov threw up his hands—"as a result we may have to launch an all-out war against Chechnya. Another terrorist attack like the one at the concert hall and I think Chechnya's days are numbered."

"How well did you know him?"

"We spent two years together, enough time to get to know someone. He's completely fearless. He never shows his anger and rarely raises his voice, which gives him a menacing quality. His calm outward demeanor often disarms people who meet him. They think he's a gentleman, always so soft-spoken. But that's just a mask. In fact he will do anything to win independence for Chechnya. He's a fanatic."

"Is that why the Russian Army killed Zakayev's family? Because he's a fanatic? Did they think that would break his will to fight?"

Abakov considered. "You Americans judge us by your own hypocritical standards. When we Russians take harsh action to protect our country and citizens, we're accused of crushing independence and democratic reforms. When

America does it, you justify it by saying you are preserving liberty and democracy. But now it's different. We are fighting a group of terrorists bent on destroying Russia. You have to meet force with force. It's the only thing Zakayev respects."

"When Zakayev disappeared from the KGB, why did you think he'd gone over to the West?"

Abakov removed his *ushanka* and rubbed his bald dome with a palm. "There had been rumors that the United States had recruited Zakayev to foment unrest in the Caucasus. That the U.S. wanted to distract Russia from protesting American involvement in the Middle East, in Syria and Iran. We have a huge Muslim population and have good reason to support them in other countries where they are fighting Western imperialism. There are rumors that the U.S. provided Chechen terrorists with money and weapons."

"Why would the U.S. do that?" Alex said.

"To make sure Zakayev succeeded. Yes, that's true. Then you could play us off against the Chechens by promising that you'd look the other way while we fought Zakayev so long as Russia looked the other way while the U.S. overthrew the regimes in Iraq and Iran. What you call a quid pro quo."

"Do you think Zakayev still has ties to the U.S.?" Scott said, drawing a look from Alex.

Abakov shrugged. "I have no proof, but yes, I think so."

The chopper bounced in rough air.

"Is it possible that Drummond was murdered because he knew something about Zakayev's ties to the U.S.?"

"The official report I filed states that the cause of death was suicide. You read it."

"Sure I did. But what about the unofficial report. The one you didn't file."

"I don't understand. What unofficial report?"

Scott tapped his head. "The one inside that policeman's brain of yours. The real one. The one that might be telling you Drummond was killed by Zakayev."

"You ask too many questions," Abakov said dismissively. He unlatched his seat belt and went forward to chat up the pilots.

Alex dropped her voice even though Abakov couldn't hear and said, "Are you going to tell him about the message you found in Frank's papers?"

"I could be shot for doing that. I could also be shot for reading it and not telling Radford that I read it."

"Do you have to tell him?"

"It all depends on what we find at the hotel in Murmansk."

"What do you think we'll find?"

"Probably nothing. But I think our friend here knows more than he's letting on."

Alex looked at Abakov, who was stooped in the open doorway behind the flight deck, looking over the pilot's shoulder, out the windshield. "That's a scary thought."

"Is it scarier than tracking fissile materials so terrorists can't build a bomb?"

"In some ways it is. You can see radioactive materials, but you can't see plots unfolding behind the scenes."

"Is that why you agreed to come with me? To see if Frank had uncovered a plot?"

"If Frank was murdered, I'd want to know why and who did it."

"I hope David Hoffman will see it that way. I didn't mean to make you uncomfortable last night when I asked if he was your lover."

She gave Scott a playful poke in the ribs. "Yes, you did. Anyway, it's still none of your business."

"Right."

"Look!" Alex pointed. "Off to the west you can just see the skyline of St. Petersburg."

Scott saw a small spike on the relatively flat horizon. It could have been anything: a mountain, a pine forest, a low cloud. "If you say so."

"I've never been to St. Petersburg. I've heard it's one of the most beautiful cities in the world."

"And indestructible too. It withstood a nine-hundred-day siege by the Nazis."

"Tells you something about the Russian character."

"Yeah, hard as nails."

Minutes later Alex dozed, her head on Scott's shoulder. The chopper lifted and dropped on a sudden gust of wind from the west, but the pilot, tacking to port, kept its nose pointed north toward the Kola Peninsula.

# 6

## Murmansk

The girl's warm breath teased Zakayev's bare shoulder. He watched her sleep and thought about what she had been through, marveled at the terrors she had survived to be with him now. He thought about what was to come and for a moment felt sad that she would never have a life beyond the one they were living at that moment. As if she knew his thoughts, her eyes opened to meet his gaze.

"I love you, Ali," she whispered against his shoulder. Her hand was on his flat belly.

A trace of scented bath talc clung to the fingertip he sketched across her hip, which felt like satin. He remembered how she had trembled with fear when he coaxed her from the shelter of the bombed-out building in Grozny where he had found her living like an animal, so emaciated that when he took her hand to help her over the rubble to freedom, fingers dug into his palm like claws. Her sunken eyes had just stared at him, perhaps expecting the worst. He knew he could help her recover physically but didn't know if he could heal her mind. But she was young and resilient and responded to his care and deep affection. How many times had he wanted to tell her he loved her but didn't dare to say the words.

They lay side by side, not talking but stroking until their breath exploded, until she moaned and rose above him, her long, black hair tumbling around his face like a tent. His tongue moistened the tips of her small, pointed breasts. His hips rose and he entered her as she pulled his head back, ran a hand through his hair, and covered his lips with a kiss. Legs stiffened, body arched, he let go at the exquisite moment when her lovely face was blemished by the convulsion of orgasm.

Her breath had returned to normal. She sat up in bed. Bars of late-afternoon sunlight falling through window blinds marched across her slim thighs and the damp, rumpled sheets. Zakayev, naked, moved about the room fiddling with his things, searching for wrinkles in the Russian naval officer's uniform he had hung up on the bathroom door. The girl's eyes roamed over his lean, pale body scarred by Russian bullets and shrapnel. The fresh white bandage over the wound on his arm almost matched the color of his skin.

"We'll leave after it's dark," Zakayev said. They had let a room in a small, moldering hotel overlooking Murmansk's busy harbor. It was a place where people didn't ask questions and avoided eye contact with strangers.

"You will look handsome in your naval uniform," she said. "I'll want to kiss you."

"A petty officer first class can't kiss an admiral," Zakayev said with mock seriousness.

They had discussed it so many times and she was eager to play her role. The uniform she would wear—navy pants, striped jumper, a traditional Russian Navy flat hat with ribbon device—lay folded neatly on a chair.

"Ali, sit here."

He let her kiss the pit of his neck, his chest and nipples, both hands. Her eyes suddenly welled up. "Ali, there isn't much time, not even a week, you said." Her voice quavered, a delicate flutter that he pretended he hadn't heard.

He appraised her with cold objectivity. "You said you were not afraid to die."

"I'm not. I chose this, so what is going to happen to me doesn't matter as long as our mission succeeds; but even so, I want to know if you . . . I want to hear you say . . ."

"Don't . . ." He got up and turned his back. Yes, he loved her, but could admit it only to himself. If he said the words she wanted to hear, everything would change. "Don't ask; don't say any more. We agreed not to. It's all arranged and nothing can happen to change it. Litvanov and his men are waiting for us." He faced her. "Now it's time for you to prepare."

She rose silently from the bed and went into the tiny bathroom. A naked bulb hanging from a twisted wire in the ceiling provided weak illumination. For a long time she stood looking at herself in the tarnished flyspecked mirror over the rusty sink. Then she picked up a pair of scissors and began cutting her hair, the long, silky strands falling like black rain.

Zakayev turned up his coat collar. A sharp wind laced with the stink of dead fish and diesel fuel sent paper and debris corkscrewing down a deserted wind tunnel of a street lined with ship chandleries and warehouses, with old packing cases, cargo pallets, and rubbish of all sorts. The wheels of heavy trucks had carved ruts in the frozen snow, which made footing treacherous. The girl slipped and almost fell but Zakayev caught her arm.

They turned off the main street into a narrow alley between darkened warehouses that rose on either side like the walls of a canyon. Zakayev found the battered wooden door, which he identified by the heavy iron crossbraces bolted to its face. The door was set into the brick wall of a warehouse over three crumbling concrete steps. He looked down the alley and saw a Guards stake-body truck parked where he was told it would be, beside the seawall fronting the harbor.

Zakayev withdrew the H&K P7 from the pocket of his overcoat and tightened his fingers around the grip, cocking the pistol. He banged on the door and waited. A gust of wind plastered the skirt of his overcoat between his legs.

Heavy boots tramped over a plank floor. Bolts snapped open and door hinges squealed. A heavyset man in shabby work clothes, a greasy cap on his close-cropped head, stood in a rectangle of light spilling into the alley from the open door.

"Were you planning to shoot me, Ali?" said Kapitan Third Rank Georgi Litvanov.

Zakayev lowered the pistol. "You look well, Georgi Alexeyevich."

They entered and Litvanov closed and bolted the door behind them, then looked them up and down. "Here, let me see you."

Zakayev shrugged out of his overcoat. The girl handed him a traditional Russian Navy garrison cap, which he put on his head at a rakish angle.

Litvanov stepped back and regarded Zakayev dressed in the uniform of a Russian *kontr-admiral*—rear admiral—complete with gold shoulder boards on the tunic and gold stripes on the sleeves.

"It's perfect!" Litvanov said. "You look just like a Russian flag officer."

Litvanov's attention swung to the girl in her peacoat, jumper, and flat hat. He inspected her outfit, nodding approval. Her big eyes and full lips, triangular face, and short hair gave her an androgynous look that was strangely appealing.

"My men could take some pointers from this one, Ali, on how to wear their uniforms properly. Ha! You are both a credit to the Russian Navy."

The girl didn't speak but smiled to show she was pleased that she'd passed muster with the captain of the submarine *K-363*.

Litvanov beckoned they should follow him up a flight of stairs to a makeshift office that had a view from a pair of dirty windows onto the darkened warehouse floor below. Litvanov had laid out black bread, salted herring, and a bottle of vodka on one of the desks.

"You had no trouble finding the place?" Litvanov said.

"No, your instructions were clear," Zakayev said. "We took an electrobus from the hotel and got off three blocks away." Zakayev looked around the office at file cabinets and equipment that included modern computers and printers. "How did you come by this place?"

"I do a little business with the owner," Litvanov said. "He's always in the market for surplus goods the Northern Fleet has no use for. Particularly titanium and stainless steel. He was in a generous mood and lent his office for our meeting. Eat."

The girl declined but Zakayev sampled the salted fish and nodded approval. "Your boat is set for departure?"

"Of course, General." Litvanov paused to light a cigarette. "The schedule is tight. I've timed our departure so we won't run into any vessels patrolling the main channel out of the Tuloma River or around Kil'din Island. Procedures have broken down and the harbor control units don't keep track of ship arrivals and departures like they used to, but now and then you get a new skipper who goes by the book. Do you follow?"

"Of course. And your crew?"

"Handpicked," Litvanov said, his voice thick from cigarette smoke, "stripped to only essential personnel. In other words, enough to operate the boat. The crew has trained nonstop for over a week while we've sat moored to a dock in Olenya Bay. They're eager to get under way. They are good men. All the high-flown lectures they receive about duty, honor, and the Motherland can't change the fact that life at sea in a submarine is hard, that we have lousy food, live among the unwashed, breathe one another's farts and smelly feet, and sleep in soggy bunks. And for this privilege we are not paid. But now that will change."

"Then there is no question that they are fully committed," Zakayev said.

Litvanov's face hardened and his eyes narrowed. A boot sole ground his cigarette into the rough floor. "Are you questioning, General, whether these men, whom I myself have trained, will follow orders?"

"It is not a question of following orders, it's a question of how dedicated they are to the cause."

Litvanov, eyes blazing, said, "*I*, Georgi Litvanov, kapitan third rank of the Russian Navy, commanding officer of the *K-363*, assure you that each of them is willing to give up his life for the cause. These men come from towns and villages all over Chechnya. There isn't a man that hasn't had a family member murdered by the Russians. I don't have to tell you, General, that if I hadn't offered them a chance to strike at the heart of Russia, they would have deserted to fight on the ground in Chechnya."

"And you, Georgi Alexeyevich?"

Litvanov lifted and dropped his shoulders. "What have I to lose? Tell me?" His eyes searched Zakayev's face. "I have a photograph of my wife and children in their coffins. My cousin sent it to me. At first I thought it was a cruel joke somebody was playing, and I wish to God it was. I had to beg for leave and even then I was granted only three days. Three days. My cousin had them buried in Sernovodsk, our ancestral village, the same as yours, General. When I got there and saw their graves, I was sick. A pile of rocks—not even a proper marker."

Litvanov downed vodka and wiped his mouth with a hand, which he then ran over his close-cropped skull. He turned his gaze on the girl. "I serve in the armed forces of a country that killed my family. I thought I had a good job, one of the best Russia could offer. I was blind to what was happening in Chechnya." He reflected for a long moment, then said, "But now I have the means to strike back—hard. So, like you, I made a decision and here I am."

Through all of this the girl said nothing even though Litvanov spoke directly to her because he knew she understood the horror of Russian occupation in Chechnya. And because he had had a daughter her age.

"We all have our reasons," Zakayev said. His mouth was a thin hard line.

"It's hard to forget. I go on sometimes."

Somewhere a rumbling diesel truck, perhaps hauling logs bound for one of the sawmills in Murmansk, made the warehouse tremble.

Zakayev said, "That sailor, Radchenko, and the American. What do you hear?"

Litvanov shoveled salted fish into his mouth and spoke while he chewed. "Nothing. No one at Olenya Bay has asked any questions. Radchenko's been listed as a deserter. His records, personal effects, everything, went to Northern Fleet Headquarters in Severomorsk. It's as if he never existed. As for the *Amerikanski,* I was told the FSB investigators looked around the hotel for less than an hour, then packed up and left town. The *michman* who discovered what Radchenko was up to is one of my best men."

A gust of wind off the harbor rattled the office window glazing. The girl shivered and hunched her shoulders.

"The weather will be cold but stay clear for another day or so," Litvanov said, dislodging a fish bone from his teeth.

"Then it's time to go. As you said, there are patrol boats."

Litvanov downed another drink then wrapped the bread and fish in newspaper He threw the waste in a trash bin and stuck the bottle of vodka in his outer coat pocket. "Security at the base is nonexistent, a joke," he said as he finished up. "A few conscripts with unloaded assault rifles. When they see your uniform, they'll be so frightened, they'll piss their pants and wave us right through without asking for identification."

"And you?" Zakayev said, looking at Litvanov's grubby outfit.

"They don't know who I am. They'll think I'm your civilian driver." He jerked a thumb at the girl. "And her, they'll just ignore because they'll think she's—he's—with you."

"Are you sure?"

"Yes, yes. The base commander's a drunk and has no idea what's going on under his own nose. They're all a bunch of drunks. How do you think we walk off with goods to barter? Trust me on that."

They stood in the alley by the bolted door adjusting to the dark, getting their bearings.

"This way," Litvanov said.

Suddenly a pair of headlight beams shot into the alley blinding them. Litvanov threw up an arm. Frozen in the hard, brilliant light, it took a moment to react.

"Get down!" He grabbed the girl and they rolled for cover behind the concrete stairs at the entrance to the warehouse as automatic weapons stuttered and bullets snapped overhead, *spang*ed off brick, metal, and wood. In the shattering silence that followed, Zakayev heard empty brass cartridge cases skittering and spinning over ice and stone. And the metallic slap of a round jacking into the chamber of an automatic pistol that he guessed was Litvanov's.

Zakayev reached back and felt around blindly. The girl raised her head a fraction. "I'm not hurt," she said. Then: "It's him. Ivan Serov."

Muzzle flashes; another burst of gunfire rattled up the alley.

Zakayev raised his head cautiously and recognized the dual nostrils of a BMW grille between the headlights. He guessed there were three shooters lurking behind the car, which was parked about twenty meters away with two wheels on the curb up against the wall of a warehouse. And one of them was Ivan Serov.

He understood now. Despite precautions they had been followed. Serov had set a trap and he had walked right into it: the narrow alley, the seawall, the harbor—a box, a killing ground. They were pinned down and cut off from the parked truck, their only means of escape. The alley was a stage, and the blinding klieg lights made it impossible for the actors to see the audience waiting for the performance to begin.

Another flash and stutter. Chunks of shattered brick and cement rained on Zakayev and the girl.

He was back in Chechnya. Russian guns cracking and popping all around him and his men. The dull thump of a rocket-propelled grenade exploding. The screams of the wounded and dying. The sharp, sweet smell of cordite mixed with the brassy odor of wet blood. His blood oozing from a horrid, searing wound on his hip turning the baked Chechen soil into red mud. They were low on water and ammo. And it was only noon. Hours to go before dark and possible escape into the hills. Litvanov, on his belly behind a large empty packing crate up against the warehouse, growled something that brought Zakayev back to the present.

"General! Who's out there? What do they want?"

"It's Ivan Serov and he wants me."

"Fuck! You said he was dead."

Zakayev said nothing.

Litvanov, flat on the ground, aimed and shot out a headlight. In response a white-hot muzzle flash bloomed in the narrow space between the car and brick wall of the warehouse. Bullets ravaged masonry, punched through windows and the packing crate, tearing out splinters of brick, glass, and wood.

Still flat and below the line of fire, Litvanov shot out another headlight. The glare they had been looking into dimmed but didn't go out, and to make a run for the truck was suicidal: They would be perfect targets lit by the beams from the two remaining headlights. The only way out was to kill Serov and his men.

Somewhere in the distance a police car siren started hee-hawing insistently.

"Hear that?" Litvanov growled over his shoulder at Zakayev. It drew another burst of fire from the shooter hunkered between the car and the wall.

Zakayev waited until he saw the man's outline back-lighted from reflections off the BMW's gleaming finish. He rested his cupped left hand, which steadied his right hand gripping the P7, on the top step. When he had the man in his sights, he fired twice. The first bullet pierced the BMW's windshield. The second bullet struck the shooter in the head like a trip-hammer. His body crashed against the car, then sprawled out into the street, weapon clattering after him.

The two remaining shooters crouched behind the car fired wildly, hosing down the street. Zakayev and the girl hugged the ground as bullets ripped overhead.

"Shit!" Litvanov scuttled backward from his hide like a crab until his feet contacted the base of the concrete steps opposite where Zakayev and the girl had taken cover.

More sirens. Somewhere a watchdog barked.

"Ali!" It was Serov. "I'm going to finish our business." His voice resonated with loathing and resignation.

Zakayev looked around. The truck was too far away. Serov was too close. The police were getting closer.

"Ali? Do you hear me? We can't sit here all night. I'll make a deal with you. A mutually beneficial deal."

Zakayev reached back and grabbed the girl's arm. "Give it to me."

"The girl can go free. But not Litvanov. He stays and we finish it."

"How does he know . . . ?" the girl said.

But Zakayev's hand closed around the Czech grenade. A URG-86, it had a four-and-a-half-second fuse. If he did it right, he could skip the grenade over the icy street and under the BMW.

He gave the pistol to the girl. "When I tell you, empty the magazine."

"Yes."

"Georgi," Zakayev called. "Stay down but be ready to run."

"What are you doing?"

"Do as I say."

"Ali?"

He nudged the girl. "Now!"

She opened fire, the bullets ricocheting off the car and howling away into the night.

Zakayev pulled the pin on the grenade, released the spoon, and, with a delicate underhand toss around the staircase, sent it skipping across the icy street toward the car.

The pistol's magazine ran dry. Zakayev hauled the girl down behind the steps as Serov and his man, ignoring the approaching police cars, opened fire with their automatic weapons.

A pinprick of light appeared under the BMW. A split second later the vehicle exploded in a huge ball of flaming gasoline. Red-hot shards of metal pinwheeled into the air and over the tops of the warehouses. The deafening explosion rocked the confined space they were in. The searing fireball rolling out of the alley forced policemen jumping out of their cars with guns drawn to dive for cover.

Zakayev, ears ringing, staggered to his feet and saw a burning shell of a car and flames licking up the side of the warehouse and curling over the roof parapet where large pieces of burning wreckage had landed. A few feet from where Zakayev stood was a smoldering tire still mounted on an alloy wheel.

More police cars arrived, but the fire that had engulfed buildings on both sides of the alley kept the officers at bay.

Zakayev, Litvanov, and the girl dashed for the truck and piled in.

"We'll take backstreets and work our way around the harbor," Litvanov said. "The main streets will soon be blocked off by the police."

A fire truck screamed by in the opposite direction, then another with police cars following.

Zakayev looked back and saw flames leaping skyward, turning the bottoms of low clouds over the harbor red.

"Anyone behind us?" Litvanov asked.

"We're clear."

Litvanov found the intersection he wanted and turned right to head north against the Tuloma River. Hunched over the wheel, Litvanov blew through his teeth and said, "General, I thought Serov was dead."

The girl, seated between them, said, "He is now."

The truck ground north, toward Olenya Bay.

Paul Friedman, the national security advisor, signaled with a subtle toss of his head and thrust of jaw, that the president of the United States was displeased.

Karl Radford entered the Oval Office and slipped into a wing chair beside the president. Friedman sat on a sofa, his knees pressed awkwardly together supporting a bundle of battered folders stamped Top Secret. The only sound in the Oval Office came from a ticking desk clock that had once belonged to Admiral Chester W. Nimitz.

An inaugural gift from Radford to the president, a Nimitz admirer, it sat on a Duncan Phyfe end table next to a bust of Nimitz.

Friedman and Radford waited while the president read a document. Radford assumed it was the briefing summary he had prepared at Friedman's direction the night before. Without looking up, the president, a handsome black man wearing a double-breasted charcoal suit, said, "Good morning, Karl."

"Good morning, Mr. President," said Radford.

The Nimitz clock ticked toward seven A.M.

The president finished reading. He put his elbows on the chair arms and made a steeple with his fingers. "This fellow, Scott," he said, speaking to Radford over the steeple top. "I thought he had orders to escort Drummond's body home, not open an independent investigation. I see here that you spoke to him."

"Yes, sir. Last night."

"What's he up to?"

"Wants to prove that Drummond was murdered. He doesn't believe the FSB report and wants to clear the man's name."

Friedman, heavyset with a head of thick, unruly hair that curled over his shirt collar, said, "I'm surprised you authorized his trip to Murmansk. Isn't that risky?"

"If I had ordered Scott to stay out of Murmansk, it would only make him suspicious," Radford said. "I felt a trip there would prove he's on a wild-goose chase. After all, there's nothing to see."

The president said, "This science attaché, Dr. Thorne. What do you know about him?"

"It's a 'her,' Mr. President," Radford replied. "I was fooled too. She worked with Drummond, knows the ropes up there on the Kola Peninsula."

"Can she be trusted?" the president asked.

"Scott vouched for her."

Friedman said, "I read Scott's file: It says he's got a reputation for taking matters into his own hands. Sounds like that's what he's doing now."

The president collapsed his steeple. "What's that all about, Karl?"

"Sir, Paul's referring to a submarine recon mission Scott undertook a year ago for the SRO into the Yellow Sea. You may remember that your predecessor ordered a special-ops team into North Korea in preparation for a preemptive strike on the Yongbyon nuclear complex. The NKs stumbled on the op before we could execute. Scott almost lost his ship trying to save a SEAL team that the NKs had trapped. He had explicit orders that if something went wrong he was to pull out and leave the team behind but didn't."

The president nodded. "I remember. Pretty gutsy, I'd say."

"But a direct violation of orders. We almost lost a Los Angeles–class nuke to the NKs. It would have been a propaganda coup for them if we had and a hell of a provocation too."

"To say nothing of the NK ship he torpedoed," Friedman added.

The president waved that aside and moved on. "I don't want this Drummond affair blowing up in my face while I'm in St. Petersburg. I'm facing some difficult negotiations, and the Russians have been playing hard ball on every issue we need to resolve."

"Scott will have departed Russia before you arrive, Mr. President. I guarantee it."

The president erected his steeple again. "See that he does, Karl," he said in a measured tone.

"Yes, sir."

Friedman shifted the load of folders from his lap to the sofa. "Anything new on Zakayev? I see he's not mentioned in the briefing's threat assessment."

"Our J-25 com intercepts have gone deaf," Radford said. "There's been no communications activity between Zakayev or his people for almost ninety-six hours."

"A worrisome thing," Friedman observed. He glanced at Radford, perhaps hoping the SRO chief would confirm this.

Radford said, "Zakayev's being hunted all over Russia, so he's probably hiding somewhere. If in fact he killed Drummond, he may still be somewhere between St. Petersburg and Murmansk. I expect he'll surface soon."

"That's what I'm afraid of." Friedman unloaded the folders onto the sofa and got to his feet. "And when he does, God help us and the Russians."

The president collapsed his new steeple and frowned. "You're overstating it, Paul."

"Am I?" Friedman said, then, as if suddenly remembering who he was addressing, he softened his tone. "I beg your pardon, Mr. President, but what I meant to say is that we underestimated Zakayev. The attack on the concert hall was a shock, something none of us could have ever imagined. We know Zakayev is unpredictable and, like a damned snake, can turn on us if he wants to. He's proven it by turning on the Russians. He's our creation and we've lost control of him. I still believe we made a serious mistake supporting him, using him to distract the Russians. And if they find out we did, it will destroy the summit and undermine our efforts to bring the Russians over to our side on a host of issues."

"Your moral outrage is duly noted," the president

said. "But you're raking over old ground. What's done is done and we can't change it. What we have to do is convince the Russians not to launch an all-out war in Chechnya and the Caucasus."

"Sir, with respect," Friedman said, "the Russians launched all-out war there ten years ago."

"I'm talking about all-out war using nuclear weapons. They've threatened to go nuclear, and if they do it could ignite World War III."

# 7

## The Novy Polyarnyy Hotel, Murmansk

Yuri Abakov opened the window blind and looked out at the TV antennas and satellite dishes on the roof of the building next door silhouetted against a red glow in the eastern sky. Earlier a dull boom had rattled the windows.

"Is that a fire?" Alex asked.

"Looks like a big one in the harbor area," Abakov confirmed.

Scott stood in the middle of the room surveying the bed, the greasy furniture, the soiled walls.

"I told you there would be nothing to see," Abakov said, sounding slightly bored.

There was nothing to indicate that two men had died in the room. And no bloodstains on the floor or the bed. Scott peeled back the coverlet and sheets and discovered a cheap, thin mattress that looked new.

"Satisfied?" Abakov said.

Scott stood with hands on hips. A wild-goose chase, and he hated to admit it. Yet, something gnawed at him. Why here? Why with Radchenko? What was he overlooking?

Alex peeked into a corner of the room at what passed for a bathroom equipped with a chipped washstand and crazed china commode. A faded floral print curtain on a rusty pole offered little privacy. "This place gives me the creeps," she said.

"It's not exactly the Sheraton Regis," said Scott.

Alex went around the room looking, touching. She stood at the door and ran a hand over the rough woodwork. She worked the doorknob and Abakov took this to mean she was anxious to leave.

"If you are finished, I suggest we go," Abakov said, closing the blind on the red-tinged sky. "We can conclude our business in Moscow tomorrow and then you can take custody of Admiral Drummond's remains."

"Scott, take a look at this," Alex said. "These door moldings are new and freshly painted. The door looks new too. So does the lock and mortise."

Scott examined the crudely executed carpentry where angles didn't match and bent nail heads protruded from scarred wood trim.

"There's a simple explanation," Abakov said, rapping his knuckles on the new door. "The old one had been forced open and had to be replaced."

"Forced open?" Scott said. "Why?"

"Admiral Drummond had taken the room for one night only. When he didn't come down the next morning to settle his bill, the porter became suspicious. He went up to check on Admiral Drummond, but when he didn't answer the door, the porter broke it open and that's when he found the two of them inside, dead."

"Why did he break it open?"

"He said the chain lock was set. As you can see, it's been replaced."

"Did you see the broken door?" Scott said.

"No. The Murmansk police reported to me that it was smashed in when they arrived."

"Smashed in?"

"The porter said he kicked it in."

"I want to make sure I understand. . . . You were called by the Murmansk police?"

"After they discovered that one of the dead men was an American attached to the U.S. Embassy. Admiral Drummond had nothing on him at the time he was found to indicate he was."

"How long after the bodies were discovered did you arrive in Murmansk to take over the case?"

"Why do you ask?"

"Just curious."

"Two days."

"Did the Murmansk police take photos of the crime scene? Of the door?"

"Of the room, not the door."

"So you never actually saw the bodies here. Just photos of them in the positions you described."

Abakov hesitated before saying, "Yes."

"I see," Scott said.

He ran a hand over the ugly green wallpaper behind the door and felt a deep, round depression in the plaster that matched the shape of a doorknob. When the door was kicked in, it had flown back and hit the wall, the doorknob leaving its deep impression in the plaster.

"It took a lot of force to do that," Alex said. "A lot."

"Didn't the porter have a passkey?" Scott said. "I mean, why break down the door?"

"It's not my hotel," Abakov said, apparently irritated at Scott's discovery of his lack of firsthand knowledge of the condition of the bodies after their discovery.

"Let's get the porter up here," Scott said. "Maybe he knows something."

"He's already told us everything he knows," Abakov said.

"Well, maybe he forgot something."

Abakov bristled.

"I'm not trying to encroach on your territory, Colonel, if that's what you're worried about. I just want to ask him a few questions."

Abakov boarded the elevator and rode it, clanking and grinding, to the lobby.

Alone in the room with Scott, Alex said, "Abakov never saw the bodies except at the Murmansk morgue. Only photos of them."

"That's right."

"Then his report is based solely on secondhand information from his investigators."

"Right again."

"Which means it's suspect."

Scott nodded.

"And you don't believe that the porter kicked the door in, do you?"

"The old man we saw downstairs? No way."

"Then who did?"

Scott ran a hand through his hair. He thought it would be so simple, but suddenly everything had been turned upside down.

"Tell me."

He looked at her. Was she reading his mind?

"It was Alikhan Zakayev, wasn't it," she said. "Or one of his men."

They heard the lift start its return trip from the lobby with Abakov and the porter on board.

"Zakayev must have known that Drummond was

hunting for him and that he was here with Radchenko," Scott said. "He killed Drummond and Radchenko and made it look like a murder-suicide."

"Jake, why fake a suicide? Why not just kill Drummond and Radchenko and get rid of their bodies?"

"Because their disappearance would raise too many questions. At least with a murder-suicide there'd be a good reason to cover up what happened."

"All right, I can buy that, but what was Drummond doing here with Radchenko, and what was he after?"

The scissors gate rattling open signaled the lift's arrival. Scott put a finger to his lips.

The porter had eyes bleary from vodka and too much TV. He looked about seventy and smelled like the hotel: unwashed and musty. He was painfully thin, with arms like sticks and tufts of white hair that stood straight up on his head as if he'd stuck his finger in a light socket.

"What's your name?" Scott asked.

The old man started at hearing an American speak good Russian. "Nikita Fyodorovich."

"May I call you Nikita?"

"That's what my friends call me." He glanced around the room with the practiced eye of an innkeeper concerned that his establishment maintain its reputation for quality. He looked at the tossed bed and frowned.

"I was told that you were the person who discovered the dead bodies in this room."

Nikita hesitated. He looked at Abakov. "Tell him," Abakov said.

"I didn't know there was another man in the room with the *Amerikanski* until I broke in."

"Why did you break in?"

Nikita fingered white beard stubble while he considered. "The American had been in the room all night and now it was the next day. When he didn't come down to pay for another day's stay, I got suspicious. Here, you always pay in advance for each day that you stay."

"Do you always break down a door when some one doesn't pay?"

Nikita had terrible breath, and when he exhaled heavily before answering, it washed over Scott. "I went up three, four times and knocked. I called to him. He didn't answer. I waited until noon before I did it. You can't ever let them go a full day without paying."

"Why didn't you use a passkey instead of breaking down the door?" Scott said.

Nikita's eyes flicked to Abakov. "I already told the police everything."

"Tell me."

"The chain lock had been set."

"You mean the American had set it?"

Scott saw a tremor affect Nikita's blue-veined hands. He linked them behind his back. "Yes, that's what it was."

"Why would he do that?"

Nikita lifted a shoulder.

"How did you break down the door?"

"I kicked it in."

"This new door is pretty thick. Was the old one this thick?"

Nikita shrugged again.

"You didn't hurt yourself–kicking it in, I mean?"

Nikita looked as if he'd been insulted. "I'm stronger than you think." He thumped his chest with a fist.

"Did anyone see you do it?"

"No."

"Weren't there other guests on this floor? Did they hear you do it? Did they come out of their rooms to see what was going on? It must have made a lot of noise."

"This isn't Moscow. They knew to mind their own business."

"I don't understand," Scott said.

"I think what he means, Jake," said Alex, "is that old habits from the Soviet era die slowly."

"I see," Scott said. "After it was all over, who fixed the door?"

"A man who does odd jobs for the hotel. He does carpentry and fixes plumbing and electricity. He's also an exterminator."

"When did he fix it?"

"The next day, after the police had finished."

"And before Colonel Abakov arrived?"

Nikita shrugged again. "We needed to rent the room."

Scott gave Nikita six hundred rubles for his trouble and watched him depart.

"He's lying," Scott said. "He couldn't have kicked in that door. He couldn't kick his way out of a paper bag."

Abakov said nothing. He tested the lock from both sides of the newly installed door with a shiny brass key tied with sturdy twine to a piece of wood with the number 312 burned into it like a brand. Satisfied that it worked properly, he stood with arms folded across his chest and sniffed, perhaps picking up the faint scent of mistaken assumptions.

"Someone kicked the door in and shot them," Scott said. "Then they told Nikita to make up a story, to get the door fixed, and to keep his mouth shut. Everyone in Murmansk knows to keep their mouths shut. As you heard Alex say, Colonel, old habits from the Soviet era die slowly."

Abakov looked shaken, as if his investigative skills had suddenly been proven worthless. The vein in his neck started throbbing impatiently. "Are you trying to make a fool of me, Captain? What do you know that you're not telling me? Who is this person you think killed Admiral Drummond?"

"Alikhan Zakayev."

Abakov stared at Scott in icy silence.

Before Abakov could speak, Scott said, "Drummond was sent to Russia to find Zakayev. That's all I can tell you. Zakayev probably knew Drummond was looking for him and he probably knew Drummond was going to meet Radchenko—not to buy sex but something else. Information. That's why he killed him or had him killed."

"What kind of information?" Abakov said with a hint of skepticism.

"There's only one kind of information Radchenko could possibly have had that would interest Frank. Information that someone, probably Zakayev, was planning to steal fissile materials from Olenya Bay."

"How would Radchenko, a seaman, have that information?" Abakov said.

"I don't know, Colonel. Perhaps he overheard something."

"Are you telling me that if Zakayev had fissile material, he could build a nuclear bomb?" He rounded on Alex. "Is that possible, Dr. Thorne?"

"Theoretically," she said, "but it would be very difficult to build a bomb. He'd need U-235 or Pu-239. But recycled naval reactor plutonium is not easily made critical; plus, he'd need a trigger and a pusher of, say, lithium deuteride and—"

"Are any fissile materials missing from Olenya Bay?" Abakov demanded.

"Not so far as I know. But one can never be one-hundred-percent sure. There's a lot of garbage laying around up there and it wouldn't be hard to steal."

"We're getting ahead of ourselves," Scott said. "Alex, did Frank ever talk to you about the possibility of terrorists getting their hands on fissile material and building a nuclear device?"

"Only in the abstract. Sure, we discussed what it would take, the techinical means and all, but we concluded it would be almost impossible to do without resources that terrorists are not likely to have, like metallurgy labs, that sort of thing. Actually, the weapon that it might be possible for them to build is a radiation bomb: a device that would spread radioactive material over a wide area and contaminate people and cities."

Abakov, stripped of skepticism, said, "How many people would die if radiation was spread over a population center by one of these bombs?"

"Depends how much radiation was released, the prevailing winds, et cetera. Under the right conditions, perhaps thousands."

"And if he were to target Moscow . . . ?" Abakov said.

"Colonel, the whole idea is pretty much impossible."

"Dr. Thorne, please believe me when I say that I know Zakayev, and for him nothing is impossible. He has contacts all over the world with men who would not hesitate to kill millions of people." Abakov's brusque manner had given way to solicitation. He was clearly shaken by what Alex had said.

Scott pictured Zakayev the terrorist assembling the raw materials needed to make a radiation bomb. He pictured a grubby clandestine workshop in some back alley in Chechnya and a group of terrorists busy putting the parts together: explosive, wiring, timers, outer explosive shell. The only thing missing might be the fission product, a highly dangerous radioactive nuclide such as strontium, cesium, or cobalt. But there was another way for them to attack their enemies that didn't require the making of a crude radiation bomb. What it required was stealing a nuclear bomb already built, but he didn't say what he was thinking.

Scott's rumination was interrupted by Abakov's chirping cell phone. An excited voice leaked past Abakov's ear planted on the phone. He went to the window blind, opened the slats with two fingers, and peered out at the red glow in the sky. "I'm looking at it now," he said to his caller. "I'll be there in ten minutes."

Abakov hung up and said, "There's been a shoot-out and car bombing in the harbor area. Several men were killed and the Murmansk police think that one of them may be Ivan Serov."

"The Russian *mafiya* chieftain?" Scott said.

"Yes," Abakov said.

"What was it you said in Moscow, Colonel? 'Where you find Serov, you often find Zakayev.' "

The car was a smoking hulk. A sickening smell hung in the air. Two corpses covered with plastic sheeting had been burned beyond recognition, their arms and legs charred stumps reaching skyward, the bodies twisted into grotesque shapes. A third corpse had been burned only below the waist, the internal organs trailing away to a black, unrecognizable mass.

Abakov pointed his foot at the corpse. "This one is a Serov lieutenant."

"How do you know?" Alex said, a hand over her nose and mouth.

The dead face was jowly and a gray tongue protruded from a wide-open mouth from which, it seemed, a scream had escaped before the man's brain died.

"There's this. . . ." Abakov squatted and pointed with a ballpoint pen to a pair of crossed daggers dripping blood tattooed on the man's biceps. The tattoo had been exposed when the man's jacket and sweater had been ripped off by the blast that destroyed the car. "We know that Serov's men wear this tattoo as proof of their blood loyalty. It means they will render their blood for him."

"Yuck."

"I'm willing to bet a week's pay that one of these other two beauties is Ivan Serov himself. It's not like him to get involved in something as crude as a shoot-out. But now I am thinking he was also involved in the shoot-out in St. Petersburg. Whatever the reason, he must have felt it had to be finished on his terms, here."

"Was it a feud with Zakayev?" Scott said.

Abakov grunted. "Anything is possible."

In his element now, Abakov shouldered between firemen rolling up hoses and stowing gear. He greeted Murmansk police officers and spoke to them in rough, clipped argot while they sifted through burnt rubble looking for evidence. Scott and Alex followed in his wake, stepping carefully over burnt wreckage from the car.

"Used to be a BMW," Abakov said over his shoulder.

He stopped to confer with an officer who then led them to the concrete steps outside the charred warehouse. Inside, a powerful beam from a flashlight played over walls and support beams as the owner of the warehouse assessed damage.

The officer showed Abakov three small, scorched automatic weapons lying on a tarp spread out on the top step of the cement staircase.

"Micro Uzis." Abakov said, poking one with the ballpoint pen. "Perfect for hosing down a room or an alley, and easily concealed." The little 9mm submachine guns had twenty-round box magazines and folding wire stocks. "They're a favorite weapon of the Russian *mafiya,*" Abakov revealed. He held up two metal objects. "Do you know what these are, Captain?"

"A safety pin and spoon from a grenade."

"A Czech grenade," Abakov said. "Rare."

"Is that what blew up the car?" Alex said.

"More than likely," Abakov said.

The police officer said something to Abakov that Scott didn't catch.

"He says," Abakov explained, "that they found spent cartridge cases around these steps in two sizes, nine-millimeter and twenty-five-caliber. The twenty-fives are probably from a Czech CZ92. Somebody put up a pretty good fight against Serov and his men. The grenade won it for them. We'll check these spent nine-millimeter cases against the ones we found in St. Petersburg. They're probably from the same weapon."

"Then you think Zakayev killed Serov," Scott said. "And got away."

Abakov shrugged. "I don't think we'll find Zakayev's corpse here."

"Can we talk?" said Scott.

"Um, sure," Alex said over the phone from her office at the embassy in Moscow. "But can you make it quick."

"Not on the phone," Scott said, sensing she was not alone in her office. "At Frank's apartment. Half an hour?"

"I'm pretty busy. . . . I told you, that's why I had to get back to Moscow."

"So you did. If it's David Hoffman you're worried about, tell him I'll explain things to him later."

"Scott, please don't–"

"Just do it."

Alex found Scott engrossed in Drummond's papers, which he was preparing for shipment to the States. He had them laid out in piles on the countertops in the kitchenette. "What's so damned important that it can't wait till after work?" she said. "You know I want to help you, but I've barely had a chance to decompress from our trip to Murmansk, David's breathing down my neck, and I've got a ton of things to do for him."

Scott brushed her objections aside with the wave of a hand. "Tell me what Frank said on the voice mail he sent you when he was in Murmansk."

"Jake, for God's sake."

"What did he say?"

Alex frowned. "I told you, nothing. Nothing I could understand. It was garbled, like cell phone calls often are."

"You must have heard him say something."

She exhaled heavily. "If you don't believe me, then listen to it yourself."

Scott brightened. "You mean that you still have it on your voice mail system?"

"I don't have it on my system, but all calls to the embassy are stored in the central security archive."

"Can Jack Slaughter find it?"

"I guess so. Ask him."

"I will."

"And I'm going back to my office."

"Wait. If Slaughter can find the message, I want you to listen to it with me."

"You don't seem to understand: I work for David

Hoffman, not Jake Scott. I can't get involved in your"—she searched for a word—"scheme."

"Scheme? You think this is a scheme? Two men are dead—murdered. Three more were killed in a shoot-out in Murmansk. Some one may have stolen fissile materials to make a crude bomb. And you think this is some scheme that I dreamed up?"

She came to him, put a hand on his arm. "Jake, I'm sorry, I didn't mean that. It was a poor choice of words."

His eyes roamed her lovely face as if committing it to memory. He heard her breathing, smelled the musky aroma of her perfume. She kept her eyes down as if immersed in a private reverie. He wondered if she had ever allowed a man into her inner life, and if she had, what kind of man he was.

"Jake, you don't understand. . . ."

"Tell me." He slipped an arm around her waist and drew her lightly against him.

"Don't." Her breath fluttered across his cheek.

"Don't what?"

She tried to move away, but he held her. "Don't complicate things any more than they already are."

Scott turned her chin up to him so he could look into her eyes. "Alex, it doesn't have to be complicated."

"But it will be and I don't want that now."

His kiss ended further protest. Her arms linked around his neck and she arched into him. When she pushed away, she allowed his hands to linger around her waist. Moisture glistened on her lips. "Jake, this is no good. That was nice, but wasn't supposed to happen."

Perhaps sensing that her comment lacked conviction, she stepped away from Scott and went to the window to look out.

"Is it David Hoffman?" Scott said.

"Not the way you mean it. I'm not in love with him."

"But he's in love with you."

At first she didn't answer. She turned from the window and, in a low voice, said, "I love this country and the people. I know this will sound melodramatic, but I believe I'm contributing something important by doing what I do to make Russia and the world safer. When Frank arrived in Moscow, I believed that he would help put an end to the nightmare we were facing on the Kola Peninsula. But then he was killed.

"I'm not a crusader nor a politician and I want to help you find Frank's killer, but I have other responsibilities too. To the people I work for and my colleagues here at the embassy. We're not always one big happy family, but it's a tight-knit group." She turned from the window to face Scott. "Does that make sense?"

"Sure," Scott said. "Look, I don't want to cause problems for you. As you said, you have to live with David after I'm gone from Moscow. But I need your help. You were the last person to hear from Frank—I know, I know, the message was garbled—but there may be something on it that will jog your memory."

Scott teetered on the brink between fantasy and reality. His experience in intelligence had taught him never to discard a scrap of information no matter how innocuous it seemed. He'd dug through Drummond's graveyard of old documents and found a link between Frank and Zakayev. Abakov saw a link between Zakayev and Serov. And there was another link between Radchenko, Drummond, and the *K-363*—which, to Scott, meant there had to be a link to her skipper, Georgi Litvanov.

He remembered something else. First rule of intelligence work: Don't jump to conclusions. Second rule of intelligence work: Construct a premise. Third rule . . .

something about logic and reason, but they had gone out the window.

"All right," Alex was saying, "let's try jogging my memory."

*"Dive the boat!"* rasped over the SC1 announcing system.

Georgi Litvanov, in the CCP—Central Command Post—with stopwatch in hand, closely monitored a series of well-orchestrated moves to get the eight-thousand-ton-displacement Akula-class nuclear attack submarine underwater as fast as possible. The singsong of orders came in full cry.

"Full dive on planes fore and aft! Make your depth one hundred meters! Both engines half speed ahead!"

Litvanov thumbed the stopwatch, noted the elapsed time, then glanced at the compass repeater. The *K-363* was on a northerly course out of Olenya Bay.

Litvanov's eyes drifted to Starshi Leitenant Karpenko, the young, wide-eyed officer of the deck, who returned Litvanov's frosty look with a hopeful gaze.

"The Russian Navy will be looking for us, you idiot!" Litvanov bellowed, his words spitting like bullets from a machine gun aimed at Karpenko. "Do you think that we can fool them into believing that we are just travelers passing in the night? No! When I give the order, I want this boat submerged in thirty seconds—not forty-five, not sixty. Do you understand?"

"Kapitan, I—"

"I, I, I," Litvanov, mocked him. "Are you deaf as well as dumb?"

Karpenko recoiled under the assault in full ear of the crew at stations in the CCP.

A sudden, shocking silence gripped the boat.

Litvanov, his coarse features twisted into a mask of

anger, looked around at his officers and crew. At Zakayev and the girl, both tucked into an unused corner of the red-lit CCP, out of the narrow traffic lanes used by the crew.

"The dive took fifty-two seconds. Why? I'll tell you why. Because you, Karpenko, ordered both engines half speed ahead instead of full speed ahead."

Karpenko croaked, "Sir, I can explain—"

"Silence!"

The sound of water dripping into the bilges echoed throughout the CCP.

Litvanov lit a cigarette with a sputtering match. After taking a few drags he said to his *starpom,* or executive officer, Kapitan-Leitenant Konstintin Veroshilov on duty at the diving station, "You will remove Karpenko from the watch bill until he can figure out how to dive this scow in thirty seconds."

Veroshilov braced. "Yes, Kapitan."

Litvanov's gaze returned to Karpenko. "Dismissed!"

Zakayev went below into the *K-363*'s innards, which stank of unwashed bodies and unflushed heads. He entered the wardroom where Litvanov was hunched over a bowl of lentil soup, a plate of herring and groats, and a bottle of vodka.

"May I join you, Kapitan?"

Litvanov, shoveling food into his mouth, washing it down with vodka, ordered the messman out of the wardroom. Zakayev took a seat on the leather upholstered banquette opposite Litvanov.

At length Litvanov, not looking up from his food at Zakayev, said, "I know what you are thinking."

He sent the vodka bottle careening across the table. Zakayev made a one-handed grab before it reached the edge. He uncorked it and filled a glass but didn't drink.

"The success of this operation hinges on how well the crew performs their duties," Litvanov went on. "We can't afford to make mistakes. Karpenko made a mistake and he has to pay a price. Being humiliated in front of your subordinates helps focus the mind. Our lives and the success of the mission depend on every man doing his job perfectly."

Zakayev knew that Litvanov was proud and dedicated and had a bedrock belief that adversity tempered a man's character. Even so, he said, "Your men are volunteers, not conscripts."

"What of it?"

"They seem on edge. Perhaps you drive them too hard."

Litvanov pushed his plate and cutlery aside. He lit a cigarette. "On the contrary, my regimen will work wonders. Like you, General, I put a high premium on dedication and sacrifice. You won't be disappointed. The mission will be successful. I guarantee it."

Zakayev believed him. He had been introduced to the *K-363*'s skeleton crew but didn't introduce the girl, in whom the men had shown only mild curiosity when she came aboard. "Because she's one of us, the old sailors' myth that a woman aboard a ship brings bad luck means nothing to them," Litvanov had quipped.

The *K-363*'s sailors, some barely out of their teens and with sparse beards, cropped hair, and eager looks, reminded Zakayev of the young men he'd commanded in Chechnya. Too embittered to believe their cause could fail, the sailors had reaffirmed their desire to sacrifice themselves to avenge their families and to destroy the hated Russians. They all drank a toast, after which they saluted Zakayev, nodded politely to the girl, and returned to their duties.

Earlier, Zakayev and the girl had boarded the *K-363* where she lay in a deep fjord at the Russian Northern Fleet Submarine Base Olenya Bay, moored to a rotting pier. The fjord, surrounded by low hills covered with scrub and birch, opened onto a dredged channel that emptied into the Barents Sea. At the head of the fjord, not far from the *K-363*'s berth and lined up like sardines in a tin, twenty rusting obsolete nuclear submarines waited their turn in the breakers' yard. Zakayev, standing in the dark on the *K-363*'s rounded, snow-covered hull and looking toward the far shore, could barely identify the bow of an old flooded diesel submarine jutting above the fjord's oil-coated water at a forty-five-degree angle, not even a buoy to mark its grave.

Starpom Veroshilov had horsed out of an open hatch and looked around, trying to see what the weather promised. "Clearing," he said mostly to himself, looking up at the night sky where, through holes ripped in the pale cloud cover, stars twinkled. "Dropping temperatures. Moderate seas."

Litvanov appeared on deck. "Starpom, sound quarters for getting under way. We stand out on the flood tide."

"Aye, Kapitan."

"What was your final muster?"

Veroshilov recited from memory. "The twenty-three men you selected are aboard. The rest—ten officers, eight warrant officers, three petty officers, ten able seamen—are ashore on liberty and will be left behind."

"Very well."

Veroshilov, after delivering this report, had gone forward to the brow, where he knelt and disconnected a thin, black drooping cable hanging between the pier and the *K-363*. The cable provided intermittent phone service to submarine headquarters at the sprawling Olenya Bay Naval Base complex. The phone rarely ever rang, and Litvanov liked it that way.

Litvanov had glanced at the Russian tricolor—white, blue, and red—snapping from a staff planted on the sail, then turned to Zakayev and said, "So, now it starts."

Shortly, Litvanov maneuvered the *K-363* away from the pier and stood down the Tuloma River under cover of darkness. He had invited Zakayev to the bridge high in the submarine's streamlined sail and, like a guide on a sightseeing cruise gliding silently down the river, pointed out the sights: darkened, abandoned warships anchored in the roadstead; two rusting and mottled radioactive waste transport ships, the *Amur* and the *Vala;* the defunct Letinskiy lighthouse at the point where the Tuloma River emptied into Kola Bay, and where balls of sleet peppered the *K-363*.

"So much for the weather report," Litvanov had said and sounded the diving siren.

Now Litvanov stood at the chart table in the CCP, laying off ranges and bearings. He studied the chart, working his jaw from side to side as if reciting a silent incantation known only to him. He said to Starpom Veroshilov, who was also the ship's navigator, "Hold this course until we pass the channel marker buoy in another"—he looked at the chronometer mounted over the chart table—"twenty minutes. Then come to course three-five-zero."

"Aye, sir," said Veroshilov, marking their course line, which, laid out, was six nautical miles due west of Kil'din Island off the Kola Peninsula.

Submerged, rigged for silent operation, the *K-363* crept northeast at five knots. Tension had risen steadily until it showed on the burnished faces of the sailors on duty in the CCP exchanging nervous glances. They knew that the *K-363*'s submerged transit of Kola Bay was a gross violation of Northern Fleet regulations and that they ran the risk of being attacked by Russian patrol boats on the lookout for intruding foreign submarines.

Litvanov tapped the chart and said, "No sign of any patrol boats. Good thing too: Those idiots might panic if they hear us and start dropping depth charges." He glanced at the girl, dressed in a pair of baggy gray regulation submarine coveralls that hid her slim figure, to gauge her reaction. She calmly held his gaze with her big, expressive eyes and said nothing.

"Where do you think they are?" Zakayev said.

Litvanov shrugged. "Maybe they heard a whale, thought it was a sub, went chasing after it, and are miles away. Or maybe they decided to hang around to catch some poor fisherman with his nets over the side in a prohibited area. You never know."

"How good is their sound equipment?"

"Fair. They have hull-mounted and dipping sonars. Torpedoes, anti-ship rockets, and guns. Nasty little bastards. But they don't maintain their equipment and they get lazy when nothing exciting ever happens. They don't have much to do, now that the *Amerikanskis* don't spy on us like they used to. During the Cold War they'd stick the noses of their Los Angeles–class boats into the Tuloma River delta and—"

"Kapitan, sonar. Sound contact bearing zero-five-zero degrees!"

Litvanov reached for a *kashtan* microphone attached

to the end of a coiled wire hanging from the overhead. "Fire Control, Kapitan. Range?"

The range had been generated from multiple bearings. "Under four thousand meters."

Litvanov pushed away from the chart table and went forward from the CCP to poke his head into the sonar room, where a spike of noise on a green waterfall slowly worked its way down a sonar screen.

"Contact drifting east-southeast, Kapitan." The senior sonarman, intent on tracking the contact, didn't look up. "Light twin-screw beat—I'd say sixty turns."

"Five knots," Litvanov said. He tugged his nose and waited.

A minute later the sonarman looked up at Litvanov. "Contact moving abaft the beam. No change in speed."

"Can you identify him?" Litvanov said.

The fire control computer searched its memory banks for a matching sound profile. "MPK patrol boat, Kapitan."

Litvanov considered. The *K-363* was more than ten minutes away from a planned course change to the northwest and into the Barents Sea. But now they had to sidestep the pesky patrol boat. "Come left ten degrees," Litvanov ordered briskly.

"Come left ten degrees, aye," from the helmsman.

Litvanov waited as the *K-363* turned and settled on her new course. "Anything?"

"Contact diminishing, Kapitan."

Veroshilov's tongue flicked across dry lips. He followed the action and made manual course adjustments on the chart, which was updated automatically by a plotter stylus moving over an acetate overlay. He also kept track using information marked on the chart of how much water lay under the keel. A Fathometer sounding would confirm it but a ping bounced off the sea bottom would reveal their position.

"Hold this course for fifteen minutes," Litvanov ordered, "then we'll come back to our original base course. By then he may be gone." He caught Zakayev's eye. "What did I tell you?"

Zakayev turned his gaze on the girl. She looked composed yet intrigued by the utter complexity of the CCP. Like snakes, cables and wiring, some thick as a man's arm, crawled over every available surface inside the hull. Men sat or stood facing control panels and consoles covered with red, green, and orange lights indicating the status of the submarine's nuclear reactor, fire control system, weapons, countermeasures, and hull integrity. Other men sat in comfortable padded chairs while they manipulated the wheels and joysticks used to control the boat's direction and attitude underwater. Throughout the entire compartment a bewildering forest of valves and levers sprouted from pipes and hydraulic lines running every which way, concocted, it seemed, by a team of plumbers gone mad.

Litvanov, arms folded, brow rutted in concentration, hovered near the periscope stand while he waited for a fresh report from sonar.

"All clear, Kapitan. Contact fading."

Litvanov gave the order to resume their earlier course. A minute later he ordered, "Come to periscope depth."

"Periscope depth, aye. Fore and aft up ten."

The *K-363* rose toward the surface.

Litvanov stood by at the night vision scope. He motioned *up* to the quartermaster of the watch. The quartermaster yanked the periscope lift handle and the heavy tube rose from its well in the deck. Litvanov slapped the scope's training handles down as soon as they appeared above the stand. Crouched, eye pressed into the rubber buffer surrounding the ocular, he rose with the scope to a standing position. First he walked the scope around 360 degrees to check for intruders, then checked his swing on the bearing where the patrol boat had been reported by sonar, slowly moving abaft the starboard quarter. He wigwagged the scope left, right, left.

Nothing.

He searched dead astern. Clear there, too, except for a gray curtain that was a snow squall crawling seaward from Kil'din Island. Another 360-degree sweep. "All clear. Down periscope."

Litvanov pushed away from the descending tube. "Come. Let's have a drink."

# 8

## U.S. Embassy, Moscow

For several hours Jack Slaughter had sat in a subbasement room facing a bank of computers and monitors at the heart of the embassy's communications center. Slaughter had entered the embassy voice mail system's Stored Program Control through COMSEC—Communications Security—and retrieved Drummond's cell phone message to Alex.

With the use of filters and modulation techniques, Slaughter had minimized many of the defects in the message caused by nulls and voids and signal fades. Scott and Alex listened through headphones to replay after replay, but only two phrases spoken by Drummond were made clear enough to understand: "I'm staying there" and "will return tomorrow."

While Slaughter experimented, he gave Scott and Alex a running commentary on the complexity of multipath effects, echo elimination, and modulated signal parameters. He spun around in his swivel chair and said, "Try it now; see if it's any better."

Scott listened carefully, but Drummond's voice, badly distorted by noise and signal fade, came through only marginally improved. "Any other ideas that might work?" he asked.

"Afraid not," Slaughter said. "I've used all the tricks I have in my black bag. Cell transmissions from the north are notoriously bad. Pity he didn't use a satellite bounce. The Russian ground relay system has very long transmission paths that badly degrade signals."

"What about his armored cell phone?" Scott said. "Why didn't he use that?"

"Good question," Slaughter said. "By the way, did you ever find it?"

"No."

"Whoever stole it, it's no good to them. It's locked."

Alex saw Scott's disappointment. "Sorry, Jake, I thought for sure we were onto something."

The phone at Slaughter's workstation chirped. He answered, punched the hold button, and said, "It's for you, Captain Scott. It's Mr. Stretzlof."

Scott and Alex found Chief of Mission Viktor Stretzlof waiting for them in a "bubble," one of the embassy's safe rooms on the second floor. He sat at the head of the long coffin-shaped mahogany conference table sipping a diet cola through a bendable straw. David Hoffman sat to Stretzlof's left facing Scott and Alex, his face set in stone.

Without preamble Stretzlof said, "For your information, Captain Scott, the use of the embassy comm center is restricted to the sending and receiving of official embassy communications. It is not to be used for any other purpose."

"Jack Slaughter helped me clear up some messaging Admiral Drummond sent to Dr. Thorne before he was murdered," Scott said. "I felt it was important to know what he was trying to tell her."

"General Radford gave me a rundown on your orders," Stretzlof said gravely. He favored suspenders and starched shirts with white collars and cuffs and blue bodies that crackled when he moved as he did now, turning to Alex then back to Scott. "It seems you've blatantly disregarded them. Furthermore, you've involved Dr. Thorne in your adventures, which, as I understand from David, has taken her away from important duties at the embassy as well as in the field. You were told by General Radford to confine your work to the return of Rear Admiral Drummond's remains and the security of his papers. Apparantly you've seen fit once again to expand your warrant."

"Mr. Stretzlof, I can explain everything–"

Stretzlof cut Alex off with a vigorous chop of his hand that made his jowls oscillate. "I want to hear Captain Scott's explanation, not yours, Dr. Thorne."

"My 'adventure,' as you call it," Scott said, "concerns the murder of an American naval officer–"

"Total conjecture on your part, Captain, isn't that so?" Stretzlof interrupted. "The official FSB report states that Drummond committed suicide."

"The FSB report is wrong."

Stretzlof showed mock surprise. "Is it, now? And I suppose you have ironclad proof to refute the FSB."

"Yes, I do have some information, and I expect to have more soon. Alex–Dr. Thorne–has assisted in the investigation. I believe Frank may have been murdered because he uncovered information about Chechen terrorist activity in Russia."

"My, my, you are quite the detective," Stretzlof said. He put his cola aside. "But General Radford's orders don't authorize you to conduct a police investigation."

"They also don't authorize you to enlist Alex to help you," Hoffman added.

"I volunteered, David," said Alex. "Because I had worked with Admiral Drummond, I thought that any information I had might be helpful to Captain Scott's investigation."

"There you go again," Stretzlof said. "Captain Scott is not here to conduct an investigation. Is that understood?"

Alex said, "Mr. Stretzlof, David, I was very skeptical when Jake told me that he believed Frank was murdered. But I've seen evidence—some of it circumstantial, I admit—that challenges the FSB report. Also, we think—"

"Alex, that's enough," Scott said.

"No, let her speak," Stretzlof said.

"I'm not authorized to reveal what we know, nor is she," Scott said.

"Really? Aren't you lucky that you are able to interpret your orders to suit your every whim."

"You've got it wrong, Mr. Stretzlof. I'm not doing any such thing and I'm not playing detective. What I am trying to do is find out why an American was murdered in Russia. If it involves terrorism, it should concern you too."

Stretzlof's face turned hard as flint. "Don't presume to tell me what should or should not concern me. I know something of your background, Captain, and you appear to have a penchant for taking matters into your own hands when the orders you've been issued don't suit."

"The facts, if you bothered to look at them, may prove your assumptions wrong," Scott said.

Hoffman cleared his throat. "Alex, Mr. Stretzlof and I have decided that you are to withdraw from further involvement in Captain Scott's assignment. Is that understood?"

"David, I–"

"Is it?" Hoffman insisted.

She nodded.

"Good. The President arrives in St. Petersburg next Wednesday. . . ."

"I know the President's schedule, David."

"Then you also know we still have a lot to do to get ready."

"And I'm doing it," Alex said, not hiding her annoyance and embarrassment at being treated like a glorified secretary.

"Don't take it out on Alex," Scott said to Hoffman. "I drafted her to work with me on this investigation and she's done a great job ."

"I told you, Scott, she works for DOE, not the U.S. Navy."

Stretzlof raised a hand. "And how far have you gotten with this 'investigation'?" he asked drily.

"I plan to report my findings to General Radford this evening."

"Yes, do that," Stretzlof said. He opened a file folder and took out a message flimsy, which he slid across the table to Scott. "This is from General Radford. You'll note that I am also an addressee."

Scott took a quick look at the message and said, "Thank you."

Stretzlof stood. "Until General Radford either countermands your present orders or modifies them in some way, and as long as you are in country, you will cease making further inquiries into Admiral Drummond's suicide. For the record, I will report this conversation to the ambassador."

They were all standing. "For the record," Scott said, "I will report this conversation to General Radford."

"Good day," said Stretzlof, departing.

Hoffman said to Alex on his way out, "There's a staff meeting at four."

Alone with Scott in the safe room, Alex said, "I'm sorry. Stretzlof could use a good kick in the balls. David too."

Scott wasn't paying attention, so she sidled up to him and said, "What does General Radford want?"

Scott showed her the message flimsy. It said, REPORT AT ONCE.

There was a knock on the door. "May I come in?"

"We're supposed to stay away from each other," Scott said.

Alex entered Drummond's apartment. She had on the down-filled vest, a silk shirt, jeans, and sneakers. Her hair looked freshly washed and she smelled good. "Professionally, not socially. Anyway, what I do on my own time is none of Viktor's or David's business."

"How'd the staff meeting go?" Scott said.

"Boring. I thought I'd find you here. What are you doing?"

"I've finished packing Frank's things." Scott pointed to several boxes sealed with special tamperproof tape sitting on the floor in the middle of the living room. There were also two zippered garment bags filled with Drummond's uniforms and civilian clothes, and a big battered aluminum suitcase. He kicked one of the boxes. "Files."

Alex looked around the apartment. "It's like Frank was never here."

"That's how Stretzlof wants it."

"Did you talk to General Radford?"

"When I'm good and ready."

"Won't that make things worse?"

Scott snorted. "What can he do? Order me back to the States without Frank's body?"

Alex hugged herself. "Have you made final arrangements?"

"The paperwork is all filled out." He pointed to it on the coffee table. "I'll give it to Abakov tomorrow. He's involved with the investigation into the two shootings, the one in St. Petersburg and the one in Murmansk." He stopped being busy and looked at her.

She met his gaze but said nothing.

"Care for a drink?" he asked. "I saw a bottle around here somewhere."

"Sure." She removed her down vest and hung it over a chair.

They sat on the sofa and drank iced vodka. Alex put her feet up on the coffee table, careful to avoid the paperwork for Abakov. "When you leave Russia, will you go back to your submarine?"

"That's up to Radford," Scott said.

"He's not your commanding officer."

"He is now. He'll have a lot to say about what happens to me after this stint in Moscow. I have a feeling he's not going to be happy with the fact that I—what was it Stretzlof said? 'Expanded my warrant.' How fucking quaint."

Alex hesitated but after reflecting, said, "What did Stretzlof mean when he said he knew about your background, about you taking matters into your own hands? Or shouldn't I ask?"

"He was referring to something I was involved in a while back. I had some problems."

"In other words, you don't want to talk about it."

Scott, hunched on the edge of the sofa, said nothing.

"I'm sorry." She came upright and put her glass on the table. "Maybe I should go."

He looked back at her. "No. Don't go." He reached for her arm to stop her.

She sat back, turning slightly so she could look at him.

Scott flopped against the cushions. "It was a special-ops mission. We almost lost some men; orders got fouled up. I did something I wasn't supposed to do and it's followed me wherever I go. Even to Moscow."

Part of his past had hurtled out of a dark place and he wasn't sure how it had happened. Her silence made him hesitate to say any more about it.

He felt her warmth against him and felt the familiar sting of desire. He tried to concentrate on reality, not fantasy, but she had aroused feelings that he thought were buried for good after Tracy had left. He regretted his earlier clumsy attempt to discover how reachable Alex was. It wasn't supposed to happen, she had said. But God, he had wanted it to.

He felt her gaze on him. "Alex, today when I—"

She put a finger to his lips. "Don't say anything."

Scott drew her head down and they kissed. Her mouth was soft and moist the way he remembered. He moved to her throat, the pit of her neck, her stomach under the open silk shirt, and ran his hands over warm, soft skin.

Alex moved to unzip her jeans. Instead, Scott took his mouth from one of her exquisitely shaped breasts and led her into the bedroom. His body ached while they stood caressing. They parted and Scott quickly shed his clothes. Alex wiggled out of her things and crawled onto the bed. They knelt naked, facing each other, exploring with their hands, enveloped by the heat of it. Slowly they sank into each other, Alex pulling Scott down to feel his mouth between her legs, his tongue in her blond triangle of pubic hair. She closed her eyes and moaned softly, then, gulping air, biting her lip, arched against his mouth and came so quickly, so explosively, that it caught Scott by surprise.

He didn't stop until she cried, "Do it! Now!" Scott, on the verge of losing control, was barely able to pull away in time to enter her and, driving deeply, empty himself before she climaxed again.

They did it again, slower this time; then, exhausted and cooling down, they lay intertwined on the narrow bed. "I didn't mean to complicate things," Alex said.

"Complicate things how?" Scott said. Eyes closed, he let his hand drift lazily over the silky curve of Alex's hip. He felt overwhelmingly contented and didn't want the moment to end. There was no one waiting for him in the States, and at that moment Tracy had never existed.

"I had an affair with David," Alex was saying, "but ended it before you arrived. He's not handled it well and he's made things uncomfortable for me."

"I've noticed."

"And you're right, he's jealous of you."

"Tell him not to be. I won't be around much longer." Scott kissed her, then sat up and swung his legs out of bed.

Alex came up behind him. He felt her cheek against his back, her breath on his skin. "This was wonderful. Don't be angry."

"I'm not angry, I'm confused."

"Over what?"

"Everything."

"That's understandable. There's so much we don't know."

"Well, we know that Zakayev, Drummond, and Radford are connected somehow."

"Are you disappointed that Frank was working for Radford?"

"Frank was just doing a job. He probably didn't know what he was involved in. They never tell you."

"But why send Frank? Did he know Zakayev?"

"I've thought about that. It's possible that it may go back a long way, when Frank was in Afghanistan."

"What do you mean?"

"A lot of it is rumor, but there may be some truth in it. There always is. Frank was damn good at planning and executing special sub ops. From there he moved on to planning special ops against the Taliban and al-Qaeda on the ground in Afghanistan. There were Chechen forces in Afghanistan, and apparently we arranged for them to feed us intelligence in return for our help in Chechnya against the Russians."

"Good God, you mean we were helping the Chechens fight the Russians? Why would we do that?"

"To keep the Russians focused on the fight against terrorism, which would justify U.S. incursions into Iran and Syria. Look, it's complicated and I only know what I told you. But it doesn't take much imagination to figure that we may have had some SRO special-ops types around Grozny, coaching the rebels."

"Would they have coached Zakayev?"

"It's possible," Scott said. "At this point in time anything is possible."

"Do the Russians know this?"

"If they did, it would blow Radford—hell, maybe even the President—right out of Washington. Especially in light of Zakayev's attack on Moscow last month."

"In other words, Zakayev's our creation."

"I wouldn't go that far."

"But we know that Radford sent Frank to Russia to find Zakayev. Maybe to head him off before he launched another terrorist attack."

"Maybe. Anyway, it's too late now for me to find out what Frank knew that got him killed. I'm out of here day after tomorrow."

"Maybe I can help you," Alex said, and kissed Scott's neck.

He turned into her. "How?"

"Maybe I can uncover information that will complete the puzzle."

"How can you do that?"

"I'm not sure exactly, but I have friends here who have access to other friends. It's a long shot, I know, but still . . ."

"Too risky. And even if you found something, what would you do with it—send me a letter, call me at home?"

"I can do better than that: I can leave a voice memo in my secure memo file and give you the code to access it."

"Secure memo file? What the hell's that?"

"It's part of the embassy voice mail system. We all have them. You call your telephone number, enter a COMSEC code, and after the prompt dial a six-digit, three-letter access code. This gets you into the memo file, then you leave a message."

"And it's totally secure?"

"Totally. It's a place to park important messages. Later you can download them to the comm center onto a CD-ROM or print them out for file. I used my memo system all the time when we were in Olenya Bay. It saves time; you don't have to sit down and type out a report or memo on a computer. If you don't need the memo, you dump it or keep it and edit it. You can access the memo file from any phone in the world. We used our special cell phones because they're compatible with the comm center's scramblers."

"Why didn't you tell me this before?"

"It didn't seem important."

Scott exhaled heavily. "Did Frank have a memo system?"

"He must have. We all have them."

"Did he use it in Olenya Bay?"

"I don't know, I suppose he did. . . . Oh my God, I see what you're getting at: Frank may have left information on his memo file about the meeting with Radchenko."

Scott saw that her skin had gone all goose bumpy. "Put something on. We've got work to do."

Scott dialed the COMSEC code Alex said would activate the memo system.

*"You have requested access to a secure communications system of the United States Embassy,"* said the recorded female voice. *"To access the system, please enter your six-digit access code, then wait for the prompt to enter your three-letter confirmation code."*

"Okay, we know Frank had a memo file," Scott said. "Now what?"

"We could ask Jack Slaughter for the access code," Alex said.

"Forget it: Stretzlof would find out and know what we're up to. We'll have to find the code ourselves. Maybe among Frank's things."

"If it is, it'd be on a plastic card," Alex said. "One smaller than a credit card."

Scott cut open one of the sealed boxes containing Drummond's papers and started pawing through them while Alex cut open another box.

"I just thought of something," she said. "Those cards are self-destructing. They fade after six weeks and you can't read them."

"Frank was here for, what, six months?" Scott said.

"Close to it. Damn."

Scott knew Frank was never careless when it came to security and wouldn't write the code on a piece of paper and carry it on him. He'd have committed the number to memory. But memory can be tricky, and important things are sometimes forgotten. So he'd have a backup in case he needed it. Then again, maybe he wouldn't need a backup.

"Can people customize their memo codes?" Scott said.

"Sure: I did, but they warn you not to use anything obvious, like birthdays and anniversaries. Why?"

"Let's try something," Scott said.

"If you're thinking of using different number and letter combinations, good luck. We tried that on Frank's computer and it didn't work, remember?"

Scott picked up the receiver and held it away from his ear so Alex could listen in while he accessed the memo system.

The recorded female voice said, "*. . . please enter your six-digit access code, then wait for the prompt to enter your three-letter confirmation code.*"

"What are you going to enter?" Alex said.

"The hull numbers of the two submarines Frank commanded: 767 and 778."

"The what?"

"I'll explain it later." Scott keyed the numbers; a tone sounded, then the voice. "*Please enter your three-letter confirmation code.*"

"I don't believe it."

He shushed her and punched in SSN.

Another tone, then: *"Access permitted. You have accessed Level One Memo Security. Observe all procedures required for the recording, hearing, and printing of memo documents. When finished, enter J-Star to print documents. Enter T-Star to hear a recorded memo in date order. Enter X-Star to initiate deletion and destruction procedures. Warning: Deletion and destruction procedures cannot be reversed after initiation!"*

Scott entered T-Star. A tick later Drummond's voice with a burst overlay from the armored cell phone came through the receiver like a jolt of electricity.

*"Record to memo at twenty hundred hours on four October oh-six . . . confirming meeting with one Andre Radchenko able seaman assigned to Russian Northern Fleet submarine* K-363 *. . . at Novy Polyarnyy Hotel in Murmansk. . . ."*

The words rushed over Scott, their force almost palpable.

*". . . Radchenko has information that I believe is genuine. . . . Chechen terrorists under command of General Alikhan Zakayev . . . repeat, Alikhan Zakayev . . ."*

Alex's hand flew to her mouth.

*". . . are planning an operation against the submarine base at Olenya Bay. . . ."*

Alex parked the borrowed Skoda in front of a graffitied apartment block on Viatskij Prospekt and doused the headlights. Kids kicked a soccer ball back and forth between the hulks of abandoned cars sitting in a trash-strewn lot illuminated by a solitary sodium vapor street lamp casting a green pallor over their game.

"You can still change your mind and return to the embassy," Scott said. "It's not too late."

"No: I said I would do it and I'm going to," Alex said. "Anyway, the hell with Stretzlof. David too."

Scott leaned over and kissed her. "Then let's go. He's waiting for us."

They climbed concrete stairs past baby carriages and trash cans. The place smelled of urine and old cooking. Babies squalled; couples argued; an American situation comedy dubbed in Russian blared from a TV. They found Abakov's apartment, a 1960s Khrushchev-era *khrusheba*, on the fifth floor and rang the bell.

The door opened and Yuri Abakov, looking exhausted, a day's growth on his face, and wearing rumpled clothes and worn carpet slippers, waved them in. His wife, a pretty young woman with a head of curly orange hair, stood in the doorway of the tiny kitchen. "My wife, Elaina," Abakov said with a perfunctory wave in her direction.

*"Dobro pojalovat! Bud'te kak doma!* Welcome. Come in. Make yourselves at home," she said.

The apartment was small, considering that Abakov, a senior FSB investigator, made a good living. But in Russia, Scott recalled, men like Abakov often went without pay for months while the bills piled up. For the Abakovs, a bigger, more modern apartment was out of the question.

In the living room a solitary window looked out over the trash-strewn lot from where the thud of the soccer ball and the shouts of kids roughhousing reached the apartment. A folded newspaper had been left on the worn cloth sofa where Abakov indicated Scott and Alex should sit. Abakov dropped into a lumpy armchair.

Elaina brought in a bottle of Gjelka vodka with its intricate blue and white label, and plates piled with smoked sturgeon, caviar, homemade pickled cucumbers, and black bread cut into triangles.

Abakov, looking anxious, watched her depart. In

English he said, "Excuse Elaina, she is young and likes to entertain, but we don't often have guests. She wanted to make chicken *tabaka,* but I told her there wouldn't be time for that."

"She's very pretty," Alex said.

"I was a widower, we met, and now I have a family."

"Thanks for seeing us on short notice," Scott said.

"You were in luck: I just returned from St. Petersburg."

"Any information on Zakayev's whereabouts?"

"None. But I was right about one thing. Those spent nine-millimeter cases we found in Murmansk came from one of the guns used in the St. Petersburg shooting. As for Zakayev, he's disappeared. You said you had something important. Let's see what you have."

Abakov kneaded his forehead while he read Drummond's memo, which Scott had printed out in the embassy comm center. Scott knew that showing the document to Abakov was a gross violation of security for which for he and Alex could be prosecuted. But there was no time to ask for clearances that might never come from the embassy or the SRO. Abakov seemed to appreciate this when he said, "You're both taking a big risk. I shouldn't be looking at this."

"The risk is worth taking if we can head off a terrorist attack."

Abakov let out a heavy breath. "What's your assessment?"

"It's clear that Zakayev is either planning to steal fissile materials or something even more dangerous."

Abakov gave Scott a sharp look. "What could be more dangerous in Zakayev's hands than stolen fissile material?"

"A nuclear submarine."

Abakov snorted. "Impossible. There's no way he can steal a submarine."

"He could if he had help."

"From whom?" Abakov said, perhaps seeing the possibility.

"Someone at Olenya Bay. Georgi Litvanov, for instance, the skipper of the *K-363,* the sub Radchenko served in."

"He'd need a crew loyal to him."

"Maybe he's got one," Scott said.

Abakov ran a hand over his bald head while digesting this. At length he said, "They have security at Russian sub bases to prevent terrorists from getting on the base."

"Not according to Alex," said Scott.

"Security at Olenya Bay is nil," Alex said. "No one guards the submarines tied up there. The sub crews are responsible for their own security. And there's no accountability. The base commander doesn't even know how many subs he has or what condition they're in. If one of them sank at a pier, he might not know it for days."

Abakov's face was grave. "Stealing fissile materials is one thing, but stealing a nuclear submarine . . ." Abakov saw Alex give a little wave and smile at someone behind him. He turned around and saw a little boy peeking around the corner from another room. "Sasha," Abakov said, "I thought you were doing your homework."

Sasha was joined by his younger sister, wearing pajamas printed with giraffes. She peeked around Sasha at Scott and Alex.

"They're so cute," said Alex.

"This is Sasha's sister, Nina," Abakov said. "Now, both of you, say good night." There was an exchange between Abakov and his wife and Elaina apologized for the interruption and shooed the children back to their room.

"Look," Scott said, "we can't just sit here, we have to move on this now. You have to alert Olenya Bay and Northern Fleet headquarters."

Abakov ran a hand over his mouth. "I can't do that."

"What the hell do you mean, you can't do that?"

"I can't alert them without having ironclad proof that this memo from Admiral Drummond is genuine, that the information in it is accurate. Otherwise no one would believe it."

"Are you saying you think Drummond may have made it up?" Alex said.

"Of course not. But Drummond is dead, officially a suicide, and so is Radchenko, who, according to this memo, had information about an operation by Zakayev against Olenya Bay."

"But you know as well as I do," Scott said, "that Drummond was murdered to prevent him from warning us about this very plan—Zakayev's plan."

"We have no proof of that. All we have is circumstantial evidence and suspicions."

"We have Drummond's memo, which proves it wasn't a homosexual rendezvous, that he didn't commit suicide and kill Radchenko. The hotel porter didn't smash in the door to Drummond's room: Zakayev did and then killed them. You have the matching shell cases that prove he was involved in the St. Petersburg shootout and the one in Murmansk that killed Serov. Their feud may even be related to the operation at Olenya Bay. What more do you need?"

"A lot more," Abakov said, his voice rising. "For instance, how and where did Radchenko get his information? Maybe he made up a story to get money out of Drummond."

"Frank wouldn't fall for that," Alex said.

"How can you be sure? Drummond was looking for Zakayev, and he would be eager for any information that would lead him to him. As for this Litvanov, we have nothing to tie him to Zakayev except the fact Radchenko was a member of his sub crew."

Alex said, "Colonel, your points are valid. So . . . would it be possible to get information about Litvanov? Maybe there's something in his record that might tie him to Zakayev."

"Yes, perhaps. But it will take time." His eyes darted over the memo while he gnawed a knuckle.

"Then you'd better think about this," said Scott. "In a few days the President of the United States and the President of Russia will hold a summit meeting in St. Petersburg."

Abakov looked intently at Scott while he listened. Sweat shone on his bald dome.

"I'm no expert on Russian subs," Scott continued, "but I know that some can launch SS-N-21 cruise missiles equipped with nuclear warheads. They have a range of over sixteen hundred nautical miles. St. Petersburg can be targeted by a submarine armed with these missiles from anywhere within an arc stretching from the Norwegian Sea to the Barents Sea."

There was a long silence. The sounds of kids playing, punting a soccer ball, scrambling over the empty trash-strewn lot, penetrated Abakov's apartment.

Abakov got slowly to his feet. "I think we'd better pay a visit to Olenya Bay."

Captain First Rank Gennadi Titov, commandant of the Russian Northern Fleet Submarine Base, Olenya Bay, rushed into his office to find Scott, Alex, and Yuri Abakov waiting for him. Titov's face looked puffy and mapped with capillaries. He appeared flustered by his tardiness and struggled to button his tunic. His chief of staff made introductions.

Titov rocked slightly on his feet as his eyes focused on Alex. "Ah, Dr. Thorne, such a pleasure to have you on board again. I always enjoy your visits–"

"This isn't a social call, Commandant," interrupted Abakov. "We're facing a possible security threat."

"So my chief of staff has informed me, Colonel," said Titov, an edge in his voice, his gaze on Abakov's forest-green FSB uniform with gold flashes and decorations. "But he said you were rather cryptic on the phone. So I ask you now: What does this security threat have to do with Olenya Bay?"

Abakov appeared a different man in uniform. His movements were crisp and economical, and his voice conveyed authority. "As you know, Commandant," said Abakov, "a sailor from this base, Able Seaman Andre Radchenko, assigned to the submarine *K-363,* was found murdered in Murmansk."

"Yes, he was found with"–he swung his gaze to Alex–"Rear Admiral Drummond. My condolences, Dr. Thorne. You were saying, Colonel?"

"We think Radchenko may have been murdered because he knew something about a terrorist plot to steal a submarine from Olenya Bay."

Titov's eyes narrowed as he processed this information. He threw back his head and gave a sharp bark of a laugh. "Who's bad joke is this? Yours, Colonel?" Another bark. "Or some idiot in the FSB with nothing better to do than dream up fantasies?"

"This is no fantasy," Abakov said calmly. "We have information that leads us to suspect that Alikhan Zakayev may be planning to steal a submarine from this base."

"Nonsense," Titov said, wiping an eye. "You don't know what you're talking about if you think a terrorist can steal a submarine." He inclined toward his chief of staff, who was as silent as a stone. "Am I right, Lieutenant?"

The aide, hanging back deferentially, tugged the hem of his wrinkled tunic and nodded.

Titov, suddenly serious, rounded on Alex. "Is this your doing?" he said through clenched teeth. "Haven't you and your Norwegian friends meddled enough in naval affairs? Perhaps you want to cause more harm by spreading rumors that we harbor terrorists in Olenya Bay. Is that what your Admiral Drummond did, spread false rumors?"

"Of course not," Alex said. "You know that Earth Safe, Admiral Drummond, and I tried our best to prevent fissile materials from falling into the hands of terrorists. We never meddled. But we can't prevent a terrorist attack on this base. It's your responsibility to provide security, not ours."

"You're out of line, Commandant," Scott said. "Don't blame Dr. Thorne for your failings. There's no security on this pigsty of a base that I can see. When we drove on, there was no guard detail at the gate to check IDs. Your active submarines lack topside security watches, and the rest have been abandoned like so much junk. Hell, half your sub fleet's rotting at the pier. The other half's not even seaworthy. Terrorists could walk right on this base and go aboard any submarine they chose."

Titov's face turned crimson. "Who do you think you are, Captain Scott, to tell me that the Russian Navy's submarine fleet is rotting? Our active submarines are the best in the world, better than your Los Angeles–class and your Seawolfs, and are in prime condition. As for terrorists stealing one of them, I tell you it's impossible."

"Not if they have help," Abakov said.

"From whom?" Titov said sharply.

"Kapitan Georgi Litvanov," Scott said.

"You're mad. Litvanov is one of the top submarine commanders in the Northern Fleet. He would never deal with terrorists."

"Did you know that he was a Chechen?" Scott asked.

Titov considered. He put a hand on his desk for support. "A Chechen . . . yes, of course I knew that. His family name was Litvanayev, but was changed to Litvanov by his father."

"Why would a Chechen be given command of a Russian nuclear submarine?" Abakov said.

"Why? Because he is loyal to Russia, just as he was loyal to the old Soviet Union. And loyal to the Navy. Kapitan Litvanov was awarded the Red Star and the Red Banner. It's well known that there was a Soviet policy of assigning certain Chechen officers to important positions in the Navy. As a young officer he was probably brought along by his seniors and eventually given command."

"Did you know that his wife and children were killed by Russian Spetsnaz in Chechnya? That he comes from the same village as the terrorist Alikhan Zakayev?" Alex said.

"What of it? And how do I know what you say is true?" Titov said, as if the import of what he had heard was finally sinking in.

"Before departing Moscow, I made inquiries of Litvanov," said Abakov. "I received a report on our way in to Olenya Bay."

Titov frowned.

"Do you know where Litvanov is?" Scott asked.

"Of course," Titov said. "He's aboard his submarine, here in Olenya Bay."

The chief of staff cleared his throat. "The *K-363* is moored in North Fjord," he added, as if his knowledge of such detail confirmed that everything was normal.

"We want to interview him," Scott said.

Titov's hand slashed the air. "I won't permit it. His loyalty is above question."

"What is not above question are the security lapses we see on the base," Abakov said. "Perhaps I should notify the commander in chief, Northern Fleet, that you are impeding an FSB investigation into why such lapses exist when Russia is fighting Chechen terrorism."

Titov's mouth tightened into a hard line. His eyes darted from Abakov to Scott to Alex. He said, "I can order the three of you thrown off this base."

Abakov said, "As you wish, Commandant."

Titov turned away and refused to meet the gaze of his chief of staff, who had an imploring look on his face. Titov lit a cigarette, took several deep drags, then mashed it out. He picked up the phone on his desk and punched a number. "Get me Kapitan Litvanov on the *K-363*. Yes, I'll wait."

Titov drummed his fingers on the desk, avoided eye contact with his visitors. Impatient, he rearranged pens, papers, files, a dirty glass and cup.

"Yes?" he said into the phone. "Well, send someone over there–now!" He slammed the phone down. "The ship-to-shore phone connection to the *K-363* is dead," he explained. "Perhaps Litvanov shifted her berth. They're looking for her. It won't take long."

Scott caught Alex's attention. She rolled her eyes toward the ceiling.

An uneasy silence descended. Titov stared at the phone as if willing it to ring. He rearranged his desk again, made a pretense of looking through paperwork.

"Litvanov has been conducting drills on board his boat," Titov said at length, to break the heavy silence. "He never let's his crew rest, even when they're in port. I wouldn't be surprised he's conducting a training exercise right now and that's why we can't locate him."

"Commandant, I understand he granted liberty to a sizable section of his crew," the chief of staff said.

Titov brightened. "There, you see: Litvanov is a reasonable man."

The thuds of trucks hauling heavy equipment over the broken-up road fronting headquarters penetrated Titov's office. Phones in the outer offices jangled. A teleprinter started up and began chattering. Titov chain-smoked. Scott examined a plan view of the base, its maze of fjords clotted with submarines slated for disposal. His rough tally came to over 110 boats. A massive and dangerous job that the Russian Navy had yet to address.

The phone burred; Titov seized it. "What?" He shot to his feet. "Impossible!" He listened to an agitated voice on the other end leaking past his ear. Stunned, he lowered the phone and faced Abakov. All the blood seemed to have drained from his face.

"The *K-363,*" Titov said. "She's vanished."

# Part Two

## THE CHASE

# 9

## Washington, D.C.

Karl Radford looked up from his coq au vin and saw the chief of the SRO security detail, apology written all over his face, enter the restaurant's private dining room.

"Darling, why do I think our evening is about to end?" said Radford's dinner companion.

Radford kissed her hand. "Be an optimist, love."

He excused himself and steered the chief into a small, unoccupied cocktail lounge off the dining room. "Let's have it."

"Sir, Captain Scott calling from Moscow. They patched him through to your car if you wish to take the call there."

"You bet I do."

Suddenly Radford's fantasy, the one he'd nurtured and refined in great detail all evening—the one in which his dinner companion steps out of her panties while he reclines on the satin-sheeted bed in her Foggy Bottom apartment—went black.

Radford sat in the backseat of an armored Mercury Marquis parked in the garage under the restaurant. He picked up the phone and heard, "Your call is cleared through, General."

Radford said, "What the hell's going on, Scott? You had orders to make contact immediately. Now Stretzlof says you're off freelancing. "

"Not so, General," Scott said.

"Then why are you in Olenya Bay. I want an explanation and I want it now."

"Yes, sir, I was about to explain everything."

For the next ten minutes Scott gave Radford a complete report. It included his discovery of the message to Drummond about Zakayev, Scott's conviction that Drummond had been murdered, and the disappearance of the *K-363*.

"Jesus Christ, how long has that sub been gone?" Radford said while making notes.

"We think two days."

"And you say that no one saw her get under way?"

"All we have is a report from an antisub unit of a three-hundred-hertz sonar trace typical of an Akula, the *K-363*, heading into the Barents Sea. Of course, it could have been one of ours. . . ."

"We have no boats operating up there. How certain are you that Zakayev is aboard that sub?"

"Everything points to it, starting with Drummond's rendezvous at Murmansk with the Russian sailor. And of course your orders that he was to make contact with Zakayev to, I presume, head him off ."

"You presume too goddamn much, Scott. You were not authorized to see those communications. That was a flagrant violation of orders for which I could have you–"

"I won't argue that point, General. Meanwhile we've got a submarine controlled by terrorists on the loose in the Barents Sea."

"What's she armed with?"

"Well, that's a bit of a mystery. Apparantly her SS-N-21 cruise missiles were off-loaded when she returned from her last patrol. As far as the base commander here can determine, they're still aboard the arsenal ship where submarine ordnance is stored. Russian Navy record-keeping is lousy and no one is sure of anything, so there's no guarantee that she put to sea without them. However, she does have a partial load of antisubmarine and antiship torpedoes—how many, no one knows. They say none have nuclear warheads."

"How can they be sure?"

"All of their nuke torpedo warheads were dismantled last year and are accounted for."

"That's a break."

"But if Zakayev wants to attack St. Petersburg, he sure as hell can't fire a torpedo into the harbor from the Barents Sea, can he?"

"So what's he planning?" Radford said.

"I don't know, General, and that's what worries me and the Russian Navy and the FSB."

"We know that the Russkie navy is in terrible shape, that they're desperately short of ships, crews, you name it. Think they can find that sub?"

"General, they have no choice, they have to."

"All right, I'll tell the President what's happened, try to convince him to cancel the summit, though I don't think he will. And if the Russians can't find that damned sub, we'll have to do it for them."

"They may give you an argument on that, one. This is unfolding in their backyard, not ours. And don't forget, the *K-363*'s had a good head start on us. Even if the Russians allow us to get involved, it'll take time to get our ASW assets organized to mount a search. All Zakayev has to do is stay one step ahead of the Russians until he's good and ready to launch missiles–if he has any–and . . . *poof,* it could be over."

"I'll alert the chairman of the Joint Chiefs and CinCLant. They'll want to try and coordinate our operations with the Russians. As for you, Scott, stay put: You're liaison on this–but goddamnit, lay off the freelancing."

Radford ordered a car for his dinner companion, made a note to send her a dozen roses, then made another call. Ten minutes later he got out of his car in front of Paul Friedman's home on Dumbarton Street in Georgetown. Two Secret Service men with crackling handheld transceivers met him at the door and checked his ID. There were undoubtedly others he couldn't see posted around the house. Admitted to Friedman's study, where cigar smoke hung in thick layers, he found the president of the United States sitting in a chair with a drink in his hand.

"Karl, good to see you," the president called, waving with his drink. He sat opposite Friedman at a small table with the remains of a sandwich and potato chips in a plate by his elbow. Drink-mixing paraphernalia and a bottle of bourbon stood on a sideboard. Papers lay strewn on the floor around the president's feet, and he stepped on some as he rose to greet Radford.

Radford knew the president sometimes visited Friedman to play poker and get away from the constraints of the White House. But instead of winning a few bucks from his national security advisor, this evening he had been preparing for his summit meeting with the Russian president.

Friedman said, "Drink, Karl?"

Radford shook his head no.

Both the president and Friedman held Radford in their gaze, measuring Radford's unease while telegraphing theirs.

"What's happened, Karl?" said Friedman.

"Trouble." Radford briefed from his notes and both the president and Friedman listened intently, not asking questions. When he finished he laid out his recommendations and a plea that the president cancel his summit meeting.

The president rose and, brushing crumbs from his lap, said, "Trouble indeed, and it seems to have a way of finding Captain Scott. Do you trust his assessment of the situation?"

"Yes, sir. He's on the scene in Olenya Bay and knows firsthand what's unfolding. I admit it seems unbelievable, but I think we have to accept that Zakayev is determined to bring down the Russian government."

"By killing me and my Russian counterpart and a couple of million Russian citizens with nuclear-tipped missiles."

"I want to reiterate, sir, what Scott said: that the Russians are sure there are no cruise missiles, nuclear or conventional, aboard that sub. Still, I think it wise to assume for the moment that there are."

"Has Zakayev and his cohort, this . . ."

"Georgi Litvanov," said Radford.

". . . made any demands either on us or the Russians?"

"No, sir, not yet," Radford said. "But we don't have time to wait for an ultimatum or to make a deal with them. The situation is unprecedented and we can't afford a mistake."

The president put his unfinished drink aside. "Okay, Karl, we'd better have a chat with Defense and the chairman of the Joint Chiefs, bring them in on this now." He turned to Friedman. "Paul, while we're at it, set up a meeting with the Russian ambassador tonight. Let's find out what they know, see how we can coordinate our efforts to head this thing off. After I've talked with the ambassador, I'll talk to the Kremlin."

"Yes, sir. I'll also contact Admiral Grishkov, C in C, Northern Fleet."

"Do you know him, Karl?"

"Yes, sir, he's a leftover from the Putin days, but a man we can work with."

"Good. What else?"

Friedman said, "Sir, I think it would be prudent to cancel the summit meeting—"

"Out of the question," the president said with conviction. "The press will say we've been blackmailed by terrorists. I'm sure the Russians would agree."

"Sir, I must protest. I agree we can't give in to terrorist demands, but the situation is too dangerous to risk a summit meeting now. In fact, announcing that you will not attend the meeting may well disrupt Zakayev's plans and forestall an attack on Russia. With all due respect, you can't risk your life and the lives of millions of innocent people. And if Zakayev does carry out his plan, the Russians may well retaliate with nuclear weapons that would devastate not only Chechnya but the entire Caucasus region. It could ignite World War III!"

"Nice speech, Paul," said the president, "but the summit meeting will take place as planned. Now, how about calling the Russian ambassador."

* * *

Zakayev closed the door of his stateroom so he could be alone. The *K-363* was so big that each officer had had his own stateroom. And because so many officers from Litvanov's crew had been left behind, there had been many empty staterooms to choose from. The one he picked was large—larger than Litvanov's—and well appointed. It had a comfortable bunk, a desk, chairs, and a head complete with a shower and fixtures worthy of a luxury hotel. The stateroom also came equipped with a video monitor slaved to the monitor in the CCP that displayed images seen through the periscope.

Zakayev sat on the edge of his bunk and unzipped a canvas duffel. He took out a small hand-tooled leather portfolio containing color photos of his wife and three children, the only ones he had of them.

Irina. Smiling, posing for the camera against their one-story whitewashed house in Caucasian Grozny. It was spring, and they had been planting flowers in the side yard. Feigning impatience with his manipulation of the old Argus C3 camera, she had brushed dark strands of hair from her face, leaving a streak of mud on a cheek that had showed up in the photo, and, she said, made her look like a *krestyanka*—a peasant. It was his favorite picture of Irina, exuding seduction and vulnerability in equal proportion. The children had joined in, and after the picture-taking session they had cleaned up and gone to Zakayev's mother's house for dinner. A week later Irina, the children, his mother were dead.

There had been warnings circulating for weeks that Russian Spetsnaz supported by armor had been probing the outskirts of Grozny in search of rebels who had attacked a Russian outpost and killed ten soldiers. No one in Zakayev's neighborhood had seemed overly concerned because the rebels being hunted had moved north.

Zakayev had been attending a strategy meeting in central Grozny with members of the Muslim Brotherhood when he received a frantic phone call from his uncle about a disaster unfolding at home. By the time he arrived, it was too late. His house, along with several others, had been leveled by Russian tanks. He found Irina, the children, and his mother lying in the side yard by the flower beds, shredded by machine-gun bullets.

Looking at their pictures now, he remembered the white-bearded village elder who had said, "For a Chechen, death is unimportant. What matters most for a Chechen is to have lived and died for your family and your people."

There was a soft knock at the door of his stateroom and a voice said, "Ali?"

He put the pictures away and opened the door.

"Would you rather be alone?" the girl asked. She had her own stateroom next to Zakayev's.

"No. Come in."

She looked at him in his dark blue submarine work coveralls, the same kind she had on except that hers were too big and had rolled-up sleeves and pant legs. "I wanted to be with you," she said. "Do you mind?"

"No, I don't mind," Zakayev said. He held her by the arms and kissed her forehead.

"You seem distracted," she said. "Are you worried about something?"

He released her and they sat on his bunk. "I've been going over our plan. In a little while Litvanov will put up a radio mast to monitor a CNN broadcast to see if the Americans have canceled the summit. If they have, it means the Americans and Russians are hunting for us because they know something is going to happen. Then we can expect to run into American and Russian naval forces, but Litvanov is good and I'm not worried about that."

She sat beside him and said, "Hold me."

He put an arm around her and she turned into him. He ached for her and for Irina and the children. The pain was bearable only because he knew that when it disappeared, he'd be free.

Litvanov glanced at the ship's chronometer. "Come to periscope depth," he ordered, adding, "zero bubble."

"Periscope depth, twenty meters, aye," repeated Starpom Veroshilov.

The planesmen manipulated their joysticks and eased the *K-363* toward the surface, employing a combination of power from the turbines and hydrodynamic action on the diving planes.

"Stand by to update your inertial computer," Litvanov barked at Veroshilov.

"Standing by, aye."

Litvanov, an eye on the unwinding depth gauge, explained to Zakayev what was happening: "We use our Molniya-3 satellite system to navigate and to target our weapons. It's linked to our Orbita ground terminals and it's accurate to within a meter anywhere on the face of the earth."

Litvanov didn't wait for confirmation that the *K-363* had reached periscope depth. "Up," he ordered. Crouched, elbows on knees, he seized the handles. The periscope drive hummed as he walked it around twice. The periscope video monitor showed the scene

Litvanov saw through the raised scope: a rising and falling sea and a few hearty gulls braving frigid weather.

"Clear," Litvanov reported. "Raise the ESM."

The electronic signals mast, its sensors able to detect radar and radio emissions from ships and aircraft, rose above the surface.

"Anything?" Litvanov asked, eye to the scope.

"A weak single sideband contact," said the electronics petty officer. "Bearing three-five-zero. Signal strength One."

"Probably a freighter," Litvanov said. He put the scope on the reported signal bearing but saw nothing. Whatever it was had hauled over the horizon, which had merged with a cloudy sky into a wall of gray.

"Down ESM," Litvanov ordered. "Raise the GPS antenna."

"Aye, Kapitan."

Veroshilov got ready to update their position with a satellite fix.

"Now, let's see what they're saying about us on CNN. Raise the antenna."

A small TV set mounted over the chart table came on, a diagonal band of light rolling up its blank screen.

As the two antennas rose, the quartermaster thumbed a stopwatch to keep track of how long they were out of the water. He reached up to an equipment rack and punched a button on a DVD recorder in time to the opening graphics and music of the CNN satellite-transmitted hourly newscast.

The news readers, a man and woman, prattled on about Wall Street, the Middle East, and a plane crash in Spain. A string of ads followed, then a weather report for western Europe.

"Come on, come on, give us what we want," Litvanov urged.

"One minute," the quartermaster intoned.

The Russian president appeared with his foreign minister.

"What's he saying?" Litvanov said. "I can't follow the English translation."

The quartermaster interpreted. "The, uh, President is looking forward to meeting with the, uh, American president in St. Petersburg. Their meeting will include, uh, discussions about the refinancing of Russian debt to the IMF, international terrorism, and the future of Chechnya."

"Did you hear that, General?" said Litvanov. "The future of Chechnya. Ha!"

CNN rolled a tape of fighting outside Grozny, then switched to a correspondent reporting from the devastated Tchaikovsky Concert Hall in Moscow, where bulldozers clawed at the wreckage.

"Two minutes."

"Enough. Retract all masts," Litvanov ordered.

The TV screen went blank.

Paul Friedman pushed aside the remains of a cheeseburger as the Secure Video TeleConference split-screen monitor flickered to life in the White House Situation Room. "Right on time," he said, wiping his hands on a linen napkin.

Karl Radford squared his note pad and pen. He saw familiar faces swim into focus: at the Pentagon, Secretary of Defense Dale Gordon and Chairman of the Joint Chiefs Admiral Jack Webster; in Norfolk, ComSubLant Carter Ellsworth; in Moscow, Admiral of the Fleet, Commander in Chief, Russian Navy,

Vyacheslav Stashinsky; in Severomorsk, Commander in Chief, Northern Fleet Russian Navy, Vice Admiral Mikhail Grishkov.

"I'd like to get right to it, gentlemen," said Friedman. "The recommendations we develop from this conference will be presented for consideration and implementation by our respective chiefs. We've all had time to read and digest the staff summaries. It's not an exaggeration to say that Chechen terrorists armed with a stolen Russian nuclear submarine, the *K-363,* pose an extraordinary threat to the world, to Russia, and to our respective leaders. Therefore, I urge that we focus our attention this morning on finding an answer to one question: Do any of you have any ideas on how this threat can be eliminated?"

There was a brief rustling of papers before C in C Stashinsky said, in heavily accented English, "I resent the implication in your summary that the Russian Navy was careless in regard to the theft of the *K-363* and that we bear sole responsibility for the crisis. The Chechen problem is not just Russia's problem alone."

"Admiral Stashinsky—" Friedman tried to interject.

"The United States," Stashinsky went on, "bears as much responsibility for this crisis as anyone."

"Admiral Stashinsky, nothing in the report implies that the Russian Navy was careless," Friedman said. "A postmortem of events leading to the theft of the *K-363* can come later. For now, perhaps you have a solution to our immediate problem that we can discuss."

Stashinsky had a face with heavy features and bushy black eyebrows that, on the video feed, gave him a menacing look. "There is only one solution and we've taken the necessary steps to ensure its success: We've ordered the deployment of antisubmarine forces into the Barents Sea. And we have taken the extra precaution of alerting the Norwegians and Swedes to our deployment, telling them it is only an exercise. It will take time, but I'm confident we will find the *K-363*. Radioing an entreaty to the pirates aboard the *K-363* to surrender won't work. The only thing that will work is brute force."

"Unfortunately, Admiral, your government has refused our assistance," Friedman said.

"We are well equipped to solve this problem without your help."

Defense Secretary Gordon, a former civil rights attorney and Wall Street banker friend of the president, said, "With the dwindling assets you all have, how in hell are you going to find, much less eliminate, one of your own submarines?"

"On the contrary," Northern Fleet C in C Grishkov snapped, "we have forces adequate to the job. What you are saying is simply untrue–"

"Mikhail," Friedman cut in, "let Secretary Gordon finish."

"What I was getting at," Gordon said, picking up his thought, "is that you're dealing with a huge area. Hell, look here."

The conference screen went blue before a detailed map of the Barents Sea area appeared.

Webster, Gordon's tag-team partner, took over. "The area you have to search, Mikhail, and search quickly," Webster said in a voice-over, "stretches from Finnmark, Norway, in the west to the mouth of the White Sea in the east, and from the Kola Peninsula in the south to the Spitsbergen Bank in the north."

"We know the area quite well," Grishkov said caustically.

Undaunted, Webster said, "Your ASW forces will take days to organize themselves and get under way. And what've you got to work with? Less than thirty MPK patrol craft, a couple of command ships, and some old Be-12 Mail amphibians, some Ka-25 helicopters, and a few Il-38 prop jobs."

*Don't rub it in,* thought Radford. He knew only too well that since the end of the Cold War, the U.S. Navy's ASW capabilities had atrophied and that both surface and submarine forces had been sharply reduced. Radford also knew that the Navy's Sound Surveillance System, SOSUS, had for all purposes been mothballed. Gordon and Webster would have to strip assets from other theaters to mount an effective search in conjunction with the Russians, if they'd allow it.

"Admiral Stashinsky, why won't you allow the U.S. Navy to lend a hand?" Gordon asked.

"Ego," Friedman whispered behind a hand to Radford, who nodded agreement. "Pure and simple."

"Don't presume to lecture us on our abilities," Grishkov snapped. "Furthermore, we are hunting for one of our own submarines and reserve the right to find and kill it. Not the U.S. Navy."

Carter Ellsworth said, "The Barents Sea isn't a private Russian lake, gentlemen, it's international waters and we're entitled to access. The U.S. has a big stake in finding the *K-363* and this band of terrorists. Your Northern Fleet doesn't have the muscle to do the job by itself, and by the time you admit it, it may be too late to head off disaster."

"Gentlemen, we're getting off track," Friedman said. "I need hard recommendations I can take to the President. We can't waste time disputing methods or end up in a turf war."

"Admiral Grishkov," said Radford, "what can you tell us about Kapitan Third Rank Georgi Litvanov that might give us a clue to how we can defeat him?"

Grishkov allowed a faint smile to reveal the pride he felt in Litvanov's skills. Terrorist or not, he was still a member of an exclusive fraternity of submariners, to which few men would ever belong.

"Litvanov is a brilliant officer and an independent thinker, which I admit is rare in the Russian submarine service. That's why he will be so hard to find and . . . eliminate." He deliberately avoided the word *kill*. "I don't know of any flaw he has that we could exploit. He's too unpredictable. And he's dedicated. He will do whatever it takes to carry out their plan. That you can be sure of."

"We know that Litvanov is a tough disciplinarian," Radford said. "Is there any way that such a trait could possibly work to our advantage?"

"I see no way it could," Grishkov said. "If you are thinking he may prove too rigid and perhaps make a mistake, don't count on it. He and his crew are too disciplined to make mistakes."

Radford had made extensive notes about Litvanov. There had to be a way. . . .

Secretary Gordon said, "Admiral, what can you tell us about the weapons aboard the *K-363?* We understand that Captain Scott received assurances from Kapitan First Rank Titov in Olenya Bay that the sub is not armed with cruise missiles, only torpedoes. Is that true?"

On the split screen Grishkov shifted uneasily in his chair and glanced at Stashinsky. "Titov, eh? Well, yes, that seems to be the case. All SS-N-21s were off-loaded when the *K-363* put in from her last patrol. I made detailed inquiries of the ordnance officers at Olenya Bay and they confirm that all the missiles are accounted for. Standard procedure requires that our boats off-load missiles but not torpedoes before docking."

"Why not torpedoes?" Radford said.

"Because it is very difficult to unload torpedoes from an Akula-class boat. As you must know from experience with your Los Angeles–class boats, it requires reconfiguration of the submarine's forward compartments and decks; being short of manpower, we try to avoid it. Sometimes we remove the detonators from the torpedoes, but not always."

Stashinsky said, "I have personally approved the decision to permit our boats to retain their torpedoes while in port."

"You're certain that the *K-363* only had torpedoes aboard when she put to sea?" Gordon said.

"Yes," said Grishkov.

"Do you know how many are aboard?" Webster said.

"We think perhaps twelve, half her normal loadout."

"And none are equipped with nuclear warheads?" Gordon said.

"Of course not. Under START III we dismantled all of our nuclear torpedo warheads and put their fissile materials under international control. The torpedoes aboard the *K-363* have conventional warheads."

"What I meant was," Gordon said, "is there any way a nuke warhead could have been lost in the shuffle and stuck on the end of a torpedo? One that's aboard the *K-363?*"

"Are you suggesting, Mr. Secretary, that we are liars—that we have violated the START III Treaty?"

"Of course not. But given the situation we're facing, we shouldn't assume anything."

"Mr. Secretary," said Grishkov, "assume what you wish. We are confident all the cruise missiles aboard the *K-363* have been accounted for, and that all of our nuclear torpedo warheads have been dismantled."

Jack Webster said, "Admiral Grishkov, with all due respect, I believe that's what you believe, but if your ordnance people are wrong and someone miscounted one of those babies, we're in trouble."

"So the only way to prevent a disaster," Friedman said, "is to find Zakayev and sink him, and what I'm hearing is that the only way to do that is to flood the Barents Sea area with ASW aircraft and surface ships, right?"

"And submarines," Ellsworth added.

"Why submarines?" Friedman asked.

"In a word, stealth."

"Do you mean a submarine could find the *K-363*, sneak up on her, and kill her?"

"One of ours could."

Friedman brightened. "Could a Russian sub do it?"

Ellsworth glanced at Webster. "Well, I don't know about that. . . ."

"Admiral Stashinsky?" said Friedman.

"Of course."

Friedman was taken aback. "Then why in God's name aren't you deploying submarines to find the *K-363?*"

Grishkov looked at Stashinsky, whose gray face had turned to stone.

Friedman understood only too well. "There is no time for dissembling, gentlemen. We are facing a crisis. If you have something to tell us, then goddamnit, tell us!"

Stashinsky tugged his red nose. "*Da.*"

Grishkov nodded to Stashinsky on video, then said sadly, almost apologetically, "We have only ten SSNs—one Severodvinsk, six Akulas, and three Sierras—active in the Northern Fleet, and the *K-363* is one of them."

Radford and Friedman exchanged surprised looks. Only ten SSNs! How did that match what SRO intelligence had been reporting? Radford wondered, and made a note to find out.

Grishkov was saying, "Three SSNs are on Atlantic patrols. In Olenya Bay, three others are undergoing refits and two are in drydock. That leaves one SSN, the *K-480*, an Akula identical to the *K-363*, ready for sea. But the *K-480*'s commander, Sergei Botkin, is a young, inexperienced *starshi leitenant*, a senior lieutenant. And there is no way Botkin could find Litvanov before Litvanov would have him in his sights. It would take an experienced submarine commander to hunt Litvanov down, and, I am sorry to say, we don't have one available in Olenya Bay."

"Yes, you do," Radford said.

Friedman seemed to be reading Radford's mind; he pointed a finger of approval at the SRO director, the equivalent of a Situation Room high-five. Ellsworth had picked up on it too.

"Captain Jake Scott is in Olenya Bay waiting for orders," Radford said. "He's an experienced submariner—as good as they come, I'm told. He also speaks Russian." He saw Ellsworth give a thumbs-up. "I say, put him aboard the *K-480* and turn him loose on Litvanov."

Stashinsky looked as if he had suffered a coronary. "*Nyet, nyet!*"

"Yes!" Ellsworth slammed the table in the Norfolk

briefing room with the palm of his hand. "Do it and he'll find that sub and sink it too."

"Impossible, impossible," Stashinsky shouted. "An American on a Russian boat? Impossible!"

"Can you hear us, Jake?" asked Ellsworth.

"Five-oh. Sorry to take so long to get back to you."

Scott, in Titov's headquarters, spoke over his armored cell phone patched through an SRO satellite to the White House Situation Room.

"Have you had time to inspect the *K-480?*" Ellsworth asked. "What's her condition?"

"Not good, but not bad. She could use a refit but, all things considered, she's still pretty well screwed together."

"What about her crew?"

"We need a replacement in engineering. The chief engineer lacks experience with nuclear reactors."

"Can Titov find a replacement?"

Scott glanced in Titov's direction. The commandant, looking exhausted, was busy rearranging his desk again. "Maybe he can round one up from another boat."

"What about this skipper, Botkin?" Ellsworth asked.

"Same, but I think with a little coaching he'll be all right. Not so the engineer."

"Do what's necessary. Litvanov's got a two-day head start on you, Jake. This is no sure thing."

"Understood, Admiral."

"Anything else you need."

Scott looked at Alex and at Abakov, who was nervously massaging his bald dome. "Yes. I want Dr. Thorne and Colonel Abakov cleared to accompany me on this mission."

"Now look, Jake . . ." Ellsworth started.

"Sorry, Admiral, but that's how it's got to be. Dr. Thorne is a nuclear physicist and she understands the hazards of radiation, and since we don't know what Zakayev is up to, I may need her expertise. Colonel Abakov knows Zakayev personally and worked with him in the old KGB. Plus, he's been the lead investigator in Admiral Drummond's death. 'Nuff said."

"Have they agreed to this or haven't you asked them yet?"

Scott met Alex's and Abakov's gazes. "They're not keen on it but know how important it is."

Ellsworth, after silently polling his confreres, said, "All right, Jake. They're your responsibility. Anything else?"

"Yes, Admiral, I want you to call David Hoffman, Dr. Thorne's boss at the embassy in Moscow, and personally clear things for her."

"Goddamnit, Jake, you know I can't tell him what we're up to."

"I'm sure you'll think of something."

Ellsworth made a face and said, "All right, I'll take it under consideration. Now, how soon can you get under way?"

"Tonight."

"Codes and comm specs?"

"We'll reconfigure our communication pack for ELF and ZEVS."

"Admiral Stashinsky has agreed to provide you with updates so you can coordinate your ops with them."

"We'll need all the help we can get."

Radford sat alone in the Situation Room, worried that the Russians might change their minds. But how could they? Jake Scott was the only real chance they had to find the *K-363* and Friedman had used up all his powers of persuasion on them. The national security advisor had departed looking drained.

Radford gathered his papers. He marveled at Scott's confidence. He had no idea whether or not Scott could pull it off, but whatever had driven him to risk his neck in that damned Yellow Sea mission was driving him now.

# 10

## The Barents Sea, inside the Hundred-Fathom Curve

"Green board," announced the *starpom.*

Sergei Botkin checked the hull opening indicator panel: Six rows of bright green lights confirmed that the *K-480* was rigged for dive.

Botkin, aware that Scott had been evaluating his every move since departing Olenya Bay, cleared his throat and commanded, "Dive the boat."

A piercing siren sounded twice, followed by "Dive! Dive!" from the lieutenant serving as Botkin's *starpom.*

Scott watched the diving operation unfold, gauging the proficiency of the young officers and men manipulating the ship's controls. There was no margin for error when operating a submarine on the surface or submerged.

"Flood forward and after groups," the *starpom* diving officer ordered. Ten-degree down bubble."

Air trapped inside the ballast tanks discharged through the vent risers with a loud *whoosh.* At once the big submarine pitched down and drove her blunt nose under the Barents Sea.

"Make your depth ninety meters," Botkin ordered.

"Ninety meters, aye, Kapitan."

Seawater chuckled over the hull, gurgled into superstructure voids, and rose quickly up the sides of the sail. A water hammer pounded, then stopped abruptly. The ship's hydraulic pump moaned in protest like a man on his deathbed. Something in the pump room under the CCP made a loud clank that Scott felt through the soles of his sea boots. And when the hull began to creak and pop under increasing water pressure, some of the newer men exchanged frightened looks.

Scott knew the *K-480* was a cranky ship and made a mental note to inspect the engineering logs to see if routine maintenance on vital equipment had been deferred, and if so for how long. That important machinery might fail when needed most was a prospect Scott knew Russian submariners, unlike their American counterparts, accepted as a fact of life. The Russian Navy had a long history of submarine disasters–sinkings, collisions, reactor mishaps–that had gone unreported. So had many of the human casualties. Not only did he have to find and kill the *K-363,* he also had to bring Alex, Abakov, and the crew back in one piece. Given the *K-480*'s condition, he wasn't at all sure the mission was survivable.

Scott glanced over his shoulder at Yuri Abakov. The colonel's face shone with sweat and his coveralls had dark stains under the arms. He watched Abakov swallow hard to equalize the pressure building up in his ears and wondered if he was having second thoughts about joining the mission, wishing instead that he was home with his wife and children in their *khrusheba* apartment.

Alex, he saw, didn't appear bothered by all the noise and confusion. She had been eager to go aboard, saying,

"There's too much at stake to back out now." For a moment Scott had allowed himself to think that her decision might also have had something to do with her feelings for him and what might be possible when this was over. Wishful thinking, he told himself.

Alex, her body English compensating for the downward tilted deck, glanced at Scott.

"Hang on tight," he mouthed over the racket of venting and flooding, the creaking and popping of the submarine's hull as it drove beneath the icy waters.

"Passing fifty meters, Kapitan."

"Very well," Botkin said.

Scott's attention shunted from Alex to a valve tagged in Russian FEED CIRCULATOR that was spewing seawater from overhead. He ordered an auxiliaryman, "Tighten the packing on that valve." Scott made another mental note, to keep an eye on it.

"Eighty meters, Kapitan."

"Ease your bubble."

The men at the diving station drew back on their joysticks, taking angle off the planes.

"Eighty-five meters, Kapitan."

A huge cockroach skittered over an instrument panel. An auxilliaryman seated at the panel lashed out and crushed the bug under his palm, then wiped the gore on his pant leg.

Scott met Botkin's gaze across the CCP. The young skipper gave him a lopsided grin, as if apologizing for the deficiencies he knew Scott had logged. Botkin had a slight build and blond hair and eyebrows so fair that they almost looked white, a look that didn't come close to matching the heroic image of a nuclear sub skipper fostered by the Russian Navy.

Scott sympathized with Botkin. He was the product of a post-Soviet navy in desperate circumstances and in such dire need of officers to command their waning fleet of nuclear submarines that the Chechen, Georgi Litvanov, had command of a weapon that he and his cohort Zakayev could use against Russia. Madness.

"Depth ninety meters, Kapitan."

The *K-480* leveled out just before reaching her ordered depth.

Botkin issued orders to the helm and the *K-480* turned onto a new heading inside the hundred-fathom curve. "You wish conference, Captain Scott?" Botkin said in English.

Scott unrolled a chart, which Botkin weighted at the corners with instruction manuals and an ash-tray. Alex, Abakov, Botkin, and the *starpom* navigator pressed in around him. The CCP was silent now except for the low whine of the gyroscope in its binnacle and the hum of fire-control computers and their cooling fans.

Scott swept a hand over the chart and said. "This is our primary search area, the Barents Sea."

"But this is a huge area to search," Abakov said.

Scott's fingers walked the chart, stepping off esti-mated distances. "Over half a million square miles."

Abakov let out a low whistle.

"Time is also a factor," Scott said. "We've only got days to find the *K-363*. The message we received from NorFleet in Severomorsk, said they had established an ASW patrol line between Spitsbergen and Novaya Zemlya." He pointed to them, an archipelago and two large islands north of the Arctic Circle off Russia's northeast coast.

"Long-range Il-38s are patrolling south toward the

Kola Peninsula. NorFleet's also inserted fifteen MPK patrol craft on a line off the coast of the Kola Peninsula."

The Kola Peninsula, a tundralike extension of the Scandinavian Peninsula, was fringed with islands and deeply indented with fjords. To the west, Norway's North Cape, the northernmost point in Europe, marked the invisible line of demarcation between the Barents Sea and the Norwegian Sea.

"NorFleet's plan is to sweep north and feed more units into the line as they tighten the search box," Scott said.

"Like a pincer," Alex said.

"Exactly."

"And how will they conduct their search?" Abakov said.

"The Il-38s will drop thousands of sonobuoys that can pick up noise from the *K-363*'s reactor coolant pumps and turbogenerators—the three-hundred-hertz tone. The patrol boats use passive towed sonar arrays. Once they make contact with the sub, they'll track her, then attack with homing torpedoes."

"But excuse me, Captain Scott," Botkin said. "Litvanov has ways of evading detection. He can run ultraquiet. If he is in deep water, there are present thermal layers that deflect sonar, while in shallow water sonar pulses scatter off the bottom and make it difficult to pick a target out of the echoes."

"Right. We're up against a clever skipper," Scott said, "in command of one of the Russian Navy's best submarines—an Akula, like the one we're aboard," he added for Alex and Abakov.

"How capable are they?" asked Abakov.

"They're comparable to the U.S. Navy's Improved 688

Los Angeles–class boats. They have a 190-megawatt nuclear reactor and can make over thirty-three knots submerged. They're 370 feet long and displace about eight thousand tons. They also have advanced sonar suites and are extremely quiet and therefore hard to detect."

"Most important, the Akulas can dive to almost two thousand feet," Botkin interjected with barely masked pride.

Abakov bent slightly at the waist to study the chart. "I understand now, but still, the *K-363* could be anywhere."

Scott said, "True, but if Zakayev has plans to attack the summit meeting in St. Petersburg, the *K-363* has to stay within range of the target. That narrows the search somewhat."

The *starpom*, sandwiched between Scott and Botkin, pointed to a marked spot in the Arctic Ocean far north of the Il-38 patrol line established by NorFleet.

"What he's pointing to," Scott said, "represents the maximum theoretical distance from which an SS-N-21 can reach its target: sixteen hundred nautical miles. But Zakayev won't stray that far. I'm willing to bet he's somewhere within a sixty-degree arc due north of Olenya Bay. And not too far from land."

"Why do you think so?" Alex asked.

"Because," Scott said, "that's what I would do if I were going to attack St. Petersburg. The attack is the only thing that matters–not playing tag with the Russian Navy. And the shorter the range to the target, the less chance there is of intercepting and destroying the missile."

"Even so, how will we ever find the *K-363?*" said Alex.

"Our best chance is to hear her, get her three-hundred-hertz sound signature on sonar. It won't be easy, but if we can find her, we can kill her."

Alex, elbows on the table, put her head in her hands. "Kill her. How?"

"Antisubmarine torpedo," Scott said.

"Okay, so we or the Russians blow the *K-363* to bits. What happens to her nuclear reactor?"

"Depends. If the reactor compartment isn't damaged, it sinks along with the rest of the ship. If it is—say, the core's blown open—the fuel assemblies will end up on the sea floor."

Alex raised her head. "You know, don't you, that the Russians have been dumping naval reactors at sea for decades. It's one of the biggest problems Earth Safe has faced. There have been thousands of cubic meters of radioactive waste dumped off the continental shelf of the Kola Peninsula. Then there's the Atlantic Ocean. In 1986, when the *K-219* went down six hundred miles east of Bermuda, she had two reactors and was armed with ballistic missiles. The missiles each had two one-megaton warheads with about two hundred pounds of plutonium, which has a half-life of about twenty thousand years. This one wreck has the potential to be an ecological disaster of epic proportions. Someday the reactors and warheads will deteriorate and their radioactive materials will eventually poison the sea. If the *K-363*'s reactor is destroyed underwater, it will be even worse."

"You're assuming it'll be destroyed," Scott said.

Alex gave Scott a look. "Can antisubmarine torpedoes differentiate between a reactor compartment and the other compartments of a submarine?"

"No. But Akulas are double-hulled boats, and antisub torpedoes are designed to penetrate the outer hull, collapse the inner hull, and flood and sink the submarine, not blow the whole ship to hell."

Abakov said, "If a torpedo hit the outer hull of the reactor compartment, would the explosion be powerful enough to destroy the reactor?"

"Not necessarily. Reactor containment vessels are designed to withstand heavy damage. Chances are the reactor would hold together."

"Then again, it might not," Alex said.

Botkin said, "Excuse me, Captain Scott, but Communications say they are receiving a ZEVS."

Communication links aboard the *K-480* had been reconfigured to receive both U.S. and Russian satellite-burst transmissions.

"ZEVS?" asked Alex.

"To communicate with submerged submarines, the U.S. and Russian navies broadcast extremely-low-frequency transmissions, known as ELF," Scott said. "The U.S. ELF transmitter is up on Michigan's upper peninsula; the Russian ELF transmitter, which they call ZEVS, is located in Archangel."

"So how do they work?"

"ELF and ZEVS transmissions can penetrate hundreds of feet below the surface of the sea to summon a submarine to periscope depth to receive coded burst transmissions from satellites in earth orbit. Trouble is, ELF data transmission rates are so damn slow that a submarine's identity code takes minutes to arrive, which forces the sub to loiter near the surface, where it's vulnerable while recovering its burst transmission."

"Request permission to come to periscope depth to receive ZEVS," said the *starpom*.

"Very well," Botkin said.

"Kapitan, please double the sonar watch," Scott said. "I don't want to be caught napping by Litvanov."

Crabbing against a setting current, the *K-363* crept down the western coast of Norway.

"Depth to keel?" Litvanov said from the periscope stand.

Veroshilov had his lower lip trapped under his front teeth. The Norwegian coast was host to graveyards of ships that had blundered into unmapped seamounts and scarps.

"Sounding!" roared Litvanov.

"Ten fathoms, Kapitan."

Litvanov racked the scope's magnification control through a series of detents into high power. "Take a look," he said, turning the scope over to Zakayev.

He saw a pair of headlights moving south on a road carved from the living rock of the peninsula that formed the western bank of Vest Fjord. On the peninsula's tip he saw a lighthouse warning seafarers of shoal water.

"See any good restaurants?" Litvanov laughed. "The Norwegians make a fantastic *fiskepudding* with haddock. Maybe we can send a man ashore to get some." He laughed again.

Zakayev wasn't amused. Litvanov had insisted on cruising in littoral waters virtually up against the Norwegian coast to avoid detection and to stand clear of commercial shipping lanes. But the fear of running aground had set the crew's teeth on edge and made Veroshilov argumentative. So far they had encountered only Norwegian and Japanese fishing boats and a few rusty coastal luggers. And Litvanov was thinking of food. Well, let him, Zakayev decided. There wasn't much time left to think of things that once made life enjoyable.

He stepped away from the scope and beckoned the girl to have a look too.

"Quick now: What do you see?"

"Lights. Strings of moving lights shimmering on the water."

The SC1 speaker hummed, then: "Kapitan—sonar contact! Bearing three-two-zero, converging."

Litvanov took a quick look at the CCP's sonar repeater with its sloping trace line and saw an unidentified contact closing in on the *K-363.* He sprang to the periscope stand and pushed the girl aside.

He saw her string of lights. Red and green running lights on a vessel standing out of Vest Fjord. To Litvanov's night-adapted eyes there was something about her top hamper. . . . He switched to infrared and a spectral image danced before his eyes: a heat bloom from the turbines and exhaust stacks of a frigate-size ship.

"Switch to narrow band sonar," Litvanov commanded.

"Aye, Kapitan."

"Come right twenty degrees."

The helmsman acknowledged Litvanov's order.

On the sonar repeater the sloped line had disappeared, replaced by a horizontal row of bouncing green spikes. The sonar system needed time to filter and compare the received sound frequencies with signatures archived for the purpose of identification.

"Periscope down."

"What is it?" Zakayev said.

Litvanov stood by the periscope stand with arms crossed on his chest, not moving a muscle. "Maybe nothing. Then again . . ."

The row of bouncing signature spikes on the CCP monitor had frozen while the computer searched its memory for a matching set. They meant nothing to Zakayev, yet had taken on a life of their own. He sensed that the next few minutes were critical to their mission.

The monitor peeped and displayed a match: overlapping green on blue spikes.

"Oslo-class frigate, Kapitan. The KNM *Narvik*, F-304."

"Periscope up. Let's have another look."

As the *K-363* slowly pulled away from the coast, Litvanov kept the scope planted on the Royal Norwegian Navy frigate. Her convergence onto the *K-363*'s track, whether by design or accident, prompted Litvanov to offer a running commentary.

"She's one of those older ASW frigates, probably equipped with variable depth sonar. ASW rockets. She's either heading out on an exercise or—" He didn't finish his thought.

"Kapitan—new contact. Bearing one-eight-zero, also converging. Sounds close."

The sonar repeater recycled to the new contact.

A minute later: "Oslo-class frigate, Kapitan. The KNM *Trondheim*, F-302. She still has that nicked prop blade on the port shaft."

Litvanov put the periscope on 180. "I've seen her before. She's in trail with the *Narvik*. Periscope down!"

"How could the Norwegians know we're here?" Zakayev said.

"They have a SOSUS—Sound Surveillance System, an underwater linked hydrophone system developed by the Americans to track our submarines. The information from the Norwegian system goes to a central operations headquarters in Stavanger, where they identify submarines from recordings of their machinery and propeller noises. The American SOSUS arrays used to be strung out on the sea bottom across choke points near Greenland, Iceland, and the U.K. Also the mid-Atlantic ridge. Even in the Barents. But we cut the cables and destroyed the arrays. The Americans finally gave up repairing them and shut down the system.

"The Norwegian system is no longer fully operational. Luckily for us, their coastal waters are strewn with rock and bottom heaves. Also, the salinity varies. Temperature layers too. Sonar is unreliable under those conditions and often gives off false alarms. This may be one. We'll soon see." Litvanov consulted the navigation chart. "We're here, just north of these two groups of small islands off the tip of Lofoten."

Veroshilov had monitored the automatic plotter responding to inputs from the ship's inertial guidance system. The plotter's stylus mounted under the backlit plotting table had recorded the *K-363*'s track, now an open-ended C on the acetate overlay marked with grid lines.

"We'll turn ninety degrees off our present track and rig for ultraquiet. If the frigates turn west, they've probably been vectored into our area."

Litvanov issued the necessary orders. One turbogenerator went offline to reduce the *K-363*'s already minimal sound signature, as did machinery and equipment not essential to her operation, such as ventilation fans and the oxygen generator that broke water down into hydrogen and oxygen.

"Will they find us?" the girl whispered to Zakayev. He put an arm around her shoulders and felt a shiver. He whispered back, "Don't worry. Litvanov knows what he's doing."

* * *

In the Combat Information Center aboard the frigate KNM *Trondheim,* Royal Norwegian Navy Kaptein-Löytnant Gunnar Dass paced the deck. He tore open a fresh pack of cigarettes and tamped one out.

"Commander–incoming Priority."

Dass turned on his heel and strode to the twittering Multex terminal. He seized the message after it had finished rolling out of the teleprinter, scanned it, then headed for the bridge. The *Trondheim*'s skipper, Orlogs-Kaptein Harald Bayer, broke off his conversation with another officer and motioned Dass to follow him into the wheelhouse out of the wind's cold fury.

"ComInC FOHK Stavanger, Captain."

Bayer read the message under a red-lit battle lamp. "So, a possible second submarine contact."

He summoned the signals yeoman, who had a clipboard with recently decoded messages. The one Bayer wanted had arrived less than an hour earlier and he gave it a quick review, then reread the message Dass had collected from the Multex.

"Perhaps this latest one is a genuine contact. Any thoughts, Mr. Dass?"

"The Russians again, trying to prove something? But what? That they can elude us?"

Bayer looked seaward, where a sliver of dawn had arrived over the coast of Norway. "The Russians tried it years ago off Sweden. The Swedes couldn't find them and were ready to admit it when the Russian sub ran aground in the Skagerrak. I don't think the Russians would risk embarrassing themselves again."

Dass looked blankly at his captain's profile. Bundled in a heavy khaki-colored bridge coat with the collar turned up, a white silk scarf at his throat, binoculars hanging from his neck on a strap, Bayer faintly resembled a European film star whose name Dass couldn't recall.

"There was an earlier advisory from Operational Headquarters that the Russians were planning an exercise," Bayer said. He thumbed the dispatches. "Yes, here it is."

"I suppose it's possible, sir, that it could be one of theirs."

"Supposing won't do, Mr. Dass. Stavanger wants us to find out."

Bayer underlined with a pen the contact coordinates in the latest message from ComInC. "Quartermaster!"

"Aye, Captain."

"Plot a course to commence a search of this area. I want an ETA."

"Aye, aye, sir."

"Signals."

"Aye, Captain," said the yeoman.

"Stand by to send a visual to *Narvik:* 'Have second unconfirmed contact. Stop. I will lead. Stop. Coordinates, course, speed, the rest. . . .' "

"Aye-aye, Captain," said the yeoman sketching notes.

Bayer paced the wheelhouse. The steel deck under foot throbbed with the rhythm of the *Trondheim*'s Laval-Ljungstrom PN 20 geared steam turbines. The sea, now dark gray, splashed and hissed along the frigate's oil-canned sides. It was going to be a gunmetal day.

Impatient, Bayer rounded. "Quartermaster?"

"Sir. Recommend course three-two-zero for ten minutes, then zero-four-one for twelve minutes. Estimated time of arrival at twenty knots is zero-five-one-zero hours."

"Very well," Bayer said. "Send it, Signals."

"Aye, aye, sir."

Then, "New course: Steer three-two-zero degrees. Both engines, turns for twenty knots. Mr. Dass."

"Sir?"

"Stand by to launch VDS arrays. Let's see if we can locate this intruder and force him to the surface."

Abakov, looking a little shocked, held a message form in one hand and with the other rubbed his bald pate. "They found the missing FSB officer in St. Petersburg."

They were seated in the wardroom. The ZEVS summons had been followed by a burst message transmitted via Northern Fleet to the *K-480* from FSB Headquarters in Moscow. Abakov sat there looking shocked.

"His body was buried behind a car repair shop in St. Petersburg. Zakayev and his men had used it as a headquarters. The man was tortured, burned. He didn't deserve that."

"I'm sorry, Yuri," Alex said, her hand on his arm.

Abakov stroked his mustache, then his bald head. "Bastards."

"How did they find him?" Scott said.

"One of Zakayev's men was spotted getting on a train in St. Petersburg and was stopped and questioned. He told them about the officer and about the shoot-out with Ivan Serov in St. Petersburg."

"Did he know anything about the plan to attack St. Petersburg?"

"No. According to this message, he expired during the interrogation and before they had a chance to ask him."

Abakov didn't explain what that meant, to "expire during interrogation," but Alex bit her lower lip and made a face.

"There's this too," Abakov said. "Forensic identified

Serov's body and those of his two men killed in Murmansk. Also, Zakayev is traveling with a young Chechen woman believed to be about seventeen or eighteen years of age. They don't know her name, only that Zakayev saved her life in Chechnya, and in return she pledged her life to him."

"What exactly does that mean?" Alex said.

"It's an old Chechen custom: You save my life, I owe you everything. Only death can break the bond. Do you understand?"

"What does this bond entail?" Alex said.

"She is his wife and must do whatever he tells her. She lives to serve him. For the rest of her life."

"You mean like a slave?"

"It's not slavery. The Chechens are a very loyal people. That's why Zakayev and Litvanov want revenge for the deaths of their families."

Alex said, "I don't care how loyal they are, it's still slavery. She's being forced to do something she may not want to do."

"I doubt it," Abakov said. "After all, she's a terrorist like the others. She probably had a hand in the Moscow bombing. Someday she'll probably strap on a bomb and blow herself up in a crowded shopping mall."

"That's an ugly thought," Alex said.

"Terrorism is an ugly business."

"It stands to reason that the girl is probably aboard the *K-363* with Zakayev," Scott said.

"Then she's probably prepared to die along with Zakayev, Litvanov, and his men," Abakov said.

A messman in a filthy white apron entered the wardroom with hot tea and canned peaches, which he served in surprisingly fine, well-preserved white china bowls.

"Yuri, what can you tell me about Zakayev?" Scott said, dipping into the peaches, which were hard and mealy but sweet. "Something that we could use against him and Litvanov."

The watch changed. In the narrow passageway outside the wardroom, sailors scuttled around each other as they headed for their bunks, the crew's mess, or their stations.

As the commotion died down Abakov said, "You have to understand how Zakayev thinks. He's unpredictable; he'll do what you don't expect. He learned his terrorist trade in Afghanistan. He was a simple army conscript when the Soviets entered that country to prop up the government and install Babrak Karmal. Because Zakayev was a Muslim, he was quick to find a niche in the Soviet security forces who needed agents to penetrate the mujahideen opposition. He was trained by the KGB, and when Karmal was kicked out, Zakayev was handpicked to organize and train KGB agents to foment infighting among the mujahideen.

"He taught them how to employ hit-and-run tactics and how to use car bombings and suicide attacks to intimidate civilians. With the Soviet Union's withdrawal from Afghanistan and the rise of the Taliban, Zakayev returned to Moscow, where he had a reputation in the KGB as a daredevil."

"Because he always did the unexpected," Scott said.

"Yes. And because he was brutal. And also willing to take the kind of risks no one else would take. When we met in 1989, I was assigned to the KGB's Second Chief Directorate, Internal Security and Counterintelligence. With the breakup of the Soviet Union, the Kremlin was determined to prevent Georgia from declaring its independence from Russia. We were working on a plan to undermine Eduard Shevardnadze, the president of Georgia. Zakayev became an advisor on guerrilla tactics. He made it clear to us that he had no patience for the plodding methods the KGB had developed and used during the Cold War: disinformation campaigns and labor unrest. Instead he urged us to bomb civilian targets in Tbilisi and other Georgian cities to prove that Georgia was sliding into anarchy under Shevardnadze. That way, he said, Russia could justify sending in troops. But then something happened that changed everything."

"The Chechen independence movement," Scott said.

"Exactly."

Abakov had more tea. "Following the failed coup in Moscow in 1991, Chechnya declared its independence. It didn't take long for the Russian Army to launch covert operations against Chechnya to prevent it from breaking away. Moscow sent Zakayev to Grozny to develop a counterinsurgency movement to bring down the Chechen government.

"But when Zakayev arrived in Chechnya, he suddenly understood what he had never understood in Afghanistan and Georgia: that his people wanted to be free of Russian rule. And when he saw what the Russians were doing in Chechnya, it didn't take him long to revolt against the KGB and the Kremlin. He switched sides and moved his family from Moscow to Grozny. There he used the same tactics he'd used in Afghanistan and Georgia, but against the Russians.

"The war escalated. After his family was killed by Spetsnaz, he vowed to bring down the Russian government. At first the Chechens didn't trust him. But when he used the same tactics he'd used against the mujahideen and the Georgians on the Russians, the Russian Army put a price on his head. Overnight he became a Chechen hero and was made a general. The Chechens believed he was invincible. He was relentless. He ambushed Russian troops, shot down their planes and helicopters, killed their commanding officers, and generally made the Russian Army look helpless. He bombed apartment houses in Moscow, blew up trains, and robbed banks. Then there was the concert hall bombing. And now St. Petersburg.

"Each time Zakayev launched an operation, he did the unexpected. And I told you before, some people say he had help from the Americans, to keep Russia weak and off balance in Chechnya while the U.S. invaded the Middle East. Zakayev is experienced and he's tough. And he's committed to the cause."

"But he's not invincible," Scott said, studying Abakov's weary face.

"No, he's not invincible. No man is."

The wardroom phone chirped. Scott grabbed it from the cradle on the bulkhead and heard Botkin say, "Captain Scott, Communications is picking up another ZEVS transmission from Archangel."

Alex and Abakov followed Scott to the radio room forward of the CCP, where a warrant officer ensconced in a small, hot cubical lined with radio and coding equipment sat hunched over his receivers.

"Definitely incoming from NorFleet" Botkin said. "We've received *D* for *Delta.*"

They hung outside the radio room while the rest of the *K-480*'s call sign, *F* for *Foxtrot* and *R* for *Romeo,* arrived and scrolled out of the printer. *Z* for *Zulu* tacked on at the end of the transmission confirmed that the message had been sent from the Russian ZEVS transmitter in Archangel, and that a burst transmission with important information had been stored for retrieval from a Molniya-3 satellite.

Alex went on ahead to the CCP, and when Scott caught up to her, he saw she was troubled.

"What's wrong?" he asked.

"I was thinking . . . that Chechen girl Yuri told us about . . ."

"What about her?"

"How did she end up on a Russian submarine with Zakayev and Litvanov? She's just a kid."

"She's also a terrorist," Scott said, his voice low so the others couldn't hear.

"She was turned into a terrorist, you mean. By the Russians. Maybe by us." She looked intently at Scott, his face slightly haggard in the harsh overhead lighting in the CCP. "Imagine growing up in a country where you have to kill to stay alive. And then pledging your life to a terrorist like Zakayev."

"It depends what side of the fence you're on. Zakayev is a hero to her and the Chechens. Obviously Washington discovered that his brand of terrorism suited their needs. Until now."

"In other words, realpolitik dictates the morality of your position."

They had entered a world where there were no clear-cut answers. It was the same world Frank Drummond had inhabited, and where he had ended up dead. To Scott, unlike Alex, the girl on board the *K-363* was only an abstract concept and no less dangerous for it. What wasn't abstract was the possibility that Zakayev, with or without her help, might blow St. Petersburg to hell.

Alex waited for him to respond to what she'd said.

"Yes," he said.

"Message for you, Captain Scott." Botkin had a decrypted printout.

After Scott read the message, he announced to Alex and Yuri Abakov, who had joined them in the CCP, "It's from Admiral Grishkov in Severomorsk. He says that all the SS-N-21 cruise missiles and nuclear torpedo warheads have been accounted for. He states categorically that there are none aboard the *K-363.*"

Alex said, "Then that changes everything."

# 11

## The Norwegian Coast

"**The bastards have deployed** their towed sonar arrays. Listen to them."

Litvanov snapped on a speaker. The *K-363*'s exceptionally sensitive MGK-503 sonar had captured not only the *kish-kish-kish-kish* of props but the overlaying and sibilant *shhh-shhh-shhh* of the towed body receptor.

"It's at the end of a cable attached to a crane and hydraulic winch mounted on the frigate's fantail. Very complicated."

"Can they hear us?" Zakayev asked.

"Depends. Those arrays aren't affected by noise from the towing ship, and they have long detection ranges. But the array flexes as it's towed through the water and can give false contacts." Litvanov snapped off the speaker. A tomblike silence returned to the CCP. "Also, it's very hard to locate a quiet-running submarine in littoral waters: too many bottom anomalies and background noises to sort out."

Litvanov studied the track of the two Norwegian frigates as it developed and was marked by Veroshilov in grease pencil on the chart overlay. The frigates had cleared the tip of Lofoten and turned northeast.

"Sonar, report," Litvanov ordered.

"Contacts bearing one-one-zero."

"Base course?"

A hesitation, then: "Zero-five-two, Kapitan."

"Steer two-two-zero," Litvanov ordered.

The *K-363* turned slowly right onto an approximate reciprocal of the course steered by the two frigates.

"Fire Control, can you estimate their separation?"

"Yes, Kapitan . . . approximately six thousand meters, staggered forty-five."

"Starpom, sounding?"

Veroshilov sweated heavily. "Chart soundings only, Kapitan. . . ."

"I know that, damnit."

"Thirty-six meters and shelving."

Litvanov spoke to Zakayev. "The Norwegians are steaming in a forty-five-degree formation, the seaward frigate out ahead. I think perhaps they are chasing ghosts, not us. If we ease on by them and they don't react, we're clear."

"We are in very shallow water, eh?" Zakayev said.

"Yes. Our charts are not up to date and it's risky to drive in so close to the beach, but that's what will make it hard for them to find us."

"And if we run aground?" Zakayev said.

Litvanov pretended that he didn't hear him.

The chairman of the Joint Chiefs, Jack Webster, at the Pentagon, and ComSubLant Carter Ellsworth, in Norfolk, appeared on the video monitor's split screen.

Paul Friedman said, "Morning, gentlemen." Then: "Admiral, Webster, care to comment on the latest Russian communiqué?"

"We dodged a bullet. The Russians too. That Akula up in the Barents Sea is essentially toothless. Sure, she's armed with torpedoes, but they can't hurt us. Now it's up to Russian NorFleet to find her and decide what they want to do."

"Admiral Ellsworth?" said Friedman.

"I agree: There's nothing Litvanov and the terrorists can do. Maybe threaten a few merchant vessels, give the Russians a good workout, but that's about all. I really don't see what they hope to accomplish. As Jack said, they're toothless."

"Admiral Webster, you have no doubts that the cruise missiles are all accounted for?" Radford asked.

"Yes, sir, I'm satisfied that they are. I spoke to Grishkov—Carter and I both did—and he was totally forthcoming about the storage and securing of their SS-N-21s, and nuke warheads for their torpedoes."

Ellsworth said, "Grishkov's report on their missile inventories included the individual weapon serial numbers and chain-of-custody documents."

"Their record-keeping isn't as sophisticated as ours," Webster said, "but there's no reason to doubt them. After all, they've got as much at stake in this as we do."

Radford said, "Jack, what's the current Russian deployment look like?"

The monitor screen went to blue, then to a full-color large-scale trapezoidal view of the northern Atlantic region, the Barents Sea, and most of eastern Europe. Red deltas representing Russian ASW forces were scattered like confetti in the Barents Sea.

"As you can see, General, Russian ASW forces are deploying from northern bases into the Barents Sea.

The graphic changed to an enlargement, the red

deltas organized in a drooping semicircle from Spitsbergen to Novaya Zemlya.

"The Russians are trying to put a noose around the *K-363* and pull it tight," Webster said. "They're not deployed as efficiently as they could be, but I think they stand a better than even chance of finding that sub. Mind, it'll be like cornering an animal who doesn't want to be captured, so don't be surprised if Litvanov strikes first. If he does, the Russians will have a good idea where he is and then can go to work on him."

"What about Scott?" Friedman said. "What role can he play now that the immediate threat to the summit has been eliminated?"

"Nothing's changed, Mr. Friedman," said Ellsworth. "The Russians still need all the help they can get. Scott is their backstop if the *K-363* tries to break out of the Barents Sea–assuming he doesn't find her first."

"But now that the threat has diminished, won't the Russians decide to recall Scott in the *K-480*? They may not want him looking over their shoulder, evaluating their capabilities in detail."

"Yes, sir, that's a definite possibility," Ellsworth said. "But until they do, Scott, as you suggest, is in a position to provide us with the answers to questions we've been asking for years. For instance, how vulnerable are those Akulas to detection, and can they be knocked out by the new homing torpedoes the Russians have developed for use against us? We've heard they had problems with them being able to discriminate between U.S. and Russian decoys. We may never have a chance like this again."

The Barents Sea graphic collapsed, and Ellsworth and Webster reappeared on the monitor.

Friedman beat a tattoo on the conference table

with a gold pen. "Admiral Ellsworth, a moment ago you said that you wanted to know if a Russian Akula can be knocked out—sunk—by these new torpedoes the Russians have."

"Yes, sir. I did."

"I take it, then, you believe the Russians will sink the *K-363,* not capture her and arrest Litvanov and Zakayev."

Ellsworth put his fine china coffee cup into its matching saucer and touched the corner of his mouth with a fingertip. "Capturing the *K-363* is a tall order, Mr. Friedman. A nuclear sub's endurance is limited only by the amount of food she can carry. Even if they find her, I don't see how they can capture her or make the terrorists surrender. If they're as dedicated to their cause as it appears they are, I believe the Russians will have no choice but to destroy that boat."

"They couldn't drive her aground and board her?"

"Even if they trapped her in shallow water, which is not likely, they'd have to devise some method to blast their way inside. I don't know that they could without killing everybody aboard and maybe the commandos who'd have to do it."

"Admiral Webster?" Friedman said.

"I'm an Airedale, not a submariner. So I defer to Carter. However, I don't think the Russians are inclined to take the terrorists prisoners, not after their attack on the concert hall in Moscow. Even if the Russians believed that they could learn something from them about future terrorist plans, I think they'll decide to make an example of them and not give them an opportunity to spout their venom in a Moscow courtroom."

Friedman said, "Admiral Ellsworth, if terrorists stole one of our subs, would we sink it?"

Ellsworth blanched. "Mr. Friedman that's not something we expect to ever deal with."

"I understand, but suppose you had to."

Ellsworth laced his fingers on his desk and looked down at them; only the top of his head appeared in the monitor. At length ComSubLant raised his head and looked directly into the video camera. He said, "I'll answer your question this way: Our submarine crews are trained never to surrender their ship. An American submarine crew, confronted with the imminent capture of their vessel by an enemy, are under strict orders to destroy it."

"They have the means on board to do so?"

"Yes," Ellsworth said grimly.

"Do Russian sub crews have a similar ability?"

"I imagine so."

"Then it's fair to say that the *K-363* will either be destroyed by the Russians or the terrorists themselves."

"Yes," Ellsworth said emphatically.

"Thank you gentlemen," Friedman said. "I won't take any more of your time."

The video screen went black.

Friedman indicated that his secretary and assistant should get a start on preparing conference summaries. The door clicked shut behind them and Friedman swiveled around in his chair to face Radford.

The national security advisor's eyes flared like lasers. "Your thoughts, Karl?"

"We're skating terribly close to the edge on this one, Paul," said Radford. "The Russians will put up a hell of a fuss if they find out we're a step ahead of them."

"But they won't find out," Friedman said.

"They will if we deploy."

"You have Scott. Use him."

"And then what? What do we tell the Russians: 'Oh, sorry, we meant to tell you what we were doing but plumb forgot to?' I don't think that will go over too well, Paul."

"What are they going to do? I'll tell you: nothing. That's right, nothing. We'll have done them a favor and they won't say a thing."

Friedman and Radford remained silent for a time, assessing options, weighing possibilities. Both men knew that they could not ignore the consequences of any future operations they authorized, not when it involved the president of the United States.

Radford checked the time. "I'm to brief the President after lunch. Let's see what you have."

Radford pressed the remote video control. Again the screen went to blue, then to an image of the western coast of Norway recorded earlier by an SRO KH-13 reconnaissance satellite that had turned reality on its head: On the screen, Norway was magenta, the Norwegian Sea pea green.

"This was taken yesterday," Radford said. "We're looking at coverage between North Cape and Vanna." He pressed a button on the remote and inserted an electronic pointer like a white arrowhead into the image. He moved the arrowhead down the coast and parked it beside a dark blue, cigar-shaped blob a few miles north of Sørøya.

"We picked this target up on a blue-green laser sweep at zero-eight-thirty."

"A submarine."

"You bet." Radford moved the arrowhead behind the form and jiggled it. "See this plume? Wake heat scarring. Typical submarine signature."

"Nuclear or diesel?"

"Could be either. What makes this target especially difficult to identify is the fact that he's in littoral waters, Norwegian littoral waters, not where you'd normally expect to find a nuke. A diesel, maybe, but not a nuke. And not a Russian Akula: They're too damn big for littoral operations."

"Then whose is it?"

Radford ignored this and changed images. "Twenty-four hours later. Now you're looking at coverage between Vanna and Andfjorden." He moved the pointer to the blue blob. "Same target but farther south this time. Whose is it? I'd like to think it's Zakayev in the *K-363.*"

"But you're not sure."

"I know what you want me to say, Paul, but I can't be certain it is the *K-363*. We've analyzed these images every way imaginable but can't make a positive ID."

Friedman levered himself out of his chair and stood looking down at Radford. "For Christ's sake, Karl, what else could it be but the *K-363?*"

"We and the Russians are not the only ones with submarine fleets. The Norwegians have diesel boats; so do the Swedes."

"Bullshit. You have those Norwegian comm intercepts. They say they had a SOSUS contact?"

"Their SOSUS is suspect."

Friedman gathered his papers. "A sub contact is a sub contact. What more do you need?"

"This. Tell me what Zakayev is up to. Why would he head south in a stolen Russian sub? He knows that his chances of survival are zero. What's he's planning that's worth the sacrifice?"

"He's a terrorist, Karl. They're irrational and don't think like us. What did they think they could gain by killing a thousand civilians in Moscow? That the Russians would capitulate? All they know how to do is kill people. They're filled with hatred. They want to die for a cause. Zakayev and his friend Litvanov want to be martyrs. Well, I'll be glad to accommodate them, because it'll solve our problem."

Radford was on his feet too. "Paul, you miss my point. A terrorist doesn't steal a Russian sub that's not armed with cruise missiles or nuclear torpedoes just to prove he can do it. No, Zakayev is planning something, and we don't have a clue what it is. That scares the hell out of me and it should scare the hell out of you too."

Admiral of the Fleet, Commander in Chief, Russian Navy, Vyacheslav Stashinsky occupied a suite of offices on the eighth floor of Russian Navy Headquarters at 6 Bolshoi Kislovskiy Prospekt, Moscow. They were as sumptuous as anything occupied by a Western industrialist or Hollywood film mogul.

Commander in Chief, Northern Fleet, Russian Navy, Admiral Mikhail Grishkov noted the impressive change of decor since his last visit to headquarters and felt a pang of jealousy. He had made do for years in Severomorsk with shabby used furniture, chipped and dirty paint work, a floor covered with cracked green and black asphalt tiles more befitting an infirmary than a naval fleet headquarters.

The fleet didn't have the money to buy fuel or spare parts for its ships or to pay its enlisted men and officers but had money to purchase rich wood paneling, deep-pile carpet, and black leather sofas and chairs for its fleet admiral. And handsomely framed commissioned paintings of Russian naval vessels—the guided-missile cruiser *Petr Velikiy*, the cruise missile attack submarine

*Kursk*, and others—to display under recessed lighting fixtures. *Someday*, thought Grishkov . . .

Stashinsky's aide, a *kapitan* first rank with a gold aiguillette, helped Grishkov out of his greatcoat and took his cap and gloves. The officer departed only after seeing that the silver pot of steaming tea and glasses in silver holders were arranged just so on the table between two armchairs in the casual seating area by the fireplace.

"Mikhail Vladimirovich," Stashinsky said, rising, coatless, from behind an enormous desk that seemed to Grishkov to be at least a half-kilometer away at the other end of the room. "So good of you to come."

Grishkov plowed through the heavy carpet and extended his hand. There was no exchange of salutes. Instead the two simply shook hands like businessmen meeting to discuss a contract. But Grishkov knew better.

Stashinsky gave nothing away, though he had a chart on his desk that he had been examining with a magnifying glass. To his greeting he added, "You are looking well, Mikhail. I hate those video cameras we use for conferencing. They make a man look old."

Stashinsky's face looked heavier than usual, and pale, Grishkov thought. "Admiral Stashinsky, I am honored," Grishkov said.

Stashinsky indicated the armchairs. Grishkov picked one and brought out a package of cigarettes filled with his favorite coarse, black Russian *makhorka* tobacco. He offered one to Stashinsky.

"I'm limited to only six a day now and I've already had three. There'll be nothing to look forward to tonight if I exceed my ration. But it won't bother me if you smoke. In fact, I wish you would."

Stashinsky poured tea; Grishkov lit and puffed on a

cigarette. Grishkov watched Stashinsky sip the hot brew and gather his thoughts while glancing at the fireplace, which held cast-iron logs and hidden gas jets that gave off blue flames.

"So, where is Litvanov and the *K-363?*" Stashinsky asked. "Has he escaped or has he disappeared."

"Disappeared?"

"You know, vanished, like a magic trick?"

Grishkov tugged at his nose. "He's out there, but we need more time to find him."

"How do you know he's still in the Barents?"

"There is no way he could have gotten past our patrol line," Grishkov insisted.

"Even though your line is full of holes?"

"We've plugged the holes as best we can. Certainly we could use more sonar, more planes, more ships, but on the whole we've kept the net pulled tight. Litvanov is good, but I don't believe he can break out. Plus, we have the *K-480* backing up our forces."

Stashinsky snorted. "A public relations stunt. I only agreed to allow the *K-480* to operate in Barents to keep the Americans off our backs."

"Can you blame them? After all, the threat to St. Petersburg seemed real enough until now."

"And now that the threat has evaporated, I want the *K-480* recalled. I won't allow an American spy on one of our own submarines reporting every move we make to Washington. Bad enough they know our strengths and weaknesses as intimately as we do. All the more reason to find Litvanov and end this terrorism business." Stashinsky allowed Grishkov to digest this then said, "Can you conclude this business with the *K-363* before the summit?"

Grishkov hid for a moment behind a cloud of burning *makhorka*. He waved the fog away and said, "I can't promise that I can. There is no way to predict how long it will take." He wondered if Stashinsky was feeling heat from the Kremlin over not just Litvanov but the embarrassment of having a first-line nuclear attack submarine stolen right from under the nose of the Russian Navy. He could only guess what fate awaited Commandant Titov. Prison, if he was lucky.

Stashinsky shifted in his chair. His gaze was fixed on the cast-iron logs and gas flames heating them cherry red. He said flatly, "Then I must tell you, Mikhail Vladimirovich, you have three days to find the submarine."

Grishkov sat up straight; cigarette ash tumbled into his lap. "Three days!"

Stashinsky's eyes flicked to Grishkov. "Those are my orders from the President. He wants my guarantee."

Grishkov lurched to his feet. The cigarette ashes rained from his lap onto the luxurious carpet under his feet. "Impossible! I can't guarantee that. We have no control over the situation up north."

"A member of the Duma has been asking questions. Apparantly someone in the FSB leaked information—erroneous information at that—about a submarine being overdue from patrol. The member thinks one of ours is missing, perhaps sunk. Which isn't so bad, actually, and better than the press finding out we thought we had a terrorist with a missile aimed at St. Petersburg."

"I'm not a politician, Admiral. I don't make promises I can't keep."

Stashinsky looked up at Grishkov looming over him. "I don't think you understand, Mikhail Vladimirovich. You have three days to find the *K-363* or I will be forced to replace you as commander of the Northern Fleet."

Grishkov looked at Stashinsky but found no empathy there. "And will you also arrest me for recommending Litvanov the Chechen for command of the *K-363?*"

"Don't be ridiculous," Stashinsky said coldly. "No one is blaming you for that."

"No? How reassuring to know that the blame will be apportioned in equal measure."

"What are you saying?"

"Will the members of the command selection board that concurred with my recommendation to retain Litvanov face a punishment board?"

"I can't answer that. Only time will tell."

"Yes, I'm sure it will," Grishkov said. "Perhaps the records of the meetings to select officers for senior command positions will conveniently disappear. And the only records left will be the ones with my signature on them."

"You are getting ahead of yourself. No one has suggested that you or anyone else is at fault."

"Mark it. They will."

"Find the *K-363* and no questions will be asked."

Grishkov smashed out his cigarette in a ceramic ashtray. "Is that how it is? Find the *K-363* in three days or face dismissal and a board of inquiry."

"The President wants the matter resolved before the summit," Stashinsky said. "That's all there is to it."

"Then tell the President that I need more ships and planes if I'm to find this devil Litvanov. Maybe then he'll understand what I've been saying for years, that the Navy is collapsing, that we don't have the tools to do our job, that we can't keep sending ships to sea that are undermanned with poorly trained conscripts, that we don't have enough food to feed our crews, or fuel, or weapons, or spare parts. You tell him that for me, Admiral. Maybe it will finally sink in to that thick Belorussian skull of his that we can't perform miracles just to impress the Americans."

"Are you finished?"

"No. Give me more ships and planes, even if you have to strip the north bare to throw everything we have into the Barents."

"I can't do that. You will have to make do with what you have."

Grishkov stared at Stashinsky.

Stashinsky ignored Grishkov's hard gaze. "Another thing: When you find the *K-363,* she is to be captured, not sunk. Is that clear?"

Grishkov looked at his boss in disbelief. "Who decided this? The Kremlin? I thought we had agreed that we will not negotiate with terrorists."

"No one has suggested negotiating with them. Anyway, those are the President's orders. And I agree with him that it would be useful to know what Zakayev's organization is up to."

"Capture them, eh?" Grishkov said dolefully.

Stashinsky, as if intrigued by the possibilities Zakayev's capture had raised, said, "Does the *K-363* have scuttling charges on board?"

"No, they were removed from all of our submarines to prevent a disgruntled crewman from setting them off while in port or even on patrol. We've arrested a number of conscripts who have threatened to set them off. It seemed the prudent thing to do."

"In that case what would you do, drop a net over the *K-363* and haul her up like a fish?"

"Perhaps. But I was thinking of something a little more sophisticated. Like the *Kursk* recovery."

"I don't understand."

"If we can find her, keep her down, drive her into shallow water, we may be able to bring in a heavy lift ship."

Grishkov pointed to the painting of the *Kursk*, hanging over the fireplace. An Oscar II–class cruise-missile attack submarine, the *Kursk*, under the command of Kapitan First Rank Gennady P. Liachin, sank when one of her own torpedoes exploded. A colossal disaster for the Russian Navy, the submarine, with 118 men aboard, sank in the Barents Sea. Months later a heavy lift ship recovered the hulk and brought it home.

Stashinsky turned his gaze from the painting of the *Kursk* to Grishkov. "You have your orders, and I have a meeting with the President later today."

"Then, with your permission, Admiral . . ." Grishkov said frostily.

Stashinsky went to his desk and buzzed his aide who immediately brought Grishkov's things.

"The *K-480,*" Stashinsky called as Grishkov departed. "I want the *Amerikanski,* Scott, out of the Barents Sea and off that submarine."

# 12

## South of Lofoten

"They're on our ass and closing in," Litvanov said.

He'd ordered baffles cleared to the right and sonar had picked up the two Norwegians dead astern. Moving closer inshore was not an option: The *K-363*'s keel was virtually scraping bottom.

"Twenty degrees right rudder," Litvanov ordered.

"Twenty degrees, aye," answered the helmsman.

Litvanov wiped his face on a sleeve. He glanced at the compass repeater, its lubber's line on 240 degrees. He waited a beat, until the line indicated 245, then ordered, "Meet her."

"Aye, meet her."

The helmsman shifted the rudder to check the *K-363*'s swing to the right.

"Steady as you go," Litvanov ordered.

"Aye, steady on two-five-zero degrees."

Again, Litvanov dabbed his face. He sought Zakayev. "We'll hold this course and let them pass across our stern as we move away." He looked at the girl. She appeared calm, but Litvanov knew she had butterflies in her stomach. They all did. "We'll be all right," he told her.

"I know that," she said. "I'm not scared."

"Fire Control," from Litvanov.

"Targets steady on course two-one-eight. Speed ten. Range five kilometers."

Zakayev, familiar now with the complexity of the CCP, looked at the digital pitometer log that showed the *K-363*'s speed through the water: three knots. Just enough speed, Litvanov had explained, to maintain control of the ship against setting currents while running ultraquiet.

The girl heard it first, coming through the hull, and cocked her head to listen.

"Screws," said Starpom Veroshilov, looking up as if trying to see what might await them topside.

The men at their stations in the CCP fell silent, listening. Overhead the steady beat of thrashing screws—*kish-kish-kish-kish*—made the submarine's hull vibrate like a tuning fork.

"Fire Control." Again from Litvanov.

"No change, Kapitan. . . . Wait!"

The *kish-kish-kish-kish-ing* changed its pitch to a higher register.

"Kapitan, targets turning toward us: new course . . . two-four-zero."

"Speed?"

"Still ten knots."

Zakayev wondered if the Norwegians' sonar had picked up a suspicious noise that bore investigation or were simply adjusting their search pattern. Either way, they were headed straight for the *K-363* and would soon overtake her.

*Kish-kish-kish-kish* . . .

Litvanov prowled the CCP. He glanced at the navigation chart, then, like Veroshilov, looked up as if trying to see the approaching frigates.

Two hundred feet above the *K-363, kish-kish-kish-kish* had merged with the *shhh-shhh-shhh* of the twin towed sonar receptor bodies strung out behind the frigates.

Zakayev's armpits felt damp. Unless Litvanov ordered a change of course—and soon—the two hunters would pass directly overhead.

"Come right to three-three-zero," Litvanov ordered as if reading the Norwegians' minds.

The *K-363* swung ninety degrees right, away from the frigates. Litvanov waited a full minute for her to complete her slow, silent turn, then ordered a 180-degree turn to the south-southeast. "Steer one-five-zero."

Zakayev watched the compass slowly unwind as the submarine reversed course. At creeping speed it took almost five minutes to complete the maneuver that ended with the *K-363*'s bow aimed at the approaching frigates.

Litvanov reached up and pulled a *kashtan* toward his mouth. "Fire Control."

"Fire Control, aye, Kapitan," said Arkady, the leading *michman,* over the SC1 comm system.

"Target acquisition."

"Set."

"Target bearings?"

"Zero-six-eight degrees, combined."

"Range?"

"Eight thousand meters."

"Set range detonation ten meters."

"Set."

"Torpedo Room: Stand by to flood tubes one and three."

Zakayev lunged across the CCP at Litvanov. Veroshilov, reacting, jumped between them. "What are you doing," Zakayev demanded.

The ratings in the CCP, shocked at Zakayev's outburst, froze at their stations with eyes fixed on their work. The girl hung back afraid to move or breathe. Only the *kish-kish-kish-kish* of props intruded.

"Preparing to fire torpedoes," Litvanov said, shouldering Veroshilov aside.

"Are you mad?"

"No, cautious. If those two frigates find us, we're finished. They'll sound a general alert, then hound us until backup units arrive, including the Russians and the Americans."

"But you can't torpedo those ships: They're Norwegian and they're neutral."

"And they're dangerous."

The SC1 squawked, "Torpedo Room standing by, Kapitan. I have green activation on two TEST 71-M torpedoes."

Gaze fixed on Zakayev's blazing eyes, Litvanov, struggling to control his fury, said into the mike, "Activate targeting sonar."

"Activated, aye. Standing by to flood tubes one and three, Kapitan."

Zakayev licked his dry lips. He was out of his depth and knew it. Litvanov was in charge and there was nothing he could do to change that. The mission was in jeopardy and in danger of being sunk along with the *K-363* itself.

The SC1 squawked again. "Fire Control, Kapitan. Ready to launch torpedoes."

Captain Bayer aboard the *Trondheim* surveyed the heaving Norwegian Sea with binoculars. He didn't expect to see a periscope at the head of a feather cutting through the water. Still, something had set off an alarm in Stavanger.

He thought he saw something rising and falling in a trough and, to brace his heavy 7x50s, planted both elbows on the windscreen. Gulls. Then he heard Sonar Officer Garborg's voice in the CIC on Two Deck boom from the bridge speaker.

"Captain, possible contact dead ahead!"

Bayer rolled on a shoulder and said, "Mr. Dass."

"Aye, sir, I have it. Range?" Dass queried CIC.

"Under eight thousand meters."

"Any matches?"

"Propagation is poor. Trace only."

"Signals!" Bayer snapped.

"Aye, sir?" said the yeoman.

"Raise *Narvik* by voice. Advise we have a contact. Bearing, et cetera. Query same."

"Aye, aye, sir."

Bayer planted his binoculars on the heaving purple sea roaring white around the *Trondheim*'s cutwater and through her hawse pipes and ground tackle. He knew there was nothing to see, but in his gut felt certain that a submarine was out there, trying to escape into deep water.

The frigate pounded hard, her decks chopping up, down, up. Bayer, braced against the windscreen, swung his glasses to starboard and saw the *Narvik* take white water over her bow. In the east the sky had failed to brighten—in fact, had gotten darker. "Damn the weather," Bayer muttered. Something to be concerned about when towing a seven-ton sonar transducer at the end of a four-inch-diameter cable fifty meters below the surface. The armored cable, forty-eight pairs of signal conductors running its length, was not indestructible, and Bayer had had one part a year ago while hogging in on a contact that turned out to be a biological. He weighed reducing speed but decided not to.

Bayer slammed the bridge speaker's Talk button with the heel of his gloved hand. "Mr. Garborg, this is the captain."

"Aye, Captain?"

"I don't appreciate your silence, Mr. Garborg. I want constant ranges and bearings."

"Aye, sir. At the moment we're getting only scatter, no positives."

"In panoramic?"

"Yes, sir."

Once again, thought Bayer, geography, salinity, time of year, sea state were favoring the enemy.

"What's your cadence?"

"One thousand to thirty thousand meters, sir."

"Well, stay at it, Mr. Garborg."

"Aye, aye, sir."

Bayer snapped the speaker off and turned to his executive officer. "Mr. Dass."

"Sir?"

"Send Mr. Mayan below to Sonar. I want them to feel his hot breath on their necks."

"Aye, aye, sir." Dass, carefully gauging each step across the heaving deck, headed for the CIC, where Weapons Officer Mayan and his technicians were busy monitoring the *Trondheim*'s fire control gear.

"Captain, *Narvik* sends," announced the signals yeoman. He wore a mike and headset trailing a long cord plugged into a remote repeater.

"Well?" Bayer said. "I'm not deaf. Give me the short version."

"From *Narvik:* 'Contact negative across three sectors. Await your advisory.' "

Bayer blew through his teeth. "Send them . . . send

them, 'Contact impaired. Maintain current pattern.' "

Bayer wanted to bully Garborg again but thought better of it. He stalked onto the port wing and looked aft. He saw a huge winch and sheave arrangement mounted on the fantail, from which the thick black VDS cable paid out from a supply spool midships and over the sheave, where it disappeared into the *Trondheim*'s boiling wake, which had spread to the horizon like a bridal veil. He looked south toward the plunging *Narvik* and saw a similar scene of gear, cables, and flying spume.

Bayer spun on his heel. "Sonar!" he bellowed into the speaker. "This is the captain. What the hell's going on down there? Do we have a contact?"

"Negative, sir." It was Mayan's voice. "Zero trace on all inputs."

"Not even biologicals?"

"Nothing, sir."

"I don't believe it."

"I beg your pardon, sir?"

Bayer looked north as he collected his thoughts. He didn't doubt that he was hunting a Russian submarine but had underestimated her skipper's determination to avoid detection, a challenge Bayer couldn't overlook. *My mistake,* he thought. *It won't happen again.*

"Kapitan, the Norwegians are turning south."

Litvanov nodded.

"Have they lost contact with us?" Zakayev said.

"They never *had* contact," Litvanov said.

Zakayev watched Starpom Veroshilov mark the double track of the Norwegian frigates on the chart, a long, sweeping U-turn that would put them on a southerly track.

"This Norwegian skipper is going to retrace his steps. By the time he gets turned around, we'll be gone."

Zakayev felt the tension ebb. The girl's color had returned.

Litvanov, all smiles, opened the SC1 mike. "Secure fire control, secure torpedo stations."

The men in the CCP relaxed. They exchanged satisfied looks and gave a thumbs-up.

Litvanov opened the mike again, "Mischa . . . where are you?"

The SC1 hummed, then the voice of the messman said, "In the galley, Kapitan."

"Mischa, break out bread and vodka for everyone."

"At once, Kapitan!"

Litvanov looked at Zakayev and the girl. They knew what he was thinking: that this would likely be one of their last celebrations.

"It's over," Alex said.

"What is?" Abakov said. He entered the wardroom and took a seat at the table with Alex and Scott. He looked tired and had red-rimmed eyes. The submerged *K-480* was twenty nautical miles due north of Gamvik, Norway, and moving south.

"We've been recalled by Northern Fleet," Scott said. He handed Abakov a message flimsy. It had arrived via Molniya-3 satellite less than ten minutes before and had been copied to Norfolk. "They want a confirmation of receipt and an ETA at Olenya Bay."

Abakov read the message. "It doesn't say they've found the *K-363*. I don't understand."

"My guess is that they don't want us looking over their shoulder anymore," Scott said.

"In other words, now that they're not worried about

nuclear missiles and torpedoes, they want to hunt down the *K-363* on their own and take all the credit." Abakov rubbed his eyes. "Just as well. I'm not cut out for this kind of work. I want to feel the earth under my feet again. Plus, the air has gotten bad."

The *K-480*'s atmosphere was heavy and thick. Scott had been quick to notice a buildup of carbon dioxide. "There's a problem with the carbon dioxide scrubber," he said.

"Where's Botkin?" Alex said.

"Working on the scrubber."

"I think that's a good idea," she said. "So we don't suffocate, I mean. And that's not all he should work on. The food is lousy. And so are the cold saltwater showers, and the cockroaches, and the garbage piled up in the galley."

Abakov said nothing, just took it all in.

"I warned you this wouldn't be a pleasure cruise. The *starpom* is helping Botkin, but we don't have a spare thermocouple or filters. The DUK garbage ejector outer door is jammed. Someone put a forty-pound sack of rotting potatoes in the chute and it got stuck. I can't do anything about the cockroaches, but one of the engine snipes has set traps. As for the saltwater showers, the freshwater holding tanks are contaminated." He watched Alex tuck strands of limp blond hair under her Russian Navy cap and studied the downy line of her jaw. "Anything else?"

"Thanks, you've made me feel so much better."

"Just a warning: It may get worse."

"What do you mean? We've just been recalled to civilization, haven't we?"

"That's what I wanted to talk about with the two of you."

Alex, her eyes as red-rimmed as Abakov's, said, "I think I see what's coming."

"Something doesn't add up," Scott said. He turned to Abakov. "Yuri, earlier you said Zakayev is unpredictable."

"He is."

"That he always does the unexpected. That he's dedicated and committed to a cause."

"True."

"Stealing a submarine is a bold act of terrorism, wouldn't you agree?"

"Yes. Especially when you consider the planning that went into it."

"What are you getting at," Alex said.

"Stealing the *K-363* only makes sense if, as we all thought, Zakayev and Litvanov had a cruise missile aboard to launch at Moscow or St. Petersburg or some other place. But they don't, so what's the point? Litvanov knows that sooner or later he'll be hunted down and sunk. What will they have proven? Nothing. Zakayev dies and his cause dies with him. It doesn't add up."

"My head is throbbing from the bad air," said Alex, "and you're making it worse, Jake, by trying to make me understand how Zakayev thinks. I can't. No one can."

Abakov said, "But Jake is right: Zakayev would die for his cause, but only if by doing so he accomplished his goal."

"And what is his goal?" Alex said. "Does anyone know. Does *he* know?"

"Of course he knows," Scott said. "And the fact that he has no nuclear missiles or torpedoes hasn't changed a thing. He's still dangerous and we still have to find him."

"The Russians will have to find him," Alex said. "We've been recalled, remember?"

"Not necessarily."

"What do you mean?" Abakov said.

"Maybe the message from NorFleet got scrambled up and we didn't receive it. Maybe we were having trouble with our radio and couldn't receive it. Maybe anything. What I'm saying is, we have to find Zakayev and can't rely on the Russians."

"Jake, you can't disobey their orders," Alex said.

"Technically the recall order is for Botkin, not me. Besides, to quit now would be admitting defeat. It would be a surrender. Look, it's risky, but we can't give up when there is still potentially so much at stake."

He wanted to tell her something, something personal, to break the spell of gloom, but when her gaze fell on him, it seemed as if she were looking right through him.

"You're the Navy's garbage man aren't you?" Alex said sharply, refocusing.

"What the hell does that mean?"

"It means they send you out to clean up their mess and fix things: bring Frank Drummond home; find the *K-363;* kill her if you can but don't fuck up. And by all means keep the mess out of sight. If you don't, well, you're expendable. Do I have it right?"

For a long moment Scott said nothing. It wasn't always like that, but then one day it was. "This is a cold-blooded business. There's no room for mistakes."

"And you've made a few."

"What do you want me to say?"

"Tell us what happened in the Yellow Sea."

There was a long silence.

Abakov rose and said, "I'll be in my stateroom."

"Stick around, Yuri," Scott said. "You might as well hear this."

The memory of that incident slammed into his consciousness with a grim fury. He started talking but didn't look at his companions. "We had arrived in Sohan Bay in the north, to deliver a SEAL team into North Korea. My sub, the *Chicago*, had an Advanced SEAL Delivery System, a mini-sub that can transport ten men and their equipment. I couldn't get inshore because of shoaling, but the SEAL team CO was okay with that. Seas were rough and I felt there was no way they'd make it unless I got them in close to the mouth of the river at Sinanju."

"What was the target?" Abakov said.

"The nuclear complex at Yongbyon."

"Oh my God," said Alex.

"The NKs said they had enough plutonium to build twenty nukes and were making threats to use them or sell them to terrorists. The SRO couldn't get reliable intelligence about what the NKs were up to, whether or not they really had any nukes or whether they were bluffing. The Russians and Swedes had installed some krypton 85 sniffers in their embassies for us that would confirm the reprocessing of uranium, but the results were inconclusive. Meanwhile, the SRO had developed a new miniature monitoring device with a satellite uplink but had no way to get it into the Yongbyon area. The devices look like a plant native to the region."

"You mean the kind of plant that grows in the ground? Like a weed?"

"Yes. Only they're made of a synthetic material and have miniature processors and transmitters, and a spike on the end that you push into the ground. The SEALs had the job of planting them."

"So, what happened?" Alex said.

What happened? He'd probably never know how the North Koreans stumbled onto the mission. Luck more than anything else, he had told himself over and over until he believed it. Some parts were still a blur, but others he remembered like they had happened yesterday.

The young SEAL lieutenant and his men had been eager to carry out their mission. Scott nosed into shallow water after launching an Unmanned Underwater Vehicle, a UUV, to probe for mines, which proved to be nonexistent. The SEALs' mini-sub lifted off the *Chicago*'s deck at night and, using North Korean coastal traffic as cover, headed for the mouth of the river.

"And that's when the NKs showed up," Scott said. Noisy as a dishwasher. That's what he remembered thinking. A goddamned Soviet Romeo-class diesel submarine built by the North Koreans from Chinese plans. It had apparently chug-chugged its way up the coast from Namp'o, submerged.

"We weren't in danger of being detected, not by that old crock. But then a frigate and two patrol craft showed up and that's when it got hot. The NKs must have had a port surveillance system to detect swimmers and swimmer delivery vehicles. When they started dropping anti-diver hand grenades, I knew the mission had been blown."

"What did you do?" Alex said.

"I had strict orders to pull out if something went wrong and to not risk the ship under any circumstances."

"In other words, you had orders to abandon the SEALs."

"In an emergency they were expendable."

"And you disobeyed orders."

Scott nodded. "I couldn't leave them behind."

"How did you get them back on board? It must have been a nightmare."

A nightmare that still haunted him. Scott had activated the laser communication-navigation system used to direct the SEALs in their mini-sub back to the *Chicago* for recovery. Then he fired two decoys simulating the noise signature of a Chinese Ming-class diesel attack submarine. The first decoy drew the two patrol craft away from the SEALs and on a wild-goose chase into the mouth of the river. The second decoy, aimed at the North Korean sub, caused so much confusion that the sub ran aground.

The frigate was another matter.

"The SEALs' mini-sub was in our beacon cone, ready to relock on deck. But the damned NK frigate got lucky and picked us up on sonar."

Scott saw the Soho-class frigate turn on her heel, and with a bone in her teeth, charge the *Chicago*. He was in a race to get the SEALs aboard and haul out into deeper water before the frigate attacked. It was a race Scott knew he would lose unless he violated all the rules, including the rules of engagement governing the mission itself.

"Snapshot, tube one! Target One!" Scott had commanded, and a moment later: "Fire!"

He remembered the pressure pulse and slam of the air piston signaling ejection of the MK-48 torpedo.

"What happened next?"

"Nothing. The North Koreans never said a word. We expected a storm to break, maybe even a declaration of war. Silence. They must have believed that they had attacked a Chinese submarine that was snooping in their territorial waters."

"But what about the frigate?"

"Sunk."

"You sunk it?"

"Blew it to bits."

"And when you returned to Norfolk, you got thrown into a meat grinder."

"You could say that. The Navy said that I had disobeyed orders, violated the rules of engagement, hazarded my ship. They even threw in a few other things while they were at it."

"But you saved the lives of those SEALs. Didn't that mean anything?"

"It did to the SEALs but not to Admiral Ellsworth. He was ready to put me against the wall when Frank Drummond stepped in."

"And now you're their garbage man," Alex said.

Paul Friedman, running late from his meeting at State, took a seat by the president's desk in the Oval Office. The president looked at his national security advisor over the tops of half-glasses and said, "What'd the Russian ambassador say, Paul?"

"In a word, *nyet.*"

The president removed the glasses and tossed them on his desk. "You were right, Karl. The Russians are going to play tough on this one."

"Did Zamorin say anything else," Radford asked Friedman, "or was he his usual inscrutable self?"

"No, sir, he was quite animated," Friedman said, speaking to the president. "Despite your entreaty that we be allowed to hunt down the *K-363,* the Russians have said no. They still reserve the right to do it themselves."

"Idiots," Radford said.

"And they absolutely refuse to rescind their recall order to the *K-480,*" Friedman said, adding, "and we won't change their minds."

"Can those Norwegian intercepts and satellite images that you have be trusted, Karl?" the president asked.

"Yes, sir. That's why we should get something in the air over the Norwegian Sea. We've got P-3Cs we can deploy from Iceland and Spain. I've talked to Gordon, and he and Webster can have something on the way, today, if we say so. We ought to get an ASW group into the Skagerrak to plug that hole. Also, Ellsworth may be able to move a couple of his SSNs into the area around Norway and Sweden."

"If we did that, Karl, it would upset the Russians," Friedman said.

"Paul, we're talking international waters," Radford protested.

Friedman, looking to the president, said, "Sir, if we bring a cordon down on that area, the Russians will explode."

"So, what are we supposed to do, Paul?" Radford said. "Just stand by and watch the Russians capture Zakayev and make him talk? Think what that would do to the summit if the Russians threw him in our faces. With all due respect, Mr. President, I still think that your decision not to cancel the summit is ill advised. Your safety is of paramount concern and until we can find and eliminate Zakayev, I'm damned uncomfortable with the situation we have."

"I appreciate your concern, Karl. But you're a tad behind the curve. The decision's been made and Zakayev or no Zakayev, I leave tomorrow. The issue is closed. As for Scott, you and Admiral Ellsworth said he has good instincts. You still think he can find Zakayev?"

"Yes to both questions. He does have good instincts, which sometimes get him in trouble," said Radford. "But Ellsworth believes that with a little help from us he can do it alone. And the Russians won't know what we're up to."

"You know Zakayev, Karl. You've worked with him, supported him in Afghanistan and in Chechnya. What kind of adversary is he?"

"He's very careful. Plans every move with care. But he's also ruthless and willing to take risks. But then, so is Scott."

"Meaning?"

"If Scott thought there was even a fifty-fifty chance that he could nail Zakayev, he'd go after him if we ordered him to."

Friedman said, "What are his chances of finding and killing the *K-363?*"

"Less than fifty-fifty."

"Then the odds are stacked against him from the start," the president said.

Radford nodded. "That's as good as it gets when it's sub versus sub."

"Where is the *K-480* now, Karl?"

"A tick north of Gamvik, Norway."

"Can we talk to Scott without the Russians knowing it?"

"Yes, sir. Well, I take that back: They'll know if we send something via ELF and burst transmission, but won't be able to read what we send."

"Can we read the Russians' burst traffic to the *K-480?*"

"Some but not all. For instance, we think they've been retransmitting their recall order every hour on the hour but Scott hasn't responded, which has the Russians in a snit. And until we tell him to, he won't budge. The Russians, I suspect, know he's deliberately delayed his response until he gets orders from us."

"Zamorin complained about that," Friedman said. "He accused us of telling Scott to ignore their communications."

"Let him," the president said. "What about this fellow Botkin, the *K-480*'s skipper? Isn't he subject to the same recall order?"

"Yes, sir, technically he is. But Scott is Botkin's CO and can therefore override him."

"I want to be absolutely clear on this point: There is no question Scott is in command of that sub."

"Sir, technically he's not in command of the sub, Botkin is. But Scott is the senior commander of the operation to find the *K-363*. Botkin, though he's the *K-480*'s skipper, is Scott's subordinate."

"Which means Botkin must follow Scott's orders."

"His operational orders, yes, sir. If I may ask, where is this going?"

The president put up a hand. "Those Norwegian intercepts. What are they telling us?"

Radford retrieved copies from his briefing folder. "It's hard to say. For sure they had contact with something on SOSUS—we picked up their fleet bulletin and unit alerts—but there's no way we can confirm it was the *K-363*."

The president rose from his chair and with arms folded, cupped his chin in a fist. "Use your crystal ball, Karl. Could that Norwegian SOSUS contact and the satellite images of wake scarring have been from the *K-363*?"

"I know what you want me to say, Mr. President: that it was the *K-363* heading south down the coast of

Norway. But I don't know if it was. There are too many variables and too many unknowns. For instance—"

The president waved that away. "Karl, cut the bullshit. Yes or no?"

"Well, I suppose it could have been the *K-363.*"

"Could have been . . . ?"

Radford exchanged looks with Friedman. The national security advisor nodded almost imperceptibly.

"What other nation's submarines are in that area?" the president said.

"None that we know of, sir."

"Then it had to be the *K-363,* right?"

Radford hesitated. "Yes, sir, in all likelihood it was." He was about to say more, but the president cut him off with another question.

"Where's he heading to?"

Again Radford hesitated before saying. "Based on what we know, I'd say the Baltic. It's the only way to reach St. Petersburg by sea."

The president returned to his desk and pointed a finger at Radford. "In that case I want you to send a message to Scott."

# 13

## The Barents Sea

Botkin was adamant. "I cannot obey this order, Captain Scott. I am Russian naval officer, not American. I only obey Russian Navy orders."

Everyone in the CCP, including Alex and Yuri Abakov, watched the scene unfold. Botkin's young *starpom,* caught in the middle, still held the decrypted message from Norfolk that had precipitated a face-off between Botkin and Scott.

"That message says we are to redeploy south and intercept the *K-363,*" Botkin said, "but I am under orders from Northern Fleet to return to Olenya Bay."

"The redeployment order from Norfolk supersedes the Olenya Bay recall, Leitenant," Scott said firmly. "Now you will shape a course to the south and get under way at flank speed."

Botkin chewed his lower lip. "I must respectfully decline to carry out your orders, sir."

Scott held Botkin's gaze for a long moment until Botkin blinked. Scott lifted the decrypt from the *starpom*'s hand. "Thank you, Starpom. Please return to your duties."

"Aye, aye, sir." He eased away from Scott, wary of triggering a storm.

"Kapitan Botkin," said Scott, "please join me in the wardroom."

Scott shouldered past the others and led the way.

Botkin followed Scott into the wardroom and said, "Captain, I–"

Scott rounded on Botkin and with his face inches from the skipper's said, "Now you listen to me. Either you follow my orders or I'll bust your balls and then relieve you of command. Do you understand?"

Botkin backed against the wardroom table and froze.

"Do you?"

"Yes."

"Yes, what?"

"Yes, Captain Scott."

"And don't ever question my orders in front of the crew. Do you understand that too?"

"Yes, Captain Scott."

Scott backed off. "Square yourself away."

Botkin mopped his face. He ran a hand over his faded coveralls, smoothing out the fabric.

"You're going to return to the CCP and give orders to turn this rust bucket south and make a run to the Baltic Sea."

"What do I tell Admiral Grishkov?"

"Leave that to me."

"Yes, Captain Scott. Uh, there's something else. . . ."

"What?"

"I can't promise that we can run at full power. Our main coolant pumps have not been overhauled in eighteen months."

"So I noticed in the engineering logs. What else?"

"The oxygen generator. It's still not working properly. The carbon dioxide burner has a faulty thermocouple."

"Do we have a spare?"

"No."

"Can we jury-rig it?"

"Pardon me?"

"Can we make a temporary fix using some other part—something from a heat exchanger manifold control?"

"Perhaps."

"Then put someone on it."

"Aye, Captain."

"Get going. We're running out of time."

"Helm, engines ahead full!" Botkin ordered.

Scott felt the deck vibrate as the *K-480* came to flank speed. Aft, the submarine's main engines spun the seven-bladed prop up to full speed, driving the submarine forward.

"Make your depth two hundred meters."

"Two hundred meters, aye, Kapitan."

Scott and the watchstanders held on as the *K-480*'s controllers at their joysticks nosed her down at a fifteen-degree angle. The hull creaked and popped under the strain of the increasing pressure of deeper water. Something not stowed properly crashed to the deck in the CCP.

Scott saw the depth gauge tick up and the pit log touch thirty knots. Mentally he urged the *K-480* on. He knew Akulas were capable of cracking thirty-four knots, but perhaps the *K-480* couldn't, given her condition. He decided he'd settle for thirty knots if the engineers could coax it from her reactor.

"Kapitan, clear baffles every two hours," Scott ordered.

"Aye, aye, sir," Botkin said.

Scott knew the Russians were occupied elsewhere. But Norfolk had warned that the Norwegians had been sniffing for contacts. With luck, the *K-480* would blow on by them. Luck: They'd need a lot of it.

The diving officer said, "Sir, passing one hundred meters."

The hull popped and groaned in protest. A water hammer made Botkin start. Embarrassed, his gaze flicked to Scott, then just as quickly to the remote sonar repeater clear of contacts.

"Sir, passing one hundred fifty meters."

"Ease your bubble," Botkin ordered.

The deck slowly leveled out. Aft, the turbines thrummed.

"I'll be in the wardroom," Scott said.

"What did you say that made Botkin change his mind?" Alex said.

"I gave him a choice: Follow my orders or swim back to Olenya Bay—without his nuts."

Abakov joined them.

"What else is on your mind, Alex?" Scott said.

Arms akimbo, she glared at him. "If you plan to break my balls, too, you'll be disappointed."

"Sorry."

Alex dropped her arms and sat down. "We need to talk."

"Shoot."

"How can we find and kill the *K-363* before she gets into the Baltic?" Alex asked. "They have a huge head start."

"They do, but we can close the gap. Here, look at this chart." He turned it around to face Alex and

Abakov. "We can run full-out for a day or more, which will allow us to catch up somewhat. After that, we'll have to slow down and pick our way south to avoid running into Norwegian ASW units. Litvanov faces the same challenge."

"Why the Norwegians?" she said.

"NorFleet sent them and the Swedes an advisory that they were going to hold exercises in northern waters. It's cover for their search operation. Trust me, the Norwegians always welcome an opportunity to eavesdrop on NorFleet activity. They worry a lot about submarine incursions into their territorial waters, so Litvanov will have to be careful because the Norwegians are good at the ASW game. And they won't hesitate to drop depth charges on targets inside their territorial waters. They've done it before and Litvanov will have to dog it along their coast to avoid detection. All of this will take time. By the same measure, we also have to be on alert so we don't get caught and depth-charged too. Assuming Litvanov can slip by the Norwegians, he still has to get through the Skag and the Katt."

Scott pointed to the Skagerrak and the Kattegat, the two broad arms of the North Sea between Norway, Sweden, and Denmark. The arms were relatively narrow and especially treacherous for a submerged submarine to transit.

"If he gets through the Skag and Katt, he's still got to get through the strait that opens to The Sound, here, and then the Baltic."

He indicated a pinched and shallow strait between western Denmark and the southern tip of Sweden, a main thoroughfare used by ships bound for the Baltic Sea. "If he can get through the strait he's home free."

"Can he?" Abakov said.

"Yes."

Alex looked at the chart. She saw the strait with its narrow traffic zones, shallow soundings in meters at low tide, treacherous shoals and sandy cusps. "How can a submarine possibly get through this thing without either running aground or being seen?"

"There are ways."

"You drink too much," Zakayev said.

"What of it?" Litvanov taunted. "There's not much time left, so what difference does it make?" He poured another glass of vodka and corked the bottle.

"It sets a bad example. When the men see you drunk, they worry. Worry weakens resolve."

Litvanov gave Zakayev a dark look. "So, you have been studying my men's psyches, eh, General?"

The girl shifted uneasily in her seat at the greasy wardroom table. The remains of boiled fish, groats, and pits from Turkish apricots lay in plates and saucers.

"Ali," she said, "Kapitan Litvanov is entitled to drink as much as he wants. This is his ship and we are his guests."

Litvanov slammed his palm on the table, which made the plates and cutlery jump. "Such a diplomat! Brilliant, isn't she? And she's right. This is my ship and I will drink as much as I want." As if to prove it, he downed the vodka and poured more.

"Listen to your wife, Ali," said Litvanov. "She knows what she's talking about. Anyway, don't worry about my crew. They don't need me to ensure their resolve. All they have to do is see that murdering pig of a president from Belarus, and they will do what they swore to do."

"Yes, Georgi, I'm sure you are right. What I'm suggesting is–"

"I know what you mean: I'm too drunk to skipper the boat. Well, the boys know what to do. That's why I picked them. I could go to sleep right here and not have a worry in the world."

Starpom Veroshilov poked his head into the room and looked around.

"Konstintin! Tell him."

"Tell him what, Kapitan?"

"Tell him how dedicated you are to this mission."

"Of course, Kapitan. We all are. The general knows that. We are professionals. We do what we say we'll do. For our families. For our country."

"See, what did I tell you?" Litvanov said.

"Kapitan . . ." Veroshilov said. "We're picking up something on ESM. Possibly a U.S. Navy P-3 Orion."

"Not a coincidence," Litvanov said. "The Americans were sure to have their noses into this. I'm surprised it took them so long. We've been picking up ZEVS transmissions every hour on the hour. Moscow is frantic to reach someone. Can you guess why? I can."

Litvanov staggered to his feet and reached up to brace against the overhead storage cabinets filled with books and instruction manuals.

"They're shitting their pants in the Kremlin because of us. You can bet on it."

"Orders, Kapitan?" said Veroshilov.

Litvanov ran a paw over his stubbly face. "Did you monitor CNN?"

"Yes. They said that the U.S. president left Andrews Air Force Base for St. Petersburg at fifteen hundred this afternoon U.S. time."

"I hope he has a nice flight. That they all have a nice flight."

Litvanov, to get his bearings, glanced at the compass

and pit log repeater on the bulkhead. "Only one contact on ESM?"

"So far."

"Well, let's not hang around here. Rig for ultraquiet and shape course for Navfjord. We'll pull in there and wait out those P-3s."

"Aye, aye, Kapitan." Veroshilov moved to carry out his orders.

"What is Navfjord?" the girl asked.

"A deepwater fjord north of Bergen," said Veroshilov. "The Americans and their P-3 Orions won't find us there."

"What about the Norwegians?" said Zakayev.

"What about them? Do you think they'll expect to find a Russian submarine parked in their backyard?"

"Perhaps Moscow alerted them," Zakayev said. "Maybe that's why we encountered those two frigates."

"No, even if Fleet Headquarters has discovered by now that we're not in the Barents Sea, and even if they know our plans, they would never tell the Norwegians to look for us. That would be too embarrassing. And the Norwegians won't say anything to Moscow about a mysterious sonar contact. It's the Americans who have a stake in the outcome, but Moscow won't want them interfering, either. Imagine if the tables were reversed and Moscow wanted to hunt for an American sub in the Caribbean, or off the east coast of the U.S. Impossible."

"But the American president is on his way to St. Petersburg," the girl said. "If they know about us, why haven't they canceled the summit?"

"My guess, little beauty, is they don't want to set off a panic," Litvanov said. "Plus, it would look bad if Washington or Moscow appeared worried."

Zakayev nodded his agreement.

"Who is Moscow frantic to reach?" the girl asked as Litvanov squeezed past.

"What?"

"You said they were signaling every hour."

Litvanov rested against the doorframe. "There's another submarine out there."

"Which one?" Zakayev asked, looking slightly alarmed.

"The one they sent to kill us."

"Periscope up," Litvanov ordered.

The portside search scope snatched in its carriage and rose.

He had dared fire a single ping from the Fathometer to confirm that the fjord was deep enough to enter and discovered almost eight hundred meters of black water beneath the keel.

Now he grasped the rising periscope handles and came upright. The scope swept across the fjord and a forest of conifers growing to water's edge. At the narrow end of the fjord, walls of living rock formed a steep-sided canyon. To Litvanov, viewing it from a low perspective, the canyon resembled a raw, prehistoric fracture in the earth's surface.

He made a careful inspection of the near shoreline for houses or roads but saw nothing to indicate there were people ashore watching the periscope head sticking up out of the middle of the fjord like a pole. On the tip of the small island guarding the mouth of the fjord, he saw a stone ruin. High-magnification revealed little more than a pile of cut rock and a partially collapsed wall. He swept past the ruin and stopped when he saw three Arctic deer crash out of the forest and suddenly freeze, their tails and ears perked up, gaze planted squarely on the fjord's shimmering waters.

Litvanov allowed himself a smile. "Periscope down. Engage hovering system. Maintain periscope depth."

"Periscope depth, aye," Veroshilov replied from the diving station. "Rigging ship for hover."

Litvanov waited until he received confirmation that the *K-363* had been properly trimmed and that the submarine, hove to, lay suspended twenty meters beneath the surface of the fjord. "Raise the ESM mast," he ordered. "Let's see if that nosy P-3 is in the area."

A brief hum of hydraulics sounded in the CCP.

"Contact, Kapitan. Narrowband spectrum. Identify as U.S. Navy type APS-118 search radar. Bearing zero-two-zero, moving left. Signal strength Five."

*"Amerikanskis?"* Zakayev said.

"Yes, probably out of Keflavík." Litvanov said. "They're flying a north-south search leg."

The girl stood beside Zakayev, her big eyes on Litvanov.

"Don't worry," he told her. "They'll soon get bored and go back to their movies and television programs. Then we can head south."

Karl Radford looked at the haggard face of Rear Admiral Grishkov. The color adjustment on the videoconference screen in Radford's Crystal City office looked slightly off: As well as looking haggard, Grishkov also looked green.

"Good morning, Mikhail," said Radford.

"Good morning to you, Karl," said Grishkov. "Thank you for setting up the conference on such short notice. This won't take long."

"Take as much time as you need, Mikhail. I know this isn't a social call."

Grishkov, in Severomorsk, where it was three A.M., hunched forward and, puffing on a cigarette while looking into a glass of steaming tea on his desk, said, "No, this is not a social call."

"What can I do for you, Mikhail?" Radford asked.

"Admiral Stashinsky does not know that I'm talking to you, Karl. Nor will he, I hope."

Radford didn't show surprise. "This is a secure network. It can't be recorded or penetrated."

"Thank you."

Radford waited, toying with the Scotch and water he habitually drank at the end of his workday.

Grishkov lifted his gaze from the tea and looked directly into the video camera on his end. "Can you tell me, please, Karl, what you've done with Captain Scott and the *K-480?*"

A brief hesitation and Radford said, "I don't know what you mean. We haven't done anything with them. I know that you recalled them. Haven't they confirmed your order?"

"No. We've been trying to raise the *K-480* via ZEVS, but they don't respond. I thought perhaps you might know why."

"This is news to me, Mikhail. You aren't suggesting that something has happened to them, are you?"

Smoke from his cigarette made Grishkov squint. "You would know that better than I. You have sources we don't have."

"We've had no casualty reports. But then, as you know, our SOSUS in that region is on standby only, not active."

"I was referring to your new laser satellites."

"They're not currently deployed in that region."

"In other words you don't know why Scott won't respond to our signals."

"Perhaps he can't."

"Yes, I've considered that they may have a communication problem. But it seems a remote possibility."

"Then I don't know what to tell you, Mikhail. I wish I could help."

"Let me ask this: Have you been in communication with them?"

Radford took a sip from his drink. His mind raced. He'd anticipated Grishkov's question because he knew that the Russians monitored but couldn't break ELF or VHF signals sent to U.S. submarines on patrol around the world. And there was no way the Russians could determine which submarines the messages had been sent to, not even the *K-480.*

"Yes, we have communicated with them."

"When was the last time?"

"The day you issued the recall order. We sent Scott an interrogatory to confirm he'd received it, and he had."

"And what did he tell you?"

"Now, Mikhail . . ."

"I'm not asking that you divulge classified information. I simply want to know: Did he confirm receipt of our recall and say he'd return to Olenya Bay?"

"Yes, that's what he said."

"That was twenty-four hours ago. The *K-480* has not returned to base, nor has Botkin broadcast his position twice daily as ordered. This officer you have aboard, Scott, he's what you Americans call a loose cannon, yes?"

"Scott wouldn't disobey a direct order."

"A direct order from you, you mean."

Radford kept his iron composure. "What are you implying, Mikhail?"

"Indulge me to think out loud, Karl. What I am

thinking is that your Captain Scott received secret orders to move south, into waters around Norway and Sweden."

"Secret orders from whom?"

Grishkov allowed a mild annoyance to temper his voice. "Someone in your government. Someone high up."

"What reason would we have to send Scott and the *K-480* south to Norway and Sweden?"

Grishkov rubbed out his cigarette. "Because you believe that's where Zakayev and Litvanov are headed."

"That's absurd and you know it. Zakayev and Litvanov are in the Barents. If you're having trouble finding them, don't blame us. We offered to help but you refused. If you've changed your mind, say so, but don't come to me with some half-assed theory that we're telling Scott to ignore your orders. That doesn't make any sense."

"No? Something seems to have gotten your serious attention, Karl. We've detected a sudden increase in P-3 surveillance flights over the Norwegian Sea and as far south as the Skag. There's also been an increase in Norwegian ASW activity. Perhaps the *K-363* is headed south—was headed south all along—and you've told Scott not to obey our recall order, and also that he is to find the *K-363* and torpedo it—torpedo it even in the Baltic if necessary."

"The Baltic? Where did you come up with that idea? What the hell's in the Baltic that you think would interest a group of terrorists in a submarine? Surely not Kaliningrad, that old broken-down base you have there. Or do you think Zakayev plans to sneak into the Gulf of Riga and sink one of your old flattops or missile cruisers? Is that it?"

Grishkov lit a fresh cigarette. He waved smoke away from in front of his face and said, "I don't know if that's it. That's why I asked for this conference. I was hoping you would tell me what happened to the *K-480* if not the *K-363*. They're both missing."

"What do you mean, the *K-363* is missing?"

"She's not in the Barents Sea."

"How do you know that?"

"Please, Karl, we poor Russians don't have half the navy or satellites America has, but we are not totally impotent. And we are not fools. We put what we have to work in the Barents Sea and have come up empty-handed. Believe me, if the *K-363* were there, we'd have found her by now."

Radford pushed back in his chair. The iced Scotch had left a ring of water in its coaster and he touched it with a fingertip. Grishkov, grasping at straws, didn't realize he'd caught one.

"I must tell you, Karl, I have only one more day in which to find the *K-363*. If I don't, Stashinsky will relieve me of command."

Radford almost felt sorry for the Russian but said nothing.

"My gut tells me that the *K-363* is not hiding in the Barents," said Grishkov. "So perhaps you will tell me now the truth. Do you know if Litvanov is making for the Baltic Sea?"

Radford had his answer ready. "No, I don't."

"I see. By the way, you know of course that the only way to reach St. Petersburg by sea is through the Baltic and the Gulf of Finland."

"Yes, I know that."

"Thank you for keeping our conversation confidential. I appreciate it."

* * *

A trip-hammer went off in his chest. He needed air but couldn't breath. Everything seemed to be moving in slow motion: his ship, his men, the North Korean frigate bearing down. He tried to warn Alex, but it was too late.

"What?"

The *starpom*'s face floated into view, "Captain Scott, sir, sorry to wake you, but you are needed in the CCP. Sonar contact."

The hum of machinery. Muted voices. The dank familiar smell of the *K-480*.

Scott, fully awake now, swung off his bunk and said. "What do you have?"

The *starpom* rattled off their course, speed, and position south of Vega, Norway. Then: "Sound has picked up two sets of screws, bearing dead ahead."

"On my way."

In the CCP, Botkin, looking pale, said, "Two ships. Norwegian frigates. Each has a towed sonar array deployed."

Tactical plot had already worked a torpedo firing solution on them.

Scott acknowledged Alex and Yuri Abakov's arrival in the CCP. He glanced at the coastal chart of Norway, its filigree of islands and fjords. "They're here," he said for their benefit, "and moving toward us. We can hear them upstairs, their VDS arrays are passive. They're definitely listening for something."

"The *K-363?*" Abakov said.

"Bet on it," Scott said.

"Then may I make an observation?"

"Go ahead."

"I'm not pretending to be a naval tactician, but from

everything I've seen so far and feel in my gut, Zakayev and Litvanov are long gone–south. The Norwegians up there are like a couple of cops looking under the bed for a robber who went out the back door. They're wasting their time looking for them and instead they're going to find us–"

A wailing APD–Air Particle Detector–alarm cut him off. A split second later a red warning light started flashing on and off.

Botkin, his face a mask of fear, froze at the periscope stand.

A recorded female voice exploded from the SC1: "Condition Red, Compartment Seven! Condition Red, Compartment Seven!"

"Decreasing pressurizer level!" warned the *starpom*. Without waiting for orders, he rang up slow speed to reduce reactor power.

"What is it?" Alex shouted over the din.

"Reactor coolant leak!" Botkin croaked.

"SCRAM the reactor!" Scott ordered.

The *starpom* activated the remote and a beat later replied, "Nothing!"

"Reactor Control Compartment!" Scott shouted. "Let's go!"

Sailors flattened themselves against machinery-lined passageways as Scott and Alex, high-stepping over watertight door coamings, dashed for the Reactor Control Compartment.

At the after end of Compartment Six they found the terrified chief engineer and main propulsion engineer gawking at the reactor control console. Their coveralls were black with sweat and they had already broken out OBAs–oxygen breathing apparatuses–and silver steam suits. Flashing red warning lights and the honking alarm made the darkened compartment look and sound like a scene from hell.

The two engineers prepared to don their old-fashioned OBAs, full-face rubber masks with glass eye ports and corrugated black hoses for plugging into belt-mounted breathing canisters or into the ship's central air system.

"Put those away," Scott commanded. "There're no poisonous fumes in here."

The men hesitated, then did as they were ordered.

"Get control of yourselves," Scott shouted.

He shouldered the frightened engineers aside. One look at the console's gauges and instruments confirmed that the APD reading had increased rapidly, that a ten-gallon-a-minute leak had erupted somewhere in the reactor's main coolant loop. The reactor should have SCRAMMED—shut down automatically—but hadn't. If the reactor wasn't shut down and the leak repaired quickly, or if the coolant makeup system couldn't provide enough water, the reactor core would run dry and overheat with catastrophic results. The *K-480* was suddenly a potential Chernobyl II.

"Why didn't the reactor SCRAM?" Scott bellowed over the hammering alarm.

"I don't know," said the boyish-looking chief engineer. "The quench plates didn't drop like they're supposed to. I-I've never seen anything like this before."

Scott knew that Russian naval reactors, like U.S. naval reactors, used hafnium plates or rods to control the reactor's power output. When the plates retracted, nuclear fission accelerated, producing heat and power. Conversely, plate insertion slowed or "quenched" the reaction by absorbing the neutrons produced during fission.

The acronym *SCRAM,* for *Safety Control Rod Axe Man,* had evolved in the early days of reactor development during World War II. Then, a single control rod simply hung from a rope over the reactor. In an emergency a man wielding an axe would cut the rope, allowing the control rod to drop into the reactor and shut it down. Now the procedure was more complicated.

Scott pointed to a pair of winking red warning lights on the inclined, waist-high section of the console. "The quench plates are still in their retracted position. The autorelease mechanism must have failed—like everything else on this ship—and shut that damn alarm off. The Norwegians are probably deaf from it by now too."

The chief engineer located and threw the switch. The sudden silence was almost overwhelming.

"Jake, core temperature is rising fast," Alex said, pointing to the large, centrally located temperature gauge set into the control panel with its switch gear and elaborate red and blue diagram of the reactor's piping system. Some branches of the diagram were flagged with yellow and black labels marked *Apasnost!*—Danger!

"Chief, initiate a manual drop," Scott ordered. "And somebody find Botkin! Tell him to get his ass in here!"

"I already tried a manual drop," said the chief. "It didn't work."

"Well, try it again."

A hand wheel protruding from the center of the console controlled the insertion rate of the plates into the reactor core. The chief twisted the wheel to its stop but the plates refused to release and drop.

"I don't understand: They should have dropped," the chief said, a hand to his sweat-matted hair. "If they don't, the reactor will overheat and melt through the bottom of the ship."

* * *

"Play it back again," said Captain Bayer.

Bayer, Dass, and the sonar watch officer, Garborg, listened to the high-pitched sound that had been processed by the towed array and recorded on the VDS system's computer.

Garborg pointed to a green sine wave displayed for analysis on a monitor. "Sir, note the regularity of the wave's peaks. Strictly mechanical—that is, it's definitely a man-made sound."

"Any idea what it is?" Bayer said.

"A signal," said Dass.

"Indeed, but what kind of signal?"

"An underwater distress signal?"

Bayer seemed to dismiss this possibility by remaining silent. Then, after considering at length, he said, "Yes, a distress signal from a submarine. A Russian submarine."

Dass and Garborg said nothing.

"*Narvik* reported hearing it too," Bayer said. "Duration?"

Garborg consulted notes. "Five minutes, eight seconds. Range estimate was ten kilometers."

"Can we get an accurate fix on the source by using *Narvik*'s and our own computed bearing?"

"We can try, sir," Garborg said. He stepped away to work on it.

"What do you think, Mr. Dass? A distress signal? Or what?"

"Or an alarm."

Bayer put a finger to his chin. "A casualty alarm. A casualty serious enough to not only set off an alarm aboard a submarine but perhaps slow her down or even worse."

"Something that would force her to surface and identify herself."

"Exactly. Let's see what Mr. Garborg comes up with. Maybe we can force the issue."

"Jake, my God, look at the core temperature," Alex said. The temperature gauge needle had crept out of the Normal range.

Botkin burst into the reactor control compartment with a wild, terrified look on his face. "The warning signals—a radiation leak—"

"A coolant leak," Scott corrected Botkin. He saw Abakov ease into the compartment behind Botkin. "Calm down."

Botkin, pointing at the temperature gauge, threw himself at the control console. The gauge's black needle wiggled at the edge of the red zone. "The fuel will melt!" he cried. "We have to surface right now!" Botkin grabbed an SC1 microphone. "We have to emergency blow—"

Scott tore the mike from Botkin's fist. "Belay that!"

"We're all going to die—"

Scott grabbed two handfuls of Botkin's coveralls and threw him against the console. "No one's going to die!"

He understood what Botkin feared, what every nuclear sub sailor feared: a core meltdown. To prevent it, someone would have to enter the reactor compartment with the reactor critical and in danger of meltdown and manually drop the quench plates.

"Chief, break out your schematics of the cooling system," Scott commanded.

The engineer threw open a locker and pawed through a pile of disorganized ring-bound manuals and folded plans. He found the one Scott wanted and flattened it out on the console.

As Scott and the two engineers conferred, Abakov said to Alex, "What are we facing?"

"If the reactor core melts down, Scandinavia and eastern Europe could face a second Chernobyl," Alex said. "The radioactivity released could contaminate a wide swath of Russia too."

Botkin heard this and wailed, "But this is a disaster."

Alex said, "At Chernobyl the reactor overheated and caused a core meltdown. Two hydrogen explosions blew the top off the reactor building, releasing deadly radioactive material into the atmosphere. Not only did it expose people in Russia to high levels of radioactivity, the radioactivity spread over northern Europe. Millions were affected."

"I remember," Abakov said. "People got sick and there were birth defects. . . ."

"Radiation damages human cells and the central nervous system. It also causes cancer and genetic defects. High doses can cause death within days or even hours of exposure. The long-term effects of lower doses are just as bad. That's why we wear dosimeters to record exposure. No dose is harmless and repeated exposures build up in the body and can have delayed effects."

"How do these reactors work, and what's involved in making this, what you call 'meltdown,' happen?" Abakov said.

"In a submarine reactor, like in a civilian nuclear power plant, enriched uranium fuel initiates a chain reaction. The nuclear fission generates heat, which turns water into steam that drives the submarine's turbines. The turbines drive turbogenerators, which in turn supply power to the props and the submarine's shipboard systems.

"The reactor itself is a kind of domed container. The reaction is self-sustaining and requires a steady flow of coolant to carry away the heat. If the coolant stops flowing, the uranium core will overheat and melt through the bottom of the reactor vessel and eventually, as the chief engineer said, through the hull of the submarine. The hot core will turn seawater into radioactive steam and blow it into the atmosphere."

"You mean like an atomic bomb?

"Not like a bomb, but just as deadly."

Botkin moaned. "My God, I don't want to believe this could happen."

Scott turned his attention from the coolant piping plan and said over his shoulder, "That's why someone has to enter the reactor compartment and manually SCRAM the reactor and find the leak, then make repairs."

Botkin seemed incapable of absorbing what had to be done and acting on it.

Scott finished his study of the reactor's cooling system and addressed the main propulsion engineer. "What's your name, sailor?"

"Leonid, sir."

"All right, Leo, stand by to shift to battery power when the turbogenerators are secured. After we SCRAM the reactor, we'll need auxiliary power."

"Aye, Captain." Leonid's hands flew over the electrical distribution panel, tripping switches and throwing control levers that opened circuits through which power would flow from the storage batteries to the emergency propulsion system's motor connect and the ship's screw.

"Jake, what about the diesel generator?" Alex said.

"The Norwegians, if they haven't already heard the alarm, will spot our snorkel. Not only that, they'll hear the engine running."

Scott knew that even if the quench plates could be lowered to shut down the reactor, they'd have to find a way to inject water into the core to cool it. And it might take hours to repair the leak in the main coolant loop. With luck they could design a work-around to isolate the leak. Meanwhile they'd need another source of power to keep the ship's systems working and the prop turning. The battery was the only source available.

"That propulsion motor is a hell of a power drainer," Scott said, his attention on the flickering ammeters. He knew the ship's repair gang had less than three hours to perform a miracle before the batteries went flat. If the batteries died, the *K-480* would also die. The choice would be to sink or to surface in Norwegian territorial waters.

Scott grabbed the SC1 mike dangling from its coiled cord. "CCP, Reactor Control."

The *starpom* answered; Scott heard the man's voice quaver. "Captain Scott, what is happening, where is the Kapitan?"

"You're taking orders from me, *starpom,*" Scott said. "After we SCRAM the reactor, stand by to answer bells on emergency propulsion."

After a brief hesitation the *starpom* replied crisply, "Aye, Kapitan. Understood."

Scott snapped the mike off and said, "Chief, where's the manual override on the quench plate control."

The chief mopped his face. "Over the reactor dome. A mechanical interlock: Once it is released with a special tool, it will open the plate clips and gravity will do the rest. But as you said, sir, someone has to enter the reactor compartment to do it."

"While the reactor is critical and leaking coolant?" Alex said. She looked stunned, as though what Scott had been saying had finally sunk in. "That's suicidal."

The *K-480*'s reactor was located midships on the lower level of Compartment Seven. The compartment had heavy shielding around it to protect the crew from radiation emitted when the reactor, a huge, domed container loaded with enriched uranium fuel, went critical. A shielded tunnel provided safe passage for the crew through Compartment Seven to the machinery spaces aft in Compartment Eight. Midway through the tunnel an airlock, like that in a spacecraft, allowed access to the reactor compartment.

Though radiation levels inside the compartment reached high levels during operation, a man wearing a steam suit and equipped with breathing apparatus could enter the compartment for a short period—under five minutes—and not receive a fatal exposure. Scott knew that it would take more than five minutes to manually drop the plates and quench the nuclear fire.

"It's the only way," the chief engineer said to Alex.

"Jake, you can't allow anyone to go in there," Alex said. "It's a death sentence."

"Someone has to," Scott said. "If we don't SCRAM the reactor we'll all be dead—and so might a lot of innocent people."

"Then surface the boat and flood the compartment. Surrender to the Norwegians."

"You don't mean that."

"Yes, I do. The hell with Zakayev."

"You wouldn't risk one life to save the ship so we can head off a terrorist attack?"

Scott stared at Alex, waiting for her answer.

"I'll do it," Abakov said. "Show me how."

They all turned to the FSB officer. "The risk is worth taking," he said.

"No, Yuri, you can't go in there," Alex said. She turned on Scott. "Jake, don't let him."

"I am the chief engineer," said Leonid. "I will go." He picked a steam suit and OBA up off the deck.

Botkin stepped away from the control console and took the suit and OBA away from Leonid. "No. It's my responsibility. I'm the commanding officer of this ship. I know how to drop the plates."

Alex started to say something to protest, but Scott trapped her arm in an iron grip.

Botkin stepped one leg at a time into the steam suit and shrugged it over his shoulders. "Chief, assemble a work party. After I drop the quench plates they can follow me in, find the leak, and repair it."

"Aye, Kapitan," said the chief engineer.

Scott said, "Kapitan, you'll need an air pack, not that OBA. It's only good for ten minutes on canister.

"We have no air packs."

Scott didn't show surprise. "Then take along a spare canister."

"I'll be done in there before I need a spare," Botkin said. "At least, I'd better be, or it will be all over."

Botkin pulled the OBA over his head and face and adjusted the suspension straps. After testing it his breath came in short bursts. "Have a decontamination team stationed outside the airlock when I come out," he said, his voice muffled behind the mask, "so I don't contaminate the whole ship."

Leonid helped Botkin get his arms into the shiny suit and zip up. He fit the rubberized material tight around the OBA mask, then hooked up a two-way throat mike for Botkin to communicate with Reactor Control. Finally, Leonid dropped the baglike hood with its rectangular window like a welder's mask over Botkin's head, threading the throat mike lead to the outside through a sealed port. Fully outfitted, Botkin looked like an astronaut. Leonid stepped back and gave him a thumbs-up.

Botkin, disoriented by the bulky gear and the limited vision it provided, waddled toward the open door, which led to the shielded tunnel and airlock. Scott put a hand on Botkin's shoulder and stopped him. Somehow the young skipper had found the inner reserves of strength he needed to enter the possible death trap waiting for him in the reactor compartment.

Scott sketched a salute. "Everything is in your hands now, Kapitan. Everything."

Botkin lifted a gloved hand, then entered the tunnel.

# Part Three

## THE BATTLE

# 14

## Over the North Atlantic

*Air Force One* streaked east at forty thousand feet. The president, shoes off, dozed in a comfortable armchair. A formidable pile of briefing folders lay untouched on the table beside him. The first lady, engrossed in a paperback novel, sat opposite her husband. She had fine features, hair like a helmet of tight curls, and skin the color of polished rosewood.

The curtain drawn across the doorway of the private stateroom fluttered. The president's wife looked up and saw Paul Friedman's face poking around the curtain.

"Sorry, Mim," Friedman said, using her nickname.

"Can't it wait?" she asked, annoyed.

Friedman shook his head

The first lady shook her head too. "Lord, there's not a moment's peace." She marked her place in the book with a finger, then gently roused the president.

He opened an eye. "We there yet?"

"No, dear, St. Petersburg is still three thousand miles away."

The president yawned, saw Friedman. "What's up,

Paul?" He glanced at the binder with a red cover in the national security advisor's hand. "Trouble?"

"Maybe. We just received a flash from Karl." He glanced at the first lady.

"Well, if you'll both excuse me," she said, "I'm going to the galley."

Alone with the president, Friedman said, "Karl's not available for a face-to-face. His verbal report says Grishkov confirmed that the Russians have been trying to raise the *K-480* and can't, and that they've been waiting for her return to Olenya Bay."

Friedman quickly sketched the conversation between Radford and Grishkov, emphasizing for the president the Russian's suspicion that the *K-363* was headed for the Baltic Sea. "Also, Grishkov faces being relieved of command over his failure to find the *K-363* in the Barents. Be that as it may, Karl denied Grishkov's accusations. And he also denied we had information that the *K-363* was headed for the Baltic."

The president digested this information, after which he said, "Did Grishkov believe him?"

"Don't know. Grishkov's an old fox. I can't imagine that Karl telling him there's no truth to his accusations would convince him that he's wrong. But you have to ask if, after talking to Karl, Grishkov is still convinced the *K-363* is heading for the Baltic, wouldn't he try to save his neck by telling Stashinsky about it?"

"In which case . . ."

"Stashinsky, assuming he believes Grishkov, will throw everything they have at the Baltic before Scott can take a shot at Zakayev."

The president got up to stretch his legs. The private stateroom he and his wife occupied was outfitted like a fine hotel suite with plush carpeting, leather-trimmed furniture, a bar, and entertainment center. It was also soundproofed, the noise of the Boeing's big turbofans only a low rumble.

"Drink, Paul?"

"No, thank you, sir."

The president poured Scotch over crackling ice and, with his back to Friedman, said, "What do the Russians have in the Baltic?"

Friedman opened the red-covered folder and found the page he wanted. "Not much since the Soviet collapse and especially after Putin's departure. Funding for deployment and new construction has all but dried up, so it's a make-do situation. Baltic Headquarters is at Kaliningrad and there's a base at Baltiysk in the Kaliningrad Oblast. Kronshtadt has a few laid-up surface combatants and a handful of elderly diesel submarines, most of which are not considered seaworthy. Also a few naval auxiliaries and coastal patrol craft, but that's about it."

The president faced Friedman. "No ASW capabilities?"

"None to speak of, other than a few PCs armed with depth charges and obsolete antiship missiles. Nothing that would bother a skipper like Litvanov."

"Or Scott?"

"Or Scott."

"Then, if I understand what you've told me, nothing's changed has it? The Russians are running around in the Barents Sea after their own tails; their Baltic fleet, if you can call it that, is a shambles; they're unsure of our intentions; and Grishkov's ass is on the line."

"Yes, sir, that about covers it."

"Then we should stay out of Scott's way and not give it away to the Russians by sending in everything we have until we have to. Karl wanted Ellsworth's SSNs in there, which is a bad idea, and you can tell him I said so. You've got two Russian subs, good guys and bad guys, and I don't want our people shooting the wrong one."

Heat. Overwhelming, suffocating heat. And steam. Botkin almost retreated from the reactor compartment back into the airlock. Instead he groped forward and, through the narrow view port in his hood, saw the overheated stainless-steel reactor vessel. It looked like a huge cauldron with a rounded lid surrounded by a forest of shiny pipes and valves. His view of it was partially obscured by clouds of radioactive steam rising through the open steel grates that formed the deck on which Botkin was standing. He looked down into a virtual snake pit of tangled pipes, risers, and fittings but couldn't see which pipe had sprung a leak.

The closer Botkin got to the reactor, the hotter it felt. Sweat poured from his body, drenching his coveralls, coating the inside of the rubber-lined steam suit. The OBA mask felt glued to his face. He wiped fog from the hood's view port with a gloved hand and only then realized that almost all of the thermal insulation on the reactor vessel and piping had, for some reason, been removed or, more likely, stripped off and stolen.

He shuffled forward against the heat and found the fixed-function control panel mounted on the reactor's starboard side. He searched for the automatic coolant feed flow indicators. Almost zero flow! His heart leaped when he saw the reactor core temperature readings: 500 degrees Celsius and climbing! A blinking red light on the cooling system's schematic warned of a low-pressure zone in the water-purification trap. Another blinking red light warned of a blowout in the main coolant loop at the booster inlet. The repair gang would have to rig a backup cooling system, then cut the seal-welded valves to bypass the blowout and repressurize the system.

Botkin's ears rang. From radiation poisoning? He tried to remember what he'd learned about radiation sickness at nuclear power school. Something about gamma radiation. And alpha particles. And rems. How many rems was he taking now? Over a hundred? Two hundred? How many were fatal? He couldn't remember anything. Except that it was forbidden under any circumstances to enter the compartment while the reactor was critical.

Botkin's ears rang because someone was talking to him on his two-way mike. He couldn't hear what they were saying over the roar of escaping steam. "Repeat!" he said under his mask. "Repeat!"

"Quench plates . . ."

The mike was strangling him. He wanted to rip it off. The hood too. The bulky suit restricted his movements. He wondered if he was dying.

"Blowout in main cooling loop at booster inlet," Botkin bawled into the mike.

"Copy." It was Scott.

He pictured the repair gang outside the compartment assembling tools and parts to make the repair. He heard "Quench plates" hiss in his ear and wanted to scream, "Yes, I know I've only got minutes left to SCRAM the reactor!"

Botkin forced himself to move.

He found the special tool needed to manually release the quench plates stowed inside a yellow locker beside the control panel. The tool, a long, nickel-plated breaker bar, had a large socket attached at one end. He hefted the tool and, half blinded by clouds of steam and with sweat pouring into his eyes, inched around the reactor vessel until he found welded rungs and handholds that gave access to the reactor's dome and the jammed quench plate release mechanism. But heat from the uninsulated reactor drove him back. His skin under the suit felt scorched; patches had stuck to the suit's heavy rubber lining.

Botkin remembered something from the training he'd undergone in a reactor compartment mockup at nuclear power school. There were few safety devices built into the reactor compartments aboard Russian submarines, but he'd seen one put to use as a practical joke to scare green officers undergoing training.

He spotted what he was looking for almost directly overhead: an emergency decontamination bathwater nozzle. But it was missing the chain pull necessary to activate the valve. Either it had never been installed or it had been "appropriated" like the reactor vessel's insulation.

If he could somehow turn the valve on and direct the water spray over himself and also onto the reactor vessel, it might cool the surface just enough to allow him to reach the quench plate mechanism without being cooked like a chicken. It would also help condense steam from the leak and facilitate repair.

Botkin, his movements severely restricted by the bulky steam suit, held on to the socket and on tiptoe swung the other end of the tool at the valve, aiming to knock the shutoff arm off its seat to release a torrent of water. He barely had enough strength to wield the heavy wrench one-handed while he clung to a welded handhold on the reactor vessel. He hoped the valve hadn't been disconnected or installed in a dry line. If it had, it was all over.

The tool clanged against the shutoff arm and

bounced off. Botkin feared it was frozen. Few systems aboard the *K-480* had ever been tested much less maintained. He tried again and this time missed and almost tumbled off the rungs. When he grabbed the handhold to keep from falling, he pitched against the reactor vessel. He sprang back, leaving a huge gob of smoking silvered rubber from his suit stuck to the vessel.

Botkin felt searing pain and knew he'd been badly burned. He thought about rems, whole-body doses, bloody stools. He thought about Scott and the others waiting for him to SCRAM the reactor.

Someone was hailing him over the two-way mike, but he ignored it.

He took a firm grip on the tool and collected himself. He knew he had only a small reserve of strength left. Breathing had gotten harder, the OBA canister nearing depletion.

"You bastard!" he shouted, and swung the tool.

A torrent of water shot from the valve and over Botkin and the reactor vessel. Surprised, Botkin almost dropped the tool into the snake pit below the grates but held on and, fighting through billowing clouds of steam, threw himself on top of the water-slickened reactor dome.

He found the quench plate mechanism and flipped up the cover protecting the lockout device. He scrabbled at the interlock with a gloved hand, the fingers like thick silver tubes that refused to bend. He felt around for the two hex bolts on the quench plate release clips and positioned the socket over the first one and, his arm a blur, cranked it open as fast as he could.

It took less than half a minute to open the clips and drop both plates into the core. A moment later he heard the reactor safety interlocks lift and felt the system wind down. He thought he saw the emergency lights flicker as the power grid stepped over to battery, but he wasn't sure. Exhausted, sick, he slid down the side of the reactor, trying not to drop the tool into the pit, and landed on hands, knees, and forehead.

Lungs bursting, he tore the hood off and gulped air heavy with water, steam, and radioactive contaminants. He heard the airlock bang open and someone calling him. But the voice was too far away to identify. And besides, he didn't give a damn anymore. He'd saved the ship and that was enough.

"Nothing." Captain Bayer held on to the ship-to-ship radio handset a moment longer than necessary, as if unwilling to concede defeat, then cradled it. "*Narvik* says they have nothing."

Executive Officer Dass looked equally perplexed. "Well, we definitely had something, sir. Whatever it was is gone."

Garborg agreed.

"Not gone, Mr. Dass, misplaced," Bayer said, looking across a freshening sea at the trim gray profile of the *Narvik* keeping station on the *Trondheim.* What Bayer didn't say was that he'd been had twice. By a Russian, he was sure.

His white teeth flashed in the gloom. "Let's get a signal to Stavanger. Tell them what we have and ask permission to shift our area south. At the very least they'll want to know what may be coming their way. Then you may signal *Narvik*, tell her we're folding our tent here and that she should haul in on VDS."

"Aye, sir," said Dass. He turned to follow Bayer's orders but stopped and said, "Gutsy bastards, aren't they, sir?"

"And damned good too." Bayer put his 7x50s to his eyes, looked south and said, "Trouble is, their boats are as quiet at the American 688s. Put a determined skipper at the helm and they can just about go anywhere, do anything they want."

"Sea's making up, Kapitan."

"Bad for them, good for us," Litvanov said. "Rough weather degrades their sonar."

"Ours too?" Zakayev said.

"Yes, but we're not hunting, we're listening."

The submarine rocked slightly from side to side from the wave action overhead. Zakayev, feeling queasy, had heard that submariners sometimes got seasick because they spent their lives submerged and weren't used to sailing in rough weather.

"Watch your depth," Litvanov commanded. "Careful we don't broach." The *K-363* inched toward the surface with Litvanov's seaman's eye planted on the depth readout. Satisfied, he commanded, "Raise the ESM mast."

A deep-seated fatigue had weakened Zakayev. The tension, the claustrophobic living conditions, the discomfort of life in a submarine, was something he hadn't anticipated. The girl was also drained, her pretty face thin and drawn, her short black hair greasy and matted against her head. Yet, she hadn't complained.

Litvanov, Zakayev had marveled, was in his element. It had almost become a game for him, and Zakayev wondered if, when the moment came for it all to end, Litvanov would regret his decision, perhaps even change his mind. Not likely, he thought, as Litvanov had from time to time reminded his crew of their responsibility to carry out what they had vowed to do. Meanwhile the game they were playing with the Norwegians kept them alert and their minds off what they would soon face.

"How will he do it?" the girl had asked Zakayev.

"Explosive charges," he had answered.

"Will they blow up the ship?"

"No, just the important parts."

"Will it take long after that?"

"An hour, maybe less."

She nodded acceptance.

"Are you frightened," he'd asked.

"I won't be if we're together."

*Together,* he thought. But it would not be pleasant, and he didn't dissuade her from believing it would be like going to sleep. However, he was prepared to help her if it came to that.

"Kapitan, ESM contact!" brought Zakayev back to the present in the CCP. "I read four X-band commercial ship search radars and two land-based. And a Decca TM radar, probably an Oslo-class frigate."

"ESM down. Sonar?" Litvanov queried.

"Radiated noise levels are heavily degraded, Kapitan. But I, too, have four contacts, perhaps a fifth. The four are definitely single-screw commercials."

Litvanov noted with satisfaction that the contacts had already been entered into the fire control system as Alpha One through Five.

"How much water under the keel?"

"Sixty meters, Kapitan," Veroshilov sang out.

"Make your depth thirty meters. Easy, and don't overshoot."

"Aye, Kapitan, thirty meters."

"Those four contacts are merchantmen heading into and out of Stavanger," Litvanov said to Zakayev. "There'll be more of them as we work south, and we'll use them to mask our entry into the Skagerrak. In the

Kattegat, we can pick up a southbound merchantman and tuck in behind, follow him right through The Sound into the Baltic. And maybe shake those damned Norsk frigates they keep sending out."

Zakayev recalled what he'd seen on a chart: two narrow bodies of water between Norway, Denmark, and Sweden, and a strait with an hourglasslike shape between Denmark and southern Sweden called The Sound. During their planning sessions in St. Petersburg, Litvanov had cautioned that to transit The Sound without being detected would be difficult and dangerous. Litvanov had said that he suspected that The Sound was sown with static sonar devices and other defenses to warn the Danes and Swedes of incursions by foreign submarines. "Can you do it?" Zakayev had asked. "Of course I can," Litvanov had bragged.

Now Litvanov commanded, "Double the sonar watch. We're closing up on Swedish waters. Starpom, you have the conn. I'll be in the wardroom."

"He'll die if we don't get him ashore," Alex said. She put a cool hand on Botkin's forehead. "Feel him. He's on fire. He needs proper medical attention." His face was red from radiation burns and swollen with edema.

Scott felt Botkin's skin but said nothing. What could he say? Botkin had known the danger he faced before he entered the reactor compartment.

"Jake, did you hear what I said?" Alex insisted.

"There's nothing I can do."

"Alex, Jake is right," said Abakov, slumped in the doorway to sick bay. The air was very bad and getting worse, and Abakov, like everyone else, showed the effects. "There's nothing we can do for Botkin except make him comfortable."

"We can't just let him die," Alex said.

"What's the standard treatment for radiation sickness?" Abakov said.

"Transfusions to bring up the white cell count, and in serious cases bone marrow transplants. But he's also got thermal as well as radiation burns, and that can lead to infection and death."

"Do we have medicine aboard? Morphine?" Abakov said.

She turned to the radio technician petty officer, who also doubled as the ship's doctor.

"Not much morphine, sir: just a half-dozen syrettes," said the petty officer, a youngster with bad skin and teeth. "That's all they allow on our submarines. We have antibiotics and burn salves. I'll do what I can for him."

"Sorry, Alex," Scott said. He motioned to the petty officer. "Give him morphine as he needs it, until it's gone."

"Aye, Kapitan."

Scott said, "Excuse me."

"Where are you going?" Alex asked.

"Aft to the reactor control compartment, then the CCP to keep track of the Norwegians."

"May I tell you something? You look like hell. You need some rest."

"We all do. But there isn't time."

"Let the engineers worry about the reactor," Alex said. "There's nothing you can do, and anyway, it hasn't been damaged."

"We had a damn close call, but the repair gang performed magnificently. I've asked for hourly reports from the chief engineer on the reactor's condition—just in case."

"Okay, but what about your condition?"

"It's nothing a fresh atmosphere wouldn't cure." He jammed a Russian Navy cap on his head and went forward.

Alex's shoulders sagged. She looked at Abakov. The policeman said, "We have to follow his orders. Jake is the *kapitan* now."

The watch stirred when Scott entered the CCP. The *starpom* came to attention, something not required by Russian or U.S. Navy regulations.

Scott said, "Your report, Starpom?"

"Watch Condition Two set throughout the ship, sir. Steering course one-seven-zero. Speed ten knots. Depth three-zero meters. Reactor normal, both turbines on line. Battery charge to finishing rate and float. At fifteen-thirty both targets retracted their towed sonar arrays and reversed course to one-six-eight. Target bearings are one-five-zero and one-five-nine. Speeds are twenty-eight knots. Range fifteen kilometers and opening out."

"Outstanding," Scott said.

"Thank you, Kapitan."

Though there were no secrets aboard a submarine, Scott had toured the ship to inform the crew of Botkin's condition and of his actions, which had prevented a disaster. And to praise them for fixing the coolant leak and preventing a disaster. He soon noticed that a profound change had come over the crew. No longer sullen and indifferent, they were eager to prove themselves capable of turning in a good performance for their American skipper. Their undisguised scorn for Botkin had evaporated, too, his heroics evoking their respect and, in some men, a sense of awe.

"Maintain present course and speed for another twenty minutes, until we're sure both targets are over the hill. Then we'll go ahead full on both engines."

"Aye, Kapitan."

"Chief electrician."

"Sir?" The chief electrician, a sailor in his late twenties and one of the oldest men on board, was standing watch at the main electrical control panel in the CCP.

"Any luck fixing the $CO_2$ scrubber?"

"I put two men on it, Kapitan. They think they can repair the burned-out element. Maslov is making what you call a 'jury-rig.' "

"Excellent."

The electrician gave Scott a lopsided grin.

Scott exited the CCP, feeling for the first time since leaving Olenya Bay, that he had a crew and a better-than-even chance of nailing the *K-363.*

At SOSUS Control, Stavanger, Norway, Petty Officer Niles Horve listened closely to the threshing machine–like sounds of ships' propellers coming through his headphones from the Skagerrak. He heard the familiar sounds made by ore carriers, container ships, fishing vessels, and ferry traffic steaming in and out of Kristiansand, a port city on the southern tip of Norway. But he also heard something else: a faint three-hundred-hertz tone. A moment later it was gone.

To neutralize interference and make a positive ID on the whisper, Horve keyed extra layers of filtration and modulation into the acoustic spectrum analyzer, then replayed what he'd just heard. Though the Norwegian SOSUS network, modeled on the U.S. Navy's version, used powerful computerized signal processors, it still required a sonar expert like Horve to identify a specific target from among the scores that daily crisscrossed Sector Five in the Skagerrak.

Horve hunched over his console and, with eyes closed, pictured the SOSUS arrays on the sea bottom. Each array consisted of a bundle of twenty-four hydrophones sealed in a tank. Each tank—there were dozens in the Skagerrak and Kattegat—had hardened links to submarine cables that transmitted data to the collection point ashore to which Horve and other technicians like him were assigned. The system was old, and even though parts of it had been shut down to save money when the Cold War ended, it still worked.

After isolating the short sound segment that had gotten his attention, Horve began the process of comparing its generated signal to the center's recognition file by merging them in the computer. As the information collected underwent instantaneous processing and updating, simple triangulation and a calculation of the time required for the sound waves to travel between individual arrays provided the target's speed and base course. The computer sped through its process and in less than a minute had a match, which it displayed as a box filled with numbers and symbols on Horve's monitor. Horve gave a start: a Russian Akula. Moving northeast at seven knots. In Norwegian territorial waters!

Horve reached for the red phone that connected him to the watch commander.

Captain Thore Jacobsen swiped his encapsulated pass through the lips of a verification terminal under the flinty gaze of the security officer on duty outside the SOSUS control node. The facility was layered with electronic sensors and a heavily armed response force. The proper authorization code appeared and the terminal peeped once. Lock bolts flew back; the door to the control node opened on silent hydraulic actuators; and

Jacobsen, the SOSUS control station's commanding officer, entered the node.

The watch commander greeted Jacobsen and led the way to a small conference room equipped with computer terminals and media drives to which Chief Horve had uploaded the material he'd analyzed and identified earlier.

"Yes, definitely an Akula," Jacobsen said, after he'd listened to the audio and viewed the signal merge.

The watch commander said, "We ran it through a dual phase and it came up positive. Awfully quiet, those Akulas. Horve was very lucky to find her, what with the noise of the weather making up."

"Good work, Chief," Jacobsen said, stepping back from the bank of computer gear.

"Thank you, Captain. I'm only sorry we couldn't snatch a longer segment to analyze."

"Couldn't pick her up again?"

"I tried but she was gone and I couldn't reacquire. I've run the tapes from Sectors Five through Eight, even into the Göteborg area, but heard nothing."

"Any chance the Russian turned back?"

"I'd have heard him if he had."

"In that case we'll see what our Swedish colleagues have to say."

"I have the message traffic you wanted from Captain Bayer, sir," the watch commander said. "We've also seen an increase in U.S. P-3 overflights."

"Thank you." Jacobsen scratched his cheek. "Seven knots. The Russian's a creeper, and in littorals at that. He's definitely trying to avoid us. What's he up to?"

Jacobsen flipped through Bayer's reports on recent contacts in the north with an elusive target. "What it means," Jacobsen said, answering his own question, "is that earlier, Bayer made contact with this same Russian. Have you run those tapes for matches, Chief?"

"Yes, sir. Thermocline degrades. No positives."

Jacobsen nodded his understanding. "That Russki's been hugging the coast all the way south. Up to no good, I'd say." He turned to the map on the wall. "Show me where you think he is now, Chief."

Horve got up and pointed to a spot on the Norwegian coast near Bergendal. "Right here."

"Very well. Put a twenty-four-hour watch on Sectors Five through Eight. Feed what you have directly to me."

"Aye, aye, sir."

"Meanwhile we'll get Bayer and his group down here. What else is available that I can recommend to ComInC?"

The watch commander said, "We have two new Norsk-class frigates on training standby in Stavanger. They could be activated."

"Very well." Jacobsen, dismayed, shook his head slowly. "The damned Russians. The Cold War's over and we still can't trust them. But maybe we can blow them to the surface and teach them a lesson."

# 15

## East of Stavanger, Norway

"How is he?" said Scott.

Botkin's skin had blistered badly and the edema had spread. His face was so swollen that he was almost unrecognizable.

"Not good," Alex said hoarsely. "He's not going to make it."

Scott refused to feel guilty. "He's on an IV. That'll help some. And he's doped up so he's not in pain."

Alex slumped forward against the upper bunk in which Botkin lay. She lowered her forehead to the back of both hands gripping the bunk's side rails. She stood like that for a long moment until Scott touched her and she lifted her head. She looked exhausted.

"Let Doc spell you."

"No, I'm all right," Alex said. Though it wasn't necessary, she adjusted the blanket covering Botkin and checked his IV.

"We've been picking up Norwegian and Swedish signals activity on ESM. Some not too far away. Thought you'd want to know."

"They're looking for us?"

"They know a submarine's in the area. They may not know there's two of us. Not yet, anyway."

Alex turned around and leaned against the bunk, a thumb hooked in the pocket of her coveralls. She looked at Scott, then looked away. With her free hand she tried to do something with her hair. "I'm sorry I look so awful."

"I like the way you look."

"Like this? Please. When this is over, I'm going to sit in a *banya* for a week." She meant the steam bath favored by Russians. "Do all submarines smell as bad as this one?"

"Did you ever hear the term *pigboat?*"

"I think so."

"In the early days of submarines it was an apt description of what sailors endured. It went out of favor during World War II, but I suppose it describes our present situation."

"I'd say so." She picked at her coveralls and wrinkled her nose.

He wanted to touch her again, but the moment for it seemed to have passed.

"How's Yuri holding up?" she asked.

"Just fine, now that the oxygenerator is back on line. He's in the CCP, taking a trick at the diving station."

"He is?"

"The *starpom*'s coaching him on the diving planes. He caught on quick. He's a natural."

"Something to tell his kids when he gets back." She caught herself. "If we get back."

"I thought you'd also want to know that heavy weather has moved in. It'll mask our movements, the *K-363*'s too. Things may get a little dicey soon."

"I know that."

He pushed away from the bunk and made to go, but

Alex put a hand on his arm. "When we get back . . ."

"We'll get back."

She kissed his streaked face. "Thanks."

"Look after Botkin," he said, and departed.

Scott stuck the point of a pair of navigation dividers into Gotland, off the eastern coast of Sweden in the Baltic Sea.

"Gotland is good cover for a submarine operating in the Baltic. Believe me, I know, because I've been there and used it to hide from Russian naval units."

The *starpom* looked up from the chart and gave Scott a nod of grudging admiration. "We were told, sir, that American submarines conducted intelligence-gathering operations in the Baltic. I didn't believe it, but now I do."

"At the same time," Scott said, "we'll be operating in a littoral zone and the limitations it imposes on sub hunting."

"Shallow coastal water," Abakov said.

"Right. Turbulence, littoral marine life, bars and channels, turbidity, and pollution. They pose risks to underwater navigation and degrade sonar. So we have to go where we expect the *K-363* to go, but try to get there first."

"And lay a trap," Abakov said.

"Not so easy to do, Kapitan," said one of the senior warrant officers.

"No. I expect they'll continue to hug the coast, which will make it hard to find them, much less head them off. If we hug the coast, we'll never catch them. Instead, I'm proposing we make a full-out dash across the Skagerrak, cut around the northern coast of Denmark at Skagen, then see if we can't pick them up as they work south, somewhere near the island of Anholt."

"But Kapitan, the Danes and Swedes will hear us, no?" said the *starpom.*

"It's a risk we have to take." Scott looked around at the eager faces of the submariners. "Very well, up periscope. Raise the ESM mast."

The mast rose; the collection panel lit up.

"Various contacts, Kapitan. Sea- and shore-based radars, VHF, UHF, commercial mostly."

Even at full dark and with a gale building, traffic was still heavy, the Skag and the Katt forming a funnel for ships heading for ports in Denmark, Sweden, and the Baltic. That same traffic could pose a hazard to submerged running if enough ship captains grew cautious and decided to anchor in the roadstead north of The Sound to ride out the storm.

"Sonar, report."

"Many contacts, Kapitan. Too numerous to differentiate. None close aboard."

Scott raised the scope to its full height to get above the heavy swells riding over the scope's head, cutting off his view. He walked the scope around and saw only an impenetrable curtain of rain beating on the heaving sea, which registered on sonar as a steady hiss like interference on a radio. He switched to infrared and saw heat blooms from the power plants of two monstrous freighters heading west.

"Down scope. Come to course zero-seven-zero. Make your depth one hundred meters. Both engines ahead full."

Scott gambled that the racket made by rain and wind on the sea would mask their turbines and passage through the water at high speed. He waited as the *K-480* nosed down and accelerated to twenty-five knots.

He stood in the CCP pitying Botkin, not feeling comfortable in his role as skipper of a Russian Akula, but nevertheless relishing the power it conferred. There was nothing that compared with the utter sense of freedom and responsibility that came with command of a submarine, even a Russian one.

"New sonar contact, Kapitan," pulled Scott from his reverie. "Faint but fast: a two-screw ship."

"Maybe an ASW frigate. Can you identify him?"

"Aye, Kapitan, definitely a frigate, possible Norsk-class, but I can't be sure."

"One of their new ones. Bearing?"

"Rain and our speed through the water is degrading the signature. . . . Bearing . . . bearing . . . one-nine-five, now one-nine-four, one-nine-three . . ."

"Dropping abaft the port beam," Scott observed.

"Gone, Kapitan."

For a moment Scott considered slowing down to get a better read on the contact but decided not to. "Let's move it. Both engines ahead flank."

"Aye, both engines ahead flank."

Annunciators clinked ahead; the engine room pointer answered bells.

The turbines spooled up; Scott felt power surge to the screw. Any worries he'd had about possible damage to the reactor vanished as the *K-480* accelerated to thirty knots.

"I swear to you, Kapitan, it was an Akula."

"You're absolutely sure?" Litvanov said.

The sonarman removed his headphones, hung them around his neck, and looked up at his captain hovering over the sonar console. "I swear, Kapitan, on my mother's grave. It was an Akula. I heard her pumps kick in. And here"—he pointed to the spikes on the screen—"I reconfigured the sonar aperture for a Norwegian Ula-class or a German Type 207 diesel submarine, but it rejected both."

"Not a Swedish boat? A Gotland- or Näcken-class? Or an American 688I?"

"No, sir, an Akula. Like us."

Litvanov considered, then said, "Do you have a bearing? He's been on a southeasterly course."

"I think zero-three-two but not constant."

"Is he closing?"

"I think so, Kapitan, but can't confirm."

"Then we'll move southeast, too, and find him." Litvanov patted the sonarman on the back. "Good, good."

"So?" Zakayev said, when Litvanov returned to the CCP.

"We seem to have company. A Russian boat. An Akula."

"How can you be sure?" the girl asked.

"I told you before that someone was after us. Moscow doesn't just happen to have an Akula nosing around in the Skag and the Katt. No, someone is out there hunting for us."

Litvanov, thinking, ran a hand over beard stubble.

"But who could be in command of the hunter?" he wondered out loud. "We have so few qualified commanders." Stumped, he looked at Zakayev. "No matter. Now that we know he's out there we can set a trap and kill him."

"Set a trap where?"

"I think," Litvanov said, "somewhere near The Sound. Submarine skippers are like cats: stealthy but curious. Do you know the old saying?"

"Yes. 'Curiosity killed the cat,' " said the girl.

"Then we'll find us a cat," Litvanov said.

* * *

Petty Officer Horve heard it but didn't want to believe it: a second Akula, this one making a high-speed dash across the Skagerrak on a southeasterly track. He listened for several minutes to her thrumming machinery and churning prop. He'd never seen a real Akula, only pictures, but was impressed with their streamlined good looks and especially the way they sat low in the water when on the surface. He'd once monitored an American Improved Los Angeles–class submarine and remembered thinking how quiet she was. But the Russian boat with her rafted machinery was quiet, too, perhaps even quieter than the American when she wanted to be. So why would this Russian be wailing away in the Skagerrak? He decided that not only couldn't the Russians be trusted, they were also crazy.

Horve waited until he had an explicit sound profile match from the acoustic spectrum analyzer showing on his monitor, then reached for the phone.

Captain Thore Jacobsen didn't like what he saw: two Akula profiles tagged A-1 and A-2.

"Not a peep from either of them in over two hours, Captain," said Horve. "Lost them."

Jacobsen massaged his nose. "Karlskrona also reports that they have no contacts," he said, referring to the Swedish Navy's headquarters. "Doesn't surprise me. Their SOSUS net is old and very thin. They've agreed to deploy two patrol craft out of Hälsingborg. If the weather clears, they may be able to give us a HKP helo."

Jacobsen turned to the wall map.

"According to our information, the tracks of both A-1 and A-2, if computed out, suggest a convergence in the vicinity of Göteborg. That's where we should concentrate our efforts."

"Commander Bayer is coming up from the south," the watch commander said. "Those two new Norsk-class frigates from Stavanger should join Bayer's group at about eighteen hundred."

"Very well," Jacobsen said. "I'll brief ComInC. Meanwhile, let's see if we can figure out what game the Russians are playing."

Captain Bayer studied the decrypted message from Stavanger. "Two contacts. They have positive IDs on two Akulas." He looked up at Executive Officer Dass, whose surprise mirrored his own. "We've been authorized to force them to surface."

"One of them must be the sub we tracked down the west coast, sir."

"Which means the bastard got by us."

Dass said nothing. Bayer was still fuming over that.

"Let's take a look," Bayer said. He headed for the CIC, Dass in tow, careful of each step he took over the heaving deck.

He pushed aside the swaying blackout curtain and rapped on the door leading to CIC, which flew open immediately. Weapons Officer Mayan and Sonar Officer Garborg met the captain.

"Just received this," said Bayer. He handed Mayan the message. Mayan read it and handed it off to Garborg.

Bayer drew a circle with his finger around the coastal area near Göteborg, Sweden. "Stavanger says this is the possible convergence area."

"Big," Dass observed.

"Indeed," Bayer agreed. "Too big. But we'll have help from *Norsk* and *Kalix*."

Mayan reread the message. "Sir, we're practically in

Swedish territorial waters. Is this all they can give us: two PCs?"

"It'll just have to do. Meantime, we have to establish a patrol line near Göteborg. As you know, gentlemen, there are no restrictions on submarines transiting these waters to reach the Baltic Sea, but they must do it while on the surface and with proper advance warning. Transiting submerged is an altogether different matter. It smacks of secrecy and also violates treaties established to prevent transit of neutral waters by belligerents in time of war."

"Sir, if we can find them, do we attack?" Garborg asked, swaying as the ship lurched underfoot.

"Yes," Bayer said, then added, "if we find them in Norwegian territorial waters." He grabbed an empty coffee mug about to fly off the heaving plot table and returned it to Garborg. "I don't want to create an international incident reminiscent of the Cold War, but we must enforce the rules."

"Might they be heading for The Sound?" Mayan said.

"Who knows what they're up to," Bayer said. "They're Russians. Russians do bizarre things. I mean, you've heard of Russian roulette, haven't you?" He tapped the chart. "When *Norsk* and *Kalix* arrive, they can anchor the western end of our patrol line. We are not to interfere with commercial traffic in any way. Also, this weather will play hell with our VDS."

Garborg grimaced, knowing how difficult it was going to be to deploy the cable and sonar receptor.

Bayer was thinking the same thing. "Mind the hands, Mr. Garborg," cautioned the captain. "I don't want to lose anyone overboard. Not for a damned Russian, I don't."

Mikhail Grishkov, dressed in good civilian clothes, got out of a black Zhiguli in front of the pair of green gates at the entrance to the Novodevichy Cemetery on Luzhnetsky Proyzed. He waited until the Zhiguli drove off to the parking lot, then crossed to the kiosk and bought a ticket to enter the cemetery.

"Tour?" asked the ticket seller.

Grishkov shook his head and, turning away and pausing for a moment, turned up the astrakhan collar of his topcoat. It was a filthy gray Moscow day threatening snow, and he was glad he wore a fedora and gloves.

Grishkov marveled at how times had changed. For more than thirty years the cemetery, without explanation, had been closed to the public. Everyone knew it had been closed because the controversial Nikita Khrushchev, after being denounced by Leonid Brezhnev, had been buried here rather than in Red Square with other Soviet leaders. During the Cold War, to visit his grave was to commit a crime against the state. Then came glasnost and with it the rehabilitation of Khrushchev and the reopening of the cemetery so ordinary citizens could visit his grave as well as the graves of famous Russians like Anton Chekhov and the composer Aleksandr Scriabin.

Admiral Stashinsky's insistence on meeting at Khrushchev's grave on such a cold day annoyed Grishkov. But then, Stashinsky had entered the navy as a midshipman only weeks after the Cuban Missile Crisis broke, when Khrushchev had Kennedy by the balls. Perhaps Stashinsky wanted to make a point about those long-ago events. Grishkov kept his head down and thought how much better to make the point someplace warm, like Stashinsky's sumptuous office, with its fireplace and hot tea.

A cold wind blowing off the Moskva River plastered dead leaves against Grishkov's trouser legs. He put his head down and held on to his fedora, which was threatening to fly away, and started down the long tree-lined walkway that led to the once-infamous gravesite at the rear of the cemetery. He acknowledged the *babushki,* grandmothers posted throughout the cemetery, no matter what the weather, to give tourists directions.

Up ahead he saw the black and white marble slab that marked Khrushchev's grave: black and white to symbolize the contrasts, it was said, if not the contradictions of Khrushchev's rule. Grishkov found the site pleasantly quiet, the only disruptions a helicopter *wok-wok-wok*ing northeast up the Moskva River and the singing of traffic on the expressway carving past the cemetery on the south.

At first Grishkov didn't see Stashinsky. Only after a group of six American tourists viewing the grave had moved on did he notice the admiral, also dressed in civilian clothes, standing with hands deep in the pockets of his topcoat.

Stashinsky seemed to sense Grishkov's presence. Or perhaps it was when a member of his security detail made his presence known to Grishkov by stepping out from behind a tall headstone nearby.

"Mikhail Vladimirovich!" Stashinsky stripped off a glove and approached Grishkov with a hand extended. "But you are alone."

Grishkov glanced at the security man. "I am used to being alone."

Stashinsky frowned. "You should take precautions. Everyone in Russia is a target today."

"I feel safe here with you, Admiral."

Stashinsky made no more of it and steered Grishkov toward Khrushchev's grave. "I used to come here fairly often, but now it's only twice a year. Thank you for indulging me."

Grishkov said nothing.

In the biting cold Stashinsky's face looked dead gray and showed patches of white beard stubble he'd missed shaving. "I want to apologize for the rude way I treated you during our last meeting. It was unfair to criticize you for things over which you have no control. I'm speaking of course about the Barents Sea operation. I spoke to the President and he understands now."

"Please, there is no need to apologize."

They came to the grave and halted. Stashinsky stood with fingers linked and head slightly bowed, looking at the cold marble. "It's ironic, don't you think, that Khrushchev was the architect of his own downfall. His denunciation of Stalin, the breach with China, the Cuban Missile Crisis. It seems an appropriate lesson for our present situation."

"What situation is that, Admiral?"

"Our confrontation with the Americans."

Their shoulders began to collect snowflakes spiraling from the sky.

"I've read everything written about Khrushchev," said Stashinsky. "He made mistakes but was a great man. Mind, I'm not suggesting we should return to those days, but there was a sense of purpose we Russians shared, especially those of us in the military. This of course was before your time, Mikhail Vladimirovich. We were fighting for the survival of our motherland against the Americans."

Grishkov said nothing.

Snowflakes clung to Stashinsky's hair. He brushed them away as he said, "The only mistake Khrushchev made was not being tough enough. He had Kennedy by the balls and let him go. Had he stuck to his plan, he could have wrung concessions out of Kennedy and could have kept our missiles in Cuba."

"And could have started a nuclear war," Grishkov said.

"I've studied the evidence and don't believe it would have come to that. Kennedy was weak and inexperienced. He was on the verge of shitting his pants and was ready to give in when Khrushchev made his fatal error."

"He overestimated Kennedy's resolve and capitulated first."

"Now you see my point."

"You think we need to get tough with the Americans over the *K-363.*"

"Of course. We know they want to find and sink the *K-363* before we do."

Grishkov noticed that the snow had started coming down heavier.

"The Americans don't want Zakayev to fall into our hands," Stashinsky said. "They want him dead."

Grishkov nodded.

"They don't want him to tell us things that might be damaging to the U.S. Things that might undermine the summit meeting and the U.S. plan to topple Iran and Syria and for which they need our cooperation. And most of all, because they don't want us to know about U.S. involvement in Chechnya and support for Zakayev."

Grishkov held Stashinsky's gaze. "I thought that rumor had been put to bed."

Stashinsky snorted again. "Rumors have a way of coming back like a bad dream. I will tell you this, Mikhail Vladimirovich: The information I have comes from the top, from one of Moscow's most senior individuals. Someone who has access to highly privileged information—information so secret that only three men other than the president have seen it."

"And you are one of them."

"It's all there. Not in black and white, mind you, no hard evidence, nothing that would stand up in a court of law. Always there are prevarications and caveats and nuances of interpretation. But if one reads between the lines and applies common sense, you can see why the Americans are so eager to get rid of Zakayev. Because they have blood on their hands."

Grishkov ran through in his mind how the people at the top might have gotten such damaging evidence of U.S. involvement with Zakayev and Chechen terrorism. But Stashinsky was saying, "The American naval officer, Drummond. It was his failure to head off Zakayev that set off the alarm for the Americans."

"Yes, I remember Drummond: murdered in questionable circumstances, in Murmansk. There was a sailor involved."

"A setup, I assure you, Mikhail Vladimirovich. Zakayev handled it. The FSB investigated and wrote a report. Now we have the *Amerikanski*, Scott, on the *K-480.*" Stashinsky growled. "The *K-480*. A Russian submarine with two Americans aboard, one of them a naval officer, the other one a woman. *A woman!* What was I thinking when I authorized it? I should have had my head examined."

"She's a scientist," Grishkov offered.

"She's a spy."

"But there's also the FSB officer, Abakov. He's Russian."

Stashinsky waved a hand. "The Americans still claim to know nothing of the *K-480*'s whereabouts. As you reported, they are putting on an act that they're looking into the possibility she's gone down."

Grishkov nodded. Stashinsky's hair was getting snowier; so was Grishkov's fedora. They saw a pair of male tourists coming toward them. One held a deployed green, white, and red Cinzano umbrella over their heads.

"We absolutely must find Zakayev and Litvanov before the Americans do," Stashinsky said. "Even if it means shifting all our forces out of the Barents Sea to the south."

"That will take days."

"Then use what you have in the Baltic. Everything. Even if you have to send in every helicopter and plane and auxiliary and oiler and barge we have. Just do it. The only thing the Americans understand is force and resolve. We have to demonstrate what we are capable of."

"I'll do what I can. But I must tell you, Admiral, we are not in good shape in the Baltic. The Americans know it too. If we do what you say, it may send the wrong signal and make us look desperate."

"On the contrary, it will clog up the Baltic and make it difficult for them to operate freely. I'm for anything that will impede their hunt for the *K-363.*"

"It may also impede our own hunt for the *K-363.*"

"We are looking for only one submarine, not an entire fleet."

"Actually, if this American, Scott, shows up, we may end up having to deal with two submarines. It could be difficult telling them apart. I wouldn't want to make a mistake and sink the wrong one. It could happen, you know. And if it did, the Americans would shit their pants."

Stashinsky smiled and pointed to Khrushchev's grave, turning white with snow. "I think Nikita would like that."

# 16

## North of Anholt

After sorting for hours through dozens of false contacts, sonar reported: "Kapitan, contact! A submarine—an Akula!"

Scott donned a pair of spare headphones and listened to it. How many times had he heard Akulas while patrolling off the Kola Peninsula, in the Atlantic Ocean off Spain, and once off the coast of South Carolina?

"Faint. Very faint. A three-hundred-hertz line bearing zero-three-two; for sure it's the *K-363.*"

Scott had slowed their headlong dash across the Skagerrak, and, north of Læsø, had started hunting for the *K-363*. At first there had been nothing to hear but the normal squeal and pop of sea life, the groaning shift of sand and bottom debris, and the sound of wind-driven waves, which provided perfect cover for a submarine.

Scott had hesitated to deploy the submarine's ultra-sensitive towed sonar array from its stowage pod on the after vertical fin, fearing that the noise it would make reeling out might alert the *K-363.* To find their target, he was relying solely on the *K-480*'s MGK-503 passive bow sonar array and the sensitive ears of his sonarmen.

The *K-363* was quiet but not totally silent. Her slowly turning seven-bladed prop created a corkscrew of collapsing bubbles and low-amplitude pressure ridges that bounced off the seabed and radiated outward from the coast. Little by little the MGK-503 sonar suite stripped away the *K-363*'s cover. A half hour into the search a green spike—a three-hundred-hertz tone—began to crawl down a video monitor in the sonar room.

"Fire Control. Range?"

"Under twenty kilometers, Kapitan."

Scott checked the bathythermograph readout. The *K-480* was enveloped in a layer of cold water, which had piped long-range sound reception from the slow-moving *K-363* into the *K-480*'s sonar.

"Bearing?"

"Three-three-zero, steady."

"Excellent. Can you nail down his base course?"

"Aye, Kapitan."

"Now let's see if we can ease on in without being detected," Scott explained to Abakov, who by now had a good grasp of tactics.

"Maybe he's already heard us," Abakov said. "And is expecting us."

"Maybe," Scott said. "But he's operating on the edge, where his sonar's ability to detect targets is degraded."

"Because he's in littoral waters?"

"Exactly. We may be able to sneak right up on him and stick a fish up his ass."

Scott glanced at the fire control console. The *K-480*'s four 650mm torpedo tubes were loaded with Type 65-76 antiship torpedoes and the 533mm tubes held TEST-71M antisubmarine acoustic wire-guided homing torpedoes. She also had six 400mm bow tubes loaded with acoustic decoys. Rows of illuminated green lights on the fire control console indicated the status of each weapon and decoy.

"Kapitan, Fire Control. Target is on base course one-five-two degrees."

Scott laid a steel rule on the chart's compass rose and saw that 152 degrees from due north pointed south-southeast to the entrance of The Sound. The *K-480*'s present course was the hypotenuse of a right-angle triangle, while the *K-363*'s course was the height. If nothing changed, the two submarines would meet at the tip of the triangle.

"He's heading for the Baltic Sea," Abakov said, looking over Scott's shoulder at the chart.

"Damn right. Starpom, call away battle stations: Pass the word by mouth. I don't want our friends in the *K-363* to hear the gongs."

"Aye, Kapitan, battle stations away."

The men in the CCP and in other parts of the submarine had been alert to the subtle changes that a submarine undergoes when tracking a target and had been hovering near their battle stations, anticipating the call. Now they sprang into action.

Scott looked around the CCP and saw the fire control plotters at work; the auxiliarymen at their manifold controls; that the diving station was fully manned and ready. Reports came in from every part of the ship. Engine room, auxiliary machinery spaces, reactor control. In the torpedo room a deck below the CCP, torpedomen had run tests on their fish and double-checked their circuits and links to the fire control station in the CCP.

"All stations manned and ready, Kapitan," the *starpom* reported.

As the *K-480* closed in and the *K-363*'s relative bearing changed, the tactical display on the fire control plotter changed with it, constantly updating information the torpedoes needed to find their target.

Scott saw Alex ease into the CCP. She'd been tending Botkin and looked exhausted. Abakov said something to her that Scott couldn't hear but saw her shake her head no.

"What's going on?" she asked Scott.

"We have sonar contact with the *K-363*. I don't know what's going to happen in the next hour or so, but you're welcome to stay here." His eyes roamed her fatigued face. "How's Botkin?"

"Same." She looked around as if seeing the CCP for the first time, its lights, its equipment, the men themselves taut with expectation. "Is this the real thing, Jake? Are you trying for a kill?"

The tension had risen until it was palpable. The men, intent on their duties, had reached the point that they were unaware of anything or anyone around them. It was the moment they had trained for, and the payoff would soon be theirs to savor. Even Alex had been affected. Consciously or not, both her hands had a white-knuckle grip on the railing around the periscope stand.

There was no need to explain. She could see for herself that something extraordinary might happen soon. Yet, Scott wondered if it could be this simple, that on his first contact with the *K-363* he might nail her with a clean shot. He knew it was never that easy and tempered his anticipation of the kill with a dose of reality. Anything could happen and probably would. Expect it and you won't be taking a torp up your own ass. . . .

"Kapitan, sonar! Multiple contacts bearing on an arc

one-two-zero through two-two-zero. . . . Norsk-class frigates . . . and . . . the Oslo-class frigates we heard before!"

Scott donned headphones and heard the noise from ships' machinery distorted by heavy seas. "You're sure?" he asked the sonarman.

"Positive, Kapitan. I have them up and matched. Look."

One set of sound profiles matched the two Oslos perfectly. The Norsk-class ships were new and Russian boats didn't yet have their individual profiles recorded but instead had signatures of their distinctive-sounding Laval-Ljungstrom gas turbine power plants. The picture had cleared slightly and Scott didn't like what he saw: a line of Norwegian ASW frigates driving the *K-480* toward the *K-363*.

Scott said, "They're going to drive us south whether we like it or not, right into the approaches to The Sound. If the Swedes haven't already been alerted, they will be now."

Abakov took a quick look at the chart. The Sound was in Swedish-Danish waters. "What about the Danes?"

"Their ASW capability is nil, so they'll rely on the Swedes to screen The Sound to prevent a submarine from getting through submerged. They can't shut it down completely because of all the commercial traffic that passes through."

Scott saw the look of concern on Abakov's face and said, "That's right, we're about to be painted into a corner."

"Kapitan, I have contact with numerous targets."

"Do you have the Akula?" asked Litvanov.

The sonarman slowly nodded. "I think so, a three-hundred-hertz tone line, but faint. Masked by the frigates and commercials. Bearing zero-nine-five. Range rate closing, fifty yards a minute. "

"Fire Control. How does that compute?"

"Range under twenty kilometers, sir, perhaps less."

Litvanov glanced at Zakayev to confirm that his description of how hard it could be to slip through The Sound might yet prove true.

Litvanov had also pointed out the hazards seafarers faced when approaching The Sound. The Russian navigation charts warned of shifting bottom conditions that affected depth, residual danger from old minefields, east-west ferry traffic between Sweden and Denmark, and dangerous setting currents. Veroshilov had also reminded Litvanov of the shallow water in the Kattegat: on average only thirty fathoms, less in the approaches to The Sound.

"We'll let that nosy bastard come to us and then spring a surprise on him," Litvanov said.

"You mean torpedo him?" Zakayev said.

"Not unless I have to," Litvanov said.

"What, then?"

But Litvanov was conferring with his sonarmen.

"Where are those frigates?"

"North, bearing now zero-nine-five."

"What kind of commercial traffic do you have?"

"Mostly single-screw diesel, Kapitan." He pointed to the waterfalls of sound crawling down the sonar screens. "Four big ones, probably container ships and ro-ros." The latter were roll-on/roll-off freighters designed to carry mixed cargoes of cars, trucks, and containers. "Targets are inbound to The Sound and in-line on a track parallel to our own. They all bear due east of Anholt."

"The weather's not slowing them down a bit," Litvanov observed. "A regular freight train. They're either heading for Hälsingborg or Copenhagen." Litvanov turned to Zakayev and the girl and grinned. "Too bad we don't have time for a visit. Copenhagen is a beautiful city."

He mounted the periscope stand.

"Periscope depth. Let's see what we have."

He was right: A freight train of ships partially obscured by rain and mist steamed past the raised periscope like ducks in a shooting gallery. Their green running lights and tiers of white lights strung along their weather decks and top hampers lit them up like a carnival midway. In high magnification and with waves breaking over the scope, Litvanov moved down the train left to right, ticking them off.

"Container ship. Next, a gas hauler." He saw the letters *LNG* for *liquid natural gas* painted on the ship's side in white letters twenty feet high, and, rising above her main deck, four huge domed containers filled with liquid gas. "Third, a ro-ro. Last, a container ship, big bastard, over a hundred and fifty thousand tons. Down periscope."

"So, what do we do?" Zakayev said.

"I like that container ship. Maybe we'll hitch a ride on her into The Sound."

Captain Bayer was pleased but also a little disappointed with his own performance. The new frigate *Kalix*, with her green crew, had made contact at long range with one of the two Akulas now due south of their current position near Anholt. He regretted his earlier decision to deploy *Trondheim*'s VDS sonar because it would restrict maneuver in confined waters. *Narvik* and *Norsk* had also started hauling in. He wanted the Russians for himself but now he would have to share them.

"We're in a hurry, Mr. Garborg," he had said, "but I don't want any casualties." Garborg appreciated Bayer's concern for the sailors who had to manhandle the gear on the ship's fantail but felt the pressure all the same. He knew Bayer was pacing the bridge, waiting for confirmation that the tow had been winched aboard.

"Anything new from *Kalix?*" Bayer asked of Executive Officer Dass.

"She still has a passive contact, sir."

"Do we have an open channel to Stavanger?"

"Yes, sir. Signals is monitoring it. They're standing by."

Bayer had already given the order to change course toward the sonar contact. There was nothing more he could do now but fret. "Sound conditions are very poor," Bayer said to Dass. "I'm surprised *Kalix* made contact at all. Surprised even more that she can hold it."

Bayer looked aft at the floodlit fantail and saw sailors in blue hard hats swarming around the winch. He watched the dripping VDS cable wrap slowly around the take-up spool. It seemed that the retrieval operation would take forever.

"What's our radar picture, Mr. Dass?" said Bayer, gaze planted aft.

"Four heavies still running south in train, Captain."

Bayer started pacing again. "Keep an eye on them. We may have to warn them off the area where that damned Akula is operating. They won't like it, but they'll have no choice."

"Aye, aye, sir."

Bayer paced another ten minutes, until he heard Garborg's report that the sonar body was out of the water. Bayer spun on his heel in mid-stride across the bridge and boomed at Dass. "Both engines ahead full. Set watch condition two."

"Aye, sir. Ahead full. Call away general quarters."

Annunciators clinked and answered. The deck shuddered underfoot. The frigate's bow rose as her screws bit in hard.

"Signals!"

"Aye, sir."

"Send to *Narvik* and *Norsk:* 'Follow on ASAP, et cetera.' Send to *Kalix:* 'Hold position until we go active on sonar, then break off VDS.' Mr. Dass."

"Sir?"

"We're at the fringe of sonar range, but you may go active in five minutes. And stand by on weapons."

"I have three pingers, Kapitan."

"The Norwegians," Scott said. "They're drawing a bead on the *K-363.*"

"What's to prevent them from drawing it on us?" Abakov said.

"Unless we can stay out of their way, nothing."

Scott studied the tactical picture. Three Norwegian frigates pinging with active sonar; the *K-363* somewhere south of the Norwegians, likely near the approach to The Sound; four merchantmen north of the *K-480*'s current position, headed for The Sound.

"If we stick our nose in there now, we're going to get depth-charged by the Norwegians. If we don't, there's a good chance Litvanov will get into The Sound before the Norwegians can head him off."

"Look here, The Sound is only three and a half miles wide," Abakov said, his face practically on the chart. "Can't the Swedes be a stopper in the bottle?"

The Sound had two narrow and shallow ship channels. In some places the water was less than ten fathoms deep. On the Danish side of The Sound at Kronborg Pynt, the southbound channel made a sharp dogleg to the left before opening up for the approach to Copenhagen. It reminded Scott of a pair of cattle chutes.

"They probably don't want to risk a submarine sinking in the channel," Scott said. "It would be better to nail the *K-363* before she gets through or before she reaches Copenhagen."

"Kapitan!" The sonarman handed Scott earphones. "Something . . . !"

Scott heard the familiar shrill pinging of the Norwegians' sonars. Between pings he heard the steady thump, thump, thump of the approaching merchantmen.

Scott said. "Yuri, give a listen. They've gone active. Won't do them much good because Akulas have an anechoic coating on their hulls that defeats active sonar. But you never know. The Norwegians might get lucky."

Abakov heard thrashing screws and the eerie, crystal-clear pings of hull-mounted sonars.

"Right full rudder, come to new course one-five-zero," Scott commanded.

"Right full rudder, aye."

The *K-480* turned to avoid the approaching frigates and merchantmen. Scott had his fingers crossed they wouldn't end up in the sonar cones beating a tattoo on the *K-363*.

"Starpom, bring her up to periscope depth. Time we take a look around."

"They found us!" Litvanov shouted.

Zakayev went white. He heard the pings thudding off

the coated hull, felt the sonic pulses rattling his brain. The girl registered his shock: A hand flew to her mouth. She knew there was no place to hide.

Litvanov glanced up as if trying to see the sonar beams that had them fingered. So much for the *K-363*'s anechoic coating. Parts of it were probably missing. He issued a tangle of orders to helm and engine room. The *K-363* sped up, turned right, and left a knuckle in the water to confuse the frigates' sonar. He counted to ten, then commanded, "Fire one LA decoy!"

It took a moment to flood the ejection tube in the bow and equalize the pressure. Then the air ram in the tube cycled and spit a noisemaker meant to sound like an American Los Angeles–class submarine into the *K-363*'s flow stream.

The *K-363* continued swinging round, away from the whining decoy. Litvanov watched the compass wind clockwise then ordered, "Meet her! Steady on course two-seven-zero! Sonar . . . ?"

"No change, Kapitan."

The pinging frigates seemed as determined as ever.

"They didn't go for it," Litvanov said. "Maybe they'll go for this. Fire Control!"

"Fire Control, aye," the *michman* at the fire control console responded, while Veroshilov supervised the input of data.

"Stand by for target acquisition."

Litvanov's gaze drifted to Zakayev. The general's face was a mask; he knew there was no alternative.

Litvanov said, "Target acquisition . . . target two."

"Target two?" from the *michman*.

"Are you deaf?" Veroshilov bellowed. "The *kapitan* said target two!"

Zakayev stirred. He'd learned how to read the sonar

contacts, but before he could protest, Litvanov cut him off. "It's the only way."

"Target two acquired, Kapitan," said the rebuked *michman.*

Overhead, the pinging grew more intense, more shrill. Zakayev heard the frigates' thrashing, angry screws bearing down from the north. He knew he and his comrades had reached a point of no return and had to fight back.

"Stand by to flood tubes one and two," Litvanov commanded.

"Standing by."

The data monitor at the fire control console blipped to a vertical white line.

"I have a firing solution and generated bearing, Kapitan," said the *michman.*

In the torpedo room, computers aboard the two 53-65 anti-surface-ship torpedoes stabilized and locked.

"Flood tubes one and two and open outer doors," Veroshilov ordered

The *michman* at the fire control console acknowledged that both outer doors had opened. He released the bail on the safety covers over the red-lighted firing buttons, then flipped both safety locks forward to their ARMED positions and watched the lighted buttons change from red to green. In the torpedo room an electrical pulse energized the air ram inside the tubes.

Litvanov glanced up into the overhead. Then at Zakayev.

The *michman*'s thick forefinger hovered over the button marked Tube One.

"Fire one!" Litvanov commanded. A moment later: "Fire two!"

* * *

Bayer forced himself to move, to make his arms and legs work, to make his mind function. The LA noisemaker hadn't fooled him: just an attempt by the Russians to cause confusion. But then he heard Garborg bellowing, "Torpedoes in the water! Torpedoes in the water starboard side bearing zero-eight-zero!"

Bayer's orders came instinctively. A split second later he felt the deck canting left under his feet, felt the *Trondheim* sheering away, heard a cup and plate shatter on deck.

The bridge speaker linked to CIC grabbed his attention when it broadcast the high-pitched up-Doppler *screee* of two homing torpedoes. *Impossible,* Bayer thought. *It's all a mistake.* He heard the ominous peeping of the torpedoes' active sonar hunting for their targets. There was no mistake.

Bayer swung his binoculars to port and saw the *Narvik* and *Norsk* also sheering away at full speed. He swung right and saw the freight train of lit-up merchant ships blithely heading south.

"Captain, torpedoes passing wide to starboard!" It was an excited Garborg in CIC. "They've missed!"

"What? How wide a miss?"

"Almost a thousand meters. . . ."

An alarm went off in Bayer's head. "Mr. Dass!"

"Sir?"

"Raise those merchantmen. Say we have an emergency. Tell them to scatter. Move!"

Dass bolted for the wheelhouse and the radiotelephone.

"Signals!"

"Sir?"

"Raise *Narvik* and *Norsk*. Tell them to reform on us and stand by for orders. Then get me Stavanger."

"Aye, Captain."

Bayer bolted after Dass into the wheelhouse. "Helmsman, come right thirty degrees," he commanded, aiming the *Trondheim* back to the line of merchantmen. In the background he heard Dass on the radiotelephone trying to raise one of the ships but getting no answer.

"Are they deaf?" Bayer said, over his shoulder at Dass. He spun around. "Quartermaster, sound the ship's siren and keep it up until we get their attention."

The *Trondheim* swung right, her bow bucking heavy seas, taking water over her strakes and forward gun mount. The line of merchant ships four kilometers away were now bisected by the *Trondheim*'s jack staff.

A sharp *whoop-whoop-whoop* made Bayer wince. Insane, he thought, a Russian submarine firing torpedoes at unarmed merchantmen. Insane or not, it was an act of war and he and his men were in it now. And so were the men on those merchant ships.

"Where's Stavanger?" he said. "Do we have Stavanger?"

"Still trying, sir. Lost our clear channel."

Bayer stood in the wheelhouse of his ship aware of the massive inflow of information being digested by computers in the Combat Information Center. And no clear channel to Stavanger to warn that a war was about to start.

Bayer raised binoculars to scan the merchant line. His mind worked at lightning speed. How fast are those torpedoes? Fifty knots. Time to target? Under three minutes.

Dass had raised someone on the radiotelephone. A signal lamp on the bridge of the lead ship began to blink on and off.

"Answer them," Bayer ordered.

The signals yeoman, a hand over the phone's mouthpiece, called, "Stavanger, Captain."

But Bayer didn't move. He stood frozen, binoculars to his eyes, staring at the big white *LNG* painted on the side of the second ship in line. He thought to give an order to the helm; to stop their headlong rush into the line of freighters, some stacked high with cargo containers. But it was the ship with four huge green domes filled with liquid natural gas that held his attention for what seemed an eternity, until the world lit up like a million suns.

A shock wave, then scorching heat hit the *Trondheim* as the LNG tanker vaporized before Bayer's eyes.

An underwater shock wave rolled the *K-480* almost on her beam ends. Scott had just enough time to shout a warning and dunk the scope before the shock wave arrived ahead of a deafening blast. He had spotted the LNG tanker, had followed the course of the two torpedoes but didn't want to believe what Litvanov intended until it was almost too late.

"Starpom, get a damage report—all compartments. See if anyone was injured."

"Aye, Kapitan."

"Yuri, lay aft to check on Alex and Botkin."

Three minutes had passed since the initial explosion. It had seemed like three hours. The CCP had not been damaged, but debris littered the deck and crunched underfoot. The dive watch had regained control of the boat, had retrimmed and leveled her out again. Satisfied that they were still seaworthy, Scott took stock of the tactical situation.

"Kapitan, I count five perhaps six contacts," reported the sonarman as Scott listened in.

One contact, a merchantman, was afloat but in two halves. The other two merchantmen, filled with cargo and with little reserve buoyancy, had sunk. Scott heard their bulkheads and hulls moaning in agony as they collapsed and as their cargo-filled compartments ruptured and filled with water. A third ship, the LNG tanker, had simply vanished.

Scott lifted an earmuff.

"These four contacts, here, sir, are the Norwegian frigates. Three of them are dead in the water; the other one is steaming south and has gone active again on sonar."

"They're hunting for the *K-363.*" As Scott watched, fresh sonar contacts from every point of the compass began to blossom on the monitors. "Search and rescue. It's getting busy up there."

"Sir, I'm sorry but I've lost the contact we had on the *K-363,*" said the sonarman.

Scott knew she had escaped, masked by noise from the sinking, collapsing ships, into The Sound.

"Rerun the torpedo run-in sequence. See if we can nail down the *K-363*'s firing point and get a trace on her."

"Aye, Kapitan." The sonarman initiated the backup-and-recall program.

Scott saw Abakov enter the CCP. "How's Alex?"

"Not hurt but shaken up. I put her in the wardroom to rest."

"Good. Botkin?"

Abakov shrugged.

"Stay with her."

"Kapitan, all compartments secure," reported the *starpom.* "No injuries."

"Very well," Scott said. He looked around at the men

in the CCP. They were at their stations waiting for orders. "Periscope depth. We'll see what's what."

A merchantman torpedoed in the Kattegat, men killed, foreign submarines operating in what was essentially Norwegian-Danish-Swedish waters. Scott winced: There would be hell to pay when the world found out.

He gave a thumbs-up. The scope rose. The video monitor rolled diagonal bars then went to points of light as the periscope head broke water. A quick walk-around confirmed what Scott had expected to see: burning debris, sweeping searchlights, a listing Norwegian frigate attended by two mates. Bobbing, twinkling points of light on the sea marking the locations of survivors equipped with flashlights.

"Down periscope. Come to course one-four-zero. Ahead slow. Rerun the video tape half-speed."

Played back, the videotape confirmed that one of the Norwegian frigates had been heavily damaged by the explosion of over six million cubic feet of liquid natural gas cooled to minus 160 degrees Celsius. Torpedoed, the gas aboard the ship had erupted with the force of a small nuclear weapon, and any vessel caught in it would have been sunk or badly damaged. The tidal wave created by the blast would have swamped smaller vessels in the vicinity and destroyed shore installations when it hit the beach.

Scott looked at the men in the CCP and knew they were thinking the same thing he was: The Chechens were determined to start a war.

Returned to the Winter Palace after a performance of Swan Lake by the Mariinsky Theater of St. Petersburg and, earlier, a tour of the restored Amber Room in Catherine the Great's summer palace, the president of the United States slipped off his theater pumps and sipped an iced Sinopskaya vodka.

"And they call Pieter the criminal capital of Russia," he said, using the name St. Petersburgers reserved for their city. "Not that I can see. I've had enough culture to last me the rest of my life. On the other hand, they do have a hell of a porn industry. Seen any live fuck shows, Paul?"

The national security advisor felt his face go hot. "No, sir." He wasn't in the mood for joking with his boss but smiled anyway. Dressed in formal wear as the president was, he stood in the middle of the room, a glass of kvass in his hand. A worried look had displaced his smile.

"Give me a minute, Paul, to catch my breath. It's been a long day and I've got three more days of meetings scheduled. And I can eat only so much caviar." The president, looking very tired, drank some vodka. "Have you heard from Subitov?" he asked, referring to the Russian defense minister.

"A half-dozen times," Friedman said. "His Norwegian counterpart, the others as well."

"What about the press?"

"Nobody's said anything yet. A reporter from *The New York Times* asked what I'd heard about it, but he seemed to believe it was an accident. I don't know how long that will hold up, but so far we're okay on it."

"Is that it, Paul? Is that what Zakayev had in mind all along? Torpedo a liquid natural gas ship and scare the hell out of the Scandinavians?"

Friedman caught the president's undisquised skepticism. "No, sir. That's not what he had in mind."

"Not something that's likely to make the Russians cave, is it?"

"Not hardly. It was a diversion to help him get away from the Norwegians."

The president mulled this, then said, "Let's find out what Karl thinks. Where are we set up?"

"In the library."

The president slipped on his pumps and stood. Two Secret Service men hovering nearby buttoned their jackets and prepared to escort him down the hall to a small private library once used by Nicholas II. To another agent holding the door open he said, "Tell the First Lady I said not to wait up for me."

Two portable video-imaging terminals sat open on a worn trestle table typical of those used by researchers working in the library. Colored cables snaked across the parquet floor linking the terminals to a compact video camera facing the president, and a secure troposcatter satellite system dish antenna. A charged-particle mesh security "bubble" had been assembled from individual panels and erected around the terminal setup.

The president drew up a chair in front of a monitor and said, "Good afternoon, Karl."

A technician started a backup recording to DVD.

"Good evening, Mr. President. Sorry to make this so late for you."

Friedman, sitting in a chair beside the president and facing the other terminal, said, "Karl, what's the latest?"

"Sir, the Norwegians have put the casualty estimate at about eighty dead, eighteen missing. We've confirmed that four ships were sunk. A fifth, the KNM *Trondheim*, a Norwegian frigate, was badly damaged. Her commanding officer and two others were killed. I have a series of satellite photos that will give you some indication of the magnitude of the explosion."

A picture came up on both terminals. Radford explained that it was a side-angle view from high orbit taken at night by the satellite's infrared cameras. The coasts of Denmark and Sweden showed up in bright blue and the Kattegat in bright green. A red heat bloom clearly visible in the center of the photo drew their attention. Radford narrated the series in which the bloom grew to enormous size until it almost touched the coast of Sweden.

"Observers as far away as Stockholm, Sweden, and Hamburg, Germany, reported seeing the flash from the explosion," Radford said. "Some thought a nuclear device had gone off. A couple of TV stations reported one had and you can imagine the panic it set off.

"So far the Norwegians have agreed to our request to say it was an accident aboard an LNG tanker. But it's got a lot of people worked up including the world's shipping lines and Lloyds of London, as well as the UN, who are demanding an immediate investigation. On the technical side we're in agreement with the Norwegians that the LNG tanker took two torpedoes. They know a Russian sub fired them and it's only a matter of time before the Norwegian Navy puts it together and figures it all out. They admitted they've been tracking what they say are two Russian subs for the last week. We know they have the SOSUS contacts to prove it. Also, our cable taps of their communications confirm their suspicions that the Russians may not be in control of their submarines. No one at ComInC Stavanger has yet mentioned the word *terrorist*, but that may only be a matter of time. And it may only be a matter of time before the Norwegians, the Swedes, even the Danes, lodge a protest."

"What about the Russians?" asked the president.

"They're pulling out of the Barents Sea and we're starting to see activity in the Baltic. Mr. President, if they aren't already asking you questions, they soon will."

"Subitov has asked for a private meeting to discuss, as he put it, 'the recent incident,' and I can't put him off. Tomorrow I'll probably hear it from the president himself."

Friedman said, "Karl, have you heard from Grishkov?"

"Not yet. But I will. Bet on it."

The president finished his vodka and set the glass aside. After a long pause he said, "What's happened to Scott?"

"We think he's either in the Kattegat or in the Baltic. We can't be certain, but I believe he's still trailing the *K-363.*"

"Any chance that the *K-363* was sunk in that incident?"

"Doubtful, sir," Radford said. "We would likely have picked it up on satellite. We have the four wrecks heat-spotted—the frigate, too—but no others."

"No traces of her on satellite imagery?"

"No, sir. Our laser satellites can't penetrate those waters. Turbidity leaves us blind."

The president turned to Friedman. "What do you think, Paul? Tell the Russians what we're up to or continue to play innocent?"

Friedman toyed with the studs in his shirt cuffs, both of which had exploded out of his coat sleeves at least half a foot. "Why let on? Let Scott finish it for us. We're that close now."

The president turned to Radford. "Karl, after you talk to Grishkov, see if you can raise Scott and get a status report."

"I'll try, but he may have his hands full right now."

The president turned back to Friedman. "Paul, I can't stonewall the Russians much longer. Subitov is no dummy. If Scott can't nail that bastard Zakayev in another day or two, it's over and we'll have to come clean."

Friedman looked as if he were in physical pain.

"Agreed that Zakayev knows too much. But I'm willing to take a risk that whether it's us or the Russians who find him, he'll end up dead."

After a prolonged silence, Friedman said, "I don't know. I just don't know."

"What don't you know, Paul?"

Radford waited silently in Virginia.

Friedman stuffed his protruding cuffs back into the coat sleeves. "I don't know what Zakayev wants."

"What he wants," said the president, "is to destroy the Russians, bring down their government. That's what he wants."

Friedman looked the president in the eye. "With respect, sir, would you, or would Karl, please tell me how? How is he going to do it? How is he going to destroy the Russians? He has no missiles, no guns, only torpedoes, and they're only good for sinking ships. He proved that when he sank a ship filled with natural gas, sank three other ships filled with a billion dollars' worth of cargo, killed scores of seamen, damaged a Norwegian warship, killed her captain, scared the hell out of a good part of Scandinavia and parts of Germany. Yes, Zakayev is a goddamn terrorist and he hates the Russians and he's run us and them around like a bunch of bloody fools. But he's not doing it for the fun of it or to prove how clever he is or that he can kick the bloody Russians in the ass any time he wants by stealing one of their goddamned submarines. He's got something planned and I don't know what it is, and frankly, sir, it scares the shit out of me and should be scaring the shit out of the Russians too."

Radford smiled, hearing his own words, slightly embellished, aped by Friedman.

Friedman compressed his lips and looked away.

"And it should scare the shit out of me, too, is that what you're trying to say, Paul?"

"I'm sorry, Mr. President. I was completely out of line. I didn't mean that."

"Sure you did. Admit it."

Friedman said nothing.

"Well, if it's any consolation, Paul, Zakayev does scare the shit out of me. All the more reason Scott has to kill him before the Russians get to him."

# 17

## Crystal City, Alexandria, Virginia

Karl Radford looked at his watch and frowned. Downstairs a car waited. In an hour he was to deliver a speech at a breakfast meeting of the Retired Intelligence Officers Association in Arlington, and Grishkov's appearance on the Secure Video Teleconference link to Severomorsk had been delayed.

While he waited he glanced at the computer monitor on his desk and his frown deepened. Displayed were PRs—Pending Replies—to encrypted messages transmitted to various units under SRO control around the world. The list wasn't long; only ten units had been flagged and two were undergoing decryption even as Radford studied the list. But at the top of the list was *Badger One,* Radford's code name for Jake Scott. Next to Scott's name was a blinking red flag that meant there had been no response to the cycle of SRO transmissions broadcast from the Wisconsin ELF facility starting late last night.

Too soon to worry, Radford told himself. Weather in the Kattegat had been bad and getting worse. The attack and its aftermath had required the rerouting of some shipping into and out of The Sound and nearby ports. Satellite photos showed a traffic jam off Falkenberg, Sweden, and another south of Copenhagen. With ships jammed like logs in a river, Scott would indeed have his hands full.

A new message appeared beside *Badger One*. The ELF transmissions had automatically recycled to once every hour instead of every half hour. Too soon to worry, Radford told himself again.

A tone chime from the SVTC got Radford's attention. A digital timer on the monitor counted down to zero and the screen brightened.

Radford cleared his throat and faced the screen. "Hello, Mikhail."

Grishkov, hunched forward on his elbows, had a sour look on his face as if the cigarette he was smoking tasted bad. "Good day, General."

Radford said, "It seems we've been talking on this thing–"

"I warned you not to take us for fools," Grishkov erupted. "The *K-363* torpedoed that LNG carrier, sank those ships, and almost sank a Norwegian frigate, killed her captain–no, don't deny it. We know your Captain Scott witnessed the attack because he has been dogging the *K-363* ever since she departed Olenya Bay. The Norwegians have lodged a protest with our ambassador in Oslo, and have threatened to take the issue to the UN. Our mistake was to fall for your ruse with the *K-480* in the first place. But that's over now. We have ordered our forces in the Baltic Sea to find and capture Zakayev and his terrorist friends."

"Aren't you overlooking something, Admiral?" Radford said frostily.

"What would that be?"

"The Germans, Poles, and Finns, to say nothing of your former republics Estonia and Latvia, which border the Baltic Sea, will want to know what you're up to when they see all that Russian naval activity."

"We are already a step ahead of you. Those countries have been informed that we are conducting exercises. Your president will be informed—today—of our intentions and of our displeasure with your actions. He will be told to refrain from any further actions that will interfere with our capture of the *K-363*, and we expect you to keep our true operations secret from the countries you have mentioned as well as others. Your president will also be informed that if Scott interferes in any way whatsoever, he will be attacked and the *K-480* sunk."

"You can't threaten us," Radford said.

"But we are not threatening you, General. We are simply saying that Captain Scott's and Dr. Thorne's presence on the *K-480* no longer imparts any U.S. authority to a Russian naval vessel. If it comes to it, Scott, Thorne, and even Colonel Abakov will be treated as pirates and, if we capture them along with Zakayev, Litvanov, and his crew, arrested."

"No one is claiming U.S. control over the *K-480*. But we have certain rights under international law."

"I am not an expert on international law, General. But as a sailor I know that the law of the sea states that pirates can be hunted down and brought to trial."

"Scott is not a pirate. And in case you've forgotten, it was you and Admiral Stashinsky who approved his status as an observer on one of your submarines, along with Dr. Thorne and Colonel Abakov."

"Yes, as observers, not as agents of the United States bent on thwarting Russian plans to deal with terrorists."

"No one's thwarting your plans, Mikhail. We can still help you find Zakayev if you'll let us."

Grishkov snorted. "Let you help us when what you want is to kill Zakayev before we can capture and question him. Isn't that so? Isn't that the reason you commandeered the *K-480?*"

Radford willed himself to retain his composure. What did Grishkov know and how thin was the ice they were skating on? "I don't understand what you're getting at. What reason would we have to kill Zakayev?"

"Because you supported Zakayev and his terrorists in Chechnya. And you are afraid he will tell us all about it when we capture him."

"Goddamnit, Mikhail, that's a lie and you know it."

Grishkov said nothing.

"You have no proof that we've ever supported Zakayev."

"I have proof."

"What proof? Where is it?"

Grishkov snorted again. He stood and, leaning on his fists, inclined toward the video camera with its wide-angle lens, which distorted his face on the monitor.

"Where is it, you ask? I'll tell you where. Out there in the Baltic Sea with your Captain Scott, hunting for the *K-363*. He's all the proof I need."

The door opened and Radford's secretary bustled into the office to find him staring at the blank SVTC screen. "General Radford, goodness, you'll be late for your meeting in Arlington."

Radford tore himself away to gather his things under her daunting gaze. "Right. I'm leaving now, Phyllis. Please have the audio summaries of my conversation with Admiral Grishkov on my desk when I return."

She helped him into his coat. "Yes, sir, you'll have them."

A bodyguard at the elevator ushered the admiral aboard. The doors hissed closed. The car dropped. Radford's stomach fluttered. He glanced at his wristwatch with four time zones displayed. He knew the president had been facing a long day of tough negotiating with the Russians in St. Petersburg. What he was going to hear would only make it worse.

Litvanov, exhausted from conning the *K-363* through The Sound behind a Liberian-flagged tanker, planted his elbows on the chart of the Baltic Sea. It had been a heart-stopping passage through shallow water teeming with ships of all sizes, and with Swedish and Danish coastal patrol boats on the lookout for submerged intruders. At one point the *K-363* had grounded on an underwater sandbar but worked free before almost being run down by a 200,000-deadweight-ton oil tanker.

Litvanov pushed his filthy cap to the back of his head and, tapping the chart, said heavily, "Here, the southern passage between Bornholm Island and the coast of Poland, is very wide and also deep, over two hundred feet. We have to be careful here, but we should be able to slip into the Baltic without being detected."

"But what about German and Polish coastal patrols?"

"From Sassnitz east, the Germans leave it to the Poles to patrol the southern Baltic. The Polish Navy has modern frigates and patrol craft as well as submarines and are good at interdicting drug runners and smugglers but not the best when it comes to hunting for submarines. And anyway, all we need is another twenty-four hours. Then, even if every country touching on the Baltic initiated War Plan Red, it will be too late."

"War Plan Red?"

"Full mobilization to deal with a seaborne threat to the region."

Zakayev ran a hand over his mouth. "I see. And what about this submarine you think is following us? Where do you plan to set a trap for him?"

"Here." Litvanov pointed to an area on the chart east of Bornholm labeled *Hazard*. "This is an old ordnance dumping ground."

"Is it dangerous?"

"Who can say. It's left over from World War II. Tons of chemical weapons and explosives captured from the Nazis that were loaded on ships and then scuttled. Over time the weapons casings have corroded and the poisons have leached into the sea. Now and then a fisherman puts his tackle over the side and snags a bomb and blows himself up. A good place to avoid, but also a good place for us to surprise this Russian skipper, whoever he is. And if he gets blown up by one of our torpedoes, the Bornholm fisherman's association might think one of their members caught a big one."

"But why bother with him?" Zakayev said. "He can't stop us now, it's too late."

"Perhaps. But this one is good. Maybe too good. And because he is good it would be a mistake to ignore him. Instead we have to kill him."

Scott waited for a southbound freighter. Toward midnight a huge container ship, battling high seas, her machinery noisy as a freight train, loomed up out of the rain.

Scott got ready to tuck the *K-480* in behind the massive ship and ride her wake into The Sound. A dangerous maneuver to perform in bad weather and close quarters, he had prepared by putting a bubble in the ballast tanks to raise the *K-480* and reduce her draft even though it meant her sail would be exposed.

The charts he'd studied indicated there were little more than twenty meters of water in mid-channel, slowly shelving to ten meters north of Helsingør, then running out again to more than twenty meters. But Russian navigation charts, Scott knew, were often out of date and this one had been printed in 1981.

"Battle stations manned and ready, Kapitan," the *starpom* reported.

With the crew at battle stations and the ship buttoned up in the unlikely event they collided with their trailblazer or, worse, ran aground, it was time to take the ride of their lives.

He waited a beat, heard the freighter's giant screw ripping through the water, felt the vessel's pressure wave against the *K-480*'s hull, then ordered, "Up scope!"

He saw a wall of steel rumbling by on the port side, saw the name *Sea Eagle* on her towering bow.

"Match speeds," Scott commanded, "turns for ten knots."

The *K-480,* drawn into the turbulence created by the freighter's passage, began to yaw from side to side. Scott snapped orders; the *K-480* swung parallel with the freighter, then slowly dropped back into her roiling wake to take up a trail position astern. He saw a Polish flag illuminated by a searchlight flying from a staff above the *Sea Eagle*'s sternpost. She was headed, he presumed, to Gdansk.

"Mind your depth!" Scott barked.

He'd assigned his most experienced planesmen and

helmsman the task of controlling the *K-480* while steaming in the *Sea Eagle*'s wake. At the diving station these men took a firmer grip on the joysticks.

Minutes later they entered the mouth of The Sound at Hornbæk. Scott noted the flashing lights at mid-channel and onshore, warning of sandbars, which meant tight quarters in the channel. But without incident they passed another landmark ashore, a tall commercial radio mast with a blinking red light at its tip.

Scott, at the periscope, monitored their progress to ensure they kept station on the *Sea Eagle*'s stern light. At first it proved difficult to balance speed and maneuver, to not creep in under her stern and into the heavy rudder post and massive thrashing propeller, or fall behind and shed the cover that the *Sea Eagle*'s mass and turbulent wake provided. Soon after they entered the chute and proceeded south, keeping station proved as easy as driving a car on a superhighway behind an eighteen-wheeler.

"Kapitan, we're approaching the first buoyage line," the *starpom* announced. "Ålsgårde lies to starboard."

"Very well." Scott spun the scope toward land and saw the coastal town of Ålsgårde. Yards from shore he spotted the lit-up factory and parking lot, which on the chart, served as a point of reference to the buoyage line bisecting the channel, its string of flashing lights warning of dangerously shallow water.

Scott stepped back from the scope. "Starpom, you have the conn. Hold our position."

The young officer hesitated for a moment, then did as he was ordered, proud that Scott had confidence in his abilities. "Aye, sir. I have the conn."

"Keep a seaman's eye open," Scott said, "in case the *Polski* suddenly slows down. Don't run up his ass."

"Aye, Kapitan. I mean, no, Kapitan."

Scott stepped to the navigation table and placed a tick mark beside the first buoyage line they'd passed. Soon they would cross another line of buoys, then a cable crossing. After that, a pinched dogleg where the chute turned southeast at Kronborg Pynt. Several kilometers below Kronborg Pynt, they'd pick up Ven, an island off the coast of Sweden where the ship channel split into eastern and western halves. Scott remembered from his earlier incursion into the Baltic Sea in the *Chicago* that during his transit around Ven, he'd had to dodge numerous ships as well as ferryboats and while doing so had almost run aground twice.

After crossing the second buoyage line a BP oil tanker, which the *starpom* estimated to be over 250,000 deadweight tons, churned through the adjoining channel in the opposite direction. Her sheer bulk and massive wake affected even the giant *Sea Eagle,* which threw her and several smaller ships and the *K-480* off course.

Alex sidled up to Scott after he finished lauding the planesmen and helmsman who had fought to keep the ship under control during the tanker's passage.

"How long will this take?" she said.

"Not long. Nervous?"

"Very. It's worse than the reactor SCRAM."

"Nothing's worse than a reactor cooling problem on a submarine. But I admit, this is hairy."

"I'm also worried about the ELF transmissions. What if they're trying to reach us to tell us they've found the *K-363* and that this is all for nothing?"

"They've been trying to communicate with us for hours, but there's nothing we can do until we clear The Sound and can stick up a mast. If they've killed the *K-363,* we'll congratulate them and turn around and go home. If not, well, we're where we need to be to do the job."

She looked at him and for a moment he had the impression she didn't approve of the way he'd conducted himself and the mission. But like it or not, it was the way it had to be. Later, when it was all over, there would be time to make her understand. But there was something else in her look, too, something deep and troubling.

"What is it, Alex, Botkin?"

"Yes . . . well, no. . . ."

"What?"

"We need to talk. I've done the calculations and—"

"What calculations?"

"Radiation dispersal downwind and—"

"Kapitan!"

Scott sprang to the *starpom*'s side at the periscope stand.

"Kapitan, the *Sea Eagle* is slowing down." The *starpom* turned the scope over to Scott.

Scott said, "You've got the conn, Starpom. Stay with it."

"Aye, Kapitan. Helm, give me turns for eight knots. Stand by to back down emergency full on both engines."

The *K-480* slowed but maintained a safe distance from the *Sea Eagle*. Turbulence flowing past the submarine's partially exposed hull and around her sail decreased, and along with it the sibilance of tumbling water.

"What's happening?" Scott said. "Can you see anything?

Running awash in the *Sea Eagle*'s wake had badly degraded sonar reception. They were deaf but, with the scope up, not blind.

"A ferry is crossing ahead of the *Sea Eagle* . . . Sweden to Denmark . . . cutting it very close. The *Sea Eagle* could have run the ferry down if she hadn't slowed."

The *starpom* did a quick 360-degree sweep. When he didn't swing back for another look at the ferry crossing to port, Scott sensed trouble.

"Something . . ." The *starpom*'s knuckles tightened on the periscope training handles. "A patrol boat . . . closing from astern. . . . Danish, I think. . . . . Range . . . under a kilometer. . . . Big bow wave. . . . He's in a hurry. . . . Searchlight's on." He looked away from the scope to Scott. The young lieutenant's sweaty face shimmered like polished bronze

Scott had two choices to escape detection by the Dane, and neither was good: break off from the *Sea Eagle,* fall back, and submerge in shallow water and risk bottoming and damaging the hull; or speed up and pull abreast of the *Sea Eagle* and hope that her great bulk would provide cover in which to hide.

Scott had only minutes to make a decision, but his instincts told him to wait, that the Danish patrol boat's skipper might have something else on his mind other than a submarine trying to sneak through The Sound.

Alex's gaze alternated between the *starpom* at the periscope and Scott standing in the middle of the CCP. Abakov, nodding, seemed to have grasped what Scott had intuited.

"He's not after us, Starpom, he's after that ferryboat for cutting ahead of the *Sea Eagle*. The ferry's captain violated the rules of the road. The ferry is the burdened vessel and is forbidden to cross ahead."

Alex looked frightened. "Jake, are you sure?"

"Starpom," he said, "what's that patrol boat doing now?"

The *starpom* had his eye to the scope. "Kapitan, you are right. He's signaling with his searchlight. And he's . . . he's sheering to starboard . . . to catch up with the ferry at Helsingør."

Scott wiped his face on a shirtsleeve. He caught the look of relief on Abakov's face.

The *K-480* exited the southbound channel at Helsingør Red and dropped from behind the *Sea Eagle*, which continued on her way, unaware she'd had company for the last two hours.

Still submerged, Scott began to ease the *K-480* toward deeper water on the eastern side of Ven. Surprisingly little traffic came their way and Scott let the *starpom* conn the boat around Ven, then farther south to Saltholm, where a tunnel under The Sound connected Malmö, Sweden, to Copenhagen, Denmark.

At Falterborev, a hook of land protruding into the Baltic from Sweden, a pair of Stockholm-class guided-missile patrol boats passed within a kilometer of the *K-480* but didn't react. A German naval oiler headed west toward Bornholm, which Scott had marked on the chart as their next objective, overtook them and steamed on by overhead.

"Once we get past Bornholm," Scott explained to the *starpom*, "we'll start our search for the *K-363.*"

After securing from battle stations, Scott had the messman break out tins of smoked sturgeon, black bread, and tea for the crew, followed by a small ration of vodka for each man. He toured the ship to praise the men for their performance during passage through The Sound. After conferring in the reactor control compartment with the chief engineer and main propulsion engineer on the status of the reactor and the repair to the main cooling loop, Scott headed to sick bay for a check on Botkin.

Alex caught up with him there.

"Jake, we have to talk," she said hoarsely, looking at Botkin's swollen profile.

"As soon as we get our communications traffic cleared up. Radioman's working on it now."

"Goddamnit, Jake, I said we need to talk. Now."

"I'm listening."

"Not here. Plus, I want Yuri to hear what I've got to say."

"If it's about"—Scott jerked his head at Botkin—"there's nothing to say."

She slowly turned and gave Scott a searing gaze. "It's not about him. It's not about us. It's about the *K-363*. It's about Zakayev and Litvanov. I told you, I've done some calculations."

Another long moment passed before Scott said, "All right, get Yuri. We can talk in my stateroom."

The room was small and they had to jockey around each other to fit inside. Scott hooked a metal chair leg with his boot and turned it around for Alex to use. He sat on his bunk while Abakov, arms folded, stood by the closed door.

"All right, I'm listening," Scott said.

Alex put steepled hands to her mouth and took a deep breath behind them before starting.

"I don't know if you'll both think I'm crazy or not, but I want you to listen carefully to what I'm going to say." She hunched her shoulders and shivered.

"The huge unanswered question that has been dogging us is what Zakayev and Litvanov are planning to do once they reach the Baltic Sea. I tried to think like they would—like any dedicated terrorist would, especially ones who had stolen a nuclear submarine. It seemed there was only one possibility: launch a cruise missile at St. Petersburg. But we know that there are no cruise missiles on board the *K-363*, only conventional torpedoes, which are not the kind of weapons a terrorist would use to attack Russia. So I asked myself: If Zakayev and Litvanov are not insane, what are they going to do?"

"No, they're not crazy," Abakov said. "They're totally rational."

"And unpredictable, you said," Alex added.

"That too."

"And that's what influenced my thinking. In other words, I tried to think in unconventional terms about what was possible." Alex hesitated for a moment, then continued. "We witnessed what Zakayev and Litvanov are capable of when they torpedoed that LNG tanker. It was devastating. Ships were sunk and sailors killed, and the blast probably terrified people in Scandinavia and Europe. They must have thought the world was ending. The terrorists did it just to throw the Norwegians off their trail, and their actions prove they'll do anything to carry out their plan."

She stopped and took another deep breath. "Stupid me, remember, I was worrying about what would happen if the *K-363* was torpedoed and her reactor blew up underwater— Wait, hear me out, Jake. Two days ago Botkin prevented a disaster when he SCRAMMED the *K-480*'s reactor. If he hadn't, the meltdown of the reactor core would have sent a plume of radioactivity over Scandinavia and northern Russia and, in time, around the world.

"Now imagine what would have happened if we had been in the Baltic Sea and had a reactor casualty we couldn't fix. Imagine there had been no Botkin to drop the quench plates, that the coolant loop couldn't be repaired, that a work-around couldn't be rigged, that the reactor overheated and that the fuel assembly melted through the bottom of this submarine and dropped into the sea like hot coals into a glass of water. But it didn't happen because you, Jake, and Botkin and the engineers knew how to prevent it. Now imagine a different scenario. Imagine a scenario where someone deliberately shuts off coolant to a submarine reactor or blows up its pumps and piping system so it will overheat and melt the fuel. I thought about the terrorist attacks on 9/11 in New York City and the effect a relatively isolated incident in Lower Manhattan had on the nation, and then I thought of New York Harbor, or Baltimore, or Long Beach."

Scott looked at Alex but said nothing.

"Sabotage?" Abakov said.

Alex, fists pressed to her forehead as if in physical pain, said, "For God's sake, don't either of you see what I'm driving at?" She threw up her hands. "Zakayev and Litvanov don't need any weapons aboard the *K-363. The submarine itself is a weapon!* Their target is St. Petersburg. And we have to warn Washington and Moscow—*now!*"

Her gaze bored into Scott and Abakov processing what she'd told them.

"Jesus Christ, don't you two get it?" she said.

"Are you telling us," Scott said as it started to dawn and his mouth went dry, "that Zakayev and Litvanov and the crew of that sub are on a suicide mission?"

"Yes, yes, yes!" Alex shot to her feet. "They're going to blow the sub's reactor in St. Petersburg! Drive the boat right up the Neva into the harbor! The radiation released will kill thousands of people. *Including the President of Russia and the President of the United States!"*

Scott, Alex, Abakov, the *starpom,* and the senior watch officers huddled around a chart of the Baltic Sea on the navigation table.

"I'm no climatologist," Alex said, "but, given the westerlies that blow over Russia from the Atlantic Ocean and North Sea, a radioactive plume released in St. Petersburg might even reach Moscow. Both cities will be uninhabitable for years."

"We learned in school," said the *starpom,* "that fifty million people live within a hundred miles of the Baltic Sea coast. It would be a disaster."

Scott said, "As you know from experience, once a reactor is starved of coolant, it overheats very quickly. If coolant is not restored, the reactor core will melt down completely in about two hours. Set in motion, and past a certain point, there's no way for the terrorists to stop it even if they were to change their minds. They'll die within hours from gross radiation exposure. What is it, Yuri?"

Abakov, his bald head reflecting light from the pantograph lamp shining on the chart, said, "I agree, Zakayev will not waste time now that he is so close to his objective. But don't forget, he can only do what Litvanov allows. In other words, Litvanov is the consummate tactician and will not do anything that will endanger the mission no matter what Zakayev wants. We saw it when he torpedoed the LNG tanker, to get the Norwegians off his back. If we trap him, he may fight back like a cornered bear rather than hide."

"I agree," Scott said, "that we're in for a fight."

He picked up and reread Radford's message that the

persistent ELF transmissions had indicated was waiting for them on an SRO communication satellite:

SERIAL 291159SRO TANGO/ALFA
FLASH FLASH FLASH
FM SRO/LANTFLT
TO COMM/BADGER ONE

//QUERY ONLY//OPAREA BRAVO SIERRA//

1. BREAK RADIO SILENCE AND REPORT STATUS K-363/ REPORT K-363 COURSE SPEED AND POSITION IF KNOWN/ UPON CONTACT ENGAGE AND DESTROY REPEAT ENGAGE AND DESTROY.

2. REPORT OWN POSITION IMMEDIATELY/ UPDATE AT FOUR HOUR INTERVALS IF POSSIBLE.

4. SRO ADVISORY//RUSS NORFLT DEPLOYMENT KALININGRAD ASW OPS VS K-363/ NORFLT FORCE SIZE AND STRUCTURE UNKNOWN/APPROPRIATE PRECAUTIONS ADVISED.

5. NCA REVIEWING STATUS BADGER ONE AND WILL AMPLIFY WHEN POSSIBLE.

6. END MESSAGE/RADFORD///

"Our only advantage now is that Zakayev and Litvanov may be distracted by the Russians moving into the Baltic," Scott said.

"I wouldn't count on it," Abakov said. As you said, he'll likely do everything he can to reach their objective, even if it means attacking them and us."

Alex turned from Abakov to Scott. "Does he know we're here?"

"I've assumed that all along," Scott said, scratching out a message on paper.

"What are you going to do?" Alex said.

"Fill Washington in."

"Will they believe it?"

"Can they afford not to?"

"I hear him."

Litvanov huddled with his sonarman. Green tendrils of captured sound at three hundred hertz from the *K-480*, designated Target Alpha, crawled down the monitor. Another contact, a plodding container ship heading north, had been designated Target Beta and ignored.

"He's working his way out of the northern passage, south of Bornholm," Litvanov said.

"Do you think he hears us?" Zakayev asked.

"If he does, we'd have seen him react. He's being cautious; perhaps he smells something."

"How far away is he?"

"Range, ten kilometers, General," answered Fire Control. "I make his speed ten knots."

"He'll walk right into our torpedoes," Veroshilov said gleefully.

Litvanov commanded, "Fire Control—target acquisition. Flood tubes three and four."

"Kapitan . . ."

Litvanov swiveled to the reserve sonarman working shoulder to shoulder with the senior man. "What is it?"

"I'm getting a slow bearing rate contact astern—pinging now, sir."

"Shit. A Russian patrol boat, I'd bet on it. Bearing."

"One-nine-one. I've got another one, sir. Same slow bearing rate. Fading. Thermal distortion.

"Range?"

"Twenty kilometers," reported Fire Control.

Litvanov watched the new contacts' tendrils move down the monitor. "They'll have to wait, but keep an eye on them. Now, let's get our friend in the Akula. Stand by to fire torpedoes."

"Sonar?" Scott barked.

"Nothing, sir, except a container ship. Very poor conditions. Very cluttered sound picture. . . ." He held up an open hand.

"What?"

The sonarman clamped the earphones to his head with both hands. "Pinging. Pinging to the north."

"Russians. They didn't waste any time. All right, let's move it. Come to periscope depth. We'll poke up a mast and send."

"Aye, Kapitan, periscope depth."

"Will the *K-363* pick up our radio burst?" Alex asked.

"They will if they have an antenna up and are listening. I don't reckon they will." Scott glanced at Alex watching the depth repeater now at thirty-one meters. Despite the sheen of perspiration and grime on her face, she was still lovely and desirable. He remembered their lovemaking in Moscow and how vulnerable she'd seemed. But reality intruded and he wondered what the reaction in Washington would be when the message that she had unraveled Zakayev's plan landed on the desks of men who had the president's ear. He had no idea what had transpired between Washington and Moscow but sensed that something had gone very wrong. Alex had gotten it right: He was their garbage man and would have to clean up this mess too.

"Approaching periscope depth, sir," said the *starpom.*

"A transient!" The senior sonarman spun around in his seat to face Scott. "A transient! Torpedo tubes flooding! Bearing zero-one-zero!"

Almost dead ahead.

"It's the *K-363,*" Scott said, then commanded, "Both engines ahead flank, right full rudder. Take her down, sixty meters. Stand by decoys! Bastard's got the drop on us."

The *K-480* accelerated hard. As she clawed for depth, the deck dropped away underfoot like an out-of-control elevator.

"Torpedo fired! I hear the launch." A moment later. "Pinging. It's hunting for us."

The Russian TEST 71-M torpedo, inbound at forty knots, had gone active.

"Both engines slow," Scott commanded. "Fire a decoy!"

A blast of air and rise of pressure against eardrums signaled that the decoy had burst from one of the *K-480*'s bow tubes and sped off at a right angle to the submarine's course.

"Left full rudder, both engines ahead full!" Scott ordered. The screw bit in, propelling the *K-480* left and away from the decoy and inbound torpedo. Scott knew that if he jumped off their present track, leaving behind both a knuckle in the water and a decoy to seduce the inbound torpedo, they would have a chance to escape.

"Sonar," Scott said, moving across the CCP. "I want the position of the *K-363*—now . . ."

"Aye, Kapitan."

". . . and stand by tubes one and two."

* * *

"He hears it, Kapitan. He speeded up and turned–ah! Decoy in the water!"

"Range to target?" Litvanov demanded.

"Under three thousand meters. . . . He cut his engines. Drifting. I've lost him, sir."

"Our torpedo is still active?"

"Still active, Kapitan."

"Do you have a bearing on his decoy?"

"Three-three-one but rapid drift to the north."

"While our target is moving south."

"Torpedo is turning north, I think chasing the decoy. . . . Yes, Kapitan, definitely chasing the decoy."

"Wasted. We'll turn south, find him and try another shot–"

The sonarman bolted upright. "Kapitan–a torpedo!" He was almost indignant. "He's fired at us."

Litvanov didn't hesitate. "Decoy–fire!"

Alex had sought cover beside Abakov. Scott wanted to tell her there was no place to hide but was too busy trying to evade the *K-363*'s torpedo. He recognized naked fear on her face–on Abakov's face too. On the faces of the men in the CCP. His mind, struggling to understand the tactical situation, made his own fear bearable.

The busy picture he had was of two submarines engaged in a dance of death with two torpedoes in the water hunting for a target and two noisemakers designed to draw them off. Even so, one of the torpedoes might get lucky and find its target.

"Transients. Flooding tanks. High-speed cavitation, Kapitan. Target's running east."

"Away from our torpedo."

When the noisemakers died, both torpedoes would

continue to hunt for targets until they either found one or their batteries ran flat.

"Sonar, where's the torpedo fired by the *K-363?*" Scott said.

"Bearing zero-one-zero, drifting right. Opening out."

Scott looked at Alex and Abakov. "You can relax. It's moving away from us. Let's hope it doesn't find that container ship."

"It was close, eh?" Abakov said, his face pale gray.

"Our decoy drew it off. His decoy will probably do the same to ours." He said to Alex, "Are you all right?"

"I can handle it," she said. "What about the message? Can we send it?"

"Not with the *K-363* firing torpedoes at us."

"Jake, we can't wait any longer. They've got to know."

The sonarman broke in. "The *K-363,* Kapitan, she's turned due north."

"Where's our fish?"

"I've lost it, sir."

"The message will have to wait. Let's get after the *K-363.*"

# 18

## St. Petersburg

The president stood by a gilt window in the north façade of the Winter Palace and gazed out over the Neva, gold in the setting sun, and at a pair of empty cruise boats moored below the Palace Embankment.

"Must be killing their business," the president said.

"I beg your pardon, sir?" said Paul Friedman.

"The FSB closed the river to traffic for the summit. The Moyka too. No tourists. Those cruise boat owners must be feeling it."

"I imagine so. But the rivers will be reopened when the summit concludes."

"I sympathize with them, Paul. There are still three days to go, and like them, I'll be glad to have this business over with."

Friedman nodded, though he wasn't sure what business the president would be glad to have over, the summit or the hunt for the *K-363* in the Baltic Sea. Both, he suspected.

The president turned away from the window and

crossed the ornate room. He loosened his tie and dropped into a baroque armchair upholstered in red and gold silk damask. A fleshy Fragonard nude cavorting with a pair of adoring nymphs gazed down at the president from over a gargantuan carved marble and gold fireplace.

"Hand me my drink, would you, Paul? Thanks. At any rate, I thought we should talk before the others arrive to discuss the Russian IMF proposal. Things are about to boil over. The President was polite and didn't bring up Grishkov's accusation about our connection to Zakayev. But it hung in the air all the same. Also, they don't buy that we've lost contact with Scott. Nothing I said convinced them it was true."

Friedman shook his head.

The president's face showed signs of stress. "Paul, they're on a hair trigger. Subitov wants to hit the Chechens now, not wait until they've captured Zakayev."

Friedman's eyebrows shot up. "Hit them how?"

"He didn't spell it out, but as you know, he's been itching to use nuclear weapons in the Caucasus. "

"He's mad."

"He has his supporters, Paul."

"They're mad too." Friedman made notes as he talked. "Does anyone around the Russian president, not in thrall to Subitov, still think they can capture Zakayev?"

"Stashinsky thinks they can. But what will it matter if Subitov has his way? They've been looking for an excuse to finish the job they started in Chechnya, and this may be it. On the other hand, if they could capture Zakayev, it might change the picture, make them less likely to act rashly."

"I tend to agree with Ellsworth, that it's going to be impossible to capture him."

"I'm with you, Paul. And I'd feel better if I knew what Scott was up to and whether or not he's even in the picture anymore. What can Karl do for us on that score?"

"Not much, sir, I'm afraid. Weather has been poor over the Baltic and SRO satellites haven't picked up a thing, even on MAD. Gordon put some P-3Cs into the Baltic, but we have to be careful we don't go head-to-head with the Russians on this. They've redeployed two Be-12s, three Il-38s, and an unknown number of Mi-14 ASW choppers shifted from the Barents operation. The Baltic is over 163,000 square miles in area, and finding a pair of subs in a sea that vast is not going to be easy. Identifying which one is Scott's is another matter altogether." Friedman hesitated, tapped a pen against his front teeth.

"What's on your mind, Paul?"

"I was thinking that if the Russians find one or both of them before we do, they may not be inclined to sort things out."

"You mean they may shoot first and ask questions later."

"Something like that."

The president got to his feet and glanced up at the enigmatic Fragonard nude and her cavorting nymphs. "You're assuming nothing bad has happened to Scott," he said to the nude. Then, to Friedman: "He told Ellsworth that that damned sub he was on was a junker, or something to that effect."

"Karl believes he's okay and so does Ellsworth."

The president, working off nervous energy, went back to the window overlooking the Neva. "I'm glad they're such optimists. I wish I could be."

"Ellsworth says it's a communications problem,"

Friedman said, turning around in his chair to speak to the president's back. "Karl agrees."

"So we wait and see if they're right."

"Yes, sir."

"And even if it is a comm problem, Scott can still find and kill Zakayev."

"Ellsworth says Scott's a survivor."

"He had better be if the Russians find him before we do and think he's Zakayev."

Zakayev faced Litvanov across the wardroom table.

"Have some." Litvanov pushed a bottle of vodka toward Zakayev.

Zakayev grabbed the bottle and put it out of Litvanov's reach. "I told you, you drink too much."

Litvanov, unshaven, dirty, his greasy cap pushed back on his head, stared at Zakayev. At length he said, "And I told you that it makes no difference because"—he swept a hand in the air—"I—all of us—will soon be dead."

Zakayev watched Litvanov's eyes flick to the girl. He knew what Litvanov saw, that she looked haggard, that her eyes were dull, her skin sallow, that she had lost weight. He knew that they all, the crew included, had undergone similar changes. Looking death in the face could do that. Better to have it over now, he had decided.

Zakayev said, "We'll never make it to St. Petersburg. I want to blow the reactor now, before the Russian patrol boats in the north get here and before that submarine finds us again."

Zakayev held Litvanov's gaze, daring him to say otherwise.

"He'll find us all right," Litvanov said wearily. The

attack and counterattack had depleted him and it showed. "He's probably less than forty kilometers away. He'll find us."

"You're obsessed with him. Admit it. What you really care about is killing this skipper in the other submarine. You don't want to destroy Russia; instead you want to destroy him. That's your new cause. Perhaps you've also changed your mind and want to return to Russia and make a clean breast of it, apologize for stealing their submarine."

Litvanov eyed the bottle of vodka, then Zakayev. "Is that what you think, General?"

"It's what I see. The longer you toy with him, the longer you can put off doing what you swore to do. What your men swore to do."

Litvanov's hands on the table balled into fists. "Are you calling me a coward?"

"Prove to me you aren't."

Litvanov half rose from his seat as the girl pushed the bottle of vodka in front of him. "Here," she said.

"I swore to blow up the reactor in St. Petersburg, not in the middle of the Baltic."

Zakayev hadn't moved an inch. "Whether we do it here or in St. Petersburg, the Russians will suffer the consequences, be blamed for it. That's good enough."

Litvanov ignored the bottle and sat down again. "You think we can just blow up the reactor, don't you." He snapped his fingers. "Poof, and it's over."

"You said we could. I believed you. Now you say we can't?"

"No," Litvanov protested, and grabbed the bottle. "What I'm saying is that unless we can eliminate that submarine closing in on us, we stand a good chance of being torpedoed before we can set the charges and destroy the reactor. He'll hear the charges go off and know exactly where we are. He'll think something happened to us and he'll be right, and he'll be here in no time and won't stop to ask if he can help us. Instead, he'll see us on the surface and attack before the reactor runs away. I told you, it will take two hours for it to melt down through the hull. We don't have that much time because he's less than an hour away from us."

"How do you know where he is?" Zakayev said.

Litvanov poured another drink. He pushed the cap farther back on his head with a thumb under the bill, then threw the drink down his throat. "Do you think," he said, eyes watering, "that we scared him away like a dog running with its tail between its legs? This man, whoever he is, is not afraid of us. It's as if he knows exactly what we intend to do."

"Then you are wasting time," Zakayev said. "Do it now. Blow the reactor, and if this Russian shows up, torpedo him. But do it now."

Litvanov rolled the empty glass between his fingers. He looked at the girl, her deep-set eyes now seemingly bigger than ever, then at Zakayev. "I'm not convinced he's a Russian."

"What are you talking about?" Zakayev said. "Of course he's a Russian."

Litvanov kept rolling the glass, his gaze planted on the girl as he spoke. "He doesn't track like a Russian skipper. He sprints and drifts, dodges and weaves, runs silent, and above all doesn't spin on his heel—what the *Amerikanskis* call our 'Crazy Ivan'—to clear baffles. Those are the tactics of an American skipper, not a Russian."

Zakayev felt his patience slipping away. The man was drunk and talking nonsense. The pressure had gotten to him and Zakayev wondered if it had gotten to the crew as well. If so, the mission was doomed. For a brief moment he considered killing Litvanov. But he realized Veroshilov might not take orders from him and he'd have to kill Veroshilov too. After that, where would it stop? Even if he killed them all, he could probably set the charges but wouldn't know where to put them. And who would drive the submarine?

"How could he be an American?" Zakayev said.

Litvanov said nothing.

"Not in a Russian Akula," Zakayev said, and got to his feet. "Impossible."

Still Litvanov said nothing.

"We're running out of time, Georgi. I'm giving you an order. Prepare your crew; tell them we are going to blow the reactor."

Litvanov nodded.

"Who will set the charges?"

"The *starpom,*" Litvanov said. "He volunteered."

"Very well, then get Veroshilov started on it. Anything else?"

Litvanov moved in slow motion. He stood, fists on the table, looking at the girl. "Perhaps I should marry you two. A ship's captain can do that, you know."

The girl looked at Zakayev, then Litvanov. "We're already married, Kapitan," she said with mock cheer.

"I didn't know that. Congratulations." Litvanov pulled his cap down over his brow and departed.

She was almost nothing in his arms. So utterly light and fragile. She clung to him like a child–like the child she still was.

"I brought this along," she said, taking her arms from around his neck. "It's all I have left." She unwrapped her parents' wedding album from the oilcloth and held it on her lap so Zakayev could see.

"I remember," he said. "It's very beautiful."

Inside were color photographs of a tall, handsome man in a square-cut suit and a slender, lovely woman in a traditional wedding dress holding a bouquet of flowers, posing for the photographer. The girl's hands caressed the photos, her fingers lingering on the faces, drawing their outlines, perhaps feeling their warmth against her hand.

Zakayev sat down beside her, their bodies touching. She seemed different, no longer a wife but a daughter. What they had shared was gone, and, he sensed, so was she. There were more pictures to see, though he'd seen them all before, knew everyone's name, their stories, and the places where they'd been taken. Friends, aunts, uncles, grandparents. Children of friends. Cousins. A friendly black-and-white dog taught to shake hands, holding up a paw.

She closed the book and leaned her head on his shoulder. "May I stay here with you, Ali?"

"Of course. I want you to."

"I'm glad it's almost over. Are you?"

"Yes."

"You're angry at Litvanov."

"Not angry, disappointed."

"You don't trust him, do you?"

"A man doesn't willingly chose to die," Zakayev said. "But even if he does, he's entitled to change his mind."

They both fell silent listening to the faint, faraway noises made by the *K-363*.

At length the girl curled up on the bunk and Zakayev covered her with a rough wool blanket. He put the album by her side so it would be there when she awoke.

He brushed a few strands of hair off her cheek and kissed her.

He changed into a pressed cammie shirt and matching pants that he'd stowed in his tourist suitcase on wheels. He laced up a pair of scarred boots and put on a canvas web belt. Then he stuck the H&K P7 automatic inside his shirt into the waistband of his cammies.

Zakayev thought about what he'd told the girl: A man doesn't willingly chose to die. But even if he does, he's entitled to change his mind. Zakayev felt the pistol's cold steel against his belly. In case Litvanov changed his mind, he'd be prepared.

The men on watch in the CCP expressed silent surprise at Zakayev's change of dress, Litvanov especially, who looked him up and down but said nothing.

"Veroshilov is preparing the charges," Litvanov said without prompting. He motioned to the men in the CCP watching, and also pointed fore and aft. "The men said they want you to know they are ready to do what they swore to do."

"Excellent," said Zakayev. "It's been an honor to serve with them. And with you, Georgi."

"Thank you, General," Litvanov said. "There's one more thing to do: monitor the hourly CNN broadcast at thirteen hundred for an update on the party going on in St. Petersburg. Also, we have a fix on the patrol boats to the north. I think they're Grishas, but it's raining and we have degraded sound conditions. There are at least four of them, perhaps as many as six, all with active sonars. They're moving south at ten knots. It's hard to tell how much time we have before they arrive in this area. It depends on how thorough they are."

"What about the submarine?"

"Nothing. That worries me. He's out there, somewhere. I know he is. He's not invisible but almost."

"Kapitan—broadcast in five minutes," a *michman* advised.

Rain lashed an angry gray Baltic. Visibility, Litvanov estimated, extended less than a kilometer, the horizon invisible. He spun the scope through 360 degrees, saw something, and froze. A four-engined plane, its props shimmering silver disks, had punched through the curtain of rain and zeroed in on the *K-363*'s periscope. In the split second it took Litvanov to react, he saw the plane's open bomb bay and a falling object strike the water.

"Emergency dive! Full down-angle on the planes! Engines ahead emergency speed!"

Pandemonium erupted in the CCP. Litvanov lost his footing as the *K-363* nosed over at a frighteningly steep angle—more than thirty degrees. He grabbed a stanchion to keep from tumbling into Veroshilov at the diving station behind the men at the controls, who had slammed their yokes forward against the stops.

The *K-363* accelerated, burrowing into water only 160 meters deep.

Zakayev held on tight to a railing but had to dodge loose gear—tools, books, a clipboard—tumbling down the slanted deck and against the legs of men at their stations and into corners and under equipment. He wondered if the girl had been tossed from her bunk and, if so, hoped she'd not been injured.

"Ease your bubble," Litvanov ordered. He was down on one knee and watching the depth gauge register ninety-six meters, the pit log fifteen knots and climbing.

"One of ours—I think. A May. Came in almost on the surface. Must have had a MAD contact—"

"Torpedo. Active sonar! Starboard side!"

Litvanov shot to his feet, bellowing, "Rudder full left! Fire a decoy!"

The submarine heeled left like a plane in a wingover. A sudden rise in air pressure and a *whoosh* signaled ejection of a noisemaker in the opposite direction of her turn.

"Torpedo bearing one-seven-eight. Active sonar."

"Fire another decoy!"

Another pressure pulse and discharge of air.

"Rudder amidships."

Zakayev took a deep breath.

The *K-363* heeled right and leveled out while still nosing down.

"Where's that torpedo?"

"Turning right—going after the decoys."

Zakayev exhaled.

"Maybe that's all he—" Litvanov said, only to be contradicted.

"Another torpedo! Active sonar! Port bow! Very close!"

"A bearing! Give me a bearing!" Litvanov exploded.

"One-one-two, Kapitan. Steady rate."

"Bastard," Litvanov hissed. "He's not giving up." He lurched forward. "Fire two decoys!" He spun toward the depth repeater and saw 110 meters. They were running out of water. "Level her out at one-twenty."

"Kapitan, I've lost the first torpedo."

"Never mind that one, where's the other one—?"

A thunderclap and the *K-363* leaped sideways. Litvanov collided with the main blow manifold and crashed to the deck on his back. Zakayev went down, too, but not before he saw a sheet of insulation fly off the hull on the port side of the CCP and shatter on deck. A moment later the CCP went black.

Zakayev, dazed, looked up and saw blue haze hanging in the air, smelled burning insulation, and heard the pop and fizz of a live cable arcing inside an electrical cabinet. The emergency battle lamps had cycled on.

He saw smoke. No, $CO_2$. A sailor crunching over debris played a fire extinguisher over a sparking panel of gauges. Another sailor slammed tripped circuit breakers back into their seats with the heel of his hand. Somewhere, rushing water filled a void. Were they sinking? He didn't think so. His cammies and skin were dotted with bits of cork hull insulation and flakes of paint knocked off bulkheads and equipment.

"Report damage!" Litvanov, standing, rubbing his backside, bellowed into the SC1.

Zakayev scrambled to his feet and brushed himself off. The pistol in his waistband had gouged his groin, but he ignored it. He pushed past sailors working to restore order and make repairs. He staggered forward, out of the CCP, into the narrow, smoky passageway in Compartment Three off which were the officers' staterooms. He made way for two sailors rushing aft with tools. He heard someone shout. Then it was quiet.

The lights flickered, went out, then came on again. The acrid smell of smoldering rubber and phenolic resin stung Zakayev's nostrils. He wiped his eyes and coughed into a fist. For a moment he thought he had gone too far but then realized he was facing the door to his stateroom.

He slid the door open on its track and stepped inside. A blade of light from the passageway knifed into the darkened room. He felt around on the bunk, still warm but empty. Heart hammering in his chest, Zakayev fumbled for the light switch over the small desk. He was terrified. And he had the memory. He saw his children in the garden in Grozny, their little bodies bled white, shredded by bullets from Russian PKMs. His wife, Irina, raped, beaten to death with rifle butts, her face unrecognizable. And he saw the girl scrabbling over the rubble in Grozny, clutching the album in one hand, reaching for his with the other. She had been crying, tears streaking her dirty cheeks.

Zakayev dropped to his knees. She was lying on her back, head tilted awkwardly to one side, an arm thrown back in a casual gesture. Like the day he had coaxed her out of the ruins in Grozny, she had been crying; miniature diamonds still clung to her long eyelashes and downy cheeks. But her dead eyes looking up at him saw nothing. A berry of dark red blood had pooled at the corner of her mouth. He wiped the blood away with a fingertip and put it on his tongue. He had always called her *devushka*—girl—even though her name was Irina.

The explosion had rattled the *K-480* stem to stern and sent the sonar traces dancing off the monitors. They had watched torpedoes chasing decoys—four straight lines on the monitors—until the lines merged into one and then heard the explosion like rolling thunder and felt the bump from the shock wave.

"What do you think?" Abakov asked. "Did they nail her?"

"No breakup noises," Scott said. "That May we saw hanging around the impact area will call in help. It's going to be hot upstairs."

"What do we do now?" Alex said. She'd gotten a second wind and had cheered when the torpedo detonated, thinking it had hit the *K-363*. Now she was subdued.

"What we don't do is try to send any messages. They'll pick up our burst. Plus, that May has a MAD stinger like our P-3Cs and can find us. And she probably has plenty of torpedoes left. And active and passive sonobuoys: Those babies are hard to avoid; they pick up everything. The one thing in our favor might be that the Russians don't know we're here. So if they do pick us up, it may confuse them and give us a chance to break away."

"But Zakayev and Litvanov know we're here," Alex said.

"Right. And they're caught in a vise between us to the southeast and the Russians to the north. We can try to squeeze the *K-363* into a box and, if the Russians don't interfere, finish them."

"By *interfere,*" Alex said, "you mean if the Russians don't attack us too."

"I don't want to fight both sides," Scott said.

"And I don't want to get sunk by the Russian Navy," Alex said.

Scott marked the position of the torpedo detonation on the chart. An ESM sweep confirmed that the May was flying over it in ever-widening circles hunting for her prey. Only a seemingly impenetrable wall of rain prevented Scott from getting a good look at the May when, on one of her passes over the target area, she hove into view for a moment over the horizon.

"The *K-363* is somewhere east of the May's flight circle. He needs deep water so he's not going to head west toward Gotland, where it's shallow, not now. We're going to ease due east and see what's what. If we're lucky, we'll pick him up maybe . . . here." He stabbed the chart with a point on a pair of dividers.

Karl Radford sat stuck in traffic on Memorial Bridge. He could see cars backed up all the way to the exit ramp to Jefferson Davis Highway and beyond.

Grishkov. He'd barely been able to contain himself. There had been an attack, maybe a kill, but even so, it would take pressure off the president and that's what Friedman wanted. Suddenly no one seemed to care about Scott, Alex Thorne, the Russian investigator Abakov, the crew of that Akula. Expendable. Ellsworth said Scott was a survivor. Maybe he'd prove it yet.

Radford checked his watch, then lifted his secure phone, waited a beat, and said, "Are we cleared through to St. Petersburg?"

"Stand by, sir."

The familiar tone, then Friedman. "Morning, Karl. The President's running late. What do you have?"

"Not much. We confirm what Grishkov said, that a Russian plane attacked a sub off Gotland, can't confirm they killed it. We have nothing on thermal imagery other than the torpedo warhead's detonation. Weather is giving us trouble with satellite coverage."

"Go on."

"We've also confirmed a report that a Russian plane, an Il-38 May like the one that attacked the sub, crashed off Saaremaa, Estonia. The Russians have diverted several ships to search for survivors."

"How many planes does that leave for ASW patrol?"

"Only two Mays. The Be-12s are worthless for ASW, obsolete as hell. So are the choppers. Their range is too short and they haven't the loiter time necessary for searching."

"And how many patrol craft?"

"Three Grishas. Three others are off searching for any survivors of that plane crash."

"Grishkov told you this?"

"He knows we can tell what's what. They have nothing to gain by denying it."

"How sure are they that it was the *K-363* that they attacked?"

"I would say reasonably."

"What about Scott. Where's he?"

"Haven't heard from him."

After a lengthy silence Friedman said, "What are the chances the Russkies nailed Zakayev?"

"I'd only be guessing."

"But he could be damaged?"

"Sure."

"Damaged, but not so bad that he can't give the Russkies the slip."

"He could do it."

Another silence.

"Then we may still need Scott to mop up for us."

"Of course. We're still broadcasting, still waiting for his response."

"I'll tell the President."

Radford's car started moving. He looked out the tinted windows toward Arlington National Cemetery and thought, in the Baltic, there had been no trace of oil or radioactive debris to prove a sub had been hit and sunk. He felt sure Zakayev was still out there. But where the hell was Scott? Suddenly his spirits sagged.

Litvanov looked genuinely shaken.

"No one is to touch her," Zakayev ordered.

"Of course not, General," said Litvanov, peering into

the stateroom at the girl's body lying on the bunk. "I'm sorry" was all Litvanov could manage.

"It was unavoidable," Zakayev said. He backed out of the room into the passageway and slid the door closed.

They faced each other in the darkened strip-lit passageway.

"Are the charges set?" Zakayev said.

"They are made up with detonators. Veroshilov has to enter the reactor compartment and rig them to the primary and secondary coolant loops." He described what would happen to Veroshilov inside the reactor compartment and the effect radiation would have on him.

"How will he set them off?"

"He won't. They're wired back to the main reactor control console to a microbox. The chief engineer has volunteered to handle that part."

"Then it's time. You will come to the surface and set them off."

Litvanov licked his lips. "There's a plane up there. They may attack."

"Not if you surface. They'll think we're surrendering."

"They may not believe it."

"Then use the radio. They'll believe what you tell them."

Litvanov wiped his mouth with the back of a hand, then started to move off. But Zakayev grabbed his arm. "No more delays, Georgi."

The entire crew, except for the chief engineer in the reactor control compartment, easily fit into the CCP while the submarine, controls on automatic and rigged for ultraquiet, hugged the bottom moving slowly eastward toward Estonia. The sailors regarded Zakayev with awe and sympathy; the girl's death had affected them deeply. When Litvanov told them it was time to set the charges, the men drifted off to their stations to be alone with their thoughts.

Litvanov heard Starpom Veroshilov say, "It has been a privilege to have you aboard, General Zakayev." He didn't wait for Zakayev to respond but headed aft to the reactor compartment to set the charges.

Litvanov turned away and ordered, "Prepare to surface."

"Kapitan—I hear a submarine blowing her tanks!"

"All engines stop," Scott commanded.

The sonarman put it on the speaker so everyone could hear the venting and blowing, the crack and pop of exploding bubbles. It took a moment for the noise to subside sufficiently to get an accurate range and bearing on the *K-363*, and for Scott to get a clearer picture of their relative positions.

"She's damn close," Scott said, surprised and tense with anticipation.

It sounded as if the surfacing boat was less than a hundred yards away from the *K-480* and perhaps a hundred feet below her.

"Why didn't we hear her?" Alex asked.

"She was hiding under a layer of seawater," Scott said, "one that's colder than the layers above. It deflects sonar. That's why we didn't hear her and why that damned May's been flying in circles scratching his ass. She's practically invisible."

"But why are they surfacing?" Alex said.

As she rose to the surface, the *K-363* would for a moment or two be level with the *K-480.*

"Kapitan—she's close aboard on the starboard side!" The excited sonarman's voice sounded ready to crack.

Scott's mind raced. He pictured the two submarines parallel to each other with little separation between their hulls, the *K-363* slowly rising above the *K-480.*

"Maybe they're going to surrender," Alex said.

Scott lurched to the diving station and ordered, "All back Emergency! Right full rudder!" A moment later: "Steady as she goes."

Alex ducked out of his way as Scott grabbed the SC1. "Target acquisition! Snap shot! Stand by tubes one and two!"

Aft, the *K-480*'s mighty engines spun to full power. The screw reversed direction and, cavitating, fought to gain purchase against the water. The submarine shuddered under the strain, her hull groaning in protest, deck plates vibrating violently.

"What is it?" Alex demanded.

"He's going to surface and blow the reactor!" Scott bellowed. "We've got to back out and shoot!"

Litvanov went white. "Impossible!" But he knew it wasn't.

"Starboard . . . she's starboard . . . abaft the beam," the sonarman had twisted around in his seat to alert Litvanov, who was shouting orders and didn't hear him.

"Open the vents! Emergency dive!"

The roar of water flooding ballast tanks and air escaping from vent risers hammered eardrums.

"Rudder, right full!" Litvanov commanded over the roar.

Zakayev almost fell as the deck dropped underfoot and the *K-363* sledded downhill. He held on and hand-over-handed it across the CCP. "What are you doing?" he demanded.

Litvanov ignored Zakayev shouting and didn't hear the sonarman screaming, "Kapitan–starboard, she's starboard!"

Zakayev grabbed Litvanov's arm and spun him around. "Surface the boat. That's an order!"

Litvanov tore his arm from Zakayev's grip. "You fool, we're practically on top of them. We can't surface. They'll blow us out of the water."

Zakayev snatched the pistol from his waistband and jammed it in Litvanov's belly. "I gave you an order."

"Fuck your orders. They're going to put a torpedo up our ass–"

The noise was a hundred times louder than two cars colliding head on at full speed. A tremendous shriek of tortured metal and of something solid ripping loose. The *K-363* heeled over, hung for a moment in space as if impaled, then, with a sudden lurch, righted herself and lay dead in the water.

# 19

## The Baltic Sea, East of Gotland

Sheets of water cascaded into the CCP from around the lower hatch, giving access to the escape trunk in the sail. Above the trunk's sealed upper hatch, a tunnel led to the bridge and the small cockpit from which the *K-480* was conned while on the surface.

"Damage report—all compartments, " Scott ordered. The collision had left everyone momentarily stunned. "On the double."

Scott pitched to the sonar console. "Where is she?"

"Gone, Kapitan. Just background noise now. But I can still hear those pinging patrol boats."

"She can't have gotten far. She may have been damaged. Find her!"

"Aye, Kapitan."

Scott caught a glimpse of Alex, wet and shivering. She saw him looking at her and blew out her cheeks.

The *starpom*, soaked, ducked out from under the freezing waterfall sluicing into the CCP from around the hatch skirt. "Sir, the upper skirt is cracked and the trunk is wrenched out of alignment at least five centimeters," he reported, illustrating that distance with thumb and finger. "The upper hatch may have been knocked off its seat in the collision."

"Which means the tunnel and upper sail structure may have been damaged. You'd better check out the periscopes."

"Aye, Kapitan."

"Can we handle this much flooding?" Alex said.

Water was backing up in the scuppers that drained the CCP into the bilges.

"Not for long. And we can't run the bilge pumps because the noise they make will give our position away."

"No sign of the *K-363?*" Abakov said.

"Nothing. For all I know we may be sitting right under her. You can bet they're looking for us."

"And the flooding?" Abakov insisted.

"The escape trunk in the sail and the tunnel above it that opens onto the bridge and cockpit may have been damaged."

"Kapitan, the scopes are jammed," the *starpom* reported. "And there is a bad leak coming in from around the attack scope's packing gland."

Scott pictured the packing blowing out and the CCP flooding fast.

"Now we're blind too," Alex said.

"But not deaf," Scott said. "Sonar's still in good shape."

The SC1 squawked with reports of minor damage from other compartments: tripped circuit breakers, leaking valves, smashed china in the crew's mess.

"Nothing we can't live with," Scott said. "I'm going to inspect the escape trunk and tunnel. I want to see the damage for myself."

"Jake, don't, it's too risky." Alex said.

"What the hell isn't?"

* * *

Scott shrugged into an orange immersion suit held open by Abakov.

"Can you wiggle through the upper hatch in that thing?" Abakov said, zipping Scott inside the bulky suit.

"I'll make it. Keep the lower hatch dogged until I'm ready to come back in—just in case."

"Just in case what?" Alex asked.

"Just in case the trunk floods."

"Jake, what if the *K-363* attacks while you're up there?" she asked.

"They're probably as shook up as we are and need time to square away. Anyway, this won't take long."

A *michman* handed Scott a portable light. Scott put a foot on a rung of the ladder under the skirt. "Starpom."

"Kapitan?"

"If something happens to me up there, you're in command."

"Aye, Kapitan. Don't worry, I have three men on sonar. If the *K-363* makes a move, we'll hear her."

Scott started up the ladder.

"Jake . . ."

He looked down at Alex's and Abakov's upturned faces.

"Be careful," she said, even though she knew it sounded lame.

"Stand aside," Scott said.

He spun the handwheel on the underside of the hatch to retract the dogs, then put his back against the wheel and carefully cracked the hatch off its seat, allowing air pressure inside the CCP to vent into the escape trunk. After decompression, he threw the hatch cover open, climbed into the trunk, and redogged the cover.

Inside the trunk a feeble caged lightbulb gave just

enough illumination for Scott to get his bearings. He switched on the portable light and shined its beam over the silver-gray walls of the trunk, and, overhead on the upper hatch and its release mechanism. He saw water leaking past the trunk's upper hatch seal and suspected that the hatch at the top of the tunnel leading to the bridge had also been damaged. If so, the tunnel itself might have been damaged. A catastrophic failure of the upper hatch or collapse of the tunnel would flood the escape trunk and the CCP. Normally the tunnel was dry to permit access topside. But if the *K-480* was ever sunk in water shallow enough to permit the crew to escape, the upper hatch, equipped with explosive bolts, would be blown open to flood the tunnel and permit egress from the escape trunk where Scott stood.

Scott heard a heavy flow of water and saw it swirling around his orange boots and out a wide crack in the floor of the trunk into the CCP below. His inspection revealed that the crack in the floor also ran up the wall of the trunk. He followed it around the circular chamber, where it petered out in a web of cracks at one of a dozen vertical rows of one-inch-diameter bolts evenly spaced around the trunk's circumference. The bolts helped anchor the chamber to heavy steel support frames inside the free-flooding sail.

He winced when he saw that the collision with the *K-363* had not only wrenched the escape trunk out of alignment but had also pulled several of the massive bolt heads through the hardened steel wall of the trunk as if it were soft cheese. Seawater poured into the trunk through the enlarged, puckered bolt holes while it also poured in from above through the sprung hatch.

Scott concluded that the overhead tunnel wasn't

flooded, a sign that the damage wasn't as great as he had feared. Otherwise water would be shooting out from around the hatch under pressure so great, it would have sliced through his immersion suit. He spun the handwheel on the upper hatch to retract the dogs and, bent double on the ladder below it, tested the hatch against a possible pressure head of seawater. When it gave easily, he cracked it open.

A torrent of icy water crashed over Scott's shoulders. He felt the ocean's cold knife through the immersion suit and knew that without it he'd be immobilized from the cold. The flood ebbed and he swung the heavy cover up and away until its lip caught the safety catch made to hold it open.

Overhead he saw a long tunnel with welded-on rungs and handholds receding into blackness. The lantern beam revealed a fan of water shooting into the tunnel under high pressure just below the sealed hatch at the tunnel's upper end. Water crashing against the tunnel's wall flowed down its length and poured from the open hatch below, into the escape trunk, and out through its cracked floor into the CCP.

Despite the texture molded into the heavy rubber gloves and boots attached to the immersion suit, Scott found it hard to get a grip on the steel rungs. The climb was slow and difficult. Water shooting into the tunnel drenched Scott and took his breath away. Halfway up he slipped and almost fell but held on with both hands to a slippery rung above his head.

He reached the underside of the upper hatch, played light over its rough steel, and saw that the hatch itself wasn't damaged but that the tunnel had been caved in and fractured, which allowed water into the tunnel. Scott didn't doubt that the tunnel would probably collapse under heavy sea pressure and flood the escape trunk and CCP.

He looked around for the emergency SC1 speaker he knew was mounted in the lower end of the tunnel. He found the large flat speaker button painted white, which he hit with the flat of his gloved hand.

"CCP, Scott!" he bellowed.

"CCP, aye. We hear you, Kapitan. Are you all right?" It was the *starpom.*

"High and dry," Scott said.

But he wasn't. Scott slipped and fell down three rungs before he got a firm grip. Slag from a rough weld on one of the rungs tore through the immersion suit and his flesh.

"Kapitan . . . ?"

"I'm okay," Scott said. "We've got damage to the trunk and upper tunnel. Can't go deep or we'll flood." He filled them in and then started back down.

Scott dropped the last fifteen feet down the tunnel and scrambled into the trunk. He unclipped the upper hatch cover, dogged it, then opened the lower hatch, unleashing a flood of freezing water onto Abakov and the *starpom* waiting for him at the base of the ladder. Scott dropped to the deck and collapsed in an orange-suited heap.

He was greeted by the *starpom*'s warning: "Kapitan, sonar contact–"

"The *K-363?"* Scott said.

"I hear a circulating pump–not a main, something else."

Abakov helped Scott out of the immersion suit. He was soaked. And bloody.

"Scott, you're injured," Alex insisted.

"Later." Scott squelched across the CCP to the sonar repeater.

"Close aboard, Kapitan," said the *starpom.*

"Bearing?"

"Weak signature. Bearing two-four-zero . . . two-three-nine . . . two-three-eight . . ."

"Dropping abaft the port beam," Scott said.

"Jake, you need some dry clothes," Alex said.

"And you need to stay out of my way, Doctor."

He ignored Alex's angry look and turned to the *starpom.* "Okay we're on zero-two-two. Let's move in nice and slow. Come right to course one-eight-zero. Let's see if we can find the *K-363* and have a talk with our friend Zakayev."

"Have a talk?" Alex, still angry, was also incredulous. "What do you mean?"

"In the U.S. Navy we call it a Gertrude: an underwater telephone that works like sonar. They're omnidirectional and short on range and security, but it's a way to communicate with another sub." He pointed to the unit equipped with a mike and headphones, mounted on the bulkhead near the diving station. "I don't know what the Russian Navy calls theirs."

"Nina," said the *starpom.*

"Let's raise them."

"Why would you want to talk to him? And what good would it do?"

"There might be time to strike a deal, to make Zakayev understand that he has no good options left."

"He won't deal," Abakov said. "I told you, he's determined to kill as many people as he can. You're wasting your time."

"Not if it'll prevent a disaster."

"But what if their Nina isn't switched on?" Alex asked. "How will they hear you?"

"It's self-activating. If we send, it'll activate their Nina and they'll hear us. They don't have to answer but I think they will."

"What makes you so sure?" Alex pressed.

Scott looked past her at Abakov. "Zakayev might be glad to hear from an old friend."

"Me?" Abakov said, looking doubtful.

"Sure."

"And what am I to say?"

"Tell him to surrender."

"And I'll say it again. Fuck your orders!"

For a small man, Zakayev proved stronger than Litvanov thought possible. He slammed his forearm into Litvanov's throat, driving him against the chart table, pinning him and sending charts and instruments flying. He jammed the short, thick barrel of the pistol into Litvanov's right ear.

Sailors watched, paralyzed, frightened by what they had seen and by Zakayev speaking to Litvanov in an unnervingly calm voice: "I gave you an order and you will obey it."

Litvanov clawed at the arm crushing his windpipe. But Zakayev only bore down harder until Litvanov dropped his hands and let them go limp at his sides.

"It doesn't matter to me how you die, Georgi," said Zakayev, "whether from radiation poisoning or from a bullet in the brain. But die you will. Now you can order Veroshilov to trigger the charges or I'll kill you and order him to do it. What matters is that we accomplish our mission, not how we do it."

"It won't work," Litvanov croaked. "The other boat is somewhere close aboard. If he gets off a torpedo shot, we'll go to the bottom like a rock and the reactor will go down with us."

"But he doesn't know exactly where we are," Zakayev said calmly.

"He's hunting for us, I tell you."

"And he hasn't found us. Are you afraid to die? Is that it?" Zakayev smelled Litvanov's sour breath and overpowering sweat.

"No, I'm not afraid to die."

"Good. Then you understand that I won't hesitate to kill you."

Zakayev kept the pistol jammed in Litvanov's ear and reached overhead with his free hand and pulled down an SC1 mike, stretching its coiled cord taut. "Give the order."

Litvanov took the mike and toggled the Talk switch. Zakayev pushed away from Litvanov, stepped back, and watched him, the pistol aimed at his chest. He motioned with it that he should call Veroshilov. Litvanov brought the mike to his mouth, but his flaring eyes gave him away. Zakayev spun around and was face-to-face with Veroshilov brandishing a heavy tool above his head.

Zakayev shot Veroshilov in the jaw, the pistol's deafening blast searing the air in the confined space of the CCP. The 9mm round tore Veroshilov's face apart below the eyes and blew him backward against the periscope stand. For a moment he stood perfectly still, his ruined face a mask of dark blood and white bone. Then his knees gave way and he crashed facedown on deck.

The tool Veroshilov had been armed with, a heavy open-ended manifold wrench, crashed with him. Only it bounced crazily like a thing alive, end over end, and collided with a run of stainless-steel pipes that rang like bells in a church steeple calling the faithful to services.

Litvanov, roaring, came at Zakayev like an out-of-control machine. Zakayev twisted away but not in time to avoid one of Litvanov's rocklike fists aimed at the side of his head. The blow delivered a shock of searing pain that made points of light dance in the smoky air before Zakayev's eyes.

Litvanov went for the pistol in Zakayev's hand. Zakayev ripped it from Litvanov's fingers and brought the barrel down on the back of his head. Litvanov, still roaring, dropped to his hands and knees, gulping for air.

Zakayev looked around at the sailors in the CCP stunned into silence, horrified by the faceless Veroshilov. He held the pistol loosely in his hand and gestured to the senior *michman,* Arkady. "*You,* prepare to surface the boat."

The warrant officer tore his eyes from Veroshilov to a groaning Litvanov with blood-matted hair, trying to sit up.

"Did you hear me?"

The warrant officer fled to the diving station to initiate the surfacing routine.

"Sonar. Where is the other submarine?"

"General, I . . ."

"Don't look at the *kapitan,* look at me when you speak."

"I-I don't hear her . . . sir."

"What do you hear?"

"Pinging to the north. There are active sonobuoys to the west, but they are fading."

Zakayev leaned against the chart table. They would surface and pretend to surrender. The Russians would think they had won. For that he didn't need Veroshilov. Or Litvanov. He only needed the chief engineer who had volunteered to blow the charges. After that, it would essentially be over.

He grabbed the SC1 mike swinging lazily at the end of its cord and, watching the crew watching him, brought it to his mouth. "Chief Engineer. This is General Zakayev speaking. Kapitan Litvanov has been injured. I am in command. Listen carefully to my orders. . . ."

Behind Zakayev, something that sounded like a cheap radio speaker filled with static made a croaking noise. A moment later a flat, mechanical-sounding voice that had been carried underwater by slow-moving sonar waves reverberated into the CCP.

"Colonel Yuri Abakov calling Colonel Alikhan Zakayev."

"It's Nina . . ." a mystified sailor said, pointing to the device.

Zakayev looked around as if expecting to see that someone he knew had entered the CCP.

"The underwater telephone," a groggy Litvanov said, pointing to the lit-up equipment mounted on the bulkhead behind Zakayev.

"Colonel Yuri Abakov calling Colonel Alikhan Zakayev," said the voice.

Zakayev stood rooted in place, the SC1 mike still in his hand listening to a voice from the past.

*"K-480* to *K-363.* This is KGB Colonel Yuri Abakov calling KGB Colonel Alikhan Zakayev."

The failed 1991 coup in Moscow. Abakov had moved up, became Colonel Abakov in the FSB, Zakayev realized, and now this. How long had they known about his plan? Days? Months?

"KGB Colonel Yuri Abakov calling KGB Colonel Alikhan Zakayev. Ali, can you read me?"

Zakayev dropped the SC1 mike and picked the Nina mike up from its cradle.

A petty officer stepped forward and adjusted the gain. "This is General Zakayev speaking." His voice rumbled through the sea, distorted but recognizable.

"Hello, Alikhan Andreyevich. It's been a long time."

"You picked a strange place to meet wouldn't you say, Yuri?"

Litvanov was on his feet, a hand to the back of his head. He waved off a sailor coming to help.

"In the middle of the Baltic. Yes. Very strange. Perhaps we can do something about that."

"What?"

"Find a place more conducive to rekindle an old friendship."

"We were never friends, Yuri. Colleagues."

"Still, it would be good to talk."

"There is nothing to talk about."

"But there is much to talk about. We may be able to settle a few things we both have on our minds. Perhaps we could even strike a mutually agreeable deal."

"There are no deals to be struck. No compromises. I suggest you tell that to your handlers in the Kremlin."

"The Kremlin. Pah! This is between you and me. . . ." Abakov's voice started to break up and fade. "Can you hear me, General?"

"I hear you. Between you and me, eh? And the Russian Navy."

"We can call off the Russian Navy if that's what's worrying you."

"So? Have they made you the captain of the *K-480,* Yuri?"

"No, not quite. The captain is an American."

Silence.

"Ali?"

"An American . . . ?"

"Yes, it's true. Captain Jake Scott, U.S. Navy."

"I knew it," Litvanov said, and reached for the mike. "Let me talk to him." Zakayev pulled the mike away from Litvanov.

"Put Captain Scott on Nina," said Zakayev.

A short crackling silence on the Nina, then, "This is Captain Jake Scott," he said in Russian.

"So, Captain Litvanov guessed right," Zakayev said. "He said an American had command of the *K-480.* Is the Russian Navy so desperate that they put Americans in charge of their ships?"

Scott said, "Tell Kapitan Litvanov that I respect his expertise as a sub driver. He's as good as any American sub driver I've ever met."

"He heard you, Captain Scott. And so you've been trailing us for a long time."

"Since you sailed from Olenya Bay."

"And who else is aboard the *K-480* with you, Captain Scott? An official from the Kremlin?"

"Dr. Alexis Thorne, first science attaché, United States Embassy. She's an expert on spent nuclear fuel and the effects of radiation poisoning. But let's not waste time, General. We know that you plan to blow the reactor aboard the *K-363* and I'm not going to give you a lecture about what that will do to the Northern Hemisphere. You already know all that. As Yuri said, maybe we can find a way out of this—if you're willing to talk."

"What about?" Zakayev said. "The Russians are just like you Americans: They make promises they have no intention of keeping. I helped the Americans when they needed leverage against the Russians, and when our collaboration became a liability they decided to kill me. Isn't that true?"

Scott didn't hesitate. "Yes, that's true."

"And your Admiral Drummond led you to me?"

"No, you did. When you sent your people to kill Frank Drummond and the sailor from your boat and make it look like they'd committed suicide. And when you killed Ivan Serov in Murmansk. It all added up after we discovered the *K-363* was missing."

A long, humming silence over the Nina.

"Tell me this," Zakayev said. "Was it because of Admiral Drummond that the Russians sent you out in one of their submarines to track us down? So you could have your revenge?"

"No. We and the Russians thought you had cruise missiles aboard and planned to attack St. Petersburg from the Barents Sea. We offered to help them track you into the Barents, but it didn't take long for us to figure out you weren't there. And when the Russians realized you had no cruise missiles to fire, they wanted to capture you. That's when we were ordered to track you south."

"And kill us."

"Yes."

Litvanov, moving around the CCP, stripped a work jacket off one of the men on watch, and covered Veroshilov. He looked around the CCP, his eyes flitting between the sonar repeater and navigation plotter, the men at their stations watching him.

"Do the Russians know what we plan to do?" Zakayev asked Scott.

"No one knows but us, which may be to your advantage if you are willing to reconsider."

"Why haven't you told them?"

"We've been too busy dodging your torpedoes."

"And if we try to escape?"

Litvanov looked at the fire control console, at the panel's settings. A hand to his head came away sticky with blood. He looked at his hand but didn't seem to comprehend. He appeared to be in a trance.

"You won't get far," Scott said. "U.S. and Russian planes are over the Baltic. And you've heard the PCs just as we have. There's no escape. And if you still think you can blow the reactor, we'll torpedo you before you can melt it down. It's your call. Kapitan Litvanov's an excellent skipper and is no fool. He knows it's over."

Zakayev threw a look over his shoulder, turned around to face a dull-eyed Litvanov.

"Georgi, did you hear that, he says—"

Litvanov's fist slammed into Zakayev's gut like a piston. Zakayev doubled over and Litvanov brought both bunched fists down on the back of his neck. The little general collapsed at Litvanov's feet. Litvanov snatched the pistol from Zakayev's hand and whirled around to show it to the men in the CCP, and that he was once again in control of the ship.

Silence rumbled over the Nina, then: "General . . . General Zakayev . . . ?"

Before his men could register shock or surprise, Litvanov snapped an order: "Sonar! Echo range active sonar. One ping!"

A split second later a pulse of pure sound like a cry from hell struck the *K-480*'s hull and rebounded. Aboard the *K-363*, targeting computers captured the range and bearing data, shot it down the line to two torpedoes waiting in their tubes. The next sound was Litvanov roaring, "Fire one!"

# 20

## The Baltic Sea, East of Gotland

"Fire one!" Scott commanded.

The sea erupted with the roar of submarine engines, whining torpedoes, and chattering decoys. There was no need to hide anymore; speed, not stealth would decide the outcome.

The sonar screens lit up with blips and flashed warnings.

"Kapitan, torpedo in the water! Starboard side!"

Scott saw it on the monitor: a heavy red line streaking away from the target blip that was the *K-363.*

After painting the *K-480* with sonar and shooting, Litvanov had sheered off the firing point. The torpedo Scott had fired at the *K-363* showed up on the monitor as a heavy green line streaking toward the *K-363.* A moment later two thin red lines signaled the launch of paired decoys from the *K-363.*

The *K-480* accelerated fiercely. She was as deep as she could go without suffering a collapse of the damaged tunnel inside the sail, and without the escape trunk splitting open and flooding the ship.

Scott knew that the two torpedoes would search in a

widening spiral until they found their targets or, confused by sound-reflecting thermal layers, homed in on the decoys. If the *K-363*'s torpedo went for the kill instead of the decoy, Scott wasn't sure that the *K-480* could outrun it.

As Scott watched, a white blossom erupted on the monitor at the point where the thick green line and one of the thin red lines had converged.

The sonarman flinched. "Shit! Our torpedo, their decoy."

The thunder of an exploding warhead rippled through the *K-480* ahead of the shock wave, which, like the hand of an unseen giant, gave the boat a hard shove.

"Can you hear his inbound fish?" Scott said.

The sonarman had to wait for the turbulence to clear, for the blast bubble to collapse and gas to disperse. Even so, and with their own sonar degraded by the *K-480*'s high-speed dash, the sonar screens were lit with a confusing tangle of overlapping lines, blips, and waterfalls. Scott knew the picture would be just as confusing aboard the *K-363*, a slight advantage he might utilize.

"Kapitan, I hear something, a decoy. . . . Ah!"

Another clap of thunder shook the boat.

Alex huddled with Scott and asked, "Did we get him?"

The sonar display still had not cleared sufficiently to provide a picture Scott could evaluate.

"I can't tell for sure. Our decoys may have seduced his fish like his seduced ours."

Overloaded with data, the computer running the *K-480*'s sonar system paused, then recycled and began reprocessing information. On the monitors, squiggles and blips that had represented torpedoes and targets turned into rows of straight lines and dots.

"Where the hell is she?" Scott queried the sonarman.

He shook his head. "I don't hear anything, sir. Only a single decoy, one of ours, I think, very faint."

"All engines stop," Scott ordered. "Rig for ultraquiet. Secure main circulating pumps. Right full rudder."

"Why are we laying to?" Alex said in a small voice as the boat wound down and began to coast. She watched the compass repeater unwind. "And why are we turning around?"

Scott preoccupied, snapped at her over his shoulder. "Litvanov leaves nothing to chance. I'm betting that he's as confused as we are and will want to know whether or not he got us."

"But won't he assume, as you did, that both torpedoes were seduced by decoys?"

"There's always that shade of doubt."

The computer system came back on line with a confusing array of targets, any one of which could be the *K-363.*

"And what if Litvanov does come back?"

Scott tore his gaze from the monitors and gave Alex a vexed look. But she had put steepled fingers to her lips and closed her eyes. Scott wondered if she was praying. He decided he'd take whatever help he could get.

Litvanov looked at the sonar monitor and saw no sign of another submarine nearby or any traces of one crashing to the seabed in pieces after being torpedoed. The waterfalls simply cascaded down the sonar monitors undisturbed. It could be a trick by the *Amerikanski,* some tactic he wasn't aware of. Litvanov blew through his teeth. An American skipper in a Russian sub. Unbelievable. What he knew about U.S. submarine doctrine dictated that the American skipper would have tried to outrun the torpedo, not go silent and rely on a decoy. But this skipper was not your typical American skipper, which made him very dangerous. Not only that, but the two torpedoes that had detonated less than three kilometers away from the *K-363*'s current position would draw Russian planes and patrol craft. Litvanov felt the box around him getting smaller. Still, he had to know.

"Both engines ahead slow," he commanded. "Helmsman, put us on a reciprocal course."

"Aye, Kapitan."

"Fire Control, shift to constant data upload and stand by."

Litvanov's eyes roamed the control panels: They still had four tubes loaded and green-lighted. Torpedo gyros and turbines spun to prelaunch.

"Ready to fire, sir."

Then something flashed at the periphery of Litvanov's vision. Zakayev on his feet, armed with the tool Veroshilov had brandished, dodged around equipment as he sprinted for the dogged watertight door in the after bulkhead of the CCP.

Litvanov hurled after him, but Zakayev was too fast. He wrenched open the door and dove through the opening. Litvanov, pistol in his fist, arrived in time to have the heavy door slam shut in his face and hear the dogs crash home.

The charges, Litvanov thought. The demolition charges.

"Ali! Ali! Ali!" screamed Litvanov after he, too, had yanked open the door and dived through the opening. He thundered down the narrow passageway and collided with the corner of a partition where the passageway jogged right and opened on the deserted after machinery space.

It was a part of the ship he rarely visited and smelled of oil, diesel, and hot metal, a place where off-duty sailors congregated to smoke dope and drink vodka when the captain wasn't aboard. The passageway continued on past the machinery space and ended at the sealed door that gave access to the reactor control compartment. On the other side of the reactor control compartment was the shielded tunnel with its airlock to the reactor compartment itself, and the set charges.

Zakayev suddenly darted into the passageway from his hide near the watertight door and hurled the heavy tool at Litvanov. It missed and caromed off the partition with a loud clang but struck Litvanov's right forearm raised to fend it off. Pain seared through his arm like a bolt of electricity, which brought him to his knees in agony. He staggered like a drunk and fell against the thin metal partition and felt it give under his weight. The pistol had skittered away and, fogged by pain, he couldn't find it.

"Ali! Ali! Ali!" he cried.

"A dropped hatch lid, Kapitan?"

"I don't think so. Play it back."

The sonarman flipped switches, adjusted gain, and punched Replay.

The clear sound of steel ringing on steel came from the speaker over the sonar monitoring station.

"Sounds like the same noise we heard before, metal on metal, like a bell," Scott said. "Not a hatch lid, something else, something lighter."

"A dropped tool?" Abakov said.

"That's what I think," Scott said. He tapped the sonarman's shoulder. "Input it to fire control."

"Aye, Kapitan."

Scott swung toward the fire control station, where data began to flow between sonar, fire control, and the torpedo room.

"You were right," Alex said. "Litvanov came back."

Scott, intent on the plot he'd scribbled on paper with the automated system down for ultraquiet, ignored her.

A moment later a barely audible sonar contact appeared as a trace on the sonar monitor.

"If it's him, Kapitan," said the sonarman, "he's maneuvering on a very low power setting. Convection cooling, no pumps."

"Yes, he's barely making steerage."

Scott saw the range to the target click down but asked anyway.

"Three kilometers, sir."

"And dead ahead," said Abakov to himself.

"At that rate it'll take him all day to get here." Scott stood back from the monitors and stretched a kink from his back. "Let's try something."

The men heard this and tensed, ready to carry out Scott's commands.

"We're going to fire a fish at him with a wide initial gyro angle and also with a sharp cutback to get the fish in behind him. There's no way he can ignore a fish in the water, even if it's not aimed directly at him initially. He'll hear it coming and haul out—fast. And that'll give the fish a target to home in on."

Alex started to say something but Scott silenced her. "By the time he gets a bearing on our torpedo and figures out where we are, we'll have moved off the firing point and put another fish in the water. Maybe up his ass."

Litvanov sagged against the knob- and switch-studded control panel connected to the auxiliary diesel generator set. He gripped the tool Zakayev had thrown, too weak to lift it. Points of light danced before his eyes. He felt slightly nauseous and wondered if he had a concussion, or worse.

Litvanov peeked around the corner of the control panel at the sealed watertight door to the reactor control compartment. He knew exactly where Zakayev was hiding, in a small storage locker used for stowing lubricants and clean cotton waste. Because he was small in stature, Zakayev could easily fit inside the locker. But he had trapped himself. And if he tried to open the watertight door, Litvanov had only to throw the tool a short distance to brain him or at least smash his backbone. Litvanov knew his arm was broken and couldn't possibly go hand-to-hand with Zakayev.

Litvanov, sitting on deck, looked up and saw an SC1 mike clipped to the edge of the auxiliary control panel. He reached up and unclipped it and, with the cable stretched out full, toggled the Talk button and called the CCP, his voice echoing throughout the ship from speakers mounted in every compartment. He knew Zakayev would hear every word he said.

"Kapitan, are you hurt? What is happening?"

He recognized the voice: the senior *michman*, Arkady.

"Who has the conn?"

"I do, Kapitan. And I've broken out small arms from the weapons locker. I'll bring them."

"No. Stay in the CCP." He took a breath. "Chief Engineer, if you are listening, this is the Kapitan. Do not trigger the charges unless I order you to. General Zakayev is no longer in charge of the mission and you will not follow any orders he issues. Arm yourself in case General Zakayev tries to enter the compartment and blow the charges himself." He toggled off. He knew that if Zakayev somehow escaped into the reactor control compartment, there was no way the chief engineer would survive a battle with the little general.

After a beat, Litvanov retoggled the mike.

"Arkady."

"Yes, Kapitan?"

"Where is the *Amerikanski?*"

"We're trying to locate him."

"And the Russian patrol boats?"

"Closing in from the north at high speed."

"They know we're here. Arkady?"

"Kapitan?"

"On contact with the *Amerikanski,* open fire."

"Aye, Kapitan."

Litvanov almost blacked out from the pain when he lifted his arm by the shirtsleeve and lowered it into his lap. He forced his head to clear and tried to think. He and Zakayev weren't enemies, they were friends. No, more than friends: soldiers fighting a brutal war. The Americans and the Russians were their enemies. Instead, here they were with time running out and the mission a shambles, fighting each other.

He blamed Zakayev, the little general who thought it would be so simple. The little general who understood nothing about maneuver at sea and about tactics, only how to ambush and kill Russian Spetsnaz. So simple, he had lectured, to drive into St. Petersburg and martyr yourself. If it had been left up to Zakayev, they'd have been sunk by now and the Russians, to celebrate, would be grinding Chechnya into dust.

"General, perhaps now you see my point!" Litvanov shouted.

Silence.

"The American is determined to kill us."

Again, silence.

"Now that he knows, he won't rest until he's finished us off. You see that, don't you?"

A voice returned from the darkness. "I see only what I

saw before, that you are obsessed with the American. It's your private war we're fighting, not the war we agreed to fight. For that, I should have killed you when I had the chance."

Litvanov mopped his face with a blood- and sweat-blackened shirtsleeve. He heard his dead wife and children calling him. But there was nothing he could do for them. He heard their screams echoing in his fatigued brain. But it wasn't their screams at all, it was a voice coming from the SC1 shouting, "Torpedo inbound!"

"He hears it," Scott said. "He's turning away, fast."

Now they had a bearing and range on the *K-363*. The fire control computer gobbled up the data and sent it to each of the torpedoes waiting in their tubes.

A new blip, then a thick red line emanating from the *K-363*, appeared on the sonar screen.

"He's fired a torpedo down the bearing of our incoming fish," Scott said, aware of Alex and Abakov watching over his shoulder.

The sonarman pointed to a curving green line. "Just as you said, Kapitan, it's cutting back abaft the *K-363*'s starboard quarter."

"Look: He's fired another one down the same bearing," Abakov said.

"Stand by to fire decoys," Scott commanded. He saw that his plan might work, that turning off their firing point would likely take them out of the *K-363*'s torpedoes' sonar range. Even so, he wanted the decoys ready i˜ needed.

Four blips looking like red-hot sparks flying up a chimney flue shot from the *K-363*, their red-lined sonar traces splayed like fingers into the wakes of the *K-363*'s outbound torpedoes. But as they watched, the torpedoes began to veer off course and curve back toward the decoys. A moment later they started wigwagging as if sniffing for a target.

"Jesus Christ," Scott said. "They fired their decoys too soon. Their own torpedoes picked them up and are on a circular run. If they don't intercept the decoys, they'll lock on the *K-363* instead."

Something nagged at Scott, something he remembered from an intelligence briefing about Russian torpedoes and their propensity for running afoul of their own decoys. Something about a faulty range tracking pinger and the lack of anti-self-homing interlocks . . .

They watched, amazed, as the two thick red lines curved around and started inching back toward the four thin red lines fanning out from the *K-363*. One of the torpedoes appeared to overrun one of the thin lines and, a split second later, exploded, the force of the underwater detonation hammering the *K-480*.

"Look! His other torpedo. What's it doing?" Alex said, shaken up and showing it.

"It got through a gap in the decoy coverage and it's looking for a target," Scott said. "It's a race now, between their fish and ours, to the *K-363*."

The red line, like the green line emanating from the *K-480*, was only inches from the *K-363*'s marker on the sonar screen. The red line was gaining.

"Can't they do anything?" Alex said, with what almost sounded to Scott like a touch of sadness in her voice.

"Too late," Scott said.

Litvanov heard sonar waves bouncing off the hull. Then a shrieking turbine and the high, rising Doppler pitch of contrarotating torpedo screws. He knew instinctively that it was their own torpedo coming in on a circular run.

He ignored Zakayev, forced himself to his feet, and burst from the machinery space where he'd lain, into the CCP. He blocked the pain from his broken arm shooting into his brain and heard himself screaming orders: "Full dive on the planes! Hard right rudder!" But the image of converging lines painted on the sonar monitor mocked Litvanov's frantic attempt to avert disaster. A cry, a mixture of despair and anger, rose from his throat.

Zakayev clawed for a moment at the door to the reactor control compartment, barred from the other side by the chief engineer. Defeated, he slumped to the deck and thought about the girl named Irina. He saw her lovely face and saw her shedding tears for her dead family. He saw Drummond and the quizzical look on his face in the hotel room in Murmansk. A joke, Drummond had thought. The sailor too. They were all dead, the bull, Serov and his men. Now it was his turn to die.

Zakayev heard the torpedo warhead punch through the hull and detonate. For an instant he felt the crushing rise in air pressure and the searing heat. And then he felt nothing.

The blast ripped through the CCP, killing everyone. Plasma roared through the ship fore and aft crushing compartments, tearing apart machinery, igniting fuel, and detonating torpedo warheads. The nuclear reactor, ripped from its moorings in one piece and thrown from the wreckage, plunged to the bottom of the Baltic Sea, trailing debris.

It was over in an instant, the fury unleashed in a gigantic bouquet of filthy water that shot more than a hundred feet in the air and, as if eager to have it finished, collapsed, leaving behind only a dome of swirling bubbles to mark the *K-363*'s grave.

* * *

The cocktail reception at the Hermitage had been under way for over an hour. Both presidents laughed and drank champagne. The Russian foreign minister drank vodka, as did the defense minister. Admiral Stashinsky, in navy mess jacket, red sash, and medals, preferred American bourbon. He listened in as the first lady of the United States, her satin-black skin set off dramatically by the white silk of her Lagerfeld mini-dress, kept the bearded Russian president hanging on her every word.

The mood was upbeat because the reports that had arrived earlier from Russian naval units in the Baltic Sea had also been upbeat. Search teams on the scene had found wreckage from the *K-363* and there was no indication that radioactive materials had escaped from the submarine's reactor.

Cigar smoke hanging across the room in thick tattered layers parted like the sea when Paul Friedman strode up to the president of the United States and, after waiting for him to finish telling a dirty joke, asked for a moment of his time.

"Sure, Paul," said the president, wiping an eye and looking around. "How about in there."

They stepped into a small anteroom off the main gallery where the party buzzed. Friedman handed the president a message from Karl Radford. At first the president just looked at it, fearing the worst, that Scott's report of the destruction of the *K-363* before the terrorists could melt down the reactor had been wrong. On his orders the Russians hadn't been told about how close they'd come to disaster, only that Zakayev and the others were dead.

"It's okay, sir," Friedman said. "I think you'll like this."

The president read the message and the look of concern on his face changed to one of sheer delight. "Do the Russians know?"

"No, sir. We just found out ourselves."

"Shall we tell them?"

"Why not?" Friedman lifted then dropped his shoulders. "The local naval commander had a fit when he found out, but what could he do? He had to provide an escort. Stashinsky may shit his pants when he hears, but it's too late now. Besides, we're friends again with the Russians."

The president returned to the reception and, after asking for quiet, said that he had an announcement to make. The rock band stopped playing and everyone gave their attention to the tall black American chief executive standing in the center of the room.

"As you all know," he said, "the historic cruiser *Aurora* is moored at the Nakhimov Naval Academy. A shot fired from one of her guns signaled the storming of the Winter Palace and the start of the Revolution of October 1917. She symbolizes, among other things, the importance the citizens of St. Petersburg place on their city's relationship to the sea, and in particular the Gulf of Finland. Over the years ships of all kinds from all corners of the world have called in St. Petersburg. In that tradition, another ship will soon arrive in St. Petersburg, and I think it is safe to say that she's the first of her kind ever to do so."

Mystified by the president's announcement, everyone present started talking at once.

The president asked for silence again and said, "Mr. President, ladies and gentlemen, I've been told that the Russian nuclear attack submarine *K-480* will arrive in St. Petersburg early tomorrow morning. I suggest that we all be present to welcome her and her crew home."

* * *

A stiff, cold breeze snapped the Russian tricolor flying from the *K-480*'s wrecked bridge. Sailors wielding a cutting torch had cut away the plating on the sail stove in by the collision with the *K-363*, blocking access to the cockpit.

At Kronshtadt the *K-480* had picked up an escort of trawlers, luggers, and private powerboats. Their skippers had been so eager to get a close-up look at the big black submarine wending her way to St. Petersburg that they had risked colliding with each other or being run down by the *K-480*'s giant bow wave. Two Russian Navy patrol craft arrived in time to restore order and provide additional escort.

Scott pointed to the low hump of Vasilevskiy Island up ahead, which split the Neva into two tributaries. Church spires and domed palaces touched by dawn had turned the island pink.

"Almost home, Yuri," Scott said. Abakov stood beside Alex, his chin in a fist resting on the black metal fairwater. "You'll soon get to see your wife and children. Remember them?"

Abakov grunted. "My wife the unhappy camper, you mean."

"And Botkin will get the treatment he needs for radiation poisoning. He's a lot tougher than I thought. He deserves a hero's welcome if anyone does."

"I hope you're right, Jake, that the Russian Navy will give him a commendation. And I hope the Russian president will be pleased to see us arrive in St. Petersburg."

"The hell with him," Scott said. "The hell with all of them. This is our chance to see the city. You said you've never been here before."

"No, never."

"So do what a tourist would do."

"You mean like returning their submarine as if it's a rental car."

"I think they'll be glad to have it back in one piece, don't you?"

"St. Petersburg is a wonderful city," Abakov said. "I can recommend some good restaurants." He looked out dreamily at the lights burning all over Vasilevskiy Island.

"Look!" Alex said pointing up the Neva. "My God, there must be hundreds of them."

A flotilla of lit-up small craft of every size and description poured from both mouths of the Neva to greet the *K-480*. Two fireboats shooting curving streams of water into the sky had created an arch for her to sail under.

"We're getting the full treatment," Abakov said as a helicopter clattered overhead.

"Scott," Alex said, "it's cold up here."

He put his arm around her and she pressed against him seeking his warmth.

"There's still a lot that I don't understand," she said, and shivered.

"I don't think we ever will."

"I was thinking about Frank," she said. "And about his wife."

"Would you like to meet her?" Scott said.

"Yes, I would. There are so many things I'd like to ask her. And to tell her." She looked up at Scott's determined profile.

"I'm taking Frank home," he said. "Come with me."

They steamed toward a glowing St. Petersburg, and into a welcoming cacophony of hooting horns, shrilling whistles, and piercing sirens.

## Acknowledgments and Sources

*War Plan Red* could not have been written without the guidance and support of many people. I'm fortunate to be represented by one of the top literary agents in the business, Ethan Ellenberg. He took me in hand, showed me how it's done, then made it happen. My deepest gratitude to the professionals at Simon & Schuster/ Pocket Books and to my editors, Kevin Smith and David Chesanow, whose expertise and editorial skill made *War Plan Red* more than I could have hoped for. And without the love and encouragement of my wife, Karen, none of this would have been possible.

Absent firsthand experience in nuclear submarines, I consulted experts who led me through the unbelievably complex world modern submariners inhabit. I want to stress, however, that while these experts—some of them naval officers who had actually commanded nuclear submarines—coached me on the facts and stressed what was possible and what was not, I am solely responsible for how those facts were used or, in some cases, ignored. I'm especially grateful to Captain Donald C. Shelton, U.S. Navy (Ret.), for his invaluable assistance and unflagging interest in *War Plan Red.*

Also, Cristina Chuen, senior research associate, Center for Nonproliferation Studies at the Monterey Institute of International Studies, who provided important information on the Russian Northern Submarine Fleet; and Nina Kudryashova and Aleksey Ogrenich, my good friends who interpreted the nuances of Russian culture and history. My thanks to Steve Ernst, Armando Rodriguez, Tom and Tina Bell, John Lord, Geof Rochester, Joanna Taylor, Jerry Cummin, Christine Sweeney, and Rear Admiral Virgil I. Hill, U.S. Navy (Ret.), all of whom provided information, counsel, and critical advice.

Reference works that were especially helpful also deserve mention. *Combat Fleets of the World* by A. D. Baker III, published by the U.S. Naval Institute Press, is the definitive work on the organization, ships, and weapons of the world's navies. It is a must for anyone interested in modern naval warfare. It is also a book worth perusing if for no other reason than to be dazzled by the thousands of different types of warships and combat aircraft in use around the globe. *Hostile Waters* by Peter Hutchthausen, Igor Kurdin, and R. Alan White is the story of a nuclear casualty aboard a Russian submarine while patrolling off the eastern seaboard of the United States. It puts the reader smack inside *K-219,* where brave men fight to save their ship and the lives of their shipmates. *K-19 the Widowmaker,* also by Peter Hutchthausen, is a gripping story (and movie) about another near-disaster at sea aboard a Russian nuclear sub. Among other things, these two books offer the close reader an opportunity to compare the vast differences, yet remarkable similarities, in lexicon and culture between the U.S. and Russian navies.

Another important work I consulted was *Chechnya* by Anatol Lieven. There I found inspiration for some of my characters and scenes and, as well, a lesson in the history of the war between Russia and Chechnya. Lieven provides riveting eyewitness accounts of the war seen by its victims as well as analysis of its origins and the terrorism it has spawned.

Finally, a special thanks to the Naval Submarine League and its quarterly, *The Submarine Review*. Chock-full of information about the U.S. and Russian submarine force, the *Review* is a veritable guide to the past, present, and future of undersea warfare.